THE LOST DUTCHMAN

MICHAEL LESSARD

PREFACE

My first book, *Christology of the Family: A Systematic Theology of Pastoral Care,* focused on the primary church (the family) as the place where we learn caregiving. *the Lost Dutchman* is a parable and a story that contains this theology. It explores the eternal importance of caring for oneself and caring for others.

The book should make the reader think about the nature of God's treasure in their heart and the treasure in others. Sometimes, we have to dig deep to find it. We receive the heart of Jesus, The Pearl of Great Price, in our baptism (Matt. 13:45-47).

The book was not written as an apologetic for the theological concept of purgatory.

It is a story that moves us to identify eternal and spiritual themes of forgiveness, love, caring, and redemption in Christ. I thank my wife, Dorothy, who has supported me in this work. It would never have been completed without her love and care. I thank Jonteel House, my sister, Barbara Jensen, and her daughter Sarah, and my mother and father, Joseph and Beatrice Lessard, who encouraged me by reading and giving glowing reviews. I thank Jesus, who gave me the dream to write a story of His. I hope you enjoy it as much as I have been blessed in writing it.

And finally, I want to give a special acknowledgement to Jill Breckenridge for her initial editing of the book.

To my loving wife Dorothy Lessard, August 28, 1943,
March 23, 2015, forever in the arms of Jesus

INTRODUCTION

The journey to the treasure in our heart is not a flight of fantasy or magic. It is a trip through the territory of our choices and history. It is built stone by stone, on sand, or on rock. Dr. Michael Turner is discovering what this journey means; his family and others too. We leave a larger footprint in the world than we know. It's every person's quest to experience God's love in their heart.

The person reading this book will find themselves in it. I believe that it will speak to you as it has to me. The book connects life and theology together, something that needs to be recultivated these days. It will cause you to hope in God's plan for your life, believe in a message of faith, and trust in God's goodness.

Dr. Michael Turner is struggling with a decision; it's to care or not to care. The choice follows him into eternity. His family too is trying to face the truth about him.

Discovering his secrets reveals a person they didn't know. His ex-wife, son, and daughter are on the journey to forgiveness. It is a difficult road filled with speed bumps and obstacles.

We'll enter into a new world of God's care, which holds a hope of glory. I hope that you will enter this world with me and find the treasure inside you. It will require a map to follow. *The Lost Dutchman* will help you find that treasure.

What a sight that lingers upon the horizon

of my dreams.

That looks out with fascination

and weds the solitary view of creation

with graceful silhouettes of mountains

lakes and streams.

I carry a knapsack of such days

full of wonder, truth and treasures.

Private collections of bundled leisure's

held together and fastened with praise!

The Flight of the Falcon

He drove to Falcon Field for the first time in years and thought of how things had changed. It looked like this whole part of town had morphed into Los Angeles. Progress had set in, and nothing looked like he remembered. *Well,* he thought, *so has this world changed.* Doctors were supposed to be the stabilizing factor, to have the answers and solve the clinical and emotional pain of their patients. It was never that simple, and now medicine held no attraction to him. The years had passed, and partners and patients had come and gone. He carried in his wallet a reminder of the inevitability of this truth, his business card that read, "Dr. Michael Turner MD, Family Practice." The wallet was a Christmas present from his daughter, Jamie. It was silver and shiny, made of Titanium. She said, "Because you are so tight with your money." He smiled when he thought about that. She had ordered it from a special catalogue. He carried it as a prized memento even though the material made it slippery. It held his business card, credit cards, money, and a key that he kept in it.

He confessed the truth only under his breath, not that anyone noticed or cared: he wanted out of the practice of medicine. There was a deep sadness in that admission—not a hopeful "looking forward to turning a new page" or "setting off in a new direction" or "quasi-retiring to do restful things," rather a solitary acquiescence to the march of time and the folly of human caring. *Perhaps that message is not so far from the surface,* he thought.

Marian had seemed to notice his depression. She'd been a patient of his for at least ten years. She'd always wanted him to go flying with her. Last week, she'd stopped by the office after he'd had a really long day, and again, she asked him to go flying with her on Saturday, and in a moment of sheer weakness, somehow to his amazement, he said yes. He didn't know why; maybe he just needed to break the rut he was in with a tiny glimmer of hope that something spontaneous might revive his spirit.

Marian was a woman who didn't understand that someone could change their mind. He had thought of calling her several times to cancel, but the idea of having that conversation was much more painful than just going along for the ride. So here he was, turning into the parking lot of the private airport that housed the small restaurant and tower surrounded by a covey of tied-down small planes. She stood at the cafe door waving at him. It was a formidable scene. He couldn't turn back now.

She was a middle-aged woman with red hair mixed in with a little white. Marian was not the type to dye her hair; no, she liked the natural look. She liked being herself, wrinkles and all. She was one of those people who abhorred pretentiousness and wanted the world to know. She had a childlike side that was charming; perhaps it was her green eyes or those freckles on her face that made her seem attractive and younger even though she was determined to defend the character of her age. She wore a pair of denim shorts, and a red blouse, and, of course, running shoes. She didn't look like a pilot. He thought maybe they could just look at the plane and have lunch. That might be a good fallback plan. The first words out of her mouth killed that idea. She said, "Hi, doc. I got us checked out with the tower, and we're all gassed up and ready to go. We can take a turn around the Superstitions over Canyon Lake and up by Globe and then head back to Phoenix. The trip should take us about an hour and a half."

Well, he thought, *no use coming up with a different plan.* He became aware of that feeling he tried not to admit but carried around like his watch all the time. Inevitably, there was no changing it, no point in discussing it; the dye had been cast, and he was going flying.

"Great, sounds like fun," he said, and even feigned a little smile.

"Let's go," she said. "I really want to show you my plane."

As she led the way, he followed behind like a dutiful little boy who had no other option but to get his haircut. Inevitability crept darkly into his consciousness: the inevitability of disappointments about the past, of unmet needs, of his limited tomorrows, and of retirement.

"Here she is," Marian said proudly as she pointed to the little white-and-blue Cessna 150 they were approaching. *Inevitability,* he thought. *that's why I don't care. What's the point if it's all pointless?* That idea had been swirling around in his head like a glass of nursed scotch; looking at it too closely never made it disappear, and drinking it never really made the pain go away.

Marian was beaming with excitement and invited him. "Hop in! I already did my preflight inspection before you got here." He tried to get into the seat without looking clumsy. He figured that he'd give himself a little better score than the last time he tried to get on a horse, but not a promising start by any means. "Are you all set and secure?" she asked.

"Yep," he said, thinking that, for some reason, he was trying to impress her with the misguided notion that he had been around private airplanes before. It seemed like two switches went on together. The first one started the engine, and the second one suddenly made Marian a pilot. She looked around with a little headset on and was in control. She wasn't the excited little girl waiting for the ice cream truck to come down her street but was the cool customer facing a task that demanded an adult with attention to detail.

As she taxied the plane to the runway, he became aware of how different she was. Here in her world, she knew the rules, knew how to talk to the tower, and had mastered a craft that required practice and precision and a kind of science that he knew nothing about. Why did he trust her? *Well, flying and medicine,* he thought, *are very much alike. Perhaps there is such a thing as pilot paternalism. The doctor knows best just how to heal the body; the pilot knows best how to take off, fly, and land.* He chuckled to himself. If that was so, he would need to jump out of this plane right now to avoid all that hubris. Oh no, too late. Before he knew it, they were at the far end of the runway. Marian leaned over and touched his arm to give some paternalistic assurance just like a doctor would and said, "Well, here we go.

After she said a few garbled words to the tower, she revved up the engine, and down the runway they went. They picked up speed, and then came that moment when the plane felt as if it was floating. They were off the ground, and they rose higher and higher. It was like they left the weight of his practice behind. His burdens dropped from the landing gear down to the desert below. Somehow, he knew that when those wheels touched back down, he would feel the weight of those burdens again. He would land back onto those familiar patterns of lost time and lost hope. They would stick to the soles of his shoes and bog him down in so much apathy that he couldn't lift a finger to care. That's all that medicine had become—just filling out forms, just a paperweight. Marian's voice shook him back into the moment. "Hey, isn't it a great day? Look at this view. I love to fly because you can see so much more of God's creation from up here. You know, it never ceases to amaze me that you can get a better picture of things when you get a different point of view." Shaking his head slightly up and down, he feigned agreement, and the view was pleasant. He looked over to her and asked, "So where are we going?"

"Oh," she said. "Over the Superstitions and up towards Globe, and then back to Phoenix. It is a nice little trip, and we can take our time, provided we stay out of the way of the big jets. They like to use the Superstitions as a vector point when they are coming into Sky Harbor. Just settle back and let me drive. Relax and enjoy the view."

"Okay," he said as he tried to settle back in the seat, only to recognize that her comment made him aware of how tense his shoulders were. Now that the initial panic had passed about taking off, he really focused to identify where they were headed and what he could see out there. First, he noticed that there was not a cloud anywhere. It was a blue and somewhat hazy Arizona sky, typical for early April. Summer was not far away, and although visibility was good, there was nothing exceptional about it. Looking down to the valley, he saw the geometric patterns of suburban subdivisions, the footprints of pools, the rooftops of businesses, and, of course, the streams of cars scurrying back and forth like ants busy doing God knows what. Up ahead was the stony forehead of the Superstition Mountains. From this high up, they looked different—somehow rougher and more barren than from down in the valley. Deep washes and gullies plunged between chiseled slabs of volcanic rock dotted with saguaro cactus and occasional Juniper and Palo Verdi trees. They must be struggling to stay alive in this foreboding wasteland. There were lots of stories about the mountains—the Lost Dutchman Mine and the gold fever that made men crazy. Many had gone up into that cathedral of stone to find a treasure, only to redeem a handful of fool's gold. *That's the attraction of the Old West, even today,* he thought. Most of the time, you come up empty, but you still keep looking. The mountains kept getting larger and larger as they flew closer to them. He could see the effects of the elements that had shaped them and had left them beautiful, majestic, and terrible. More and more details emerged from beneath the shadows, and each one drew his eyes deeper into the vaulted canyons and weathered terrain below.

"There is Weavers Needle just ahead of us," Marian said, pointing to a tall spear of rock that rose straight up six hundred feet. "You know that the Pima Indians didn't like these mountains, and the soldiers at old Fort McDowell in the 1880s named them the Superstitions because the Indians acted so weird about them. It's said that the Apaches believed there was a cave in this mountain that led down into the lower world and all the wind in the dust storms that hit the valley were created there. "We are going to have to climb a little as we go northeast because the mountains get higher once we get a little further away from the air traffic into Sky Harbor. Right now, we can't go above five thousand feet. Sometimes, flying gets rough because there are different air currents around the mountains that can make the ride a little bumpy." She glanced over at him and gave him one of those reassuring looks that said without words, *Don't worry. I know what I am doing, even if it doesn't feel that way.* He was about to reply when things got real bumpy fast. There was a pop and a muffled bang, and then the engine sputtered, and then the prop stopped turning. All of a sudden, it became quiet. There was no sound of the engine. In its place came fear and terror.

To her credit, Marian acted exactly as she'd been trained. She ran through her emergency checklist and tried to restart the engine. When nothing happened, she recognized that they had only a few minutes to find a place to land. They were only 1500 feet above the mountain, and they were dropping at 500 feet a minute. That meant the mountain was coming toward them very fast, and it wouldn't be a pleasant meeting. Marian had frantically called Falcon Field and had gotten the attention of one of the air traffic controllers. She had reported that they were in trouble and had given her best guess as to their location. Then she managed to speak, saying, "We have to find a place to land right now!" She said this coolly, in a matter-of-fact way that seemed to brush away the terror and fear for the moment. "Look," she said. "There's a small wash down in the bottom of that ravine. We'll have to try there."

If she had time to fly over the area first and make a go-around, she would have noticed that it was a gulch full of large boulders hidden by cactus and scrubby bushes. She would have seen that if she overshot this hazard, the wash ended in the face of the rising mountain and that she was actually going upstream, not down. But she didn't have time for any of that; the plane was going down, and that was it.

"Doc, we are going to land, but it may be more like a crash. It's nice to know I have a doctor on board. I may need your services. It might be a good idea to pray right about now and hold on."

He'd been in disbelief when the engine quit, but now, as the ground seemed to rise up to swallow them, adrenalin and fear ran together right down into the pit of his stomach and then up to collect in his throat. He couldn't say anything because he couldn't spit out any words. All he could do was hold his breath, an unconscious nod to the fact that they were going down. Down went the little Cessna. Now, they could both see the minefield of rocks that stood between them and safety. They first clipped the tops of two large Junipers, which didn't slow them down much. Before they could touch down, the gulch ended. What loomed ahead was no soft sandy wash; that hope disappeared when they confronted the sheer flat face of rock that had taken its place. There was no escape. They were going to hit it straight on!

There was no crashing sound or white light. Instead, he saw a small opening like the mouth of a cave approach him. It was black and empty. As it grew closer, it developed tentacles like an octopus's that reached out to him. They had no color. They were lonely arms, full of pain and regret. They came closer, trying to wrap him up in their darkness. They were sucking the life out of him, seeking to extinguish every bit of his humanity. He felt the terror of their isolation moving over him, probing, trying to steal into his soul. He cried out with all the will he had left to resist the onslaught, a loud cry that poured out from his memory that echoed all the way down to the valley of his youth, to the treasure chest of his lost ideals. It rang out loud without words. It carried one hope.

"GOD HELP ME!"

There is an angel at my shoulder; guardian of virtue and love.

There is an angel at my shoulder; who wears grace like a glove.

There is an angel at my shoulder; he protects me day and night.

There is an angel at my shoulder; God's sentry of glory and might.

In times of hurt or fear; he whispers, "God's love is here."

In times of victories that I have won; he
whispers, "God's glory to His Son."

Someday I will meet my friend and thank him for the truth he said,

and he will introduce me to a place prepared for me and you.

A Heavenly Host

It took a moment for him to bring where he was into focus, like the day he got his first pair of glasses when he was in fourth grade. When he put them on, all of a sudden, the world looked clear, new, and vibrant. He had wondered then, "How can the world be so different from the blurry one I've known?" It felt like that now. He found himself staring down the hall of the medical building where he had his office. He walked down to the door wondering, *How did I get here?* He remembered flying with Marian, or was that a dream? He got to his suite and started fumbling in his pockets, looking for his keys but couldn't find them. As a matter of fact, his pockets were completely empty. *That's odd,* he thought. He looked up and saw something on the door to his office. It was a notice that read,

> Our office is closed because of the death of Dr. Michael Turner, tragically killed in a plane crash that also took the life of one of our patients, Marian Anderson. Dr. John Brothwell is taking Dr. Turner's patients. Please call his office to set up an appointment. Thank you.

He was shocked. He looked down and checked himself out from head to toes. He was in one piece. Nothing was missing, although it was only a cursory exam. He was sure that he was alive, but at the same time, he was aware that something was different. He had the strong feeling that he was out of sync with this world.

The place he knew had left him behind; something new was calling out to him. He wasn't afraid or worried about this new place; he was somehow ready to accept it. He had seen glimpses of this transition with his patients when a spouse died. At first, there was grief and sorrow, but then came the dawning, the realization that life moved on, and somehow, living meant changing and adapting to a life without them. Now, it seemed that this transition meant that he had to step away from his partnership with the familiar to a new frontier. He felt ready and okay with that idea. He looked to his right, and at the end of the hallway where the west wall is, there also was a wide transparent stairway with three steps. At the top of the steps was a man standing, inviting him to come up. Michael quickly approached the stairway and looked up at the man. He was dressed in a bright white suit. When you fixed your attention on any single part, it seemed to contain every color of the rainbow. The whole effect was like a shimmering incandescent globe.

"Hello, Michael," he said with warmth in his voice that indicated they were friends, because it sounded so familiar and comfortable. "Come on up. I want to introduce you to your new practice." It was an effortless climb, and when he got to the top step, a whole new world opened up to him. It was a beautiful pastoral scene of a green grassy meadow, and at the end of the field was a series of white bungalows and other small apartments arranged in a semicircular configuration. A large main building was three stories high with a big veranda out front. Mature oak and maple trees shaded each building. Behind the houses were layers of green rolling hills that reminded him of Ohio. Behind the hills were majestic snow-covered peaks that looked like the Rocky Mountains. The sky was pale blue with an occasional puffy white cloud floating by. Michael felt a vibrant energy about the place. Yet it wasn't perfect. There were several run-down buildings. There was someone repairing a fence that had broken. An old tractor was parked in a shed that probably was built for horses. The overall view produced a warm, inviting atmosphere. It also had a familiar sense of comfort and peace. He took a few steps and walked into a field of tall grass, which reached up to his knees. With each step, a sweet aroma rose up from the ground. It was an experience that gave him sudden joy—a bubbly feeling that with each step, he entered into a new world that wanted and needed him, a far cry from the world he left behind. Perhaps, he thought, that was why they crashed; if they had safely landed on the runway, he would have been trapped with all the cares and sorrows that gravity had produced in his heart. Now, he would never have to live being bogged down and depressed. No wonder they never made it back to the airport, back to the familiar, to the inevitable. The idea briefly flew across his mind; for a moment, he felt something new and wonderful. He felt happy.

He looked over at his companion. Michael should have been full of questions; as a scientist and doctor, there were so many to ask. He knew now that whatever questions he had, the angel next to him would answer. In that short ascent, a new sensation flooded into his consciousness. *Trust, that's it. Trust. I don't know where I am or what is going on or what I am to do,* he thought, *but the angel will tell me when I need to know.* They walked together a little further, and then the angel stopped and looked at him and said, "I am here to welcome you to your new home. This place is a working farm. What we are growing is not wheat or oats or corn. We work on people's hearts. Around you are a number of people who still need a Doctor. I know it seems strange when they have passed through life and are now living in a new world, but many of them are stuck between time and forever. They feel the same way they felt before they came here. Just like in your practice, many of the patients you saw had no real illness or treatable disease. They just needed someone to listen and to care about them. Your patients here at the farm need your service to care for them and help them heal. This leads us to you. Michael, you are on a similar quest. I am very familiar with the story of your life, how you wished to leave the practice of medicine because you had given up caring for anyone. It is my prayer for you that God will bless you with a caring heart again and that you can discover how to receive and give love. It can happen to you here at the farm. I must tell you that you were rescued by that prayer that came from your heart just as you crashed into the mountain. God's grace broke through. We almost lost you forever."

As if to punctuate the fact, his companion put his hand on his shoulder to cement both the gravity of that situation and his reassurance that things would be all right now. When he touched him, Michael knew who he was instantly. That touch had been on his shoulder before. It was a familiar touch, one that stabilized his heart when it was broken the night his high school girl friend dumped him. He had felt it when he failed to pass his medical boards and had to take them over. It was a subtle touch. It had been easy to discount as a simple human reaction to stress. But now he remembered that touch and knew that he had not been alone. His angel had been with him in times of joy and sadness. He was there at the birth of his children, and now they were finally introduced. Suddenly, with the touch on his shoulder came the awareness of his angel's name, Ayin.

With a sense of acknowledgement that passed between them, Ayin continued, "I know that it is difficult for you to have faith, but it is a prerequisite at the farm. You had to have some of it to call out to God at your most desperate moment. That faith is now with you, and it will grow if you let it. With each person that comes for your help, ask God what to do, and He will guide you. Consider it a kind of insurance policy for doing the right thing, the loving thing."

They began walking up to the main building and soon stepped onto the veranda. From there, they strolled into a large room with comfortable-looking chairs—waiting room, he thought—and then through another door that had his name on it, "Dr. Michel Turner MD." They stepped into his office. It reminded him of his pediatrician's office when he was a child. It looked straight from the sixties: examining table, sink, a small stool with wheels, two chairs, a chrome medicine cart on wheels, a small jar of cotton balls and tongue depressors, stethoscope, cabinets above and below the sink, and floor tile from that era, a blood pressure cuff, and a large oxygen cylinder with an oxygen mask. On the walls were medical charts showing in detail the digestive system; another one on the opposite wall, the respiratory system. On the countertop under the cabinets were patient-information brochures in clear plastic holders about diabetes, gout, arthritis, and asthma. There were several boxes of plastic gloves, and on the inside of the door, hanging from a hook, was a white medical coat with his name above the breast pocket. Light came in from a small widow on the opposite wall, and there was an examination light that hung down from the ceiling not far from a pull down eye chart. It reminded him of the time when medicine was still practiced as an art—no intrusion with Medicare or big insurance plans or defensive medicine because every doctor is afraid of being sued. It is strictly between the doctor and the patient. The diagnosis and the treatment rest on their decisions and their relationship.

Ayin said, "I hope you like your office. I have been instructed to tell you to come up with your diagnosis of these patients. I will not give you too much more information for now. Here are a couple of important things you need to know about this place. Every farm has a caretaker. Yours is named Josh. He will maintain the environment, so don't hesitate to visit with him and get to know him. He is available for any questions or needs you may have. He is the guy you saw fixing the fence as we walked in. "Also, Michael, this property has limits. You can walk and explore the area if you wish, out if you go too far, you will find yourself walking back toward the main house, just like when we first walked in. The reason is that the work needing to be done here requires persistence, even when there is a natural resistance to run away or hide. Speaking of that, there is one place you must not go. I am telling you about it so that you might know where there is danger. On the far side of the property, at the base of a large limestone outcropping, is a small cave. It leads to Perdition. It is a cold and vacant place, and only one old tree grows nearby. If you choose to go down into that cave, you will descend into a realm that would make escape unlikely. We could lose you forever. Please stay away from there." Ayin looked intently at Michael and punctuated the remark with a slight pat on the back.

"Now I have to go. The Lord has given me a new assignment. I will stop by every now and then to see how you are doing. There is no need to go with me. Just stay here and make yourself at home. This whole house is for you to stay in. Enjoy it. God bless you. I'll be seeing you." With that, Ayin turned, walked out the front door, and disappeared.

As far as Michael was concerned, it was an abrupt exit. He was just beginning to accept his new home when his only friend left on some other—how did he put it—"assignment," whatever that meant. Well, he decided not to dwell on disappointments. *Maybe I'll just check out the place.* He walked toward the front door, and there on the left was a large great room. It had a rustic look with large wooden chairs, a big heavy-looking coffee table you could put your feet on, and oak end tables with Tiffany lamps on them, a long leather couch in the middle of the room, and a huge fireplace on the eastern wall. It was like a hunting lodge in the mountains. It even had a grandfather clock that obviously didn't work since the pendulum did not swing. He thought about that; there is no way to measure hours, minutes, and seconds. Time is limited by materiality. He thought about the timeless life he would now experience. What did it mean in this new world to "make yourself at home?" Something told him that this was not meant to be a final destination but a transition place. He had a job to do; he didn't understand it, but he became very aware that he would do his best for the patients in his care. That was an idea that had died long ago, well before he arrived here.

Michael was still focusing his attention on the great room. He didn't see her peering in the front window, looking at him from outside on the veranda, those crystal-blue eyes observing him with a kind of innocent fascination. He somehow felt her look and turned around to see if someone was there. He didn't see anyone, but he knew he was under observation. Just then, he heard a faint knock at the door. *Well,* he thought to himself, *my first patient. Hmm… that didn't take long.*

There is a Portal, a door that opens,

a natural wonder that I see.

The soul of the earth that bore,

upon creations breast a nugget of eternity.

A precious gift that Apaches knew,

the mother's milk of blessings.

The dappled colors of granite hues,

and moss covered cliffs to nest in.

The Seekers

Sergeant Kelly Bright worked for the Phoenix Police Department. He was flying a chopper monitoring traffic on the eastbound 60 Freeway heading out toward Mesa when he got a call from his dispatcher informing him that there had likely been a small plane crash in the Superstition Mountains. The pilot had radioed Falcon Field with a mayday emergency, giving a proximate location of their last known position. The tower had tried to raise them, but there had been no further communication. Sgt. Bright put his helicopter in a sharp bank and headed northeast. In the seat next to him was a young officer, Tim Horne, who was observing and learning the ropes of traffic control. He felt a rush of excitement at the idea of finding a downed aircraft in the mountains. Tim had a boyish face, a patchy reddish beard that barely needed shaving, and lots of red hair that tended to fly in every direction. Anything would be better, he thought, than watching traffic, which is as boring as watching paint dry. Kelly was close to retiring from the police force. He learned his trade of flying helicopters in Vietnam when he'd arrived at the end of the war to evacuate military and civilian personnel during the fall of Saigon. That experience burned a hole in his memory, which still woke him up with nightmares and cold sweats. He was tall and had chiseled facial features that were punctuated by a strong chin. He looked his age with crow's feet around his eyes, leathery skin, and a receded hairline. He had brown eyes and salt-and-pepper hair.

Kelly talked again with the dispatcher and got a little more information. It had happened an hour or so ago. If the plane had gone down, which was likely, there might be some tell tale smoke that would help locate the crash. Small planes also have emergency locator transmitters (ELT) that will send out a signal in case of a crash for rescuers to follow. With any luck, they would find the plane without needing the ELT. They climbed as they approached the mountains and headed over to Weavers Needle. When they got there, Tim called out, "Hey, sarge, that looks like some smoke coming up from the other side of that ridge."

"Yeah, I see it. I think you're right," Kelly said. He slowed the chopper down as they came over the ridge. There was a wash below, and it might have been the place where they tried to set the plane down. They followed it a little further and had to make a hard left turn to avoid the steep wall of rock that surprised them.

"Whoa! Where did that come from?" Kelly said in a tone that indicated fear and close call all at once. He said, "That was close. We almost bought the farm." Tim looked back over his right shoulder and said, "See, back down there. It looks like they did."

Kelly replied, "It sure does. I'll circle around, and we can get a better look." Kelly put the chopper in a tight circle and came around carefully, aware of how quickly that sheer rock wall could sneak up on another victim. He hovered the aircraft so they could peer down and evaluate the crash site. The first thing they saw that resembled any part of a plane was the crumpled-up tail section. It looked to him like the plane had hit the face of the rock wall about ten to twelve feet above the wash. That had ended their journey suddenly and fatally. The pilot had probably never seen it coming. They must have been blindsided. There had been an explosion. Bits of metal were spread all over. Some bushes had caught fire, but there was no grass here. It had just burned itself out. It didn't look like anybody could have survived this crash. Still, Kelly decided to make a slow circle around the site to see if there had been any survivors. He didn't see anything moving except a few jackrabbits. There was no place to land, so he called the tower at Falcon Field. He reported that they'd found the plane with no sign of the pilot or passengers.

Kelly said, "Well, I don't think there is anything we can do here. They're going to have to send a team in by foot or horseback. It's just too rough and steep. Maybe the sheriff can find an old prospector to lead them in there. Anyway, I'm glad I'm not the one going down there trying to put together all the parts of what happened. Spread over God knows where." His young protégé nodded and said, "Yeah, it's not anything I would want to do either. What are we going to do now?"

Kelly replied, "We'll head back to Falcon Field and check in when we get there. We'll have to file a report for the county sheriff and give them as exact location." He banked the chopper over and headed back to Mesa.

Once word got out that there had been a plane crash in the Superstitions, a series of actions began to build on top of each other like a shuffled deck of cards. Marian Anderson was identified as the pilot. Her flight plan was reviewed, and it was noted that she had checked the box that indicated she had one passenger on board. The conversations between her and the tower were traced, replayed and edited together, and transcribed. The National Transportation and Safety Board was notified along with the Pinal County Sheriff's Department. A team would be assembled to go to the crash site and begin the process of sorting out the details of what happened.

Identifying the passenger would be settled so that the relatives or next of kin could be notified. Some of the procedures were hampered by the very fact that the crash had happened on the weekend and some relatives or next of kin could not be reached until Monday. The news media was contacted to inform the public of the crash in case someone had any useful information. Names were withheld to give time to confirm the information and to investigate the site. Chanel 10 news sent a helicopter over the crash and filed a short report on the evening news.

Hunter Grayson had just finished dinner and was going to sit down and watch the baseball game. He had a scotch and water in his hand and plans for a relaxing evening of nothing to do when the phone rang.

"Hey, Hunter, how are you doing?" It was his coworker at the NTSB in Washington DC, Ed Fox.

"Hi, Ed, I'm okay. What can I do for you?"

"Well, the commander in chief called me and told me that the Pinal County Sheriff's Office in Arizona had called him and told him there had been a private plane crash in the Superstition Mountains. He asked me ifl wanted to take the investigation. You know that I have two cases I'm working on. I told him that you had just finished that case out by Tucson where that crop duster pilot had been killed. He said that he would call you later. I am just giving you a heads-up."

"Gee, thanks, Ed," Hunter said with a sarcastic tone that probably let Ed know that he was ticked off. Ed felt a real sense of pleasure at Hunter's feigned enthusiasm.

"What are friends for?" Ed said with a hint of satisfaction. "Anyway, if your wife will let you stay up with the big kids, the boss said that Chanel 10 Fox News sent out a chopper and got some pictures for the evening report. You can check out their website. Knowing the media, they probably will accuse the pilot of flying in illegal aliens or running drugs or some such thing."

"Maybe they were looking for that Lost Dutchman Gold Mine," Hunter said.

Ed asked, "What's that about?"

"Oh, when I was down in Tucson, somebody told me a story that goes back to when Arizona was a territory. There was this old German miner who used to show up in Phoenix every so often with lots of gold. He said that he had a mine up in those mountains. Well, when he headed back up there, people would try to follow him. He was real good at getting them lost, or he would just lose them in the canyons. When he died in Phoenix, no one knew where the mine was or where he got the gold. So people headed up there to find it. Lots of people had maps that were supposed to lead to it. Some folks even got killed fighting over their claims. To this day, no one has ever found it."

"Hell, yeah, wouldn't that be a great story?" Ed said wryly, dismissing the question. "Oh, by the way, the boss said there was a passenger. The pilot noted that on her flight plan. One of the regulars at the cafe said that he saw the pilot and a male passenger get into the plane and watched them taxi off."

Hunter chimed back, "Well, that makes suicide less likely. Probably was some mechanical failure."

Ed replied, "The boss said that the terrain is really rough and that you'll have to hike in. Be sure to bring your walking boots and plenty of water. You're going to need them."

"I appreciate your concern for my welfare, Ed," Hunter said with a tone of sarcastic acquiescence. Hunter knew that he would hear from his boss, John Tyler, and sure enough, just after he hung up, his pager went off. He also knew that whatever John would say, Ed had already told him. Ed loved being that person who is first to know and first to tell.

Hunter was to head up the "Go Team," which was made up of two other young investigators from the NTSB who needed some field experience. They would leave immediately for Phoenix then head to the crash site. He was booked on the next red-eye leaving tonight and arriving, because of the time change, around two hours later. He was not excited about telling his wife, Natalie, the news. He knew that she would not be happy. He was right. Plans had to be changed, scheduled altered, and good-byes said. The kids would be told in the morning that Dad was called to work and would be gone for a few weeks. He thought, *Thank God I have my equipment ready to go.* He focused his mind on the big duffel bag that carried all his tools. He took a quick shower and, as he shaved, took a minute to look at himself in the mirror. He was aging, at forty-nine, and it was definitely happening too fast for his liking. He was working on a good tan from being in Tucson; even his light brown hair had bleached out a little from the Arizona sun. When he saw the bags under his eyes, he became aware of how tired he looked and felt.

The drive to Washington National Airport was uneventful. There wasn't much traffic this late at night. Things always got more intense, however, the closer you got to the airport: traffic, energy, stress, needing to be at the right place at the right time, boarding passes, security, all made for more anxiety. Maybe, he thought, everyone feels an unconscious awareness of the possibility that this could be my last trip. As safe as airlines are, accidents happen, and Hunter knew that all too well. He was like a physician who fights against the illness that has made the patient sick. The doctor works hard for the patient to recover. The doc knows better than anyone the reality of human mortality. Most of the time, patients do recover, but sometimes they don't. Despite the FAA's and the NTSB's hard work and best efforts, rules, and laws, crashes happen. Despite all the training and attention to flight instruction and preparation, people still get killed. There is always a story. When you get behind the events that caused the crash, somehow, that story emerges. Or like a miner, he saw his job as digging down into the story, to follow it from its end to its beginning. Most of the time, huge errors begin with tiny mistakes, small poor judgments, or slight mechanical flaws. True, sometimes there's a catastrophic event that is overwhelming and unforeseen, but most of the time, it's the small stuff that kills the patient. Hunter was good at his job. He didn't like this part of it though. Suddenly, his mind switched gears; it was his turn in line. The Delta agent asked him for his ID, and she asked where he was going and if he had baggage. She printed out his ticket and handed it to him with the instruction of his plane's departure gate. He turned around to head for his flight. He still had to pass the line on his way out, and waiting their turn was the rest of his crew. He nodded and pointed his chin to his right, to Brenda Marshall and Jerry Goldman, which meant, "I will be waiting for you, and we can walk over to security together." They nodded back to indicate that they had gotten the message.

They were both in their midtwenties; Hunter had worked with them separately on other cases. This would be the first crash site that they would work on together as a team. While he was waiting, he went through his checklist on both. *Let's see. Brenda is competent and has an engaging personality. She can be a bit edgy trying to prove that she's as good as anyone in her field. I wonder,* he thought, *if that's because she's black or a woman or both or if she's just wired that way. Anyway, I'll have to be aware of that soft spot. Where there is protection, there is some pain.* She was fit at about 5'4", 130 or so pounds, with short black hair, a rounder face, and big brown almond eyes. She seemed younger than she was, although right now, she didn't seem too well put together. With a little makeover, she would be quite attractive.

Jerry, on the other hand, was the youngest rookie of the team. He would be the holder of the group: "Here, Jerry, hold this, go get that, or measure this." Jerry wouldn't like it, but he had to pay his dues, and part of that was learning what to do and when to do it. He struck Hunter as a Jewish pragmatist. He would go along to get along. He instinctively knew the expectations and seemed okay with them. Jerry was about five feet ten and 160 pounds. He had a wiry body type and features that complimented his heritage: a long face, large nose, thin lips, brown eyes, short hair, and a long neck with a protruding Adam's apple.

They came over to Hunter after they got their tickets.

"Well, boss, funny meeting you here at the airport. I guess we get to go on a plane ride to Arizona," Jerry said.

Brenda responded, "I bet you boys always get to fly off and have fun. Well, I'm onto you, and for the hell of it, I thought I might come along and play too."

Hunter gave an "Oh brother" look up at the ceiling and decided that he would play along with this little charade and said, "Now, kids, behave yourselves or you will have no dinner until we get the Phoenix."

Jerry added, "That's just fine with me. I get airsick anyway."

The three of them sauntered down to security to check in. Then they went to the gate and gave their ticket to the flight attendant. She tore off the stub and handed it back to them. They walked down the ramp that led them to the door of the plane and went inside.

He found his seat and shifting from side to side, tried to get comfortable, wondering what they would discover in the Superstitions Mountains.

It is hard to keep your eye on the prize!

The temptation to chase the good opinion of men

and bury your talents in the sand of disillusion.

Walk away and forget why you started

to run in the first place.

I have to tackle the shadow of what if's and

the shallow exhaustion of human acceptance,

and enter the quiet

echo of my heartbeat,

and plunge into

The Resurrection!

Patients

Michael walked across the room and opened the screen door. There stood a girl—she was about ten years old, wearing a pair of jeans, a pale blue blouse, and sneakers—looking up at him. She had long blond hair tied back into a ponytail, blue eyes, short turned-up nose, and a cookies-and-cream complexion. She was all the more precious with a few freckles tossed in for good measure. She had an air of fun and possibilities wrapped in her rather measured smile.

"Hi, are you the new Doctor?" she asked.

"Well, yes," he said. "I suppose I am."

"It's about time we got ourselves a Doctor. The last one we had disappeared and never came back."

"Really?" Michael said, wanting her to go on.

"Yeah, my mom said he was real young and handsome. Mom said that I was just born, and it was too long ago for me to remember, but we did have a doctor once."

"What's your name?"

"Cindy Crier," she replied with a tone that indicated she was not happy about her last name. "We live in that little white house under that big Elm tree. I have a swing that hangs down from that tree that Josh put up for me. I love to go there in the afternoon and just swing back and forth. I know I'm not going anywhere, but I feel like something is happening. I think that if I swing long enough and fast enough, I just might grow up. But as you can see, it hasn't happened yet."

"Do you have any friends here?"

"Oh, yes," Cindy said as she shook her head. "There's Josh, of course. He's always around to talk to. There's another boy down the street. His name is Billy. He's a little smaller than I am. He lives in that house that looks like nobody lives there." Cindy pointed to a gray weathered house on the other side of the path that led to the main house.

"Sometimes, Billy and his father will come out and play catch in their backyard. Then there is Mr. Delbert Finwicky, as he likes to introduce himself. He's funny. Everybody knows him, but they don't really pay him any mind. I guess it's because we are private people, at least that's what my mother says, and we are not to pry into other people's business. Well, he lives in that white house down the road there." She pointed to a little white house with lots of pretty bright flowers around it. "Then there's John and Mary Smith. My mother says it's very sad because they lost a baby and have never gotten over it. It must be true because when you see them and say hi, they always look sad. I don't think I've ever seen them smile. It's strange, like they're in their own world and nobody else is included. Why do you think that is, Doctor? Why do people forget to believe that something good could happen? Why do people give up hoping for something better?"

"You know, Cindy, that's a very good question. It doesn't have an easy answer." Now it seemed it was Cindy's turn to ask questions. He'd anticipated her next one. "My name is Dr. Michael Turner, and an angel named Ayin brought me here. He told me I was to be the doctor for all the people at the farm. I have an office in this house and a place to live and lots of room to have visitors and even parties." It was an idea that caught both of them by surprise. Michael wanted to take back his words as soon as they left his mouth.

"You mean we could have a party here?" Cindy exclaimed. Excitement entered the room, and they both felt a sudden burst of energy.

"Wow! That would be great!" Cindy continued. "We have never had one of those. I can hardly wait to tell my mom. Boy, will she be surprised."

Michael tried to calm down the enthusiasm, asking himself, *Why did I even suggest such an idea?* He should be meeting his patients, gradually getting to know them.

"Well, ah, maybe we should, ah, think about this before we get all excited," Michael stammered. Cindy, with typical adolescent intensity, turned and ran out the door.

When she hit the front porch, she remembered her manners, turned around, and said, "Thank you, Dr. Turner!" and away she went running all the way to her house.

Michael watched in amazement, thinking, *What have I done? I have inserted hope where it didn't belong.* Still, he thought it felt good to see Cindy so excited. He remembered getting the news of his wife's first pregnancy with that same intensity though he did not show it; he should have. His training had made him dispassionate and clinical, but it was too late to go back and tell her how excited he was, both proud and amazed.

Between Cindy and her mother, word got around that there was a new doctor living in the big house. He had an office and was open for business. The important news, of course, was that he was going to have a party for everyone. It would be a kind of open house, and everyone would be invited. The news brought an initial set of responses. The Smiths said they would attend just because everyone else would be there. Of course, Cindy and her mother were going. Mr. Finwicky would gladly come since he liked parties, anytime and anywhere. Josh, the caretaker, said he would help with preparations and serving. The only folks not informed were Billy and Morgan Slack. Nobody wanted to go over to their house to invite them. Cindy's mom decided that if the doctor wanted an open house, he should go over personally to invite them. Word of her decision was to be delivered by Mr. Finwicky.

Michael had plunked himself down in an oversized leather chair in the living room of his house. He was thinking about how to undo what he had unknowingly started when there was a sharp knock at his front door. He slowly got up and walked over to see who it was. He opened the screen door to find a short and rather round middle-aged man with a ruddy complexion looking up at him. Michael's first reaction was to laugh out loud. He put his hand in front of his face and feigned a cough.

"Yes," Michael said. "Can I help you?" On closer inspection, it even got funnier. The man wore a light brown plaid suit with a vest and sported a large red bow tie. He held a brown derby hat in his hand and had a bright white carnation tucked in his lapel. He had large bushy eyebrows and dimples in each cheek. His potbelly protruded out so you could see his white shirt with a button that should have been fastened sticking out under his too-small vest and suspenders. He wore brown pants and brown patent leather shoes.

"Hello, Dr. Turner, I presume. My name is Delbert Finwicky. I bring greetings from Mrs. Odelia Crier and the rest of the illustrious manage a to is speaking in the French propere of the community not limited to but contained within the borders of wherever we are, so to speak. Greetings, I say again to you, our new doctor!" He spoke loudly like he was on stage so that his voice would carry down the lane to those who might be listening. He made a deep bow and twirled his hat at the same time. It was an astonishing introduction. Michael thought, *If I hadn't died already, this would have killed me.*

He tried to keep a straight face and replied in a way that mirrored the theatrical tone of his guest, "It is a pleasure to make your acquaintance, Mr. Finwicky. Please come in, and we shall have a short visit."

Mr. Finwicky slightly turned his head toward the road then looked up and loudly replied, "Well, thank you, Doctor, for your delightful invitation to enter your office and domicile." Michael invited him to have a seat in the living room.

Once seated, Mr. Finwicky said, "Thank you again, good Doctor, for welcoming me into your humble abode."

Michael sat in a chair across from him and replied, "It's nice to meet you. I have heard about you from Miss Cindy Crier. She said that you have a good sense of humor."

Mr. Finwicky responded, "She is a delightful child, full of life and energy. Doctor, let me get to the subject of my visitation. It is this parte de jour that I came to inquire about. I love to have a good time as you can probably tell from my engaging personality and flawless attire. Unfortunately, Cindy's mother Odelia is not so pleasant. She is one of those people who thinks change is a snake to be stepped on and obliterated." He wrenched up his face to mimic what the snake must be going through as it's stepped on. He made two fists twisting close together going in opposite directions. (It appeared that Mr. Finwicky had personal experience.) "I, on the other hand, relish change and novelty. Why? Anyone can see that I am a trendsetter." Michael tried hard to hold back the laughter he felt welling up inside of him. "It is in this regard that the Widow Crier sought out my services to have social intercourse with you about this affair you are planning. I take it that it is intended as a formal introduction of your arrival and your services to our 'august camaraderie a pottage.' It is, therefore, the opinion of a majority of the assembly that you should be the one to invite the Slacks to your party since they are currently incontinento delicto as it were. You would probably be more likely to gain their consent than any of us."

Michael was quick to defend himself. "Mr. Finwicky, thank you for your salutation and felicity. I have not settled on the reason for such a gathering. It was only an idea that came up as a possibility in a discussion I had with Miss Crier. When she heard me mention it, she ran with it, literally, all the way home to tell her mother before I could stop her."

"I see," said Mr. Finwicky. "It seems we have entertained this bash, I mean 'parte de jour, under false imprimaturs.' That's most unfortunate." Then he stopped and tapped the top of his hat while his mind raced to ponder the situation. "I think, however, that you should go through with the event. The reasons are many people have already committed in principle to attend. Residents could meet you, and that would be advantageous. Finally, Miss Crier would be sadly disappointed if it is postponed or cancelled. For the reasons mentioned herewith, it might be that the pain of calling it off would be greater than the pain of having it, an 'ennui' dilemma, full of irony."

"Mr. Finwicky, I think that your counsel is correct," Michael said. "In fact, I see the only course left is to have the party. I appreciate your insight into the situation. May I ask again for your considered opinion if I need your advice?"

Mr. Finwicky repeated incredulously, "You see a benefit in my advice?"

"Oh, yes, I do," Michael replied. There was a pause, and Michael sensed that if he remained quiet, something important would come out. It seemed that the gentleman's next words were stuck in his throat trying to be spoken.

"I would consider it a pleasure to be of assistance to you." Then suddenly, the moment arrived. "You may not know this, but people around here hardly take me seriously. In fact, as much as I try to be noticed, I am often ignored." Silence set in, and Michael saw Mr. Finwicky's eyes tear up. "They think that they can dismiss me because I am so happy-go-lucky and accommodating. However, Doctor, I have sensitive nature, especially about being discounted. It hurts my heart."

Michael was taken aback. He felt a combination of pity and sorrow, which caused him to pause and take notice of the revelation. It was as if a naked man had run across the stage and something was unexpectedly laid bare. It exposed him—not as a humorous character, but a vulnerable person. It made Michael suddenly conscious that under the layers of self protection, everyone is naked.

Michael said, "How long have you had this heartburn?"

Mr. Finwicky replied, "Oh, it seems forever."

Michael said, "I can give you some antiacid for that."

Delbert responded with unusual candor, "Why, you already have, my good doctor. You already have." Delbert reverted into character as if in rehearsal for a play. He stood up and moved quickly to the door then opened it and said loud enough to be heard down the way, "Thank you, Dr. Turner, for your fine entertainment of my conveyance of our concerns relative to your parte de jour. I will endeavor to my utmost to maintain the careful enigma of our conversation in relative confidence!"

Giving a slight bow and a wink, which communicated a mutual agreement, he turned and walked out the door and through the veranda and down the lane, singing under his breath a song that Michael could not identify.

Michael left the front door open, closed the screen door, turned, and took a couple of steps toward the living room and let out a big belly laugh. It was a laugh like he hadn't had in a long time. It seemed to come from his toes and filled his lungs with a kind of nitrous oxide of humor and relief. The laugh was so pronounced that he needed to bend over and put his hands on his knees to fully enjoy the moment and breathe it in.

Then he heard a knock on his screen door. He tried to look through it, but he couldn't see who was on the other side, so he said loudly, "Come on in," as he tried to get a handle on his laughter. In walked a tall thin young dark-haired man dressed in blue jeans and a chambray shirt. He wore work boots and gloves and an old weathered hat more than used to sweat. He had a short beard and sensitive soft brown eyes. Michael noticed he wore a leather belt around his waist and a small chain of keys dangled at his side. He invited his guest to come into the parlor.

"If you don't mind, sir, I'd just as soon stay out here since I'm a bit dirty from workin' out in the pasture. My name is Josh. I just heard about the party y'all are planning from Mr. Finwicky."

Michael noticed that Josh had a southern accent and spoke at a slower pace.

"Well, Josh, what do you think about it?"

"Oh, I think that it's a real good idea. If you don't mind, I can get a few friends to put it together if you need a little help with stuff."

"Josh," Michael said, "that would be a great. I heard that you are the caretaker. I also heard that you are familiar with the way things operate. If we were going to have a party, how do we get everyone together?"

Josh replied, "As you probably figured out, things don't work the same as you knew before. For example, we got no time to worry about. Generally, things get notified by a messenger blowin' a horn. When they hear it, everyone will know to come on over to the big house for the party. There's no need to worry. Everything will be just fine. We all will have some real good grub and some fine wine and some heavenly music. I can assure you of that. Doc, just you leave it up to me. Nobody will be disappointed. Hey, there is one thing though. I heard that you are headed over to the Slacks to invite them. They can be a little unfriendly. You might want me to go over with you."

Michael thought about Josh's invitation and said, "Thanks, Josh, but I think I'll go down there and check it out on my own first, then if I need your help, I will get in touch with you."

"Suit yourself, Doc. You know people are fickle. You'd think that they'd know that you can't get sweet water and bitter water from the same spigot." He paused and then continued, "See yah, Dr. Turner, unless I hear from you. Remember to listen for the sound of the trumpet." He turned and opened the screen door and headed down the path. Michael thought Josh to be a charming young man. He is definitely a godsend. He speculated, *I wonder what he was talking about with that spigot story?*

Michael had no reason to delay. He decided to head over to the Slacks' house and invite them to the party. He walked down the path that led past the Criers house and walked over from there to the Slacks home, which was somewhat hidden behind a large clump of trees. He saw that no one was outside. He would have knocked on the front door. As he approached the house, he felt curious and fearful. He thought to himself that these folks must like the natural look since it was obvious that nobody had ever tried to paint the house or trim the bushes. He knocked on the front door, but there was no answer. He knocked again harder, but there was still no response. He looked around the front of the house and saw a young boy peering at him through the front window. The boy disappeared when he realized that he was noticed. Michael could hear the sound of small running steps approaching from inside the house. The door opened about halfway. He looked down to see a boy, maybe seven years old, with messy brown hair and a precocious smile looking up at him. The boy wore a pair of well-worn jeans with holes in the knees, a white T-shirt, and tennis shoes.

"Hey, who are you?" the boy asked in a high-pitched voice.

Michael replied, "I'm the new Doctor. My name is Michael Turner. I came to visit you and your dad. Is your father home?"

The boy said, "Sure, he's home. He's always home, and so am I. Do you want me to go get him for you?"

"Yes, I would like that very much," Michael said. The boy was gone in a flash, running from the sound of his fast footfalls to get his dad. He could hear a few loud mumbles from inside the house, which sounded like his message was not well received by Mr. Slack. He was still outside when Mr. Slack's silhouette came into view as he opened the door all the way. The conversation did not begin well.

Mr. Slack spoke first without any concern for the feelings of the person at his front door and said, "I'm Morgan Slack. Who are you, and what do you want?"

Michael felt the chill of hostility trying to settle in his heart. His first reaction was to come back with an intense response. *After all, I have been around a few difficult customers before. Who cares whether he comes or not?* Still, somehow, he managed to breathe in an air of confidence, which warmed his spirit and gave him a smile.

"Hello, Mr. Slack. My name is Dr. Michael Turner, and I am new to the farm. May I come in and explain the reason for my visit?"

"Oh, all right," Mr. Slack said. "What can it hurt? Don't expect us to be offering you any hospitality. Billy and I are both busy with study, scientific inquiry, and our intellectual pursuits."

"Thank you for your time, Mr. Slack," Michael said as he crossed the threshold and stepped into a large room full of books, charts, and papers piled up and strewn about. Michael got a better picture of Morgan Slack once inside the house. He was a middle-aged man with heavy dark stubble and handsome manly features. His strong chin, square jaw, straight nose, medium build, and tall frame anchored an energetic countenance.

"Mr. Slack—"

"Just call me Morgan, Doctor. This guy next to me is my son, Billy."

"Thank you, Morgan. It's nice to meet you too, Billy." He felt a thaw of warmth arrive with these words. He thought, *His bark is bigger than his bite.* He still felt a bit guarded. "I came by today first to meet you guys and for another reason. I want to invite you to a party at the house on the hill. I hope you will come. I want to meet everyone on the farm and to have a chance to get better acquainted."

"What do you think, Billy? Should we go?"

"Hey, Dad, it would be great to go to Dr. Turner's party!" Billy exclaimed.

"Well, I think that settles it. We will plan on being there. Oh, except that we are right in the middle of studying the philosophy of Thomas Aquinas in the *Summa Theologica.* It is most enlightening. I don't see how we can come and continue our study, do you, Billy? What do you think, Dr. Turner? You are a person of education and decorum. How can we possibly break our contract to ourselves to develop intellectually and spiritually?"

Michael looked at Billy and saw the disappointment as tears flooded his eyes and dripped down his cheeks. Billy was stymied by this sudden twist from his father. The idea of attending the party was just another remote broken promise. He said nothing, only nodded his head, which indicated surrender. Michael needed an ingenious reply. He knew that Morgan had employed a practiced strategy of avoidance.

Michael countered, "You know, Morgan, somebody just told me that you cannot get good water and bad water from the same spigot. I have been trying to figure out why he told me that. Perhaps it was for you and Billy. If Thomas Aquinas is a good philosopher, then applying his ideas and his principles would be an excellent way of mastering them. I recall that Thomas used a discussion format to explore each question. You could test your knowledge of those principles by attending my party. There, people can be studied by discussing their attitudes and opinions."

Billy was quick to respond to the challenge. "Oh yeah, Dad, let's take old Thomas Aquinas off the shelf. I want to see if we really can use his ideas." Now it was Morgan's turn to be surprised.

Michael asked, "Will both of you come for sure when the messenger blows his horn?" Morgan looked crestfallen. It was not often that he had been outmaneuvered.

"Well, I suppose that we can attend for the purpose of education and enlightenment."

"Good," Michael replied with a real sense of satisfaction. "It is settled then, and I will see you at the party. Good-bye, Morgan and Billy." With that, he quickly turned and went out the door. He waved and continued up the path to his house before Morgan could come up with some other reason not to attend the party.

As he approached the big house, he saw Ayin waiting for him on the veranda.

A high rise home

for bees, bugs and birds.

Things that crawl, climb,

fly, slide and wiggle.

Moments of shade

and of sweetness

prickly, stickery

swelled by rain

burnt by sun.

A desert home,

for God's creatures,

that play and run.

A Sad Good-bye

The Pinal Sheriff's Department had a pretty good idea who the pilot was, but finding out the name of the passenger was more difficult. The Mesa Police Department was also contacted. The NTSB investigators were arriving early Sunday morning from Washington DC. Somebody had the idea of checking the parking lot near the cafe. A witness had seen the pilot and a man leave together. The license numbers of the cars that had been there overnight were checked against other pilots' flight plans. If necessary, they were contacted to make sure that they were all right and to rule them out as the person they were trying to identify. Only two cars, a blue Buick Regal and a white Chevy Malibu, seemed to qualify as belonging to the two missing persons. Marion Anderson's car was the Chevy Malibu. A sheriff's locksmith opened both cars and checked them for any information. In the glove box of the Regal, he found a registration and insurance card and an owner's manual along with the dealership where it was purchased. The car belonged to a Dr. Michael Turner of Phoenix, Arizona. His address and phone numbers were verified. The department did a background search to find out who his next of kin were. He had no warrants, and apart from a few past traffic tickets, he appeared to be a model citizen. No names were released to the press as yet. It was becoming apparent that Marian Anderson and Dr. Michael Turner were the two persons in the plane that crashed and that they were both killed. This fact could not be made with certainty until a team went to the crash site and gathered evidence to support a final determination. The two persons were still considered missing at this point. Meanwhile, the team from the NTSB had arrived and was preparing with a couple of experienced hikers from the sheriff's department to go to the crash site as soon as they could. The Tucson Police Department was contacted and given the task of notifying the next of kin in Dr. Turner's family—a daughter and a son.

It was a loud knock at the door of Jamie Turner's dorm room at the University of Arizona that woke her from a sound sleep. Sunday is supposed to be a day of rest, and this afternoon, she had planned to do just that. Her roommate, Sharon, and her boyfriend had gone out for the day. Jamie was going to make the most of her private time. She went to the door ready to defend her right to expect some peace and quiet and not be bothered. When she opened the door, there stood two Tucson police officers. One was a few inches taller than she was. He was Hispanic with a crew cut and had a stocky build. He gave the impression of someone whose skin was a little too tight for his body and wore his uniform the same way. He was sweating. The other one was taller and stood slightly behind him. It was a hot spring day, and the Arizona sun was beginning to wrestle the coolness out of the afternoons. Soon, summer would arrive and settle the matter.

Jesse looked at her, noticing that her tank top and shorts were filled out by her well-proportioned feminine figure. She was petite, with light brown hair tied up in a bun. She had a small delicate mouth and brown eyes.

Jesse asked, "Are you Jamie Turner, and is your father Dr. Michael Turner?"

She replied, "Yes, I am Jamie Turner, and my dad's name is Michael Turner. Is there a problem, officers?" She felt a pang of fear and confusion rise up inside her; now it was her turn to sweat.

"Miss Turner, I am Officer Jessie Hernandez, and here is my identification. This is Officer Steiner. We are from the Tucson Police Department." She glanced at his credentials. He added, "May we come in?"

"Oh, sure. Come on in," she said as she opened the door. Officer Hernandez took several steps into the room, and she invited him to sit down on a small couch while the other policeman stood. Jamie took her seat in a rocking chair across from him.

"Miss Turner, when was the last time you talked to your father?"

"I saw him last week at a school function here at the university. I think it was last Wednesday night." She began to feel troubled and increasingly fearful about this visit.

"Have you talked to him since then by phone or e-mail or by texting?"

"No," Jamie replied. "I haven't talked to him since that evening. Officer, is he all right?"

"Well, Miss Turner," he paused, and she noticed that he had something to say that was difficult to talk about. He was looking down and had his hat in his hand, nervously fiddling with it.

"You see, there was this accident that happened. A small plane crashed in the Superstition Mountains yesterday afternoon. The pilot was a woman whose name was Marian Anderson. She had a passenger with her. We are pretty sure that it was your father, Dr. Michael Turner. The crash was devastating. We believe that no one survived. I must tell you that we have not confirmed this yet. We will be sending a team to the crash site, but because of the difficult terrain, it will probably take several days to confirm. My job is to inform you that our evidence of the pilot's flight plan and helicopter observation and our preliminary investigation leads us to these conclusions. We have also found your father's car, a blue 2005 Buick Regal registered in his name, at the Falcon Field Cafe parking lot. We believe that he drove it there and left with Marion Anderson to go on a short flight. I am very sorry to have to deliver this sad and painful news to you."

She was stunned. "Are you saying that my father is dead?"

Officer Hernandez replied, "That has not been confirmed, but yes, we think that he was killed in the plane crash."

"Oh my god!" she said and put her hands on both sides of her head, rocking back and forth and repeating, "It can't be. Oh my god! No, no, no!"

Jesse wanted to do something, to give her a hug or some mystical words to console her. Instead, he felt tethered to the couch, immobilized by her sorrow and grief. *I will always be remembered far bringing the bad news,* he thought. Yet at the same time, he was aware that the only appropriate thing to do was to remain in this role. His job was to stay outside the envelope of giving anything other than the bad news. Hopefully, loving people in her life would be the ones to offer her comfort. She began to cry in deep grief. It was the kind of sobbing that set your teeth on edge. It produced a sound that cut into his heart. He just listened and prayed. What else was there to do?

Eventually, she looked up at him through her tears, her nose running.

She asked in a very loud voice, "What happened? Why is my father dead?"

"Miss Turner, as I said before, we don't know what happened. We have a group of professionals who will go to the crash site and try to figure out what happened and why it happened."

Jamie replied, "I want to go!" Jessie was caught of guard by her statement.

"Miss Turner, that is a job for experts. It's rough country, and they have a task that requires special training. I don't think they would allow a family member to go." He felt trapped, like he was just giving an excuse and Jamie seemed to be one of those women who wanted see for herself.

Before she could argue, he asked, "Is there any way to get a hold of your brother? We have tried his phone. The number that we have is not in service. We have no current address."

"Oh," she said. "David can be hard to find. He's my older brother and has had a difficult time settling down. He moves from place to place working odd jobs and never stays long anywhere. He calls me once a month or so. I'm due for a call from him pretty soon."

"Since we can't locate him, would you notify him for us?" Jesse asked.

"Yes, I will do that."

"Miss Turner, do you have somebody you can call to come and be with you?" he inquired.

"Yes, I do. Have you talked to my mother?"

"We understand that your father is divorced, so no, we have not talked to anyone other than you from your family." He noticed that she was shaking and said, "We have a volunteer chaplain if you would like some spiritual support or some volunteer grief counselors through the department."

"No, I'll be all right. I just need to make a few phone calls," she replied, wiping the tears from her eyes. She excused herself, got up, and went to the bathroom to wash her face. When she returned, she said, "It's okay if you need to go. I'll get my mom to come over."

Jesse stood up from the couch. He knew that they were being dismissed, so he gave her some written information about who to call for follow-up questions. He also said that the coroner's office would be in touch when the identification part of the investigation was complete so her family could make funeral arrangements. After he and his partner gave her their final words of sympathy, they turned, and Jesse slowly closed the door behind them. They could still hear her crying as they walked down the hall. When they took the elevator from the fourth floor to the lobby and walked outside to the parking lot, neither of them said a word.

Bob broke the silence as they drove away. "How did you think it went?"

Jesse replied, "It was pretty bad. She seems like a nice young lady, and I wish I didn't have to be the one to tell her."

Bob replied softly, "It's about time to head back to the office and fill out our reports. Maybe we can get a bite on our way in.

"Sure," Jesse said, although he didn't feel hungry at the moment. Since he wasn't driving, he was content with looking out the window. He thought about what had just happened, about how fragile life is. Delivering such terrible news, it was a melancholic flight into the human condition. Tragedy collided with reality and left behind only grief. He knew for sure that one young woman would never have her father see her graduate, walk her down the aisle, babysit her kids, or have her family over for Christmas. From now on, there would always be an empty chair.

As soon as they left, Jamie called her mother. Mary Allred Turner had just arrived home from late afternoon grocery shopping when the phone rang. It was her daughter, Jamie, and it was obvious that something was very wrong. Jamie had insisted that her mother come over to her dorm at the university. She had something that she needed to tell her, but she didn't did not want to discuss it over the phone.

Mary jumped into her car and headed to the U of A. She lived across town, in Tucson, so it would take her about twenty minutes to get there. Her thoughts were racing with bad news scenarios, mostly having to do with David. She tried to put the worst ones out of her mind and just pay attention to the road. She finally got to the dorm and went up to Jamie's floor. She knocked at the door and went into her daughter's tiny apartment. Jamie stood up from her rocking chair and gave her mother a big long hug. She was very distressed and couldn't stop crying.

Mary said, "Jamie, what's happened? What's wrong?"

"Mom, it's Dad. He was killed in a plane crash yesterday."

"What?" Mary exclaimed.

"Mom, it's true. Two officers from the Tucson Police Department came to tell me. They left that stuff on the coffee table with their supervisor's card. I called you as soon as they left. Evidently, Dad went on a sightseeing flight with one of his patients, a woman I guess. The officer said something went wrong and they crashed in the, Superstition Mountains. He said that the crash was real bad. There will be an investigation to find out what happened. They can't confirm anything until they get to the crash site. Mom, Dad is dead!" she said loudly, tears streaming down her face.

Mary wanted to cry too. Instead, she found her reaction to the news very strange. Although her mind told her she should cry, she just felt numb. All of a sudden, her world had changed, and nothing felt familiar or secure. Yet all she could say to her daughter was, "My god! I can't believe it."

At first, she thought that she was just in shock. Then she realized the reason for her lack of emotion. She had already cried all her tears during their divorce. Mary had never understood the reason for their breakup. Did he have some kind of midlife crisis? Was it out of boredom or some kind of empty nest thing? It was true that they had grown apart. He didn't want to work on recovering their life together. It was like he thought it would be too difficult and he had given up caring on a variety of levels. Mary's tears had all been spent on this diet of feeling disappointed, betrayed, lonely, rejected, and hurt. The divorce had been settled about ten months ago; still, the hunger of the loss gnawed at her soul and fed her heart with unresolved grief. She did not want to 'admit that Michael's death might stop the emotional desiccation. Would it put an end to the "what ifs" that so often tormented her heart and mind, or would it make them worse?

Jamie, noticing her mother's disengagement, said, "Mom, are you all right?" It seemed to Jamie that her mother had emotionally checked out. Mary was always a proper lady. Although she had a more matronly figure now, you could still see her proportional feminine shape. No matter where she was, her auburn hair was always carefully curled. She tended to glide rather than walk. She still had attractive features, few wrinkles, and bright brown eyes.

"Honey," she replied, "I don't know how I feel right now. Yes, I'm okay, but you might get a different answer in a few hours. Jamie, I just need a little time to let this settle and become truth. I can't seem to get past the feeling that it just isn't real. The idea that your father would go flying with some woman is beyond me. Michael was always so predictable, not a person to do things at the spur of the moment."

Mary had recently become aware that things she believed about her ex-husband did not necessarily describe him. Throughout the divorce, she discovered that he was capable of acting out of character. Here was another example of Michael not acting the way she thought he would. Perhaps it was just his predictable behavior that she had gotten used to. Maybe it was that she assumed she knew him. What she thought she knew were just empty patterns, vacant attachments to the past. Now it was too late to explore that territory. The thought of their relational deprivation made her angry and frustrated. The numb feeling began to circulate in her head. Mary swallowed hard and sighed as she exhaled, trying to catch her breath. She was familiar with this feeling. It had made a home in her heart long ago. Now it was back. It felt like death, and so it was, but it was too painful to stay too long in this state of suspended mortality.

Mary asked, "Have you heard from David? How do we get in touch with him?"

"Mom, I don't know how to reach him. He usually calls me once a month to check in. I haven't heard from him yet. The officer said that since we have a better chance to talk to him, he would leave telling David to us. I'll call you, Mom, after I hear from him. How do you think he will handle this?"

"You know, that's a hard question to answer. David and your father had a difficult relationship. We will just have to do what we can to support him. I think that it's important for him to come back to Arizona so that we can deal with this together."

"Mom," Jamie replied, "you know that he will probably give a bunch of excuses why he can't come."

"Well," Mary said, "we will just have to do our best to get him to change his mind if need be."

Mary stayed at Jamie's room until her roommate came back. They talked about what to do in the next couple of days. Mary had moved from Phoenix after the divorce; she told herself to be closer to Jamie. She really wanted to get away from the familiar life they had built together in Phoenix. Now with all the details that had to be taken care of, Mary was being plunged back into it like it or not. She would call Michael's office early tomorrow morning and tell the staff. She was sure that he had patients and appointments lined up. She would contact her attorney and check out what she could or could not be involved in financially and personally. Michael's father and mother were deceased. Jamie would contact her friends in Phoenix and pick a day when the family could drive down there together.

By the time Mary got back to her condo, it was late and she was tired. She took off her shoes and just fell onto the bed exhausted and numb. Suddenly and without warning, the tears began to flow. Her lips quivered, and she cried and then sobbed. Emotion flooded her mind like waves crashing on the shore of her memory with the pounding sense of inevitability. The sadness ebbed and flowed. A long day of unexpected grief ended with the tide gone out and no water left in the harbor, only beached boats sitting high and dry, waiting with hope for the tide to come in again.

Springs of water that washes away the tides of pain.

Springs of water that breaks out from the

intractable earth.

Springs of water upon my brow that cools my skin

and makes me thirst

Springs of water that bubble and foam

dancing in the Spirit to my eternal home

Tempest

As the NTSB team flew westward, a low pressure storm moved off the coast of California, crossed the Colorado River, and moved eastward at dazzling speed. It packed a punch of rain and wind. The storm was a deep system of low pressure. It was cold from its birth waters in the Arctic. It barreled into Arizona, sweeping away all the stable warm air and replacing it with its chilling progeny.

For Hunter and his team, the flight to Phoenix was uneventful. They were met at Sky Harbor by the Mesa Police Department VIP van and driver and taken to Mesa. On the way to their hotel, the driver informed them of the terrible weather conditions that would be greeting them in the morning. Everyone had tried to sleep on the plane, knowing what jet lag meant. The unanimous opinion was that sleep had been hard to come by. Forty-five minutes later, they arrived at the Holiday Inn near Falcon Field.

They were registered and told that they should be ready by 7:30 a.m. That gave them four hours to get some sleep. There would be another driver to take them to the field in the morning. The group gathered around the back of the van to get their stuff. Looks that said without words what Hunter thought were shared.

Just great. This is going to be a real pain. He felt the sense of irony at being in the Holiday Inn. It was nothing like a holiday that waited for them tomorrow on the mountain.

Everyone silently got to the lobby and headed their own way to get what sleep they could. It seemed like he had just lain down in bed when the hotel phone rang to wake him up. The team assembled with the usual murmuring about lack of sleep as they put their stuff back in the van and headed to Falcon Field. The weather had turned cold and windy. It wasn't real cloudy yet. Visibility was down because of all the dust the wind was kicking up. It blew in strong gusts of well over forty miles per hour. Hunter understood what all this meant, and so did his team. It would be impossible to have a chopper drop them near the crash site because of the windy conditions. He also knew that they needed to get there before the rain hit and washed out most of the evidence. The weather and the terrain seemed to be conspiring against them, creating a kind of pressure that made their task far more urgent and dangerous. Hunter's mind focused on that word *pressure.* He thought, *Ask a pro golfer to make a two-foot putt and they would make one hundred out of one hundred without any pressure. Add pressure like a major championship behind that same small putt, chances are they will miss it. Pressure can make for a great performance, or it can create havoc. Well, my job is to make sure my team works together when the pressure is on.* It seemed that the Superstitions were living up to their name. The elements and the mountains would test his team. They would look to him to lead and guide them safely in and out. As they piled out of the van at the Falcon Field parking lot, he was determined to do just that.

They were escorted to a large room in the administration office in a building outside of the tower complex. There were chairs around a large table in the middle of the conference room. It had glass on two sides, which opened to another larger room with empty chairs around small tables with computers on each desk. On the back of each chair was a vest with names of departments within the county that would respond to some kind of emergency. On the walls were several large and small TVs that monitored the news and updates on weather and any other information that might impact public safety.

Three men waited for them to find a place to sit after handshakes were exchanged. When everyone on the team had sat down, the older sheriff, a heavy set man with very white hair and mustache, began to speak. "Thank you for doing this investigation. My name is Jayson Moore. I am responsible as the county sheriff's liaison working with your team to make sure you have everything you need to get this job done. This is one of the Pinal County centers established after 9/11 to respond to any kind of emergency. Here, we have the best communications assets close to where you are going and other resources if needed. We will work out of this facility. I'm joined by two sheriff posse members. To my right is Steve Stark, and Ray Solano is to my left. Both of these men have extensive experience in the Superstition Mountains. They often work with the department, looking for lost hikers or extracting folks who get hurt up there. They know the trails and can handle pack animals. They will go with you to give you the on-the-ground support you need. We will keep tabs on your progress here and give you any assistance or information that you may require.

"We are expecting a very large storm to move into our area tonight, no later than tomorrow morning. Already, we have unsatisfactory wind conditions to take you near the crash site by helicopter. That means that you will have to walk in. You will take two pack horses with you to carry some of your gear, and you will have to backpack the rest. Steve and Ray have already looked over the GPS information on the site and anticipate a full day's hike from the trailhead to get to the crash. Cell phones won't likely work up there, so you will be given maps for location and radios to stay in communication with us. I will turn the briefing over to Steve. He will let you know about things to be aware of."

Hunter focused his attention on him. He was a handsome young man with short hair, deep blue eyes, and a tan that witnessed to lots of time spent outdoors. He was about six feet tall and didn't look like he had an ounce of fat anywhere. His clothes made him look like a park ranger, and he held on to a floppy hat. Hunter felt that Steve had an air of confidence and humility. *Interesting contrasts,* he thought.

Steve looked at the group and said "hello." After an uncomfortable pause, he said, "Uh, please look at this map on the wall. I have circled where we are going. You all will have a copy of this map to take with you. We will enter the Superstition Wilderness by following this trail." His finger followed a trail marking on the map. "It is a well-used route into the area. We will get together at the Peralta trailhead. It will be an easy hike some of the way. We will have to leave the trail about here, going up toward Frog Creek and then to Fish Creek"—pointing to a spot on the map—"and head down into this small canyon here. We will face some difficulties hiking in there. It will be steep in some places, with lots of boulders. The desert is a hostile environment. Almost every bush or tree or cactus has thorns. The rattlers have come out of hibernation, and you will have to pay attention to where you step. If it rains real hard, that wash down where the plane is could become a raging river real quick. Try to stay within view of each other. You would be surprised at how thick the vegetation can be in some places. Finally, there are bugs galore. Most of them will sting you if you give them half a chance. I don't think that we will run into too many people. Anyone with any sense is getting out of the Superstitions, not going into them with this storm about to hit. With any luck, we can get out of there before it gets too bad. Ray, do you have anything you want to say?" Steve asked.

Hunter looked over and gave his attention to the other guide. He was shorter, about five nine, Hispanic, with thick black short hair. Ray was dressed in nearly the same outfit. He was about the same age, maybe a little younger. It was clear that Steve was running the show.

"No, I don't have too much to say, except be sure to stay together. Getting lost would be a real problem for everyone. If you do run into trouble, don't keep it a secret. Let us know if we need to help you."

"Thanks, Ray," Steve said. "You will be driven to the trailhead, and we will meet you there. We already have the horses on the way, and the backpacks will be there as well. Does anyone have any questions?" It was Hunter's turn to be in charge. He felt angry that introductions of his team were skipped over.

"Deputy Stark, this is my team, Agents Brenda Marshall, Jerry Goldman, and I'm Agent Hunter Grayson. It's my understanding that you are in charge of getting us in and out. I am in charge while we are at the crash site doing the investigation, is that correct?"

"Yes, sir," Steve replied.

Hunter spoke with a measured tone, which indicated that he didn't like being patronized. "My team and I have experience in the elements. We can carry our own weight. We have already had a chance to look over the topography from the data that was sent to us. I think that we are ready to head out there, if you are." Hunter thought, *Nothing wrong with a good old pissing contest to start a trip into the Superstition Mountains.* An hour and a half later, they were all at the Peralta trailhead checking their equipment, making sure they had enough food water and warm clothing for the hike. The pack horses were loaded with the supplies. They headed up and into the mountains single file, with Steve in the front and Ray leading the horses and bringing up the rear. It felt like the weather had turned colder. Each step seemed to whip up a stronger wind of resistance. Dark clouds began to roll in. It was a gradual climb at first, with a well-worn trail to follow, and they moved at a fairly brisk pace. By noon, they had covered several miles.

The landscape had changed from saguaro cactus, ocotillo, catclaw, mesquite, and paloverde, to juniper, sage, chaparral, and manzanita. The mountains were tall spires of lava and ash. Many were eroded and rounded; they looked like petrified clouds that had somehow touched earth and turned to stone. It was a place that held tightly onto its mysteries. Whatever happened there needed to be sought after and uncovered. Finding out the truth would take digging and relentless effort. Nothing in these mountains came easy, nor would they give up their secrets without a good prospector's eye. Hunter realized as they went further into the wilderness that there were hundreds, maybe thousands, of sagas extruded into these cliffs. He and his team were seeking after just one story, a short one that was lost and needed to be told somewhere in a fractured canyon.

Steve Stark was getting worried. He had been in every corner of this range of mountains before. He knew where they were going, and he figured it would take them another four hours to get there. He wondered if the weather would hold off long enough for them to find the crash site? It was likely that they would run out of daylight by the time they got to the wreck. That meant that the day after would be the soonest they could collect evidence. If it rained real hard overnight, it would be very difficult to get this job done. The desert was very dry, and a hard rain would simply fill up the washes. There would be no safe way to continue with the investigation. He did give himself a little smile as he thought, at least it wasn't summer; 110 degrees and a dust storm would have been much worse. Still, what they were facing was bad enough. They were going into terrain where there were no marked trails. There might have been a few years ago, but with the cutbacks in funding for this national park, many trails had simply gotten overgrown. He decided that this was a good time to have a powwow with the troops.

They came to an open spot that would allow them to gather around, so Steve stopped and called for them to stop and take a break. The first person to come up to him was Hunter.

"What do you think? Can we make it to the crash site before dark?" he asked. Steve shook his head up and down and said, "If we keep up this pace and the rain holds off, I think there is a good chance that we will find it before dark." By this time, everyone had gathered around, and Steve spoke up loudly for everyone to hear. "As I was telling Hunter, chances are good that we can get to the plane crash before dark. We are going to have to travel into country that is pretty wild. We will have to climb over and around some boulders. We'll be following some stream beds and washes. That will slow us down, but it should at least free us from trying to get through a lot of tall brush and cactus. There are some springs that should have some water for the horses. If it starts to rain real hard and the washes start to flow, all bets are off. We will have to get there by going up to higher ground. Anything you want to add, Ray?"

"Only be sure to keep the person in front of you in sight."

Brenda Marshall piped up, "So this is what you boys do for fun, and all this time, I thought you said this was work. No wonder I didn't get invited to one of these parties before."

"Hey, Hunter," Jerry chimed in, "why did you invite her anyway? She already thinks she knows everything." There were a few big grins at that.

Hunter fired back, "Well, Jerry, don't you know? I brought her along just in case you needed a nursemaid."

Ray laughed and said something under his breath in Spanish. Brenda immediately shot back, "I'm no nursemaid for that man." She pointed at Jerry. "He will just have to take care of himself."

"Now that's a novel idea," Hunter replied. "How about we all try that?"

"Okay," Steve said, pointing to a steep ravine, "We need to go down there. Let's go."

Hunter thought, *If anything, Steve is a man of his word.* The next couple of hours were tedious and rigorous. The wind, the dark clouds, and an occasional boom of thunder in the distance created an ominous feeling of dread.

They made it over to Frog Creek and found a little water there for the horses. They rested briefly under an old beat-up cottonwood tree. Walking in sandy washes and over lots of large and small rocks made his legs and feet hurt. They were all beginning to tire. His back ached from carrying his pack. If they had been able to take their time and really enjoy the trip, they could have appreciated the beauty all around them. Instead, it was an obstacle course that wore them down and attacked their resolve. Like runners, they didn't take time to notice the crowd; they just kept their eye on the finish line.

Hunter had become aware of how difficult it was to keep the guy ahead of you and the person behind you in sight. He had felt that rush of adrenalin wash over him several times when the person ahead had been hidden by some obstacle. Each time, before Hunter had to call out, they had suddenly reappeared. It had relieved his heart from the fear, anxiety, and embarrassment of getting lost.

They got to Fish Creek after two more hours of difficult hiking. Hunter knew that the plane should not be too far ahead. Steve had told him that there were some caves and mines in the area. He could have easily climbed up to explore several caves he saw from the creek bed. He reminded himself that the hike was not to explore the mountains; it was to find a missing plane and the people who flew it. He was determined to stay focused on the reason they were here. It was getting darker. Hunter was aware that they had only about an hour of gray light left. They turned up steeply onto some boulders and around a small bend in the creek, and there sticking up was the crumpled blue-and-white tail section of a small plane.

They had come across it quite suddenly, and it surprised everyone. It was compressed and looked like a big *X*. Steve got there first since he was out front. Slowly, the rest of the team came up. They gathered below it and looked and chatted about finally getting there. Steve felt a huge sense of relief at the discovery. He thought, *No one had gotten hurt or lost.* They had arrived at the site before dark. So far, the trip had gone pretty much according to plan. Just then, the wind howled loudly through the canyon, arid it began to rain.

The layered world that I perceive;

exposes the orange and the ebony.

Piled high upon the crumpled earth;

patterned by nature at its birth.

I am determined by the notions I believe;

trusting the template of God's love in me.

The Schley One

Michael hopped up on the veranda, and Ayin greeted him. "It is good to see you, my friend," he said.

"It's good to see you too. What brings you over here to see me? Are you making a friendly visit, or is this a house call?" Michael replied with a big smile to match.

Ayin gave a look that told him that something important was going to be discussed. After a short pause, he said, "Michael, there are no secrets in heaven. Everyone's life is an open book. That much intimacy takes a little getting used to. It's not easy for a person who has secrets to admit them and to trust them to others. Part of what happens at the farm is that people learn to face their secrets. God's love can shine on them and heal them. You have witnessed in your practice the power secrets have to cause physical and emotional pain, and even death. Many people here are suffering the effects of what their secrets have done to them. An infection, for example, can be waiting in secret for the opportune moment, when the person is under stress, to become symptomatic. If the person ignores the sickness or denies its reality, the patient can get worse or even die. There is a person who has a very powerful secret that has made him very lonely and sick. He lives here on the farm, but no one else knows he exists. He has hidden himself and kept away from others. We are going over to find him and talk to him."

Michael was not real excited about this idea. His experience told him that if a person didn't want to be found, it was best to leave them alone. He had learned this lesson with his son, David. Everything he had tried to do to help him only made the situation worse. He had finally given up trying. A sense of regret and fear knotted up in his shoulders. With each step they took, Michael felt that old tinge of guilt bog down his momentum. Ayin was very perceptive and stopped and looked back at him and said, "You don't want to go, do you?" Michael looked down at the ground, embarrassed at being so obvious. Denial would not work with Ayin.

"No, not really. I will, however, do my best to follow you. My experience tells me that trying to help someone who doesn't want it is a waste of energy. I heard somewhere that God helps those who help themselves. Isn't that true?"

"No, Michael, that's a lie. God helps those who ask Him and call out to Him. Otherwise, you would not be here. We would have lost you. It is because God is generous and kind that we must go out to Mr. Schley." Ayin's tone was soft and tender, which indicated that there was some hope for a person in such pain. It required more than a script for Valium. It did require a visit. Michael's training taught him that just because the patient was resistant, it didn't mean that there was no help for him.

"You go ahead, and I will try to keep up." It was funny Michael thought whatever was weighing him down seemed to get lighter and lighter as they walked. Somehow, speaking about his resistance melted its burden off his shoulders. He tried to grasp the sense of it. The word *comfort* came to mind. Yes, that's it. He thought he felt comforted by admitting his fear of failure.

They came to a small clearing in a large group of trees. A gentle breeze was blowing, and light was filtering through the trees, giving off a kind of hazy glow. In the middle of the clearing was a small fire. Sitting on an old log was a young man. He looked to be in his early twenties. He did not see them approaching. He eventually looked up and saw them. Immediately, he got up, ran, and hid behind a large oak tree. Michael was startled by the panic and fear that he witnessed. He had seen that kind of fear response before, usually when a patient had just received some unexpected bad news.

"You have cancer," or "You need dialysis," or "There i s nothing more we can do." The flight mechanism just takes over, and everyone looks for a big oak tree to hide behind. They think maybe the cancer will disappear or the heart will miraculously get better, that somehow, they will get back to a normal life and not need therapy. They even try out some weird treatments that they think might work. Eventually, nothing does work. The disease continues its inevitable march to its final destination. He thought that was why he wanted out of medicine. It had become a fatalistic dance that led to the same place. He did feel something for this young man hiding behind the tree. He was not so different. Michael had his own tree to hide behind with his wife and his son. What was the emotion that began to bubble up inside him? What was the word he tried to name? Then it came to him like someone whispered in his ear quietly, tenderly—the word *compassion*. He felt compassion.

Ayin called out, "Hi, Brad, I bought a new person for you to meet."

"I don't need to meet anyone new. Why don't you just turn around and take whoever it is with you back to the farm? I told you, Ayin, to leave me alone!" His voice got louder and the tone was emphatic as he yelled from behind the tree.

"Now you know, Brad, that I promised to stop by every so often. Hiding behind that tree won't make me leave. As a matter of fact, it will make me stay longer. Besides, it's impolite not to acknowledge a new person. So come out from there, and let's see each other and visit."

There was a long pause. At first, Michael thought it was a shadow cast by the tree. He soon realized it was a shadowy person leaning against it. He slowly took a few more steps toward them and entered the light. Michael could see him much more clearly. He was a young man, about twenty years old. Michael was taken aback because he was about the same age as his son, David. He was dark with an unshaven beard. He was plainly dressed with jeans and an old red plaid shirt. He had his arms tightly folded around his chest like a shield of protection. He didn't make direct eye contact but seemed to be looking down at their feet. Ayin didn't wait for any awkward silence.

He said, "Brad, I want you to meet Dr. Michael Turner. He is the new doctor at the farm. He is hosting a party at the big house. I'll let him tell you about it." Ayin looked over, nodding to Michael to elaborate.

"Uh, well," Michael stammered, "all the people at the farm have said they are coming. Ayin told me that there was one person that I didn't know that needed to be invited. He told me about you and brought me here for us to meet." Michael continued, "I want to invite you personally to come to my party and get acquainted. Josh is going to take care of catering the event."

"Who is Josh?" Bradley asked. "I don't know anybody by that name."

Michael was surprised. "He is the caretaker and fix-it guy at the farm."

"I don't remember meeting him. It's not important anyway."

Michael responded, "Well, this will be an opportunity for you to meet him along with some other people."

Ayin interjected, "I think that you would have a good time. Just listen for the sound of the trumpet and head on up to the main house."

"I'll try, but I am not going to make any promises. Darn it, Ayin. You know that I don't like people very much." Bradley said with a louder tone and higher pitch, "What did they ever do for me but be a disappointment." The statement communicated a great deal of pain. Michael felt his back and shoulders tighten up again. Ayin felt it too because Michael noticed a hint of sorrow in his face.

Ayin said, "Brad, you know that this is not a hiding place but a healing place. I think now is your chance to get to meet some people and let them come into your life too." Ayin took a couple of steps closer to him.

"I told you that I will try to show up. I would appreciate it if you two would just leave me alone." It seemed to Michael that this was a well-rehearsed rejection that led nowhere. It was a script he knew all too well from his own son. It hurt to hear it.

"Brad," Ayin replied, "if we had left you alone, you would be in a very bad place. I don't think that you really want that, do you?"

"No, I don't think so," Brad said softly.

"Then we will be expecting you, right?"

"Okay, uh-huh. Sure, I'll be there." With that, Bradley turned and headed back to the fire and sat down at the big log. It was clear that the interview was over.

Michael said, "It was nice to meet you, Mr. Schley." And they turned and headed back to the big house.

Michael was the first one to speak, "Well, I thought that went well, don't you?" His tone was a bit sarcastic.

"Actually, Michael," Ayin replied, "it did go better than I expected."

Michael was flabbergasted. "It did? I don't see how you can say that. Our friend Bradley Schley made it very clear that he didn't want any part of going to some party."

"True, but he did promise to attend, and that's a first for him."

Michael responded, "I'm not sure if I believe him or if it would be a good thing for him to show up. He has such a bundle of resentments and hurts. He must have a very sad secret that he is holding on to." He felt that twinge of compassion nestle into his heart.

"It would be safe to say that," Ayin said. They arrived at the steps leading up to the veranda of the main house. "You are the doctor. What would you prescribe for his condition?" Before Michael could answer the question, they heard the loud sound of the trumpet echo all around them.

Upon the champion's way is the journey to meet the

starlight horizon;

calibrated movements that measure the earth's

dimensions and tomorrows.

We wait upon the day when the meter of our future

will guide our hearts to God's pavilion!

The Journey Home

David had arrived in Colorado three months ago. He had gotten hired onto a big ranch near Denver. He liked working outside. The rolling hills and grass, lands of the countryside, were home to all kinds of animals. It seemed to match his temperament. The weather was as unpredictable as he liked to be. Working with the livestock seemed to give him a chance to sweat out his frustrations. Nobody he worked with thought that he would be there for long-meaning no one really expected more of a commitment than he was willing to give. The work required only his attention, not his loyalty. David smiled as he thought about the sense of freedom in his vagabond life. He knew that the feeling was fleeting. Just when he thought he had attained it, the ground seemed to shift, and the freedom was gone. There always seemed to be that other side of his brain that reminded him of the trap. It was a voice that spoke of expectations and disappointments. It was his father's voice. When he heard it, he pulled against the rope. He bolted out the door to escape, hoping to find freedom again. It had taken him down the road of drugs and alcohol into the dark places of life. The hope of freedom had almost been extinguished, but not quite. He was now betting on it again, but at least this time, he was sober. To be fair, his life was not always difficult. His sister, Jamie, seemed to understand. He could talk to her with more honesty than his mother. She knew about some of his struggles. Jamie had always accepted the fact that he was seeking something elusive. Even though they were quite opposite in temperament, she somehow seemed to grasp the premise of his dissatisfaction. Her life choices were very different, yet David was sure of her good will.

He usually called her about this time of month, and for some reason, he felt a sense of urgency to get in touch with her. It was about time for him to move on. He had a little money saved up, enough to head down the road again. He hadn't given his two-week notice, but there was really no need for him to stay. The tug in his heart's tether felt like the beginning of a new journey coming on, so he headed over to the boss's house to use their phone. He had been given the use of the phone for long distance after 8:00 p.m. David had gotten all the work done. If he was asked, he felt confident that he could answer any questions. He knocked at the screen door and found it open and walked in. Nobody seemed to be home. He heard talking and laughter coming from out back and realized that everybody was in the backyard probably having a barbecue.

Great, he thought. *I have the phone to myself with no interruptions.* He smiled and pulled his wallet out of his back pocket and found the piece of paper with Jamie's phone number, dialed it, and it started to ring.

After a few rings, Jamie answered, "Hello."

"Hi, Jamie, it's David. How are you?"

"David, I didn't know how to get in touch with you. How did you know to call? Mom and I have been trying to reach you. We didn't know where you were or are or anything."

David immediately realized that something was not right. Jamie's voice sounded relieved, but something very serious had happened, and David began to feel afraid.

He replied, "Sis, what's the matter?"

"Oh, David, something has happened to dad. A couple of policemen from Tucson came by Sunday and told me that he was missing."

"What?" David said loudly and incredulously. "What do you mean 'missing'?"

"They said that dad had evidently gone flying with some lady in her private plane. Something happened, and the plane crashed and that they were killed." Her voice cracked and, she began to sob over the phone.

"Jamie, there has to be some kind of mistake. I don't believe it. The idea of Dad doing something like that is totally impossible! Dad just wouldn't do it." David was just stunned. "What does Mom say? Is she there?"

Jamie replied, "No, she went back to her condo. We both want you to come to Tucson. We need to be together. Mom said that we can send you some money if you need it. Please come home." He could feel her grief reach out to him. Now was not the time to demand his freedom; it was not the time to exert his right of refusal. Something had happened to his father, and he needed to be home. There was that tug of the rope again. This time, he would just let it be; bolting against it would just make the pain worse.

"Jamie, I will catch a flight, tomorrow. I'll call you back and give you my flight information, and we can talk about this some more when I get there." They said their good-byes, and he hung up the phone. He knew that there were many things to talk about and questions to ask. Right now, he couldn't even think of one. He felt like someone had hit him in his ribs and he'd lost his air. Taking in a big breath seemed to hurt, and he stood there, a stranger in someone else's house, suddenly alone, sad that the man he blamed for his problems had suddenly disappeared. A cold shudder came upon him, and a loud sigh escaped from his throat. Like an animal, he was trapped and could not escape.

David had no problem getting a flight and called Jamie with the information she needed to pick him up in Tucson. A coworker took him to the Denver airport. He went through security, went to the boarding gate, got on the plane, and found his seat. He was on the aisle, so he was able to stick his long legs out, revealing his cowboy boots. They were airborne in no time, and he was heading to Arizona. His mind raced as he thought about heading home. He was going back to the emptiness that drove him away and back to the past. Maybe he could summon the courage to confront his pain. Maybe now that it was all mixed in with a big helping of grief and regret, he could somehow spit it out.

Shadows in the cave are not what they would seem.

They are but clues that manifest as Plato knew;

timeless metaphors, playing among our fantasies

and dreams.

A Clue

It wasn't a hard rain that began to fall on Hunter and his team. It did bring with it the definite intent to become ugly. Low black clouds were rolling in. It was getting darker. The temperature had dropped. A blustery wind with strong gusts brought with it a pelting drizzle. Qyickly, everyone began to do the job that they were trained for. Ray helped Brenda and Jerry unload their equipment from the horses. Steve went up the wash to reconnoiter the situation and to look for a good place to pitch camp. Hunter climbed up the wash to examine the accident and see if he could find any remains of the pilot and her passenger. He had already called in by radio and told the dispatcher that they had arrived at the crash site. He had also inquired about the weather and was told that the cold front had moved in. *No kidding,* he thought sarcastically. *What a surprise.* It was going to bring rain starting tonight and through tomorrow. They were predicting up to two or three inches in their area.

Hunter's first view of the site gave the impression that the crash was catastrophic. The plane had evidently exploded on impact. It had hit a wall of stone about ten feet up the face of a sheer slab of rock. The tail was the largest part of the plane left intact. It was crumpled and had been thrown back by the force of the explosion. Pieces of the little Cessna were strewn all around and shredded like aluminum tissue paper. There had been a fire that had charred the ground. Most of the wreckage he could see seemed to have been engulfed in the fire. It would be difficult not only to identify the people killed but to find their remains. He knew that a complete investigation would take several days. It was becoming obvious that they didn't have several days. The weather was not going to cooperate. Being in a desert wash and soaked by a storm with lightning and thunder all around was asking for trouble. They might only have an hour, if that, before they would have to find higher ground. Hunter called out to Jerry and Brenda to quickly bring over the camera and measuring tape, parkas, and the other equipment along with the body bags.

Up in the watershed, the rain had poured down with a violent intensity. It was as if nature had decided to hurl down its water in a desperate attempt to make up for all it had withheld. The parched hard ground had no defense but to push back against it and sent it cascading down, filling the washes. Quickly, the muddy water rolled down the mountain side, pushing aside all resistance. It was coming, uprooting, churning, and drowning.

The rain rolled in like waves of the sea. There would be a breaker of wind, and the rain would come in. Then it would let up as if the storms undertow was building upon itself, only to rush in again with more wind and rain. Each wave left behind more little tidal pools of water, collecting around the rocks in the creek.

Brenda had brought over their rain gear just in time. Hunter decided that they would take as many pictures as possible so they could compare them with what they might find washed downstream in the morning. The team took some pictures and was moving down the creek to take more.

They suddenly heard the loud report of three gun shots. *Bang, bang,* and *bang.* Hunter was startled by the sound. He instantly knew that they had to abandon the search. Ray took the horses to higher ground, and they all scrambled to do the same. Steve had signaled them to get out of there. A wall of water was roaring down the creek. It was coming with a terrible fury.

The rocks in the wash were already very slippery. Jerry lost his footing and fell. He yelled out for help. Hunter and Brenda rushed over to him. He had cried out in pain from a twisted ankle and bleeding left knee. Hunter became a human crutch. Jerry got up on one foot and leaned on him for support.

Hunter said, "I've got you, Jerry! Brenda, pick up the camera and the stuff that Jerry was carrying. Let's get out of here!"

Jerry said, "Gee, chief, can't you see that's what I'm trying to do?" Suddenly, it seemed funny, and they all started laughing. Maybe it was a release of tension, maybe it was the sight of three grown people slipping and sliding up the side of a steep ravine in the middle of nowhere, maybe it was the danger, but for whatever reason, it was hilarious. The humor of it all seemed to help them concentrate on climbing up and out of there.

Just in time. Down the wash came a torrent of water, taking everything with it. The creek was full of fast-moving brown runoff. It filled both banks and then some.

Thank God, Hunter thought, *we have Steve's warning shots. We're high enough to be out of immediate danger.* Or so he thought.

The rain hit with a punch of vengeance at being underestimated. The full fury was arriving, and it was definitely going to stay a while.

Jerry needed medical attention. They had to find a dry place to care for him and wait out the storm. Hunter looked up the side of the ravine. Coming down toward them was Steve. He moved with catlike assurance. He knew how to make slipping and sliding in the mud a kind of choreography of the mountain. Steve reached Hunter and Jerry.

"What happened to you?" Steve asked.

Jerry replied, "I fell rescuing the crew from the flood down in the wash."

"Yeah, he was a real hero," Brenda echoed with a tone of sarcasm.

Hunter spoke up and said to Steve, "Look. We need to get out of here and out of this weather. You got any ideas?"

"I saw a pretty good-sized cave on my way back here. It's not too difficult to get to. Let's put Jerry on one of the pack horses, and I'll show yah where it is."

Ray brought over the horses, and they managed to get Jerry on a big ole gray horse, which seemed to understand the gravity of the situation. Off they went following Steve up and along the side of the small arroyo. They walked for about fifteen minutes. Hunter spotted a good-sized outcropping of granite.

Steve yelled loudly and pointed toward the rock and said, "It's in there. I'll go in first and check it out for rattlers and other animals before y'all go in."

Hunter and the rest of the team could clearly see the opening of the cave nestled in between two large slabs of granite. Steve took the small flashlight that he usually carried in his vest and stooped down and looked inside. He went in, and Hunter couldn't see him. A few minutes later, he came out and gave his opinion that the cave was okay.

First, they got Jerry off the horse, and Ray helped him into the cave. One by one, they went in. Hunter had to stoop down a little, but once past the entrance, it opened up like a small A-framed cabin. He could easily stand up. There was plenty of room for the whole team. They quickly set up some lanterns, which made the size of the room discernable. Sand had been blown in where the rock floor would be. The cave was dry and had a kind of musty smell. Ray was the last one in after he tethered the horses to a nearby tree. When he came in, there was a corporate sigh of relief. Everyone was out of the rain and wind. It included the sense of safety that arrived from being out of immediate danger.

Hunter spoke up first, "Jerry, let's take a look at that leg. We need to take off your parka, this boot, and your pants."

"Okay, chief, it really hurts."

Steve and Ray went back outside and tag-teamed in the rest of their gear from the horses.

Hunter and Brenda took off their parkas, and Brenda went looking for the first aid kit.

She found it in a pile of stuff that Steve and Ray had just brought in along with a bedroll.

"Here you go, Hunter," Brenda said. "I think we have what we need here." She opened the bedroll. Jerry was leaning against the side of the cave. Hunter knelt down and untied Jerry's boot and took that off first. Jerry grimaced in pain while that was done. He undid his belt and zipper and pushed down his pants revealing a pair of white boxer shorts. Now was not the time for modesty. If Jerry was embarrassed, he hid it well. Hunter sat him down on the bedroll and put his leg out straight. He could see that his ankle was already quite swollen. The knee had a good-sized gash that was still oozing blood. Nothing appeared broken.

Hunter said, "Brenda, let's see what we have to treat this cut first." She opened the first aid kit and found the topical antibiotic ointment, gauze, and bandages and handed them to Hunter. She brought over her canteen. Hunter poured the water over the cut and patted it dry then applied the antibiotic and wrapped the knee with a bandage.

"Good job there, doc. It looks like you know what you're doing," Brenda said.

"I've had a little practice with the kids. Plus, I've been in the field a few times when a little medic training has been useful. Now let's look at that ankle. Oh, man, it looks like at least a real bad sprain. It will need an x-ray to tell if it's fractured. We can splint it and wrap it real good. Jerry, you will have to keep this leg elevated as much as possible. Can you take aspirin?"

"Yeah, I can take that. No problem."

"Good," Hunter replied as he wrapped his ankle. "Because that's all we have for pain."

Brenda went over to the gear and found something to prop up Jerry's leg.

"You know," she said with a big grin, "turns out you might need a nursemaid after all. I'm glad we got one thing settled though."

Jerry looked over at her with a disapproving stare and furrowed brow. "What's that?"

"Well," she said, "the question of whether you are a briefs or a boxer kind of guy has been answered. Personally, I was hoping for something a little more entertaining."

"I am sorry to disappoint you," Jerry said in a sarcastic tone." Of course, good girls wouldn't make a big deal about it."

"I never said I was good," she piped back over her shoulder as she sauntered back to the other side of the cave to get her gear organized.

Hunter thought this little flirtation was just too funny. How it brought to mind those moments with Natalie before infatuation revealed itself as love. He always remembered those days with fondness. Right now was really not the time or the place for this kind of emotional tussle. It was fun to watch it play out just as long as it didn't get in the way of the job. So what to do about it? Nothing. The Superstitions had just taken care of that.

The wind and the rain had died down to a steady rhythm. Hunter motioned Brenda over and said, "Jerry, I want you to go over what you photographed. Write down any impressions and thoughts you might have from what you saw at the site. Brenda, you were taking measurements. What did you see, and what conclusions would you draw from your observations? Please write them down. I will do the same. Let's have a meeting on this case in an hour or so, okay?" It was a rhetorical okay because it was not up for discussion. He passed out some small pads of paper and pens that he had packed.

They both shook their heads and said at the same time, "Sure."

Hunter thought, Well, that should keep them busy for a little while." He walked over to Steve and Ray. They had staked out a part of the cave further back for themselves. They had their bedrolls out and were sitting on them, discussing the day's events.

Hunter spoke up as he approached them, "I really want to thank you guys for your help back there. Steve, those warning shots really got our attention and saved our butts. I know that water coming down a wash in the desert can be a big problem. I had no idea that it could be so sudden and so terrible. Finding this cave was a godsend. No way could we have set up camp out there." He pointed outside the cave. "I appreciate your help, Ray, with the horses and getting us out of there. Without you, I think we would all be swimming or worse."

"Its just part of the job, you know." Steve had a long twig in his hand and was writing on the sand, looking down as he spoke.

He looked up at Hunter and said, "How's Jerry doing? Do you think that his leg is broke?"

"It's hard to say without an x-ray. We have to treat it like it is. We got some of the information we needed but not near enough for a proper investigation. We will put our heads together in a little while and see where we go from here. Jerry's health is a big issue, and the site being underwater or washed out, I don't see a reason to stay. We can check around in the morning if the weather is better. We do have to get Jerry medical attention."

Steve interjected, "I did call in by radio and got the dispatcher a little while ago. I told her about our situation. They can get some help in for Jerry if we need it. I said that you would decide what to do about that. They are expecting a call tomorrow morning."

"What do you guys think? Are we safe in here?" Hunter asked.

Steve responded, "We checked for snakes, and aside from some badger tracks and some sidewinder tracks, I think it's safe, except maybe for some scorpions and black widows trying to get out of the rain."

Ray interrupted, "Steve, you almost forgot about the most dangerous critter of all." He tilted his head over to one side like he was using it to point to something.

"Oh yeah, I did." He lifted his lantern up from the ground with one hand and pointed his stick over toward the back of the cave. Hunter felt his muscles tighten.

"See there." The lantern illuminated two Coors beer cans up against some rocks. "I think that is the most dangerous beast that we have to deal with too."

Ray replied, "You know?"

Hunter said, "Just when you think you are far away from civilization out in the wild, beer cans bring you back to the realization that you are never far from it."

Steve answered, "These mountains have been scoured by people looking for something. It might be the old Dutchman's gold or some kind of adventure or like us looking for evidence of a crash. People looking for something usually make some kind of discovery, even if it wasn't exactly what they started out to find. Hell, we might be sitting on top of the Lost Dutchman's Mine right now. It could be right under our nose. We would never know it.

"There is a story about an army scout and part-time miner named Ed Schieffelin who left Fort Huachuca looking for silver in 1877 inside Apache territory. A friend of his told him that if he went there, all he would find is his tombstone. Well, he took a big risk.

He did find a huge deposit of silver. He named the town that grew up around that mine Tombstone. Some newspaper guy asked him what was the best part of the experience. He said, 'It wasn't becoming wealthy or famous. It was about the looking and the excitement of making the find.' I think he lost all his money and ended up in Oregon looking for another mother lode. The point is, we have taken a risk, and we are looking for what happened and maybe why it happened to these two people. I hope your team finds something that makes it worthwhile."

Hunter gazed down at the two men reclining on their sleeping bags and said, "I hope we can! It seems like the elements are against us." He shrugged his shoulders. "We will try to find that nugget of the truth and come up with some answers. Maybe we can piece it together somehow. Gentlemen, I need to prepare for a meeting with the rest of the team. You are invited."

"No, thanks," Steve replied. "We need to get a little shut-eye."

"Yeah," Ray interjected. "I need to get some sleep too. Tomorrow will be a busy day."

Hunter headed back to his part of the cave and started to write down his notes. He had been wrestling with something that seemed to bother him like a big bug that kept running into a light. Something was just beneath the surface of his consciousness, and it was coming around again. What was bothering him? Something seemed out of place. Then it hit him. Why was he in this place? Why did the pilot fly into this part of the wilderness? She should have gone around this area. In fact, this crash site was far from her flight plan. She had to turn from her original course to a much more difficult one. The mountains here are taller. She would have had to climb to clear them. The terrain was much rougher, the updrafts and downdrafts more unpredictable and intense. They were further from civilization if something did happen. If they did run into mechanical problems, there really was no flat place to land. This brought him back to his first question: why did she make the decision to depart from her original flight plan? He would never know for sure. He could, however, make an educated guess. He picked up his pad of paper along with a pencil and scribbled down some thoughts and initial impressions.

The wind and the rain were finally letting up outside when they met around Jerry. Brenda sat on one side of him, and Hunter on the other. They had brought over a couple of lanterns. Their light produced a kind of eerie quality in the cave. Jerry immediately picked up on the ambiance and said, as if he was in charge, "The reason I brought you all together—"

"Cool it, Jerry," Hunter exclaimed. He was in no mood to kid around anymore tonight. He was tired and feeling grumpy.

"Look. Let's get down to business and then get some sleep. We are going to need it. Brenda, let's start with you."

"We did find a few major pieces of the plane. It definitely was a Cessna 150. The engine block, part of the prop, crumpled tail section with the noted aircraft ID numbers, indicated it was the aircraft owned by Marian Anderson. The measurements taken so far indicate that the plane hit the rock face and exploded on impact. The force of the explosion sent out pieces of the plane everywhere. I only had a chance to measure some of the largest parts that were found. The force of the explosion sent them thirty to forty feet downstream, depending on size and weight. Many of the fragments of the plane showed discoloration consistent with fire and burning. The ground and vegetation around the site appeared charred. My impressions based on these facts are that the plane hit the rock face and exploded on impact. How it got there is more difficult to discern. It is unlikely that the intention of the pilot was to hit the rock face. It's more likely that she hit something coming down that pushed the plane left, probably a treetop. If we had time to get back in there, we could estimate her angle of attack and maybe even find the tree she hit. It is also likely that she had no options and no way to check what she was facing trying to land here. That's what I've got right now."

Hunter looked up from the notes he was taking. "Jerry."

"Pretty much the same as Brenda. I took as many pictures as I could with the measurements that she was taking. I mostly followed her around until we had to get out of there. One thing that struck me, though, were how few personal effects there were that seemed to survive the crash and explosion. It was like two people just disappeared."

It was Hunter's turn. "I could not locate any remains. If we had more time before the storm hit, we might have been able to find them. The problems are, it took time to get here, which gave animals time to disturb the site, the explosion and fire probably incinerated part of most of the remains, the rain and water corning down the creek likely washed away most of the evidence for identification of the victims.

"I have questions about why she was so off course. The possible explanations are that she wanted to show or see some different scenery or she made a wrong turn or got confused about her position. Since she was able to notify the tower and give a pretty good description of her location, it's unlikely that she got lost or made a wrong turn. It is more likely that she decided to veer from her course for her own reasons. Whatever those reasons were, they left her with few options once the plane got into trouble.

"What caused the engine to fail, as she noted on her call to the tower, is not known. It will take a collection of as many parts as possible to figure out why that happened. We have a lot of questions to answer. The evidence we have to draw conclusions from is very meager at this point."

Hunter continued in a very business like tone, "Here is how we should move forward. I think the weather forecast is that it will clear up tomorrow. Brenda and I will go back to the site and see if we can find any evidence that identifies the pilot and passenger directly. Jerry, you need to get medical attention. Ray will take you out by horseback to a place to be picked up by helicopter and taken back to Mesa. Steve will move the camp closer to the site and communicate with the sheriff's department. They will have to send some more posse members down here to take the pieces of the plane to a hanger in Mesa for evaluation. Brenda and I will remain here to collect more data and coordinated the removal of the wreckage. There may be some minor changes, but that's how I think we should play it." Hunter asked for questions, but it was obvious to everyone that decisions had been made and that was it.

Hunter said, "Let's get some sleep." He turned and let out a big sigh and taking a lantern with him, walked over to his sleeping bag and lay down.

Hunter was up early and so was Steve. They talked about the agenda for the day and with a few small exceptions, agreed to the process that Hunter had described. Breakfast consisted of an MRE, a military term for "Meals Ready to Eat." an energy bar, water, and coffee. Hunter and Brenda went down to the crash site. It was a beautiful morning. The air had a sweet smell of creosote, so common in the southwest. Everything was clean, like the high desert had washed all the dust off and put on a bright, clean set of clothes. It was also amazing how quickly the desert emptied itself. There were some muddy spots and pools of water, but they could be avoided. The cicadas made a loud z sound in the trees, and bugs were flying all around. Nature had found its voice. Hunter hoped that they would be able to find some evidence that would help the families cope with their loss. They got down to the creek and followed it until they spied the tail of the plane. It wasn't sticking up like before. It was lying flat in the streambed, ensconced in mud and debris. The creek was still running, but the water was way down.

Hunter said, "Let's head down there and look around."

"Sure," Brenda replied.

They had wandered almost down to the creek bed, avoiding muddy areas by walking on the rocks. It took a great deal of looking down and balance to not fall and end up on their butts. Just before Hunter was about to step over to a big rock, he saw something shiny sticking out of the mud.

"What's that?" he exclaimed. Brenda was next to him and looked over and saw it too.

"I don't know. Can you get it?"

"Yes, I think so," Hunter replied. He bent over and used another big rock to hold on to as he put his hand in the mud and pulled out the object. It was a wallet. It was made out of some kind of metal. It was silver and shiny except for the part that had been in the mud. They were both excited. Here was possibly the first item that belonged to someone from the crash.

"Let's take it back up to camp," Hunter said. "Clean it and see if anything is left inside."

Steve had located a new camp site. Both he and Ray had brought the gear over and were busy setting up camp close by the wash. They had even taken Jerry with them. Ray had made him a crutch from a tree limb. His ankle was black and blue and green and still very painful. His knee looked better. It was less swollen, and the cut was healing. Once the camp was moved, Ray was going to take him on horseback to a flat place about two hours' walk from the camp, where a helicopter would pick up Jerry and drop off a few supplies.

"Hey, we found something!" Hunter exclaimed as they climbed up toward the camp. He couldn't remember being this excited about finding a piece of evidence before. Steve and Ray dropped what they were doing and walked down to him.

"What is it?" he asked as they met.

"It's a wallet," Hunter said, "We need to clean it and find out what's inside."

They quickly retrieved a small plastic washtub and put some water in it.

"Do you think we should just let it dry and clean it?" Brenda asked.

Hunter replied with excitement in his voice. "It's already been in the water and the mud. Let's go ahead and carefully run the water over it." It was like panning for gold. With each cleaning, more and more of the wallet emerged until almost all the mud was washed away. Inside was a compartment that held a plastic driver's license. It had been protected by the metal material of the wallet. Although browned and tinged by heat, it clearly bore the name of Michael Turner. It gave an address and a driver's license number. The picture was unrecognizable. There was something else inside in another compartment. It was stuck to the wallet from the heat, but with a little careful coxing, it came out. It was a key.

Hunter said, "It looks like a key to a bank deposit box." He held it up to the light and examined it closely. "What a funny place to keep a key. Well, it might help the family with their paperwork. What's most important is that this evidence identifies the passenger and connects him to the crash. Ray, take this wallet, driver's license, and key with you when you drop off Jerry. Have him give it to the sheriff's department to be logged in as evidence and returned to the family. I think the sooner they get it, the better."

Hunter put the items in a plastic bag and gave it to Ray. Soon, he and Jerry set off for their rendezvous with the helicopter. Hunter walked back down to the crash site wondering if they would find anything else.

Sometimes I think I'm back to where I've been

time repeats certain themes.

I feel the tug of the wheel of life come back round again,

Like a planet orbiting my dreams

The gravity of life is not in the knowledge of such things;

it is the Holy Spirit circling my heart

with 'ah' bright Wings

Parte De Jour

The horn sounded again. It was an unmistakable invitation. It carried a sense of urgency and a profound feeling of joyful expectation. The horn sounded a third time, and the people came down the lane to the doctor's house. Michael and Ayin were standing on the porch together.

Ayin said, "Michael, I have to go. This is your party. I think that you will have a good experience meeting your patients."

"Wait," Michael said. "Can't you stay for some of it?"

"No, they really need to be with you and you with them."

"You know, I could use a little angelic help here."

"Michael, it will be good. I'm sure."

Michael was tempted to say "Just great!" sarcastically, but he didn't say that or the word *chicken,* which normally would have tumbled out of his mouth. Ayin seemed to know of his inner conflict. He disappeared wearing a look of contentment, leaving Michael to face the music alone.

The first person to get to the veranda was, of course, Cindy Crier. She ran up the steps and, without saying hello, enthusiastically put her arms around him. His initial response was to back away. He looked down at her with some of that professional reservation, which was more like protection. He noticed that she was wearing a red dress that was a little too old for her. Cindy's hair was braided and wrapped around her head. It was shaped like a little crown.

She looked up at him with a big smile and said, "Oh, thank you, Dr. Turner, for having the party. I am so excited about it. It will be wonderful." Her enthusiasm reminded him of his daughter, Jamie. She was always willing to take on a new opportunity. Jamie had a way of somehow turning a task into an adventure. He felt himself warming up to the idea of meeting everyone. Looking at her made him feel paternal and needed, just like with his own daughter.

"Where is your mother?" he asked, changing the subject. "You know, I haven't met her yet."

"She's coming. She has to walk with a cane because she has a bad back that slows her down. I wanted to come early to see everything."

He thought, *Maybe I can help her with that.* He was surprised by how naturally that idea came into his mind.

"Well then, Miss Cindy, may I escort you into the house so that we both can see everything?"

With that, he took her hand and placed it through his arm. He guided her from the veranda into the living room. It was full of soft light. In the middle of the room, where the furniture had been, there was a big table set with fine china, silverware, and crystal goblets all on a bright white tablecloth. The room seemed to glow. All the colors of things were more intense. The beauty of it made them both breathe in the moment and exhale a warm sigh.

"How beautiful it is. It's perfect," Cindy said. "How did you do all this?"

"Don't look at me, Cindy. I am as amazed as you are. I asked Josh to help with the party. He was the one who did all this. I wonder where he is. I want to thank him."

He must have come up quietly behind them. "Doctor," he said in a muted tone, "how do you like it?"

Michael still had Cindy's arm through his. They both turned and looked at Josh. He was wearing a full chef's white outfit: one of those big bulbous hats, a white tunic shirt, white pants, and white gloves. He even had on white shoes.

"Josh, it's great! There are no words to describe how fantastic it is. Thank you for the party," Michael said.

"Yes," Cindy interjected. "Mr. Josh, it is wonderful."

He replied with his southern drawl. "Y'all really like it? That makes me real happy. Let me tell you what the menu is for dinner. We are going to start with appetizers of quail pate served with on matzo with grape preserves, a tossed salad with our house vinaigrette dressing and homemade bread. The main course is a choice of roast of lamb with a honey mustard glaze, poached lake trout with a special cucumber sauce, or flame-broiled beef kebabs served on a bed of brown rice. Dessert is a fig flambe pudding. Of course, we will serve plenty of our house wine. The meal also includes lots of our fine local olives. I hope y'all will like it."

"Josh, I think this will be a great hit. I know that I am very impressed and amazed."

Just then, there was a loud rap at the screen door of the veranda. Michael knew who it was. He thought that would be Mr. Finwicky.

He said, "Please excuse me," and turned toward the veranda and left Cindy and Josh to talk to each other. He was right. Michael heard that voice that could only belong to Delbert Finwicky. Mr. Finwicky called out through the screen door, "Is anyone attending this domicile?"

"Yes, I'm coming, Delbert," Michael replied. He opened the screen door, and there he was. "Mr. Finwicky, I am so glad to have you back over to my home."

"Dr. Turner, it is a pleasure to be with you. I am quite honored to be invited to your parte de jour. I believe the rest of our gentry are on their way. I, being the most limber and athletic, got here way ahead of the others." Michael discerned that something was different about him. First, he was dressed in a more subdued fashion, wearing a light blue suit and pink tie. His potbelly still stuck out, leaving that same gap in his white shirt that strained against a tight button. Second, he was not as flighty and nervous as his first interview playing for some other audience. Third, he seemed to be less theatrical than at their first meeting. A smile still came to Michael's face upon their reacquaintance. He felt a real sense of joy at shaking his hand and inviting him into the house.

"You know, Delbert, that I have been looking forward to our meeting again."

"You have? Well, Doctor, that is very nice of you to say. I must confess that I have been looking forward to this party too."

"Come in, and let me show you the wonderful arrangements that Josh has made for our gala event," Michael said with a touch of his own theatrical embellishment. "Josh and Miss Cindy Crier are already here." They took a few steps through the veranda and entered into the dining room.

Mr. Finwicky let out a long "ah" as he saw the beautiful setting that Josh had prepared. "Doctor, this takes my breath away. It is a wonder, sir, a wonder. How did you do it?"

"It's the work of our caretaker, Josh. He set the whole thing up at my bequest. Little did I know that he would provide such an elegant table d'hote."

Delbert replied, "I must express my appreciation to him for this wonderful banquet."

"Oh, Miss Cindy Crier, it is so nice to see you."

Just then, there was another knock at the door.

Michael said to them, "There is someone else at the door. Please excuse me." He looked down at himself and discovered he had a white dinner jacket on and black pants and shoes, a white shirt, and a black bowtie and cuff links. There was a bright red flower in his lapel. The whole ensemble fit him so well that he was totally unaware of it.

Well, he thought, *this must be the first monkey suit that fits the monkey.* He laughed to himself as he got to the door of the veranda. He opened the screen door, and there was a young attractive couple holding hands. The young man said in a halting quiet way, "Hello, I am John Smith, and this is my wife, Mary."

He was wearing a black suit and tie, black shoes, and a white shirt. His wife was in a black gown and shoes. Their attire matched their dark hair and eyes. It communicated an air of mystery and sorrow.

"Hello, and welcome to my home and office. I am Dr. Michael Turner, and I'm so glad that you are here. Mr. Finwicky, Miss Crier, and Josh are in the dining room. I hope you enjoy the party."

John and Mary followed Michael. They stepped into the dinning room as he watched them look over all the setting's stunning details. He had a sense that the room glowed a little more with the addition of each new person. Michael was about to introduce the couple when Cindy took over and welcomed them first. Her excitement and the sweetness in her voice made her the perfect hostess. It was a role that was made for her; she took to it with unfettered joy.

There was another knock at the door. Cindy had clearly taken over the duties of being in charge of hospitality. He was now free to turn and move quickly to the veranda and answer the door.

Morgan and Billy Slack stood there looking at him. "Welcome, gentlemen," Michael said with a good bit of enthusiasm. He was actually glad to see them. Both looked right past him over his right shoulder, focusing their attention to the goings-on inside.

"Hi, Doctor," Billy said.

Before he could go on, his father interrupted. "Thank you for your invitation, Doctor. Billy and I are here purely to observe the nature of such gatherings and to discuss the purpose of social interactions and the complex behaviors of people to such an environment."

"I see," replied Michael. "Then will you please come with me into the dining room, where you can begin your experiment?" Michael encouraged them by sweeping his hand forward for them to go ahead of him, and he put his hands on their shoulders once they passed him and kind of steered them into the dining room. They both seemed tense and slightly resistant. Then it hit him; they were both unfamiliar with this kind of social experience. It was clear that Morgan, more than Billy, felt awkward. He didn't seem to know what to expect or how to behave.

Their choice of clothing was interesting. Billy wore a white shirt with a black tie and black high-water pants, like he was growing right out of them. He had on black shoes and socks. His brown hair was slicked back. He looked restrained like a reptile that needed to shed its skin. Morgan was all business. He was straight as a ramrod and uptight as one in the barrel of a rifle. It was as if he expected some terrible event to happen. Where Billy was uncomfortable in his clothes, Morgan was uncomfortable with himself and others. He wore a brown suit, blue tie, and ivory shirt.

Cindy was looking for a new assignment. The Slacks fit the bill. She spritely walked up to them as they entered the room, and Michael did the introductions.

"Miss Cindy Crier, may I introduce Mr. Morgan Slack and his son, Billy. They have accepted my invitation to our party. I am very happy to have them with us. They are both scientists and are here to research the nature of social gatherings and their benefits. I trust, Cindy, that you will introduce them to the other guests."

She came over and grasped both their hands with hers. She flashed a big smile and said, "Oh yes, Dr. Turner, I would be glad to do that. Gentlemen, please come with me, and I will introduce you first to Josh, our chef, and the rest of our friends." Michael was surprised by how she sounded so grown up, not like she was trying on a new role. *No,* he thought, *she has discovered something about herself that enhanced her personality. She is somehow more mature and self-confident.* He could tell at the same time that there was definitely some positive chemistry between Cindy and Billy. She had grasped his hand and then put it through her arm, leading him over first to Josh and to Mr. Finwicky. Morgan walked slightly behind them, looking a little out of place. *It could be very interesting watching those two,* Michael thought.

There was a faint knock at the veranda screen door. He knew that there were only two people yet to arrive. He thought, *That must be Odelia Crier.* She had probably come last so that she could make a grand entrance. She was unaware that someone else would likely claim that honor—that is, if he came at all.

He answered the door. He had been right. They both stood there for a moment and looked each other over.

Quickly, she gathered her composure and said, "I am Mrs. Odelia Crier. You must be our new Doctor."

"Yes," he replied. "I am Dr. Michael Turner. I am very glad to meet you. Welcome to my home. Let me show you in." He saw that she was using a wooden cane to lean on. She had a pronounced limp on her left leg. Odelia was wearing a beige business suit and matching shoes with a pink blouse and matching skirt and jacket. She had a matronly figure and was not a beautiful woman, but she was sophisticated, knowing how to accent her physical attributes. Her red hair was pulled back like her daughter's. She carried a self-confident demeanor. He thought that Odelia was one of those people who were hard to impress. They are often too busy keeping score of their own expectations to be taken by surprise. Yet as he shook her hand and escorted her into the dining area, the atmosphere definitely had taken her off guard.

"Oh, Doctor, this is a very beautiful table. I must tell you that I am quite amazed. The decor is wonderful. You have my congratulations," she said as she eyed the room up and down and all the people in it.

"Thank you, Mrs. Crier. I am glad that you approve. I must tell you that our caretaker, Josh, put this all together for us."

"Really? That is truly amazing! I didn't know that he was up to this kind of work."

Michael looked over to Josh, who seemed to be getting ready to serve the drinks and appetizers.

"He has quite a meal planned for us. I don't want to give away all that he has prepared. I think that he can best describe the menu. However, I will tell you that it will be very special."

Just then, Cindy came over from talking to Mr. Finwicky and Billy and said, "Hello, Mother. Isn't it all wonderful? Josh and Dr. Turner have provided a really great opportunity for us to meet one another. I think it's great!"

"Yes, I can see your point, child. We haven't had a party since the young doctor was here. He left so soon that none of us ever got together, socially I mean. We have just stayed in our own little worlds, dealing with our own problems and keeping to ourselves."

She looked down at her leg and sighed. It was an unsaid expectation that Michael was supposed to notice her discomfort and inquire about her leg.

"Tell me, Mrs. Crier, what happened to your leg? I see that you need a cane. Were you hurt in an accident or is this some kind of chronic problem?"

"Thank you for noticing, Doctor," she said with a touch of sarcasm. It made him remember Delbert's admonition that she knew how to put someone in their place. "I think that we should set up an appointment so that we can discuss the matter privately."

"It would be a pleasure to listen and to help you if I can."

"I don't know if anyone can help me with this," she replied. "Some things you just have to adjust to. That is what I have done. Still, perhaps there is a small hope for some kind of improvement."

Michael looked up, and next to him was Josh holding a tray with glasses of wine for everyone. It was understood that each person should take one. He quickly served the drinks and poured a glass for himself.

He said, "I hope that y'all enjoy the food that has been prepared. I have had the help of a few angelic visitors."

It seemed a natural place for Michael to say a few words. Delbert cleared his throat, which had the intended effect of getting everyone's attention.

He took the floor and said, "Ladies and gentlemen, it is a real pleasure to be here with you and our new doctor. I am sure that we are glad to have his services if any of us should find ourselves incontinento de-lick-toe. Dr. Turner, we welcome you here, and we rejoice at your propitious assignation. Would you please share with us a few remarks?" He pointed an outstretched hand and waved it with a flourish and a short bow.

Michael felt a little awkward at this unexpected request to perform, yet he quickly rescued the moment.

"When Miss Crier and I came up with this idea, I wasn't sure that it would work out. I am glad now that I took the opportunity to host this party. I want to extend my appreciation to our chef, Josh, for this wonderful billet a faire and decoration." He pointed a little stiffly to the table and the walls. "I look forward to getting to know you all a little better. If you need me, I am usually around here at my office. Thank you, and God bless you." He looked around the room and was given a pleasant round of modest applause. He noticed that the only people who did not enter into it were the Smiths. They had already staked a claim for a spot in one of the corners and were too busy carrying on their own conversation, which excluded everybody else.

What an interesting group of misfits, he thought. *I wonder how they all got here. Probably the same way I did with a prayer of desperation. It's a good thing that God seems to pay attention to those, or at least He did in my case.*

He noticed that Odelia Crier was corning toward him, seeming to carry a concern that was too big for her to hold in. She limped like the top part of her was trying to race the bottom half as she leaned heavily on her cane. He waited for all the parts to arrive, which, of course, they eventually did.

"Mrs. Crier, it seems like you have something on your mind," Michael said with a slight questioning look, which indicated he was curious.

"Doctor, do you know that Mr. Slack and his son are going around writing things down about the party?" Her voice cracked, and she held a harsh stare at him. "Why, they are asking questions about the event and our personal feelings about it. I thought that I was being interrogated the way they went on. Well, I think they are rude and need to be reprimanded or asked to leave."

"Mrs. Crier, it was told to me that I should personally invite them, so when I met them, it became clear that their attendance would require a motive that would interest them. I suggested that they could come to evaluate scientifically the nature of social discourse. They accepted with the understanding that they could interview the guests. I have noticed their attention to this task and especially Billy's single-minded devotion to interview Miss Cindy. I think that this is a very good development. They seem to be really hitting it off."

She recoiled and looked for her daughter, who was standing at the end of the long dining room table talking to Billy with rapt attention. She took in a big gulp of air and breathlessly said, "Well, I'll go stop that."

"Oh, Odelia," he said brashly, "you don't need to be concerned. They are just kids having a good time. They have a whole room of chaperones. Besides, I have something I want to discuss with you." She suddenly shifted gears with that tidbit of information, and her curiosity got the better of her. Her indignation over the Slacks took a backseat to what the Doctor wanted to talk about. He paused and moved a little closer, knowing that he had hooked her interest.

"Did you know that there is another person here that nobody knows about?" he said quietly.

"That is preposterous, Doctor! I know everyone who is here, and unless there has been another new arrival like yourself, nobody else lives here." Her look and the tone of her voice indicated that she would not easily accept what he was about to tell her.

"I know for a fact that someone else lives here because I met him. His name is Bradley Schley. I invited him to our party, and he said he would be here. I don't think that he will actually show up, but you never know he might surprise me." Odelia looked shocked as she replied, "You must be joking. How come I, uh, we, have never met him?" she asked with an air of disbelief that also indicted a tinge of disapproval.

"Well, I think that he is more reclusive than any of our other guests. He probably has some reasons why he has avoided everyone. If he shows up, you can ask him your questions."

"Don't worry, Doctor, if he comes, I intend to," Odelia replied. She made a quick glance around the room. Michael wasn't sure if she was looking for Mr. Schley to quiz or if she was just curious to meet the person who had upstaged her or both.

The event was progressing wonderfully. The appetizers and wine had been served, and everyone was talking to each other. Odelia had even taken some time to visit with Mr. Finwicky. Somehow, Morgan Slack had managed to break into the Smiths conversation.

He seemed determined to discover what their story was and why they were so content to be left alone. Michael thought he was like one of those cheesy malpractice lawyers gathering data to build a case.

Meanwhile, Cindy and Billy continued to focus their attention on one another. She has definitely put aside her role as hostess. It was clear, he thought, that she had gotten a much better offer. Michael was just about to join Delbert and Odelia when Josh came up next to him.

"We are just about ready to serve the main course. There is one empty chair. You think that our reluctant friend might be outside waiting for an invite?" he said with a whisper. "I just bet that if you went outside for a stroll, you might just run into each other. Remember, guys like him don't come out of the rain unless their waterlogged."

With that admonition, Michael turned and walked to the veranda to head outside for some serious looking around. He left shaking his head, wondering what Josh was trying to say. Michael crossed the veranda and noticed, as he opened the screen door and stepped outside, that it was dusk. *Strange,* he thought. *The daylight has turned gray.* Everything was colored over with a huge shadow. It was like many evenings in his boyhood home in Ohio. He could smell the aroma of cut hay and felt a chill in the air. It reminded him of other late summers that resisted the stealthy approaching fall.

The realization slowly crept into his consciousness, and then it hit. This experience required this setting. He hadn't thought about it till now. The farm was whatever he needed it to be. Sunny, temperate, dawn, or dusky—it perfectly matched the moment and the mood. It was like a theater that had all the lights, sounds, colors, and sights to match the requirements of the characters. Its job was to heighten the experience and reveal its significance, as he looked around and asked himself what was he feeling and thinking about meeting Mr. Schley.

Ayin had told him that Bradley Schley was a man of secrets. He lived outside the rest of the community. He lived in the shadows. The advent of dusk fit him so well. Secrets are not black or white but mostly gray. They can hide true intentions and cover over the truth. Secrets are the in-between place of light and dark. They are that place where temptations are born and often where sin is conceived. It's the perfect place for Mr. Schley to live. Michael remembered their first meeting. Bradley had been like a shadow cast by the tree. He's very hard to spot. Ayin had only seen him because he knew what to look for.

There was a question that germinated in his mind. Was this setting for Mr. Schley's benefit, or was it for him? He began to ponder that idea and looked down at the ground. He didn't notice the shadow that moved differently from the others. It was like the wind was coming from another direction. Michael lifted up his head and saw nothing unusual, and yet he knew there was. The shadow man approached him from the left and slowly came closer and closer.

A move is an action that is a change of place,

change contains the possibilities of good or bad.

Today or tomorrow reveals the captured space,

that time deletes from the hair upon our head.

With No Mercy

Transitions

David's flight had been uneventful. He landed in Phoenix and changed planes and took a puddle jumper to Tucson. People down there called it the "Old Pueblo." It certainly was not his old pueblo. He didn't like the town much, probably because it was a place of ambiguities. Was it a city or a town? Was it America or Mexico? Was it rural or cosmopolitan? The plane descended to land, and Tucson awaited him with all its confusions. Soon, he would be seeing Jamie and his mom, and the Old Pueblo would suddenly be all too real.

Jamie had arranged to meet David at the luggage claim area. His plane was right on time. Good old Chandler Air they must have had a tailwind. She smiled as she parked the car and walked toward the terminal. It was a pleasant day. The sun had not yet become the oppressive force of summer that would hold the desert hostage. The slightly cool breeze gave hope for the moment that spring would hold off the beast. She was so glad that David was coming home. She was really happy that she didn't have to beg him. He had simply made arrangements, and he was coming home, even if it meant going to Tucson.

Mom had decided to fill her morning with distractions, so it was up to Jamie to pick up David. She was grateful to be the first to see him. Jamie thought how confused her feelings were. Normally, she would be excited. The reason why he was coming, though, was painful—not to see her or catch up on life experiences or kick around for a few days. He was here because Dad would never be here again. She felt the sadness return with that thought, and tears began to well up in her eyes. Jamie looked around in the commotion of the baggage area, trying to find David and change the direction of her thoughts and focus on the task at hand. It was busy but not packed. After a few minutes, she realized that he was not here yet.

Jamie saw him first. He was sauntering down the walkway that led to the baggage carousels. She recognized that loping stride of his that was slow but somehow graceful. His last picture showed him sporting a full mustache and bushy beard. She was glad to see he had shaved it off. He was tall and lanky. He wore, of course, a faded pair of jeans and a white long sleeved shirt with a leather vest, cowboy hat, and boots. David had dark black hair and brown eyes. When he smiled, she could slightly see the outside edges of dimples on both cheeks. He had a strong jaw and straight nose, which fit the rest of his face. She thought how handsome he was and that her friends would be falling all over themselves to meet him.

He saw Jamie as he headed toward the baggage carousel. He couldn't see her face, just the top of her head in the crowd, but he knew that it was her. They walked toward each other. David reached out and gave her a big hug. She felt tiny in his arms.

She said, "David, it's good to see you. I am so glad you're here."

"Me too," he said.

David stood back and looked at her. Jamie was much the same. Her hair was shorter. It was a little blonder than he remembered. She still had that round coquettish face and green eyes. She had a little mouth that fit her face and a long neck and a petite figure that made her both attractive and alluring. She was wearing a light blue sundress with a yellow blouse and white sandals. *It's too bad,* he thought, *that Da Vinci had only the Mona Lisa to paint because Jamie would have been a better subject.*

"Here's my bag coming around. Let's get out of here so we can talk." He pointed to a big black duffel bag on the carousel that looked like it had been around. David went over and snatched it up like it was as light as a feather.

"Where are you parked?" he asked.

Jamie replied, "Follow me," and off they went.

It didn't take them long to get to her car. It was a perfect car for her, a white VW Rabbit. He thought it interesting how people and cars tended to match each other. David threw the duffel bag into the back of the car, opened the passenger door, and slid his long frame into the seat. They headed out of the airport and in no time were on that part of the highway that required only a modicum of attention.

David was the first to speak. "Jamie, could you tell me what happened and how you found out about the accident?"

She thought that the way he phrased the question was a little odd. It made her feel like he was a prosecuting attorney and she was the confused and probably bewildered witness. She decided to be as accurate with the time line as possible, beginning on that Sunday afternoon when the two officers came to her door at the dorm with the bad news. She tried to remember the sequence of facts, but other emotions and impressions poured out too. David would stop her occasionally and inquire about some detail, but mostly, he just listened. She was afraid that despite her best efforts, she still came across as a dizzy blond. They were almost to Mom's condo when she finished her testimony. Jamie felt a sense of relief, like a weight had been removed from her shoulders. She realized that this was the first time she had gone over the whole thing with anyone. It was like going to confession—telling what happened made her burden lighter. Keeping some of her attention on the road had provided a chance for her to get outside her grief and get a little perspective.

"Jamie," David said after a few minutes of silence, "what you've told me makes sense, except for one thing. I don't know why Dad would go flying. You know how hevalued predictability and security. I just can't understand how he agreed to go with this lady on a plane ride. It is so out of Dad's comfort zone."

"You know, David, I thought about that too, but the evidence points to only one conclusion. For some reason, he did. I don't know why. We will probably never know the answer to that question. I've wondered about a bunch of strange coincidences. You know, Dad came to take me to a play at the university. It was the Wednesday before the plane crash. He really wanted to go see it. So we made a night of it, dinner and the play. It was dreary and painful. Not the dinner—I mean, the play was depressing. It was *A Long Day's journey into Night* by some guy named O'Neill, I think. I was ready to leave after the first act. Dad was determined to see the whole thing. It was like he was experiencing something about himself. You know how he gets that 'can't you see I'm busy' look. Well, there was something very much like that on his face but a sadness too. A couple of times, I looked over at him, and I thought I saw tears in his eyes. I don't think I ever saw him cry before. It was strange. We said our good-byes after the play. He seemed okay, but I have thought about that evening quite a bit. I asked Mom about Dad's childhood, and she replayed that familiar story that his parents had been killed in a car crash coming back from a party. He and his brother and sister had been raised by his grandparents. She said that his grandfather died of heart problems, and his grandmother a year later, of cancer before he completed med school. His family had split up after their deaths, and he didn't know where his brother or sister lived. It's a lonely story.

"I couldn't help but think that there was more to it. The play is about a broken home and family. The mother is an addict, and the rest of the family sort of revolves around her. Maybe Dad's family was like that in some way." Jamie pulled into the gated community in the Tucson Foothills. "Here we are."

Time had just flown by, and now it was pushing them onward to the next thing.

David wondered if Jamie was giving an invitation to really talk about Dad, or was she just nibbling around the edges? Should he just blurt out how he felt about his father or wait and see what would emerge? He quickly decided to wait and gauge the emotional landscape. Jamie already knew some of his feelings anyway from past conversations. He knew that Jamie was closer to Dad and that she was grieving.

Well, he thought, *so am I.*

She punched in the access code at the gate, and it opened. They drove through and made a turn at the first street on the right. It led to a long row of white single-story Mexican colonial-style homes connected together by a common wall and adjoining two car garages.

"Mom should be home by now," she said and parked the car on the street in front of the condo. He got his duffel bag out from the back, and they both walked up to the front door. Jamie had a key and opened the door and called out.

"Mom, we're here."

There was no response at first, then from the back of the house, David heard his mother's voice. "I'll be right there."

He knew that voice. It sounded warm and inviting. It was such a pleasant voice that it made him realize how much he had missed it and the person behind it. She walked in from what he thought was the bedroom into the living room. His mother had a way of making an understated welcome that often gave the impression she had some special information that she would discuss later. Instead, she rushed up to him and gave him a big hug.

"Davie, I am so glad you have come home. I can't believe that this has happened to your father. It is just the most difficult and painful time for all of us. It has taken me several days to face the reality that he is gone."

"I'm struggling with that too, Mom."

She stood back and put her hand out. Jamie came over and grabbed it. Together, they walked over to the couch and sat down next to each other, still holding hands. David found a wingback chair across from them to sit in. It was too small for him and made him feel restrained. He noticed that his mother began to cry. Jamie realized it at the same time. She got a Kleenex box on an end table, went over, and brought it to her.

David recognized at that moment how Jamie was just a younger version of her mother. He had gotten his father's stronger manly features, and Jamie had her mother's rounder facial characteristics. Their mom was a little over five feet tall and a little heavier than he remembered. A description of her shape would be matronly. She was wearing a red blouse and a blue denim skirt and wore some Indian silver jewelry, a turquoise necklace, and a couple of red coral bracelets. She had her hair pulled back in a bun, which was a curious contrast with her subtle face. Her hair was still light brown mostly, but there were lines of gray running through it.

"Mom," David said as he broke the silence. "I need to have some answers. Do you have any more information about what happened?"

Before she could respond, Jamie said, "David, the NTSB is doing an investigation to find out what caused the crash. They sent a team from Washington. They are gathering all the evidence they can from the crash to figure out what happened. They said that they would release any of Dad's personal stuff to us. One of their agents called and said that he would be coming to Tucson to meet with us."

"Jamie," Mary interrupted, "I got a call just a little while ago from an Officer Hernandez. He said that he had met you several days ago here at your dorm."

"He was one of the policemen who told me about Dad. What did he have to say?" It was Jamie's turn to interrupt.

"He said that they did find something that belonged to Dad and that he and an NTSB agent would bring it over for identification. It has already been catalogued or something."

"What is it?" Jamie asked with a tone of frustration and curiosity.

"He didn't say, only that it belonged to your father. He said he would be here in about half an hour."

The next twenty or thirty minutes were spent talking about some of the questions they would like to ask the agent and catching up on travels and impressions of the city, school, and vacations. It was abruptly halted with a ring of the doorbell. David was closest, so he went to the door and opened it.

"Hello, I am Officer Jessie Hernandez with the City of Tucson Police Department, and this is Agent Jerry Goldman with the NTSB. I was given this address and contact phone number by Miss Jamie Turner. I called earlier—"

"Yes, Officer Hernandez," Jamie replied before David could open his mouth. She quickly approached him and ushered him and Agent Goldman into the living room. Jamie noticed that the agent was wearing a walking boot and was limping. She introduced her family and invited them to sit down. David had pulled out a couple of chairs from the dining room table before they arrived. He had folded himself back into the wingback chair. David observed that Officer Hernandez tried to look at everyone but was obviously more interested in looking at Jamie. He was stocky and had very Hispanic features. Next to him sat Agent Goldman. He was thin and had a nasal high-pitched voice that matched his torso. They looked like Mutt and Jeff. Agent Goldman was trying to make eye contact with everyone in the room. It seemed a little rehearsed, like he had practiced this kind of interview before but now it was all too real. David thought, *When people are under stress, they always fall back on their training.*

Jesse was glad that Jamie was there. He'd hoped to see her again and not just be the bearer of bad news but to help provide some closure. He could tell by her welcome, and the way she looked at him, that she harbored no bad feelings. Jesse felt his shoulders relax with that assessment.

Still, he stammered as he started, "L-1-let me, uh, first say that I am very sorry for your loss. As you know, there has been a team working at the site of the crash from the NTSB, National Transportation and Safety Board. It is their charge to investigate and provide a written report of the crash and its likely causes. Agent Goldman is here from that team."

Jaime and David introduced themselves, and David introduced his mother.

Agent Goldman spoke up, "I want to express my sympathy at your loss and assure you that everything is being done to recover as much evidence from the crash as possible. I am part of a three-person crew that flew in from Washington to examine the site. Our team leader is Agent Hunter Grayson. The other member of the team is Agent Brenda Marshall. They have found several items belonging to the passenger we believe to be from Dr. Michael Turner. I am authorized to bring this to you for identification." He pulled a small plastic bag with a silver object inside from his inside coat pocket. "We believe that this was your father's wallet. There are two items also included, a signed driver's license and a key that was found inside. It appears to be a key to a safe deposit box or something like that. Do you recognize it?"

Jamie spoke up first. "Yes, I do. It looks like the wallet I gave him for Christmas. It's made of titanium, and I got it for him over the internet." She laughed through the tears, which now ran down her cheeks. "I made a big deal about Dad being so tight with his money and stuff like that. He got a kick out of it too." The agent got up and walked over to her. Jamie took it from him like it was a precious newborn. She removed it from its plastic cradle and carefully opened it.

"This looks like his driver's license, but I have never seen this key before. Mom, do you know about this key?"

Mary replied, "No, honey, I have never seen that before."

Agent Goldman continued, "I know that you must have a lot of questions. I have been to the site of the accident. You might recall the terrible weather that weekend. We tried to get to the crash as fast as possible. It's in a very difficult location. We had to get horses and guides to get to it. We discovered that the crash had been catastrophic. There had been an explosion and fire as result of the apparent collision of the plane with the sheer face of a mountain. We know from the communication logs between the pilot and the tower at Falcon Field that the pilot, Miss Marian Anderson, said that she had complete engine failure. Why that happened, we are trying to figure out."

Jerry Goldman began to fumble with his words, so he paused and said after a deep breath, "One of the things we do at the NTSB is to investigate the backgrounds of anyone hurt or killed in a plane crash. This is standard procedure for a variety of reasons that I won't go into right now. We do a far more detailed background check than most agencies. There are a few things we need to understand about Dr. Turner that have come up as a result of our investigation. What can you tell me about his past?"

Love is an exodus that prods and propels me on:

I pass it over to you and we carry it along.

Like a runner, who after the race feels as if he's

running still.

We move upon the swiftness of God's ever striding

grace ascending another hill,

knowing that there is no race to run on Egypt's

foreign soil.

So I set upon my journey's prize and pray God to win

my soul

Passover

Michael knew that Bradley Schley was close by. It was no surprise that he heard his voice before he saw him.

"Hello, Dr. Turner. I told you I would show up," he said with a low gravelly voice.

"I've been down here. Of course, no one ever saw me or even looked to see me. They are all too busy, concerned about themselves. Just like you."

Michael was trying to hear where the voice was coming from. It sounded like just behind him, near the side of the veranda. There was a pile of wood there, and he decided that the sound came from behind it.

He turned and said, "You know I can't see you. Would you please come out from behind the woodpile and talk to me."

"Sure, I'll come out if you will." Slowly, he stood up and walked out from behind the obstacle.

"What do you mean by that?" Michael asked.

"We all have our little secrets, don't we? You have the doctor thing working for you. No problems, no hardships. You just have all the answers, don't you, Dr. Turner? What happens when the secrets add up to a pile of pain and regret, like I have to live with? What do you do then? No medicine can cure it, and no narcotic can blot it out."

He took a couple of steps, and the light from the veranda provided a backdrop that exposed his silhouette.

"It is easy to consign me to the shadows of life, to that gray grave of loneliness and despair. So many people have put me in that spot. Do you still want me to come to your party? What purpose would it serve except to satisfy your curiosity? Ayin had told me that you were coming."

Ayin said, "I'm to leave what I am accustomed to and experience life differently."

He said, "It's a necessary step for me to take to come into the light. So, Doctor, here I am, trying to take that step."

He was wearing a blue chambray shirt, blue jeans with a leather belt, and boots. Michael thought that he dressed like some of the prisoners he treated in his residency days at the old county hospital.

"Brad, I think that it is a good idea. I can appreciate how difficult that such a step would be for you. I am willing to help."

Michael felt an emotion he had forgotten. It had lingered in his memory from his youth. He tried to name that feeling, and it quickly jumped into his mind; he felt compassion. All at once, he wanted to put his hand on this man's shoulder and reassure him. Taking such a risk would not be impossible. Instead, he did what he considered professional. He waited for the patient to make the first move. He felt some disappointment with himself. He lacked the freedom to care. His medical distance had always worked for him. It was a virtue to remain aloof and detached; somehow, it didn't fit this experience and this place.

"What do we do now, Doctor?" Bradley asked. His voice had taken on a softer tone.

"Why don't we walk in together, and I will introduce you to everyone. Now that you have arrived, Josh will serve the dinner. Come with me."

Michael could feel Bradley's hesitation, as if the shadows were beckoning him to stay hidden. He took several determined strides with Michael up the three steps, opening the screen door and trudging onto the veranda. It was about twenty-five feet to the parlor and the festivities. They both reached the doorway and were immediately noticed by Josh, who whispered, "It's good to see you, Mr. Schley."

Word passed from guest to guest, and all conversation stopped. At this point, Michael took over.

"Ladies and gentlemen, let me introduce to you Mr. Bradley Schley. I am very happy that he has come to be with us at the party. I know that many have never met him before. It is true that he has been reclusive. His decision to come to the party says a lot about his desire to become a part of our community. I know that you will make him feel welcome."

Cindy immediately came over with her new friend, Billy, and they introduced themselves and whisked him off to meet everyone. He reluctantly followed them like an animal that pulled against its master's leash. Too late now to resist; there were no shadows to hide in. The bright light in the room made that impossible.

Michael had just relinquished Bradley Schley to Cindy Crier's care when Josh came up to him and said, "Would you please invite everyone to come to the table? You're the host of the party. You should be the one to offer the blessing."

He felt awkward and uncomfortable with Josh's request. Michael had always relied on his wife, Mary, to-do the praying.

I guess around here, he thought, it was his job to learn how. He knew that Josh was right and that he needed to take charge of gathering his guests around the table. He tried to get everyone's attention by raising his voice, but the room had gotten increasingly loud, so he started banging on his wine goblet loudly with a spoon. It got everybody's attention. Michael invited them to take their seats.

"Ladies and gentlemen, I am so grateful that you have decided to come to my little get-together. I want to thank Josh for putting this party together, both the decorations and the meal. I am also grateful for Miss Cindy Crier and Mr. Delbert Finwicky for encouraging me to host this soiree. Josh reminded me that a brief prayer is in order.

"Dear God, bless this food and our fellowship. Thank you for the benefits of your love and grace. Help us to always be grateful for your blessings so that we may bless one another. Amen."

There was a stillness in the room that touched each person, a quiet realization that those benefits are on display and that they were very grand indeed. Delbert Finwicky suddenly stood at the other end of the table and said with his usual loud theatrical flair, "Ladies and gentlemen, I am very glad that the distinguished Dr. Michael Turner has arrived to care for our illnesses. He has already ministered some elixir of kindness to me. I offer a toast to him. May his glass of caring for others never run dry. May he find true happiness here in our company. I am reminded of that famous Latin saying, 'Hie magnum me us nostrum releaus hoc end emeus.' With these final words, Delbert raised his glass and said, "To Dr. Turner." There were some pleasant applause and a few "hear, hears" from the rest of the assembly.

Dinner was served. It was a wonderful repast. Everyone remarked how the food was delicious and satisfying. All seemed to enjoy their conversations. It surprised Michael how at ease he felt with everything. Even Mr. Schley seemed to endure the personal interactions. He sat next to Cindy, with Billy at her right hand and Bradley on the left. It was obvious that she had become the belle of the ball. He enjoyed observing her adolescent flirtatiousness.

Mr. Slack had even put down his notepad to eat. He was sitting next to the Smiths. Michael could see that they had gotten along. Something seemed to make them compatible. He didn't know what that was. He was happy that they had hit it off. He had been concerned that they would not have anyone to talk to.

Josh came by to visit him after the main course was served. Michael was sitting down, and he came and stood next to him and whispered, "I hope the event has been a blessing to y'all. It was the first time that there has been a celebration here. I have to say that I had a good time putting it all together. It was a real change from my usual chores."

"It was a blessing for everyone, Josh," Michael replied. "Most importantly, it helped break the ice. People got a chance to talk and to get to know each other. I have enough experience from my previous patients that things can get a bit intense when it comes to something like a person's health care. I am really glad that I don't have to file a lot of paperwork and go over useless reports. It feels really good to just help someone. The patient wants someone who is willing to listen. I was a little lacking in that essential skill. I wanted to get them out the door so I could see the next patient. I had forgotten they were persons with more than a symptom or a sickness. I feel so free to be a doctor without insurance requirements, Medicare guidelines, liability insurance, and the pressure to have an immediate fix to all the patient's problems."

Josh shook his head in agreement. "Ya know, that reminds me of a fella who made a lot of money and decided to buy three houses. One was for the summer in the high country, where it was cool. One was in the desert, where it was warm in the winter, and another one was near the ocean so he could go fish'n whenever he wanted to. He spent about four months of the year in each place. He had himself a great time year after year except for one time, when he got real sick. You see, he was never in one place long enough to get to know his neighbors or build friendships either in town or in church. Oh, he watched those evangelists on TV when he needed to feel religious, but no, sir, since nobody knew him when he was ill and desperate and in need of a friend, he was alone."

Michael exclaimed, "Josh, that's a sad, sad story."

"Well, not every story has a happy ending."

"You take these folks here. None of um have ever really talked to each other except to complain. They like giving me orders, but they don't put themselves out for anyone else. They have been content to just be in their own space, until this party. Maybe that's your job here, Doc, to help them uncover a sense of belonging. I would definitely say that would be a big first step."

"Josh, how do I do that? I am still trying to figure that out for myself."

"Well, Doc, you're a smart guy. It will come to you, I'm sure. I must say, you got off to a good start here. I'll be around if you need me. Excuse me. I need to serve desert."

Josh stood up turned and walked back to the kitchen. Michael patted his shoulder as he left. It was meant to be a sign of appreciation for all he had done. Instead, Michael was the one affected. It was as if a warm connection had been communicated. He knew that he could trust Josh. It was a freeing moment of validation. The feeling had come upon him quite unexpectedly.

Delbert Finwicky had managed to sit next to him at the table. He kept the conversation moving along and funny. His humor full of misplaced words and facial contortions along with the wine had almost everyone laughing. Michael felt a real joy in participating in the repartee.

Odelia was having a hard time with Delbert's sudden rise in prominence. She felt jealous. *Aren't I the one who requires attention? After all,* she thought, *I am the one who has the most social acumen. Delbert and the rest of the quests are nice people to be sure, but after all, they lack my breeding and sensibility.* Odelia decided it was time to change the direction of the table talk to more serious topics. She was getting tired of all the laughter. She had never found humor to be all that important. Humor required a turn of phrase that was unexpected. It required a surprise. Odelia didn't like surprises any more than she liked jokes. Serious men and women accomplished great things not by surprises or whimsy. No, serious people made a habit of predictability. A person had to know what they had and how to make it grow. No personal fortune or great enterprise or artistic creation came by surprise. It came by discipline and hard work.

"Dr. Turner," she said with a loud voice, "many of us at the table are curious about what you intend to do to help us get well. There is some reason why we are not reaching our full destiny. I am speaking about our home with God. Perhaps it is some physical flaw or weakness of character that has branded us as not ready to ascend to that heavenly plane. Perhaps it's something of the earth that has us bound to this place. Perhaps it is, well, who knows. Anyway, here we are, and here you are. What can you give us that can make us feel better? What tonic or medicine or potion can effect this transformation that invites us but in the same breath holds us back?"

"That's a good question," Michael replied thoughtfully. "It's not easy to answer. The fact is, I don't know the answer. I think that if we worked together, something good will happen. I am just getting to know you. The party is our first attempt at becoming acquainted. I feel that the answer is right here for all of us to discover. Will you help me be your Doctor by working with me? I would like to have a chance to meet with each of you privately. It might be a first step to attain that destination of health you desire."

Delbert stood up at once and said, "I, for one, will participate in this exercise." He made a fist, and pumping his bicep pointed at Michael. "I think we should all make a strong affirmation to adopt Dr. Turner's plan."

There was a general acceptance of the idea by almost everyone in the room. Only one person did not say anything. He had slipped into the room when Delbert had taken the floor. The guests slowly began to head to their houses as if by some agreed-upon signal. There were cordial handshakes as they left. All expressed how happy they were at being together at the party. Michael thought he was alone. As he turned around, a surprise awaited him.

I saw no temple in the city, for its temple is the Lord God the Almighty and the lamb. And the city has no need of sun or moon to shine on it, for the glory of God is its light, and its lamp is the Lamb. The nations shall walk by its light, and the kings of the earth will bring their glory into it. Its gates will never be shut by day—and there will be no night there. (Revelations 21:22-27, NRSV)

We come upon that city of dazzling lights.

The Jerusalem of brilliance born in the womb of creation;

a ring of glory that surrounds us with God's holy reflection

where there is no need of days or nights.

Revelations

"What exactly are you getting at?" David interjected. "What about my dad's past interests you?" he asked with a tone that contained an edge of agitation.

Jerry immediately felt the emotional chill, so he paused and said, "I know that this is a difficult time for all of you. We do need to work together to find out what happened and, if possible, why it happened. I believe that we want the same things. It's just that we have discovered some facts about your father, and we wondered if you knew about them. If you will just answer my questions for now."

Jamie replied, "What do you want to know?"

"We understand that he was fifty-eight years old and that he was born in Ohio. It always helps to know what a person was like." Jerry took a picture from the end table next to him. It was a photo taken for some special occasion. It had the family all together. It was a handsome group. Everyone was full of smiles. *Probably a graduation,* he thought. Jerry looked intently on one particular person in the picture. Dr. Michael Turner was a tall distinguished-looking man. He had gray hair, blue eyes, and a trace of dimples on both cheeks with strong masculine features. He appeared stiff in the photo, and although he seemed to be trying to smile, it was not an easy task for him.

Jamie felt the need to defend her father, so she said with a resolute tone, "My father was a great man. He had a wonderful reputation in the community. He went out of his way to help people, and he was a good father."

"I am sure he was," Jerry said, realizing that it sounded and felt a little patronizing. "I guess I want to know, was he an easygoing kind of guy? Could you get close to him, or was he hard to get to know."

David chimed in, "My father was gone a lot with his practice. Sometimes, things fell through the cracks."

"What kind of things?"

"Mostly time with us and with Mom. There was an emotional distance. He would never say he loved us or went out of his way to express emotions or affection. He was like that to everyone. That's why I think it was so odd that he should go flying with one of his patients. He prided himself on keeping his professional distance. I guess it was the way he handled everything personal. I mean he just was that way." David thought perhaps this guy knows something that would explain his father's coldness and even touch his own painful past. It was hard to talk to this stranger. How ironic that this investigator might know his father better than he did. Maybe it was because his father was a stranger too; no loyalty was required.

After an uncomfortable silence, Mary spoke up in a quiet and measured voice, "It is true, Agent Goldman, that Michael was a difficult person to get close to. I tried for twenty-seven years. It wasn't that we got divorced last year because we hated each other or there were affairs. I just got tired of trying, trying to get his attention, trying to get his approval, affirmation, and support. I came to the realization that I would never really get those things from him. For some reason, it took me a long time to accept that fact. I needed to make that pain stop, so I moved to Tucson to be close to my daughter and change the priorities of my life. Oh, he would tell me that he missed me once in a while, but he would never tell me what he missed." There were tears appearing from the corners of her eyes; there were more where those came from, a lot more.

Jerry was stunned by the candor of these answers. It was obvious that this woman was still grieving the loss of this relationship, and now it was lost forever. He felt sorry for her and the family. It made what he was going to have to tell them more difficult.

"Did your ex-husband ever talk about his childhood?" he asked, breaking the uncomfortable silence.

"He told me that his mother and father were killed in a car crash and that the family was split up. He was raised by his grandparents. They are both deceased," Mary said in a matter-of-fact sort of tone.

Whenever he was nervous, Jerry found himself stammering. Trying to control the nervousness just made it worse. It always was an embarrassment.

"No, no, no, that's not exactly what happened. Frr-from our investigation, we have found out a slightly different story," he said this to minimize the hurt. "I don't think you knew that Dr. Turner changed his name when he got to be eighteen. His birth name was Stephen Hughes. He was the son of William Hughes, and his mother's maiden name was Beth Smith. He had a brother, Samuel, and a sister, Mindy. They were five and two years old at the time of the accident that took their lives."

"What are you talking about?" Jamie exclaimed.

Mary interjected, "Jamie, your father was a very private man. Sometimes, when you are away from a situation and its stress, you begin to wonder. Recently, I let myself begin to suspect that there was something he was hiding. Please go on, Agent Goldman."

"According to our investigation, Michael's father sold household products and wasn't around much. The couple were divorced in 1966, when Stephen, I mean Michael, was ten years old. Evidently, the demands of being a single mom were hard on the family. It seems that Dr. Turner's mother was emotionally very fragile.

"The story is that there was a terrible fire in the house they lived in. The two little children, Michael's brother and sister, Samuel and Mindy, were killed, and Michael's mother Beth survived. He was at school. When he got home, the damage had been done."

David asked, "How did it happen?"

"The likely cause of the fire was an electrical short, followed by a fire upstairs. The wiring was old and substandard. There were a couple of other things that made this tragedy worse. Michael's mother was in shock, and she suffered some brain and lung trauma because of smoke inhalation. She was unable to give a consistent recollection of what happened. She became more and more depressed and delusional. Eventually, she had to be hospitalized at the County Psych Hospital. She never got out of institutional care. The other thing that happened was that people began to speculate that she was behind the accident. They thought she wanted to take their lives and hers too, that she was crazy like a fox, that she acted that way to avoid prosecution, or that she was so guilt-ridden by her actions that she just went crazy. She did admit to using codeine for pain. It was confirmed during the investigation that it was a prescribed medication from her physician. Michael moved in with his grandparents on his mother's side and lived with them in the same little town of Pipersville, Ohio, until he graduated high school. Their names were Ronald and Doris Smith. Do you have any questions so far?" It was quiet. Everyone was shocked and speechless.

"There's more?" Jamie blurted out. Jerry replied, "Yes, quite a bit more."

"Why is this important for us to know?" David said with a tone of disbelief. He was leaning forward with his head in his hands.

"It is important. We will get into the crash, and it will begin to make some sense. There are still some unanswered questions. We were hoping that you could help us."

David interrupted. "What kind of questions?"

"We will get to those," Jerry said. "First, I don't want us to get ahead of ourselves. Please bear with me." He felt insecure and irritated with the interruptions, like the interview was somehow getting away from him.

"Okay," David answered as he sat back in his chair.

"Let me say that we are not trying to hurt you. This is a devastating loss for all of you. We only want to help. Like any investigation, sometimes, difficult questions have to be asked. It is not something Officer Hernandez or I like to do. Still, we have to ask these questions so that we can close this case and give you some answers.

"I was saying… Upon graduation, he went to college and got his BS at University of Ohio and medical degree at Vanderbilt University. There must have been some money collected from insurance that went to his mother Mary. All that stuff you probably know."

"Yes," Mary confirmed. "I met him at Vanderbilt. We started dating and got married a year later." Her tone indicated a slow methodical cadence of memory. "What happened to his mother?" Mary asked quietly, almost in a whisper.

"She lived in the county psych ward for about ten years. Government cutbacks closed the facility, and Michael moved her to a nursing home outside of town by the name of Hillcrest Rehabilitation Center. She lived there until her death last year."

Mary's voice got louder, and she pointed her finger and shook it like she was arguing with someone. Mental connections were being made. "We got divorced last year. I had the papers served when he got back from his trip to Ohio." She cried. "Oh my god. Oh no, that explains it. Every year, he went back to Ohio on a vacation by himself for a week or two. Michael was adamant that he spend time alone. He said that he was going to some fishing lodge. He rented it out each year. It had no phone or communication, and he liked it that way. He really went to see his mother. Oh my god, he never told me. Why wouldn't he tell me?"

Her voice trailed off like the air had gone out of the room. Breathing in and out of necessity only made the deprivation more acute. She finally took enough small breaths to say, "He never brought anything home. He would say that he gave his fish away to people around there who needed food. Michael would come back from those trips more disengaged than usual. It took him several weeks to get back to his usual level of isolation. It must have worn on him to see his mother. I just chalked it up to him, being alone too much. Oh my goodness." There was another long uncomfortable breathless silence.

Jerry interrupted the quiet and continued, "I have to tell you our team is quite positive that Dr. Turner was killed in the plane crash. We have the evidence of the wallet that you have identified as his. We have an eye witness seeing a man of his description go with Marian Anderson, boarding her Cessna 150, and taking off. We have the flight plan. We have his car in the parking lot with registration and insurance with his name as the owner. Our team was unable to find any samples of blood, hair, or bone from the crash site yet that could be tested to match his DNA for certain identification. The reason is that the plane exploded when it hit the side of a rock cliff, followed by a storm that washed away a lot of the evidence."

"You are sure then," Jamie said as she began to sob.

"We are as sure as we can be with this circumstantial evidence that Dr. Turner was killed in the plane crash. I am very sorry."

Officer Hernandez saw this as an opening to say something. "I met Miss Turner before. I want to express my sympathy to all of you at your loss."

David asked, "Does this mean we can begin to plan a funeral for my dad?"

Jerry replied, "Yes, I think that you can pending a signed death certificate from the medical examiners office."

There was a long quiet pause only punctuated by Jamie's muffled sobs.

David said, "You mentioned some other things. Is there anything about the crash we should know?"

"We collected some of the plane's wreckage, and our investigation is leading us to determine that a mechanical failure likely caused the crash. We are perplexed by several small puzzles. Why was the pilot flying so low? Why was she so far off course going toward an area that had few, if any, flat areas to land a plane if she got into trouble? I am wondering if he ever mentioned a patient of his named Marian Anderson to any of you." He looked around the room, and everyone was shaking their heads.

"I take it that he never talked about her."

"No," David said loudly. "He hardly ever talked about his patients. That is strictly confidential." David thought, *This guy is beginning to bug me.*

Jerry knew that the next few questions would be difficult, and he felt the tension in his neck. He decided to take a few slow, measured breaths. "Did Dr. Turner do anything out of character recently? Anything that made you wonder if he was depressed?" he asked and looked around the room. He noticed that Jamie looked up at him. She had stopped crying. She pressed her lips tightly and furrowed her brow.

She looked puzzled as she spoke. "He did something that was odd. The Wednesday of that week, he came down to the university to see me. He said that there was a play at the theater he wanted to see and invited me out to dinner for some father-and-daughter time. He had never done that before. Anyway, we met and went to the play after an early dinner. It was a really sad story, *A Long Days Journey into Night,* by some guy named O'Neill. I could hardly wait for it to end, but Dad was really into it. There were several times when I was bored that I just watched him. I'm sure he had tears in his eyes on more than one occasion. That was surprising too. Dad never liked to express emotion or talk about feelings. Something in that play was very important to him."

Jerry followed up, "What was his mood like?"

"I would say he was quiet and thoughtful. My dad was usually quiet, but this was a different kind of thoughtful. Not the kind that is sizing up the situation or looking for an opportunity, no, this was like looking to understand something. Maybe there was a lot in the play that reminded him of his past."

"Thank you for sharing that with me. Sometimes, talking about something that might seem small can really help in the investigation when you put the whole picture together."

"Will what I just told you help the investigation?"

"We are just now putting the pieces together. We will add this piece to the other bits of information we've discovered. Hopefully, a clearer picture will emerge than what we have right now. Do you have any other questions?"

There was just too much pain in the room. Nothing could be said, and nothing could be asked. There was just grief, sorrow, and confusion to deal with. It was a pervasive uncomfortable immobility.

"Here is my card, and you can call me if you have any information or questions that come to mind." With that, the agent got up and hobbled to each person with his card and handed it to them. It was clear that the interview was over for now. Office Hernandez got up too. They were about to head to the door when David spoke up.

"Agent Goldman, were you at the crash site?" David had gotten up too and had moved closer to the two men.

"Yes, I was there. That's how I got this." He pointed down to his walking boot. "We had fl.=own in and headed down there by horseback and on foot. We found the wreckage of the plane. We started taking measurements and collecting evidence when it started pouring rain. The crash site was mostly in a wash, and before you knew it, water came rushing down. We were lucky just to get out of there in time not to get killed. It's a shame that most of the evidence we hoped to find got washed downstream. It was like God himself was against us. Anyway, I fell and sprained my ankle. So they brought me back to Mesa. Now I am responsible for working with the families and coordinating the investigation and recovery of evidence so that a report can be put together and issued."

David asked, "What do we do?"

"That is really up to you to decide. I have given you the only personal effects of Dr. Turner that we have recovered from the crash site. Our report will be available for you when it is completed. I am so sorry for your loss. I wish that we had been able to recover more physical evidence to help you with closure. The county medical examiner will likely issue a death certificate because we were not able to find any human remains."

Agent Goldman and Officer Hernandez turned and began to head to the front door. Mary quickly got up and met them. She gently opened the door and said, "Thank you for coming and visiting with us."

They both turned, nodded, and left. Mary quietly closed the door and leaned against it as if she was somehow holding back a great flood and was exhausted. She was hoping that the tsunami of pain would pass over them somehow.

It's important to know where you are.

The proximate distance to there,

The direction you are looking from.

The point of view from here;

I can see the grandeur of God's Creation.

It is His handshake that invites His Company

Everywhere

I am here too!

Acts

Robert Hughes had just finished checking out the sport's page of the *Phoenix Republic*. As usual, all the local teams were vying for the crown of most mediocre. He was depressed over the city's inability to demand success. Being an insurance investigator and adjustor wasn't very exciting. It meant paperwork and clients with headaches, accent on headaches. *Oh well, it's a living,* he thought. *And it has been good to me.* He had made a comfortable life in his line of work. Like so many baby boomers, he was still working after he should have retired. He had always prided himself on meticulous details, but lately, he had found it harder and harder to concentrate. He wanted something to change, something to happen, but nothing was going to, and that was it.

Images began to swirl in his head. Things just seemed to be in a big blender that broke down thoughts and feelings until something emerged that held his attention, only to slide back into the soup of forgetfulness. He was at home with his wife, Janice. Things were safe. He enjoyed pretty good health for a guy of almost seventy. It was the same for her, although they had both become aware that they were slowing down, accent on the slow. It was just life, and they had lived it pretty well: three grown children, five grandchildren, and a great grandchild on the way. Not too bad for the only man in his family to really settle down. He was the last survivor of three other brothers who lived life hard, fast, and loose.

He had a nice office at home, which allowed him some friendly space to work. Familiar surroundings seemed to calm his mind and settle him. This afternoon, he had picked up a new file from the home office to look at. It was a case that had been on the evening news. A plane crashed in the Superstitions, and the pilot and passenger were killed. Bob settled back in his chair and opened the file. The pilot's name was Marian Anderson, and her family had filed a claim with American National Causality and Life Insurance Co. Inside were copies of the policy, forms, and paperwork that she signed. There was a history of payments made from an automatic withdrawal from her personal checking account. It all looked in order. Enclosed were phone numbers with the Pinal County Sheriff's Department. The name of the lead agent with the NTSB team investigating the crash was Hunter Grayson.

He said to himself, "I don't think I ever worked a case with that guy."

That is a funny name, he thought, *far an investigator, kind of like being a doctor with a name of...* Oh, he remembered that story he heard at the office about this doctor who moved into a small town whose last name was Payne. There was already a doctor there whose last name was Kophin. The two doctors often covered for each other. If you were the patient, you may have to choose between Payne or Kophin. He started to smile and said to himself, "That would be a hard choice, but my money is on Payne over Kophin any day." He just laughed out loud.

Janice heard all the commotion and yelled out from the kitchen, "What's so funny?"

She was busy planning her latest culinary adventure. Lately, the escapades had produced many interesting diversions but few satisfying destinations.

"It's okay, honey. I'm just talking to myself again."

He hoped she would get back to making her own noise of rattling pans and boiling water so that he could return to mumbling to himself, accent on the mumble.

"Back to the task at hand," he said as he picked up the file again. "Let's see what they have found so far."

The case had been opened about ten days ago. The NTSB report was still in progress, but preliminary indications were that the primary cause of the crash was a sudden mechanical failure along with some pilot error. It was likely that there would be a payout of the policy. There was an identified passenger, a Dr. Michael Turner. The crash was in a remote area of the Superstition Mountains. Parts that were salvaged from the crash site were being stored and examined at Falcon Field. There was a phone number and an address and directions so he could go and look at the wreckage.

Of course, he would have to interview the two families. He would put together his own findings before the policy would be paid out. He knew that the NTSB did a thorough background check on both Marian Anderson and Dr. Michael Turner. He didn't have a copy of that report yet. "Hmm… That is unusual," he said. "Most of the time, it's right here. I will have to ask them to fax it to me when I get down there tomorrow. I'll need to call first." He would have to go over the tapes from the tower, find out who was maintaining the aircraft, and interview them. It was tedious work, not the kind of work meant for just anyone. He had years of practice with these kinds of claims, yet he found himself sympathetic to the family's grief. It's so painful to lose a parent or a child so suddenly, without warning. His mind wandered to gratitude. "Thank God Janice and I have never had to deal with a loss like that."

He decided to put the file away for now and go into the kitchen and see what culinary adventure Janice was preparing for dinner. He wasn't absolutely sure, but from the aroma, it likely included onions. "Hmm, my favorite," he mumbled to himself carefully under his breath. "Onions on the half shell." Bob Hughes put himself together the next morning. He grabbed a cup of coffee from the expensive latte machine that made every kind of coffee you could ever want, if you could figure it out. Janice had bought it. She had somehow managed to make straight coffee for him this morning. He was grateful. It wasn't half bad. Sometimes, the good old simple stuff is the best. He poured himself a cup for the road and took the rest and put it in a thermos for later. God knows when Janice would be inspired to make him simple coffee again. He would have to rely on her good graces. He wasn't about to touch that machine. It might go off and cream everyone who tried to approach it to shut it off. Like HAL on that movie the *2001: A Space Odyssey.* The mental image of that made him laugh out loud.

"What's so funny?" Janice loudly exclaimed from their bedroom.

"Oh, nothing. I'll see you later, honey. I'm off to Falcon Field. It will take me a good hour just to get there. I'll give you a call later to let you know when I'll be home."

Hunter Grayson had made it back to civilization. Boy, was he grateful. He caught up on some needed sleep, had a long conversation with Natalie and the kids, showered, and had a good hot breakfast. He and his team had worked about a week collecting pieces of debris. The last three days, they had begun working on sifting through the bits of evidence and pulling out a story of the crash. It was really like a story. The crash had its secrets. The evidence, the details themselves, would reveal what was hidden. Hunter knew his job. He was patient and thorough and knew not to make rash judgments.

Today, he was meeting with an insurance adjustor and investigator named Bob Hughes. It was a bother to meet with these guys. He knew that it was necessary for them to be included in the investigation for their clients and, in this case, for him too. The morning was already heating up, and in an hour or so, any coolness in the breeze would be baked out. The oven of summer was getting fired up. He walked around to the front of the hangar at just the right time to see a blue Chevy Malibu driving up. It matched the color of the sky perfectly, and for a moment, he wondered if it was a mirage. The sound of the engine and the approaching sound of the tires brought him back to his senses. The car stopped, and the driver's side door opened; out popped a portly man wearing a white dress shirt and brown slacks and shoes but no tie. He quickly slammed the door and sauntered over.

"Hi, I am Bob Hughes. I'm here to see Agent Hunter Grayson."

"Hello, Bob. I'm Hunter. It's nice to meet you." They shook hands, and they both moved in tandem toward the hangar.

"Did you have any trouble finding this place?"

"Oh, no, you gave good directions. I have been out here a few times but not for several years." Bob continued to make small talk about the heat and the summer monsoons. Hunter carefully observed him while they walked. Bob Hughes had gray hair that was much thinner on the top of his head, blue eyes that had puffy bags under them, a sharp chin and square jaw, a well-proportioned straight nose, and thin lips. He was overweight but not grossly, although his shape was more pudgy, suggesting lots oftime sitting down and probably more than a few beers to keep him in that position. He had a deep resonant sound to his voice that made him easy to listen to. They got to the door of the hangar. It was open, and there was a strong breeze blowing through, which caught Bob off guard. They walked in and encountered pieces of the plane that had been recovered being evaluated by the other members of Hunter's team.

Bob wanted the small talk to be over. He thought, *Let's get down to business so I can go home and begin to put my report together. I sure don't want to spend the rest of my day out here.* "What do you think caused this to happen?" He stood with one hand on his hip while slowly shaking the other hand at the wreckage.

"We think it was a mechanical failure, probably a fuel or oil system failure. Usually, if it's the oil, there is plenty of evidence of that. We have some oil on the parts of the cowling and shards of windshield but not a lot. I think we are leaning more towards a failure of the carburetor. We have no evidence of foul play or that this was in any way planned. We still have several unanswered questions. Why was the pilot so off course from her flight plan, and why was she flying in an area that left her with no place of land if there was a problem? That could be considered a pilot error, but not a gross one. Maybe she just wanted to show off her flying skills to her passenger. Maybe she wanted to give him the thrill of seeing the landscape. God knows why she made these choices, but for some reason, she did. It left her few options."

Bob replied, "So here we are."

"Yes, here we are."

"There is something that I need to tell you about," Hunter said quietly.

"What's that?" Bob asked with a touch of curiosity.

"You know that we do an extensive background check on the pilot and the passengers, much like your company before it insures someone. Being the government, we do have, access to information that you might not."

"Is there something you need to tell me about the pilot that might affect our policy?"

"No, Bob, not about the pilot. There is something about the passenger that affects you."

"What do you mean affects me?"

"We knew that you would likely be the one sent to do your company's investigation. We were banking on it. The name of the passenger was Dr. Michael Turner, but that was his name after he changed it from Stephen Hughes."

"What?"

Hunter gave this news time to sink in. "Bob, let's go over here and sit down." Hunter led him over to a couple folding chairs that had been arranged in a larger circle for some meeting. He just plopped down with his head down, and his eyes closed trying to make sense of what he just heard.

He put his arms around himself as if he was trying to give himself a hug.

"We are sure that Dr. Michael Turner was your nephew."

"Let me get this right. Are you saying that Dr. Turner is really my brother Bill's son?"

"Yes, I am."

"Are you serious? It can't be."

"We have investigated this, and we are positive it is the same person."

"Oh my god. How strange is that? I can't believe it."

"Bob, I can appreciate that this must be a shock," Hunter replied softly.

"Can I get you some water, or a Coke?"

"No, but in my car is a thermos of coffee. The car's open. It's on the front seat."

"I'll get somebody to get it for you."

Hunter motioned for Brenda to come over and go on the errand. He noticed that Bob's breath was a little labored.

"Are you all right?" he asked.

"Oh, yes, I'm okay. I don't know why this has affected me so much. I really never met him. I hardly knew he existed. It is just so strange to come to do an investigation to find out that it's partly about you and your family."

Brenda came back in a few minutes with the thermos. "Here you go. Is there anything else I can get for you?" she said in a sarcastic tone that let Hunter know that she was none too pleased at having been told to go get the large white man's coffee.

Hunter just slowly shook his head. He watched Bob pour his coffee, and from the aroma, it already had been sweetened with a little alcohol.

"What can you tell me about your brother?"

"I was the youngest in the family, and Bill was the oldest. He left home when I was very little. I have few memories of him. Anything I learned about him came from my mom and dad and by my other brothers. I knew that he had been married twice. The first one ended in divorce with no children. It only lasted a few years. The second ended in divorce too. He did have three children with her."

"Did you know about the accident?" Hunter interrupted.

"Yes, I was told that one of the boys had survived and was living with her side of the family. I didn't get all the details, but there was a lot of suspicion and anger directed toward the mother. My brother was not interested in getting involved in that mess. I think that he just wanted out of the marriage. He handled that, like he handled everything else, by disappearing."

"We know that he died only five years later."

"He had a massive heart attack and died going to get some medicine at a drugstore. My parents weren't surprised. Bill lived a life that they did not approve of. It was a life that had few, if any, commitments and no expectations."

Hunter sat across from him and saw the pain on his face. There was a long silence. He could see that Bob was blinking a lot, trying to hold back the tears that were glistening on the edges of his eyes. He wondered if it was the tears he was fighting to control or if there was something else just over his emotional horizon that Hunter could not see.

Bob broke the uncomfortable quiet, "Did Dr. Turner have a family?" It dawned on him. *That's why some of the usual personal information was not in the file.* "You knew that I would figure this out, and you needed to be the ones to tell me. It's probably because there is a conflict of interest if I were to know this and be investigating the case. There's a financial benefit to the families of both the pilot and the passenger. My evaluation of the policy and its payout could be compromised."

Hunter looked straight at Bob and said emphatically, "Yes, you're right. We needed to let you know about this. We know that you will have to report this to your boss so that another investigator can be assigned."

"Now that I know about the relationship, I have to report it."

"You asked about Dr. Turner's family. He has two adult children, David and Jamie, and an ex-wife by the name of Mary. She and the daughter Jamie live in Tucson, and their son, David, kind of kicks around. Last known whereabouts was in Colorado. Somehow, they got in touch with him. One of my team agents Jerry Goldman met last Friday with the family in Tucson. The son was there."

Bob's mind began to go around faster and faster until it ran right into a blank, like somebody who had walked into a glass door. All of a sudden, he couldn't think clearly. He decided to focus on just one thing at a time. Bob looked up and said, "Once I get a new insurance investigator on the case, I would like to meet the family. I think it would help me fill a big empty spot in my history. I don't want to say I missed my brother. The fact that I never missed him leaves me with a big 'should have' in its place, and perhaps that's what I miss. There's a lot for me to process right now."

His voice tailed off, and there was an awkward pause. He finally shook himself back into the moment and asked, "Is there anything else that you think I might need to know?"

Hunter replied, "Yes, there is. We recovered a wallet that belonged to Dr. Turner. It was the only item we found of his that survived the crash. Inside was a key. Agent Goldman gave it to the family last Friday. There are pictures of it in the file. It looks like a key to a safe deposit box. Maybe there are things in that box that might help you with closure about your brother and his family. You can take this folder with you. We have the originals. The NTSB will be making a final report that will be available to the new investigator. The families address and phone number is in the file. If you choose to reach out to them, I would be careful. When Agent Goldman met with them, it was obvious that they knew nothing about our victim's previous name and life. That information came as a complete shock to them. If you want to contact them, please do it with care and sensitivity. Let me say that my team and I are very sorry for your loss. I wish we could have found them alive."

It seemed like a natural time to move on. They both stood up, and there was a handshake and some pats on the back. Bob drained the coffee from his cup and screwed it back on the thermos. He tucked it under his arm, turned, and trundled back to the car. He felt the hot breeze catch him and weaken his legs. He knew that his car would feel like an oven. Once the air conditioner started to catch up, he would eventually cool off. It would be a long ride home. Maybe this sadness would feel the same after the hot breath of the loss cooled; time would pass, and he would be comfortable again; His mind raced. He just might discover something about himself, if he knew more about Dr. Turner. There always had been that gnawing feeling that grabbed hold of a painful secret abandonment. It seemed to come from nowhere. Suddenly, he would feel like someone hit him in the pit of his stomach. He would lose his air and begin to pant. It wasn't a heart attack. It was perhaps just anxiety. Was it something else?

"I will have to go and meet them." He pulled off to the side of the road and opened the file on the front seat and picked up his cell phone to make a call.

The Amen, the faithful Witness and true, the source of God's creation has this to say; "Here I stand, knocking at the door. If anyone hears me calling and opens the door, I will enter his house and have supper with him, and he with me." Rev. 3:14-21

An opened invitation requires I break the seal.

look inside and see my name written by the host.

It proves to me the sentiments are real.

Sent and delivered by the post.

Once or Twice

Michael didn't see him. He turned and almost ran into him. He was a man dressed in a white tunic with gold brocade around the edges. He didn't budge. The whole effect was to put them both very close to each other. He didn't back up. Michael let out a small gasp and decided to stand his ground too. The man had a pleasant smile and clear blue eyes. He was a full head shorter than Michael. He had a personality that seemed to engage you without having to say anything, which made up for his short stature. He had white hair and looked somehow like a cross between Raymond Massey and Lionel Barrymore—two of his favorite actors who both played doctors in the movies. He had bags under his eyes, which were evidence of long days and nights of work and experience in caring for the sick. The furrowed brow and chiseled features were like scars that he wore, marking a life given over to a vocation that demanded long hours and selflessness. He looked Michael straight in the eye and said, "Well, I must say that you need training. What I saw was a rather mediocre example of medical practice." For a moment, he sounded like Dr. Frank Purcell at St. Martha's Hospital, where he did part of his residency. He remembered how hard he was to please. He was fair and demanding. Frank always stressed the importance of caring for each patient no matter how difficult they could make it.

"And who may I ask are you?"

"I am Dr. Luke. I have been called to be your preceptor. You are Dr. Turner." He pointed to Michael's chest. "I will be here when you need me and sometimes when you think that you don't, to guide you into the art of loving and caring for your patients."

"I thought that Ayin was going to show me the ropes?"

"Oh no, not at all. He will stop by, but I am going to be your attending. Don't get me wrong. Ayin is a wonderful angel, but to deal with the human condition, you need someone who's been there," he said with an air of confidence and compassion.

"So I take it that you have had some experience in the medical field?"

"Oh yes," Luke replied. "I have been around a long time. I practiced in Palestine and later throughout the Mediterranean. I have seen medicine develop into the modern era."

"With all due respect, Doctor, I have been in practice for a good long while myself, and I don't think I need a nursemaid."

As soon as those words left his mouth, Michael regretted them. He was embarrassed by his own arrogance. Before he could apologize, Dr. Luke replied forcefully and calmly, "I am not here to be your nursemaid but to help you. We both know that you have developed some habits that have limited your ability to care for your patients. These have been, shall we say, less than optimal. Those will have to change so that you can care for your patients and not just tolerate them. If you were so happy and accomplished in your life of medicine, why did you want out so badly?"

Michael looked down at him. "I see you have read my chart."

"Yes, I have! I can mentor you through this experience if you will let me. You know that one of the great misnomers in medicine is the term 'private practice.' Just think of it. Your schooling in college, your training in the hospital, both internship and residency, was not private. It rested on the training, education, and collaboration with others. Medicine is not about being a private party, a superman able to fix everything with your own skill and knowledge. It is about being a community of colleagues and a partner with God. From now on, through this process, I hope that you will discover that truth."

Michael was flabbergasted. Just when he was settling in and making some progress, a new wrinkle had emerged. He was totally taken by surprise at this development.

"Whose idea was this?" Michael asked.

"Let's put it this way. I have been appointed by the highest authority." He pointed upward. "I think that you are stuck with me."

Michael decided that the direct confrontational approach was not working. It was apparent that Luke outranked him, and he probably knew what he was talking about. His face mirrored what was best in the profession, tireless effort, wisdom, and a strong internal identity. It matched his external character and demeanor.

"Doctor Luke, may I suggest that we start over?" Michael entreated. By now, they had both backed up a bit. "I can see that you intend to help me and that I can learn a lot from you. I was just surprised. That's all."

"Why, of course we can, Michael. I believe we can become wonderful colleagues that can help these people." Luke moved closer and put his hand on Michael's shoulder. "You will discover how to care for these people and how caring is the best medicine of all."

Luke looked up directly into Michael's eyes, and Michael looked back into his. In those eyes, he saw the tender compassion of medicine. He looked into the exhilaration at the moment of birth, the sorrow of a treatment that failed. The death of an old patient, holding a hand that needed tenderness, hundreds, perhaps thousands, of IVs, examinations, worries, late nights, long days, and much more all wrapped together and tied to those eyes that looked into his and said, "I have been there and more."

He knew that Luke was looking into his soul too, seeking answers to the questions "Do you know?" "Have you been there?" "Do you still care?" He became aware that he felt something new, or was it just forgotten? Looking into those eyes had brought the feeling to mind, and there it was. What was it? He searched down into his heart, and the word came to him. He felt empathy. It wasn't sympathy or being sorry for or anything like that. The feeling was conducted by a common understanding from a common experience. They both had been there, both been vulnerable to the pain of others and to their own. Michael was aware that for Luke, it had deepened his soul with spiritual fortitude and compassion. His experience, on the other hand, had jaded him and caused him to put on a kind of protective armor. He knew that being a doctor was far more than what he had settled for. No wonder he'd wanted to give it up.

Luke looked away first, like he had learned everything he needed to know. He was ready to move on. Nothing had been said, yet there was an understanding between them that tied them on a common course.

"Dr. Turner, are you prepared for your first patient?" Luke had turned and was looking down the path that led to his house and office. "I think that someone will be coming up that path to your door. Who do you think it will be?"

Michael replied, "I think it will be Miss Odelia Crier."

"What makes you think that it will be her?"

"Well, she seems the most anxious to visit with me. She complained of pain in her hip. She told me that she had gone to other physicians and had not gotten a diagnosis and relief from her pain. She is the most symptomatic of all the people here with a pronounced limp on the right leg. She also has a disposition that could make her difficult to treat. She is highly critical and probably not very compliant with treatment, which brings me to my next question. How is this going to work?"

Luke closed his eyes like he was trying to visualize something. When he opened them, he seemed to have an answer. "I think that the way we should proceed is for you to take the lead and introduce me as a fellow physician. It would be important for the patient to give consent for me to be with you. I will say very little during the patient's visit. Once they have left, we will debrief the encounter. I will try to give you good council about the case and perhaps how best to treat them."

"I think that I get the picture, Doctor. I understand that my work with the patient may need your expert evaluation. I can assure you that any insights you might have would be most welcome." Michael said this with a touch of sarcasm that could easily be denied if questioned. He should have felt sense of satisfaction with the little "gotcha" he had just sent. Instead of enjoying the wry comment, he felt sorry for his attitude. This time, he did get his apology out immediately. "Doctor, look, I am sorry I said that. The tone of that comment of mine was not very nice, nor was it professional. Please forgive me. I'm a little defensive about my medical practice." Michael was looking down at the floor like a kid who got his hand caught in the cookie jar. When he looked at him, Luke had a big smile on his face.

"Not to worry, Doctor," Luke replied. "I think we can get through this. I believe that you will get to trust me once you know me and we have worked together."

Michael turned slightly and looked out toward the path leading up to his office. He could see Odelia Crier coming toward them, limping up the hill. Michael turned back to Luke and said, "I agree to your plan. Guess who is coming up the hill. If you said Odelia Crier, you would be right."

'We played the flute for you and THE SOUND

MEANT I HAD TO CHOOSE

You did not dance; IN THE MOVEMENT AND

THE MOMENT OF SOLITUDE

We wailed and you did not KNOW THAT THE

LOSS MADE ME

weep" AND WALK THE ROAD TO BETHANY.

Matthew 11:17 (NRSV)

Numbers

He had always considered himself a man who carefully weighed the pros and cons of every decision. He had become more impulsive lately, which caught him off guard. Right now was one of those unrehearsed moments of spontaneity. Calling felt like a risky thing to do. He had pulled his car over off the shoulder of the highway. He decided with little further thought to punch in the number that Agent Grayson gave him on his cell phone. He felt a wave of excitement, like a kid doing something daring he knew his parents would not approve of. He heard the phone ring, and he half hoped that no one would answer so he could hang up.

Instead, he heard a man's voice say "hello."

"Hello," Bob replied. "You don't know me. I'm the insurance adjustor that was assigned to Dr. Michael Turner's case. My name is Bob Hughes. Who am I speaking to?"

"I'm Dr. Turner's son, David. What is this about?" There was an understandable protective tone in his voice.

"David, I have discovered some information about your father that I am reluctant to discuss over the phone. I have spent most of the morning at Falcon Field with the NTSB agents who are investigating the crash. It's not bad information. I don't want to alarm you or your family. I do need to discuss this, however, in person. Is it possible for me to come to Tucson and meet you all?"

"Hang on. Let me see." There was some whispering in the background. "Yeah, it's okay with everyone. When can you get here?"

"I'm heading out from Mesa, so I could be there in an hour and a half. I have your mother's address and your phone number. I know Tucson and about where you are. IfI get lost, I can always call you from my cell."

"We have your phone number on our caller ID. We will see you in a couple of hours."

"Yes, I'll see you then."

He hung up and called Janice to let her know he would be home late and not to wait up for him; he would get a burger on his way home. He didn't tell her he was going to Tucson. He was glad about one thing though he dreaded the long drive; he would be spared the requirement of eating tonight's gourmet experiment. He knew it would be waiting for him in the refrigerator.

He remembered the last line from the movie *Gone with the Wind.* "Oh well, tomorrow is another day," he said to himself with a quick smile. Bob got on the interstate and headed south to Tucson. There wasn't a cloud in the sky. He felt a sense of anticipation and excitement the closer he got to the Old Pueblo. He didn't know what he would find. He was doing something for the first time in a long time that wasn't scripted by the home office. It wasn't expected or even very wise. He was determined to move forward as he guided his car toward an intersection of hope and discovery. Maybe he would learn what caused him to react with anxiety and panic whenever he thought about his childhood. It wasn't clear what he would find once he began to dig into his past. It just felt right somehow to see what treasure, if any, he could uncover. What might this new claim produce?

David had passed on the conversation with the insurance adjustor and let everyone know that he was coming over in two hours. He remembered that his name was Bob something (he had said it so fast). Jamie had just gotten back from the grocery store. He helped her bring in all the food they would need for the rest of the week. It was timely to hear from the insurance agent because that had been one of the questions that had come up. David and Jamie knew that they would have to go over to their dad's apartment and look for papers and financial stuff. Mary had already contacted Michael's attorney Joe Spagnolo to inquire about his Last Will and Testament. He had expressed his surprise to learn about Michael's death. He said that there was a will and that it would have to go to the probate court for review. Mr. Spagnolo seemed uneasy about discussing it further without his own review of its details. He said that he'd be glad to have the family come over to his office in Phoenix in a week or so to discuss the terms of the Will, its execution, and its resources. He was happy to hear from Mary that all the family was together in Tucson. They had just gotten off the phone with Mr. Spagnolo when the insurance adjustor called. He now became the next hot button issue that the family would have to focus on.

There always seemed to be at least one family meeting a day. The phone call from the insurance guy and Michael's attorney set the agenda of Michael's estate to be front and center. Mary had assumed that since their divorce, she would not expect the bulk of his estate to go to her. It was most likely going to the children.

Two hours later, the doorbell rang, and David went to answer it. There was an overweight man with a face that seemed vaguely familiar. He looked sad and serious. He wore a white shirt, a loose blue tie, tan pants, and brown shoes.

"Hello," the man said. "My name is Bob Hughes. I called you a couple of hours ago."

"Yes, we have been looking forward to meeting you. Please come in. I'm David, and this is my sister, Jamie, and my mother, Mary." Handshakes were exchanged, and Bob sat down across from Mary and Jamie, who shared a couch, and David, who sat in a wingback chair. Bob sat in a large leather recliner.

"I imagine you are wondering who I am and why I'm here. I am an insurance investigator with American Casualty and Life Insurance Company." He gave his business card to David. "We carry the insurance policy for the plane and the pilot and passengers on the aircraft that Marian Anderson was flying. We have to do an investigation of any claims on that policy. I have come into some surprising information as part of that investigation that I need to talk to you about. I met with the lead NTSB agent preparing the report on the crash this morning. He told me that their background search discovered that Dr. Turner had another name before he changed it. His name was Stephen Hughes. He was the natural son of my brother William Hughes. I was stunned by this news. My brother Bill died some time ago. He did have a son named Stephen. I never knew your father, but I knew of him. I was not close to my brother. We were separated by many years. He was the oldest, and I the youngest."

David interjected. "Do you believe them, the NTSB?"

"Yes, I do. I have never found them to be wrong about that sort of thing. I have been amazed by this news. That's why I am here. I just had to meet with you. I think that if we put our heads together, maybe we could make some sense of all this."

"We had a visit from an Agent Goldman last Friday.

He told us about my father's name change. Did you know about that?"

Bob felt uncomfortable. For a moment, he wondered if this was such a good idea.

He was the one who usually asked the questions. It felt strange to be on the other side of the inquiry.

He replied, "I was told about that conversation. I thought that since you had been informed, it would be okay for me to meet you."

Bob could sense doubt flittering around the room. He realized that he would probably feel the same way if the roles were reversed.

"I can understand your disbelief. I feel the same way too," he said. There was an uneasy silence that seemed to go on for an eternity.

Jamie was the first to respond. "Thank you for coming to meet with us. I want you to know that I believe you. I think that any information you can share with us about my father's natural family would be a real help to us. You can appreciate how confused we are with this news about my dad's life. We need all the background and texture of his story. It hurts to know that he believed he had to keep this all secret." She seemed to be talking to everyone in the room. Her voice was quiet yet strong and determined at the same time. She looked right at Bob. "I have to tell you that finding out about my father's past makes me feel hurt. He didn't think he could tell my mother or any of us the real story of his life. That makes it a painful betrayal along with a tragic accident."

Bob could feel the anguish in her voice. His experience in the field told him that tears of grief were coming.

Mary interjected, "I just don't know how a person can keep a secret like this for so long. Not once in our marriage did I suspect. Oh, there were a few times when I thought maybe there was another woman in his life. I remember thinking that if there was someone else, at least we would have something to fight about. You know that we were divorced. It doesn't happen without a reason. Perhaps this is the biggest one. I just really didn't know him. After all our years together, he was a stranger. I have learned more about him over these last few days than in the other twenty-five years. I find that very sad and humiliating."

Bob thought that he had to come clean with his story and bring his own vulnerability in line with theirs. "I need to tell you that I don't know why I'm here. I have never had something like this happen to me. I felt compelled to meet you as soon as I could. Believe me that this is totally out of character for me. Your descriptions of Dr. Turner's professionalism and personality could be me. I guess that we have certain family traits that are similar. I will be passing this case on to another agent. I want you all to know that I'm not here to represent my company. I am here for a deeply personal reason. I've been suffering from a gnawing feeling that something in my life needed to be dealt with. It has been a private anxiety that I couldn't get a handle on. I thought it was retirement or a midlife crisis, or maybe I was just feeling my own mortality. I'm beginning to think that part of what I'm dealing with is my family's story.

Bob's confession seemed to calm some of the distrust in the room. You could see everyone seemed to sit back and relax a little more. It gave everyone a chance to emotionally exhale.

The conversation moved to gathering information about both sides of the family—the history of the Turners and the Hughes. Bob shared that his research indicated that Oscar Hughes immigrated to the United States in 1861 from Holland. He was a cobbler by trade. Hughes was probably not his Dutch name, but he likely took it when he arrived in America. He had married a German woman named Wilma Von Eich. They had a large family of eight children. There are ancestors spread all around the country. Bob was embarrassed by how little he knew about his brother. He was not of much help in providing more details about Michael / Stephen or about his brother Bill. He was able to tell them about his own relationship with his parents, and he filled them in on his own wife and children. Bob also learned about the Turners.

It was decided, after a couple of hours of conversation, to order some pizza and have it delivered. Everyone got up and moved around, got fresh drinks, and went to the restroom if needed. He got to talk privately with David while all this was happening. They stood facing one another near the kitchen island. Bob had begun to feel at home with these people. They were all respectful and intelligent. David was staring down at his Coke like there was something in it. He broke his reverie by saying, "Bob, did you know that they found my dad's wallet and inside was a key to something maybe a safe deposit box?"

"Yes, Agent Grayson mentioned it to me. Why do you ask?"

"I was thinking that since we are waiting for the medical examiner to issue a formal death certificate, we have a key that opens a box that might contain something about my dad's life. Agent Goldman told us that Dad's hometown was Pipersville, Ohio. If he was there this past year, perhaps there is a bank with a box that mates this key. If we can locate that box and unlock it, we might get some answers. Maybe there are some people there who might know about what happened. Certainly, there must be some written records about him and his family and the accident. You have the expertise with these things in your line of work. I was wondering if you might go with me to Ohio. It sounds like you could be interested for your own reasons too. I can bring this up after dinner for discussion."

A light went on for Bob. "I think that would be a great idea." He put his hand on David's shoulder and softly said, "I think that we can work this out. I have some time off coming, and my wife always is looking to have a little time with the grandchildren and our kids. I am sure we can figure out the details."

With that, the doorbell rang. Jamie answered it. The pizza had arrived.

The old mission church that the settlers found was no

secret…

The Spanish Franciscans had brought it on their backs.

It was here before the settlers came. The Indians knew

about it.

They had seen its power to bring life;

Now we have settled where it was planted with love

and sacrifice.

The Criers' Tale

Odelia Crier ambled up the path with a pronounced limp on her left leg. She leaned on a thin wooden cane. She had her gray hair up in a bun and wore a one-piece denim dress and black shoes. She seemed to be laboring as if it was hard for her to catch her breath. She saw Dr. Turner through the porch screen already talking to someone old and distinguished. He had a head of white hair. He wore a strange white toga-looking outfit with a golden embroidered edge all around. She climbed the three steps up to the veranda, and Michael opened the screen door and invited her in.

"Welcome, Odelia. Let me introduce Dr. Luke. He is going to provide some professional support for me in my practice. He has lots of experience treating patients in this, shall we say, environment. I hope you don't mind if he sits in with us?"

"Well, Dr. Turner, this is highly irregular. I thought I would be seeing you alone. It is my expectation that I should be afforded full patient confidentiality," she said this with a tone of righteous indignation.

Luke replied, "Madam, I can assure you that you will be treated very well by Dr. Turner. I can also say that your concerns for confidentiality will be completely respected."

"What is your name again, sir?" Odelia asked with a hint of curiosity and resistance in her voice.

"Madam, my name is Dr. Luke. That will have to suffice for now."

"Well, Dr. Luke, I am not sure if I can trust you. What choice do I have if I want to be treated for my illness? It is quite interesting, though, that we have gone from having no doctor to having two doctors."

Michael quipped, "I guess that should reassure you twice as much?" He knew that lie should not have said that just then. He was trying to put a little humor into the conversation; instead, he had provided a whole bunch of new ammunition. He was not surprised when Odelia took and fired one of those bullets. She straightened up and said loudly with a twinge of anger, "That may be true in your mind, Dr. Turner, but I have a lot of experience in health care. I have found that it is more likely to be twice as incompetent. If you two are just going to ignore me or say it's in my head like so many others, then I will leave right now!"

Luke quietly and carefully responded by saying, "Mrs. Crier, it may be completely understandable that you feel that way. It sounds like the medical profession has let you down. Negative experiences can—"

"Let me down," she repeated. "Oh, yes, it has. I put my whole faith in it. I have tried every remedy that was prescribed for my back. I have had every treatment and test known to man, and nothing has helped."

Michael observed her carefully as she spoke. Odelia had a staccato way of speaking. She clipped the end of her words like there was a rush to get to the next one. She had strong features that were partly feminine but, at the same time, gave off a masculine kind of assertiveness. He thought that she was a perfectionist and abided no less from others. Failure to meet her standards meant swift execution since she was already judge and jury. He looked at those deep furrows on her forehead and thought how insecure she must feel to have developed such emotional armor.

Michael interrupted her diatribe against the medical profession by interjecting, "Mrs. Crier, I don't think you came to see me to discuss the failures of modern medicine. Believe me, I couldn't agree with you more. What I want to know is about your symptoms. Are you in pain right now? Where does it hurt?"

"Yes, I am," she replied. She made a slight sigh, like finally the discussion had moved to a subject with which she was well acquainted. Now she was in control.

She took a deep breath and said, "It mostly hurts down my left leg. It's a dull pain that can get sharp like a knife if i twist or bend over or make some sudden move."

"Odelia, let's leave the veranda and go into my office to discuss this. Dr. Luke will come with us."

"Oh, don't worry about me. I will only say anything if I am asked," Luke replied.

The three of them walked across the veranda and into the house. Michael led them to his exam room. There was one small chair, a stool on wheels, and, of course, an exam table in the room. Michael stepped down the hall and quickly brought in another chair from his other office. They had enough room to huddle together in a small semicircle. Michael encouraged Odelia to sit in one of the chairs.

"Sometimes, it hurts less to stand. If I need to get up, you will understand," she said rhetorically. Odelia slowly fit herself into the chair, making some groans that let everyone know that she was in pain. "I just hope I can get up again somehow," she said. He thought that she was hunting for some sympathy, and Michael was a little reluctant to give her any. He could fire off a few bullets in reply, but unlike Odelia, he decided not to. He chose to maintain a professional interest in her situation.

"Since we live here, it really doesn't matter how long this has gone on. Can you tell me what surgeries or treatments have you had on your back?"

"I believe that I have had three surgeries-one on a disk, followed by a disk removal, and a spinal fusion. Doctors say that there is nothing wrong with my hip or knee. The tests show no deterioration in the joints. They tell me that my organs, heart, and everything else are just fine. I have been told that all my pain is because of my back problem. It should have been fixed. Nothing that has been done has improved it. On the contrary, it's only gotten worse."

Michael felt a manipulation coming on. "The implication was that you're probably just like the other doctors, unable to make things better." He could sense that feeling of hopelessness make a chilling appearance. His first reaction was to try to reassure her that he would do his best. Hopefully, she would get some relief. He was aware that Luke was watching him too. He decided to keep himself focused on her problems. He blocked out everything that was trying to cloud his mind. He concentrated. Instead of a defensive statement, out popped a question.

"Ms. Crier, what do you expect me to do for you?" It had an instantaneous effect. She sat up in her chair and said, "I expect you to find a cure for my pain. I would like to have a fuller life without all this pain and suffering."

Michael shot back, "We are in a place that eliminates all bodily pain. There are no broken bones, heart attacks, rheumatism, gout, or anything like bacteria to make us sick. So what do you think the pain in your back comes from?"

"I don't know. I am here hoping to find some answers to this misery," she said with a tone of indignation.

Michael replied thoughtfully, "You probably have had an accident, for example, where you cut yourself. I know I have had things like that happen. Let's think about that for a moment. If you hurt yourself, you get out the ointment and a bandage and wrap the wound so it will not get infected and heal. Have you ever asked yourself where the pain of something like that goes? I mean think for a moment about it. I bet that if you recalled the last time you accidentally hurt yourself, you might remember it so well that you could feel the pain all over again even though the cut has been healed for some time. Maybe your experience of pain is like that. There may not be anything wrong with your back anatomically. It may be the place where you dump all the pain of cuts, bruises, hurts, disappointments, and anger. Have you ever prayed about that?" Before she could answer, Michael continued, "Maybe the pain is not in your head or in your back but in your heart."

The idea touched a sore spot in his soul. He thought, *How many patients did I treat with the wrong kind of medicine? What they really needed was the elixir of human compassion.*

She responded to his statement, saying, "But, Doctor, I am a perfectly happy woman." Her tone was quiet, and she said it as if she was trying to convince herself. "I know I can be demanding and demonstrative. I am not always pleased by the outcomes even when I get my way." Then she looked down at her feet.

Michael could see that something was happening. Her brown eyes seemed to dart back and forth, up and down, as if her mind was trying to find something. It was something important and perhaps hard to say. He felt compassion for her. He took a risk and moved his chair closer to her. He reached out his hand and touched the top of hers, which was on her knee.

"Odelia," Michael said, "if we could touch that pain in your back and it could talk to us, what would it say?"

There was quiet and then a kind of inner struggle. Her neck got red and so did her face. The words were coming to the surface like heat and ash of a volcano.

"It would say… it would say… I am lonely and afraid. Nobody ever appreciated all the hard work I did to get noticed, and no one cared. Not my mother or my father, not anyone! Only I cared, and that is not good enough!" She bent over and put her head in her hands and began to sob.

Michael was amazed. The fortress was crumbling right in front of him. Nothing like this had ever happened to him before. It was as if he had lanced a boil and all the fluid drained out, and with it all the infection, only he had not used a scalpel, just a few caring questions. Why had no one told him about this in medical school? Maybe they had. Maybe he was just not ready to hear it. He was too busy being the perfect student. Like Odelia's compulsive perfectionism, he could see some similar characteristics in his personality.

I guess nobody's story is all that unique, he thought to himself.

When Odelia looked up at him, there was a different quality in her face. Gone were the furrowed lines on her brow. Gone were the darting eyes that couldn't rest. A warm softness and calmness had taken up residence in its place. She made a long sigh, which acknowledged the transformation. Michael thought, *She is not yet a butterfly, but Odelia has definitely broken out of her self-imposed cocoon.*

"Dr. Turner, what just happened?" Odelia asked. The question had not a hint of anger or fear. The tone was soft, and it indicated that she was not going to build a defense from the answer. She was trying to explain her vulnerability. She had no context that could help her understand this glimpse into herself.

"I'm not sure." Michael had just as many questions as she did. Like someone waking up from anesthesia, there was this awareness of things coming back into focus. Odelia knew that something unexpected had happened, and in her world, that was unacceptable. She felt very confused.

"Doctor, if you don't mind, I think I will head back home." She got up swiftly by using the arm and back of the chair. Michael had not seen that coming. He half stood up and said something about being careful.

"Oh, I will be careful," she said quietly and mumbled, "Please excuse me. I have some things I need to sort out."

Michael couldn't follow up with any more questions. Odelia was already out of his office and heading for the veranda. He bolted to catch up with her.

"Odelia, if you would like to have another meeting, just let me know," he said loudly, hoping that his words would catch up with her before she was too far down the path. The screen door slammed as she hurried to her house.

Michael felt as if he had failed, but he couldn't explain why. He slowly turned and saw Luke a few steps behind him. He was leaning on a cane. He quickly straightened up and grabbed it and walked over to him.

"I guess she forgot something," he said and gave the cane to Michael. "I don't think that she will need it anymore." Michael was stunned. He hadn't noticed that she had left it behind. He was the one who was confused. He took it from Luke and studied his face. It wasn't disapproving or patronizing; rather, he was smiling and nodding in approval. He felt safe enough to ask the obvious question. "Why did she leave so quickly? What happened?" Luke looked up and paused to reflect on the question.

"First of all, you did some fine work with this woman. I don't want you to miss that truth. She left your office without her crutch. That is a great thing. You know, of course, that it wasn't because of you but because of God's help. I was praying for both of you. It was a real blessing to witness the Lord's grace working in her soul."

Michael interrupted and asked again, "Then why did she leave so fast?"

Luke touched his hand that held the cane. "Sometimes, when a person lets go of an emotional or spiritual crutch, the physical symptoms disappear. Odelia had a condition in her life that she carried in her spirit. You listened to her, and she told you about it. She was looking for you to help her understand what that pain had done to her. When you said you didn't know what happened, she -lost confidence in you. She was so confused. She felt the need to escape the inner conflict. She knows consciously that the conflict exists, and that is a big step toward inner healing."

"I didn't know what happened or how to translate it for her," Michael said in frustration as he turned the cane in his hand and pounded it on the floor. It made a noise like a muffled scream each time it struck, like something wounded. He felt a tension or a twist of torque go up from his hand to his arm, shoulder, and to his back. He quickly dropped the thing on the floor. He looked down at it. What he saw was a thin brown snake that hissed and slithered through a small warped gap between the screen door and the doorjamb. It went down the steps and headed outside.

Michael shouted, "Luke, we should go and kill that thing."

"No, Michael, there's no need to do that. It's on its way back to the Cave of Perdition, where its friends are."

"I feel sad that things ended with Odelia the way they did."

"Don't worry, Doctor. Her therapy is not over. You have only applied the first treatment. I can tell you from some experience that the patient is likely on the road to recovery." He smiled and shook his hand.

"You will need to give God glory for that.

"I do, Dr. Luke?"

"Oh, yes, you do, Michael. God does His best work when we don't solely rely only on our knowledge or human wisdom."

Michael felt appreciative. "Doctor, I can see why you are here. I do need to be trained."

Luke put his hand on Michael's shoulder again and said, "We can't afford to get too pleased with ourselves." He pointed with the other hand down the path. "Here comes your next patient."

There is a church

It's not a building.

It's not a something.

It's a Someone.

We build it Stone by Stone,

Love upon Love,

Moment by Moment,

Choice by Choice.

It's a Temple of decision built by action or vacated by

neglect.

There is a Church

It's in you and me

A holy place
The Trinity.

The Journey to the Treasure

It hadn't taken very long to make the decision. There was quick agreement with everyone that a trip to Pipersville, Ohio, was necessary. Bob had headed home after dinner and arrived back in Phoenix around 9:00 p.m. It was dark when he got there. The evening air was cool. He looked up as he got out of his car. The night sky was gray and opaque with all the city lights. He tumbled the keys in his hand looking for the right one to the front door. Janice was up waiting for him. He had told her on his cell phone that he needed to discuss a case he was working on. That had raised her curiosity since he rarely discussed any of his cases with her. He opened the door, put down his briefcase, closed it, and strolled into the living room, where she was waiting. She stood up, met him halfway, and gave him a big hug. It was one of those hugs that said "Welcome home."

She was a full-figured woman and was almost his height. Most of her hair was gray. It was cut in a way that framed her face. It was a nice look for her. They fit together in a comfortable way too, like a pair of well-worn gloves that had been through hard work and sweat. They both had to grab on to life with those gloves, and neither was ready to lay them down.

She looked at him and said, "I was worried. You didn't want to talk to me about something that happened today until you got home. Is everything all right?"

"Oh, yes, everything is fine. I didn't want to worry you," he said with a tone of remorse because, of course, he knew he did. "It's just that I didn't want to talk to you about this without being able to look at you."

She felt anxiety well up in her stomach. "Well, what is it?"

Bob sat down in the sofa, and she sat next to him. "You know the case I was working on is about a plane crash in the Superstitions two weeks ago. Our policy was purchased by the pilot, and she had a passenger on board. I met the NTSB agents at Falcon Field. It seems that the passenger's name before he changed it was Stephen Hughes. He was my nephew. He was the son of my brother Bill."

"Really? How do they know that?"

"Honey, trust me. They know," he said sarcastically. "They wanted me to know for personal reasons and because I would have to arrange for another investigator. They gave me the contact information for the family, who lived in Tucson."

"Did you call the home office?"

"Of course I did. That's not the point," he said with some urgency. "You see, I had their phone number, and I called them and went down there this afternoon. I met with them, and they are all very nice. The ex-wife is Mary, and their son is David and a daughter named Jamie. Their last name is Turner. My nephew's name after he changed it was Dr. Michael Turner. He had become a successful physician and practiced family medicine for many years."

He could tell that Jan was confused. She would always crinkle up her nose and clench her lips together when things didn't make sense. It usually worked on the kids when they were spinning a tale. She would give them that look, and pretty soon, they would be explaining themselves until she would catch them in a lie. He knew that look all to well.

"Honey, I know this seems weird, but that's what happened," he said, trying to reassure her. Somehow, he felt like one of the kids. He wanted her to be convinced that he was telling her the truth, and this time, he was.

She asked incredulously, "Did they know anything about who he was before?"

He was a bit put off by the question. "Honey, they didn't know anything about our family at all until they were notified by the

NTSB last week. Here is the strangest thing. It seems that the only thing that survived the crash was his wallet. Inside was a key to a safe deposit box. We might be able to piece together some of my family history and theirs if we made a trip to Pipersville, Ohio, and looked around."

The intensity in his voice indicated to Janice that he wanted to do an investigation of his own. She nodded as if to say, *Go on.*

"I discussed the idea with their family, and they would like to send the son, David, with me to look into things."

Janice said, "It sounds like you really want to go. How long will you be away?"

"I have some vacation time coming. I was thinking that we could make it a trip for both of us. You could go visit the kids and grandkids, and in a few days, I could meet you. I don't think it would take me more than three or four days in Ohio. What do you think?"

Janice knew that it was already decided. She nodded her head again and said, "Sure, that sounds okay."

"Great! I will put it together. Thanks, honey," he exclaimed and slapped both knees with his hands as he pushed on them, stood up, and then bent over and gave her a kiss. He changed the subject and said, "What's for dinner? I'm hungry. One piece of pizza just doesn't stick with me."

The next day, phone calls and e-mails were exchanged between Tucson and Phoenix. Calendars were consulted, schedules rearranged, reservations made, and money spent.

It was decided that David would fly up to Phoenix tomorrow. They would meet up at Sky Harbor and catch the Phoenix to-Cleveland flight at 11:00 a.m., Wednesday, on US Air. It was a good thing that both families had some frequent flyer miles. That saved them more than a few dollars. There was a Holiday Inn in Pipersville where they would stay. They would rent a car in Cleveland. They gave themselves three days to do the investigation. David would then fly back to Tucson, and Bob would fly out to Dallas to join Janice and spend some time with their grandchildren.

David met up with him at ten thirty at the boarding gate for the flight to Cleveland, just as they had planned the day before.

"Hi, David," Bob said loudly as he waved to get his attention. David nodded in acknowledgement and walked over to him.

"How was your flight from Tucson?"

"Uneventful," David replied matter-of-factly.

"Well, it was good timing. We are just about to board. It doesn't look like the plane will be full. Maybe we can arrange to sit together," Bob said with a tone that indicated that the idea needed a yes or no from him.

"Yeah, sure," David answered.

There was something about this older guy that David liked. He tried to figure out what it was. It could be the family resemblance or his slow pace and style. He seemed to have something that made David like and trust him. Bob was easy to be around. He didn't talk too much. He seemed to listen effortlessly and without pretense. He reminded him of someone, not his father or anyone in his family. Then it hit him. He reminded him of a ranch foreman in Texas, Jarvis Henry, who had helped him out of a few tough spots. He always seemed to show up with a word of encouragement, needed or not.

Jarvis could charm the rattles right off a diamond back. He could tell stories and reveled in making sure that no one took themselves too seriously. He had bailed him out of jail when he had gotten too "frisky," as he put it, one night when he had tied one on at the Wander Inn Bar and Grill. He had smoothed things out with the owner on a couple of other occasions when his behavior had deserved fiery consequences. Even when he wanted to put up his guard and cling to his usual distrustful boundaries, he would find himself agreeing with Bob and following him.

The stewardess let them sit together once they were safely in the air. They settled in for a long flight. There was that small talk about the weather in Ohio, how hot Phoenix was compared to Tucson, and about the work they both did. Bob leaned over and asked one of those leading questions that could have been an interrogation in any other circumstance but, considering the situation, was almost expected. "What do you hope to find out about your father?"

David knew that his secret resentments would have to come out sooner or later. He felt like a big stone was sitting on his heart. It needed to be rolled away. Maybe now was the time to give it a push. Bits of the story had escaped before when he was drunk and feeling sorry for himself. He'd tried to find someone interested enough to listen. It was never the whole story. He had to admit that with all the new revelations, his script needed to be revised. New facts had settled into his consciousness like a shade going up and letting in more light. The illumination had exposed areas of his father's private pain. He wanted to make sure that they would not be overheard.

The lady across the aisle had an unruly child to attend to. There was an empty row of seats in front of them. There were two youngsters interested in listening to their music, not noticing or caring about the guys sitting in front of them.

"Bob, I don't really know what I am looking for. I want to know why he treated me and my mother the way he did. We were never able to communicate or connect with each other. I have had a lot of time to think about why we were so angry. I just disappointed him because I wasn't going to live my life in his shadow." He continued forcefully, "My father had a way of undermining my choices. I think in his mind, he believed he was helping me. I felt he was manipulating me to be what he wanted. Dad set a high bar of perfection. I could never measure up to it. When the reality hit me that trying to change his mind was impossible, I just had to leave so I could be my own man."

"Those are not uncommon clashes between fathers and sons. Was there something that happened that made your relationship so painful?"

"It wasn't one thing but the multiplication of things. I could never figure out what I did that displeased him. I am beginning to see that maybe it wasn't about me but about him. It's ironic that the investigation revealed so much about my dad. You know more complexities about him than I ever knew. It must have been difficult for him to keep this all locked up inside and keep it hidden. He must have carried a deep sense of shame with him every day. I thought that the lack of bonding between us was my fault. I am beginning to understand that bonding was something he did not do well. He survived well in medicine by having the answers and staying aloof. It was a perfect hiding place for him. He could make a good living, have a reason to be absent, and have a solid reputation in the community. It was ideal for a man who had problems with his past."

It got quiet. It was an uncomfortable silence that implied there was more to talk about but enough had been said for now.

It was David's turn to ask a few questions. "I have told you about what I hope to find. What about you? What are you looking for?"

"You know, David, I'm not entirely sure either. All my life, I have felt empty, and unsettled when it comes to my family. I think it has something to do with my brother. He died, and I can't talk to him about the gaps in our family history. The emptiness sometimes cuts into my heart to remind me that I feel the painful deficit. I have a wonderful wife and three children who are fine adults. We have five grandchildren and our first great-grandchild on the way. Life has been pretty good. Still, I have this feeling. It could be that I am just entering into retirement or empty nest or something like that. I have questions that need to be answered, questions that are like that key you are bringing. You hope to unlock something, a safe deposit box, and open up your dad's story, his life. Maybe we can unlock that past together and find out more about ourselves in the process. Your father is gone and so is my brother. Many of the people who were alive then have passed away. You and I are here, and our families are here. What I hope to find is not my story. It has already been written, at least most of it. No, what I hope to find is what my story means, how it fits together with my family. I'm not expecting anything, but I have hope."

David was taken aback by what Bob had said. His candor was inviting. Trading vulnerabilities often leads to more and deeper sharing. David felt the sense of apprehension at that idea. He was his father's son after all. Being too open can be taken as weakness. It had happened to him before. He decided to sleep on it. "We both have reasons to be on this trip. It sounds like we will probably come back and revisit this conversation again. I could use a little nap before we get to Cleveland, okay?"

"Sure," Bob replied. He was surprised by the quick change of direction. "It might be a good idea for both of us to get some rest."

David had already put his seat back and tucked a pillow that he got from the stewardess under his head.

Bob folded his arms across his chest and tried to get comfortable. He felt restless. The seat was too narrow for his girth. It made him aware of how much weight he needed to lose. Bob looked out the window. Thirty-five thousand feet below was the ground, waiting for them to return to its breast. It was solid, immovable. It had swallowed up his nephew. It had reached out its hand of attraction. The closer you came to it, the more it changed. It took on the characteristics of the people who shaped it, farmed it, built over it, and under it. The reality of that idea made him feel strangely curious and excited. He closed his eyes, but trying to sleep seemed a goal beyond reach. He wondered what they would find when they arrived in Pipersville.

He must have been a fisherman, to put out from the shore,

to leave the land and coast *along the sea.*

look up and see the cross that held the sail,

to capture the tide of wind *across the sea.*

Follow in the Master's boat and weather the tumult,

of waves highs and lows and navigate *upon the sea.*

He must have been a fisherman, humbled, persistent

Vulnerable to what he knew about himself

Whenever *he sailed the sea*

The Slack Story

Michael was surprised to see Morgan and Billy Slack approaching the veranda. He could tell that it was not something Billy wanted to do. Morgan had him by the collar and was pulling him along. They were kicking up some dust on the path. He could hear Morgan say, "Look, I told you we were going to the Doctor's office, and that's what we are going to do."

Billy yelled back, "Dad, I told you I'm fine. Nothing is wrong."

"Well, we will just see about that," Morgan loudly replied. "Now come along, or so help me, I will drag you there."

Michael realized that there had been some changes. Billy looked to be a whole head taller than he remembered. His clothes seemed a bit too small, especially his high-water jeans. He looked like a thin clumsy teenager. Morgan's face was flushed. He had the appearance of someone who was enraged and frustrated. They somehow arrived at the steps to the veranda, and Michael opened the screen door and invited them in.

Michael said, "Please come in."

"Well, the Doctor is inviting you inside. Go on, Billy." Reluctantly he walked up the three steps like someone who was going to the gallows. Morgan followed right behind him to make sure he didn't try to escape.

Morgan was so intent that he didn't notice that Dr. Turner had a guest. Before Michael could even introduce Luke, Morgan said, "I can't explain it. I am telling you, Doctor, something has to be done about it."

"Done about what?" Michael asked.

"Billy has not been acting normally. He doesn't attend to his studies, makes no effort to focus on our educational projects at all. All he wants to do is visit with Cindy Crier. I tell you, Doctor, something has gotten into his head." Morgan's tone had a loud high-pitched sound that clearly indicated he had a full head of steam.

Michael interrupted him and said, "Morgan, I can tell you are upset. Let me introduce Dr. Luke. He is here to give me some assistance. Perhaps he would visit with Billy while you and I go into my office." Luke shook his head up and down in agreement.

Michael looked over at Billy, who shook his head up and down too with a shrug that feigned resistance but confirmed the need for rescue, even if it was with a stranger.

"Okay, sure. Billy, you wait here until I come and get you."

They walked into the house and down the hall into Michael's office.

"What has you so upset, Morgan?"

"Look, Doctor, Billy's mother left us quite unexpectedly. I have been trying the best I can to raise him. I have endeavored to educate him into the world of facts and science. You are a man of science and discipline. You understand the importance of study and knowledge. When his mother abandoned us, I decided that since people cannot be trusted, then we would trust the truth of science. Since we arrived, Billy and I have enjoyed the peace and quiet to focus on our scientific pursuits. There's been a change that I cannot understand nor do I like. He's chosen to visit with Cindy Crier instead of working on our intellectual discoveries. I've been shocked to realize how little knowledge seems to have sunk in from all our research and study. He's often distracted. I ask him to do the littlest thing, and he usually says he will get to it in a while. I tell you, if I waited for him a little while, it would take forever. 'Whenever' is beginning to be his favorite saying. I used to get respectful obedience. Now all I get is obfuscation and procrastination." He started pacing and waving his arms. "Can you explain that, Doctor? Well, can you?"

Michael was trying not to laugh at this display of parental confusion. "If you're asking my opinion, I would be glad to give you any help I can," he said wryly. "Have you ever read any books on the subject of parenting?"

"No," Morgan replied. His tone softened.

"I think you should. Being a good father requires training about child development, discipline, communication, and other skills. I would be glad to supply a bibliography for you." He was reminded of all those issues he experienced with his own children. He had handled some well; others not so well. His son, David's, adolescence had posed a real double bind for him. He had felt much like Morgan. Their relationship had made him feel mostly confused and frustrated.

"Billy is probably going through a stage of growing up that might be difficult for you to appreciate. It's probably going to be difficult for both of you."

Morgan sat down in a chair and looked at the floor. He was mumbling under his breath. He looked up at Michael and said, "Doctor, you're right. I think I just have been reacting and not thinking this thing through. Billy is supposed to grow up. I just never thought it would happen here. I have to admit that there are changes taking place that cannot be explained any other way. What am I supposed to do?" Morgan lamented.

"Morgan, you can do this. It's not impossible. Believe me. I have had a little experience with my own children. Somehow, both of you will survive and even grow."

"Dr. Turner, that is reassuring to know," he said with a tinge of sarcasm.

"You're right too, Morgan," Michael said. "Something is happening between Cindy and Billy. It need not be a bad thing. It could be a very wonderful thing. Like any parent, you will have to wait and see and be patient. The truth tends to work itself out. I hope you know that because you were disappointed and rejected by your wife, it doesn't mean that Billy and Cindy will have the same outcome. They are two different people." He punctuated this last remark with a more demonstrative tone and an outstretched palm.

"Yes, I know," Morgan's initial anger had subsided. His tone was softer and reflective.

"Morgan, while you are thinking about this, I am going to go talk to Billy, if that's okay with you."

"Sure, that's okay."

Michael turned and left the office. He closed the door and walked over to the veranda. Luke and Billy were not there. He heard voices in the living room and headed there. They were sitting across from each other. He didn't know what they had discussed. There seemed to be a comfortable feeling in the air. Billy got up when he saw Michael and walked toward him, while Luke remained sitting on the sofa.

"Is everything all right, Doctor?" Billy asked.

"Yes, I think so."

"Dr. Turner, I told my dad that I was going to continue to see Cindy. I don't want to hide that fact. I want him to know. I want everything to be out in the open."

"Billy, I think that is an honorable thing. It's going to take your father some adjustments to learn to accept the changes that are happing in your relationship. You might try to understand his point of view. He didn't expect that you would grow up so fast. Parents are often not ready for their children to grow up. It's a shock when it begins to happen. It can cause a lot of hard feelings if there is no understanding from both sides. I know from my own experience."

"You know, Doctor, that is what Cindy told me. She keeps saying things like 'Try to understand your father from his point of view.' She just blows me away sometimes with her compassion. She gives me a whole new way of looking at things."

"Billy, it's a good idea for you and your dad to talk about this. What do you think?" Michael asked rhetorically. "You might try some of the ideas that Cindy has been saying with him. Your father is just down the hall in my office, first door on the right. Why don't you go and knock on the door and visit with him? You guys probably need to talk together. I think that he might be willing to listen. After all, he was a teenager once too."

"Thanks, Dr. Turner. I think I will do just that." There was a maturity in his determined demeanor as he firmly shook Michael's hand and turned and walked to the door. He hesitated then knocked on it and walked in.

Michael stood there watching and listening just in case it got loud and hostile again. It didn't do either. He decided to go and visit with Luke in the parlor. Just as he got there, Billy and Morgan came out of the office. Billy had his arm around his father's waist, like he was playfully trying to put some halfhearted wrestling hold on him. Morgan laughed and dragged both of them into the parlor.

Morgan said, "Dr. Turner, we will be going home. I want to thank both of you for helping us. Can I come over and see you if I need a few more parenting tips?"

"Of course, you can see me whenever you want." Michael had a big smile on his face. Morgan and Billy turned and crossed the veranda and went out the screen door and headed down the path.

Michael watched them with a sympathetic fascination that included a flood of memories of his own. His mind settled on how he raised his children. The conflict between Morgan and Billy brought to mind his failures and successes with the kids. There emerged upon this reflection a feeling of regret. He had missed something, and it was an important something. It wasn't a small miss either. Not like turning down the wrong street or losing a small piece of paper that had an address or phone number. It was more like missing the Grand Canyon. The realization broke through his soul's rose-colored glasses. "I should have told them that I loved them, that I was proud of them and how much of a blessing they were to me. I never did. It's too late to tell them now."

Michael looked up and scanned the room for Luke. He was standing right next to him. He had his hand on Michael's shoulder. His eyes were closed like he was concentrating on something. It startled him.

"What are you doing, Luke?" Michael asked.

"I am praying for you," Luke said softly.

"Sure, I can use all the prayers I can get."

"Michael, it can be difficult sometimes to separate your own experience from your patients'. There are often many similarities between the two. I thought that you did a very good job of making the situation safer. You separated the two parties. You listened, and I think your diagnosis was correct. Billy is growing up, and that is a confusing and difficult reality for both of them. The issue I want to explore is how it affected you. It probably reminded you of your relationship patterns. It's important to tell the people closest to us that we love them. Why don't we do that when it is so necessary? It could be that we are just afraid and insecure. It might be the fear of rejection or the fear of unexpected demands. It could be the fear of losing our autonomy or freedom. Fear can have a paralytic quality on our ability to make good choices. It can rob the person of the experience of facing life head on. A fearful person is usually looking for the closest exit. They want to leave behind responsibilities, commitments, and, ultimately, life."

Michael replied, "Were you reading my mind? What you just described is what I was thinking."

"Michael, around here, loving thoughts tends to get communicated or felt somehow."

"What do you mean 'loving thoughts'?"

Luke's blue eyes were fastened on Michael, and his face seemed full of caring. "Love comes through an honest self assessment. Truth is nothing to hide from or escape."

"It's true, Luke, that I would have liked for things to have been different, especially with my wife and son. How can I change that now? It's too late."

"You might be asking the wrong question," Luke replied. "Being the physician to these people could help you come to terms with your life."

Luke turned and looked down the path. "Dr. Turner, I see a vivacious young woman coming up the hill. I believe she might be your next patient."

Michael peered over Luke's shoulder and saw Cindy Crier quickly walking up the path to his house.

Porcelain blue runs into azure. Dappled pigments inspire

a collage of tints and hues ripe with frosted clouds

that swirl and fly by

like wispy handprints one on top of another they scoot

across earth's canvas; collecting on the edges till they dry.

I look up into that sacred space and feel the hot, cold,

windy, still, beauty of the sky.

Facts and Figures

Hunter had put together a detailed list of important facts gleaned from the wreckage. He was beginning to narrow down a likely scenario of what caused the crash and why it was so catastrophic. A copy of the aircraft logbook had been recovered from Marian Anderson's house. She had a two-bedroom condo that was shared by her cat. Her mother and sister had keys to the place. They had been very helpful in finding the information he needed. The logbook had identified who the mechanic was and how often the plane had been serviced. The log confirmed that Marian had kept to a regular maintenance schedule. She had the logbook up-to-date as well. Hunter could tell that she flew at least every couple of weeks. She had lots of hours logged. Marian seemed to enjoy taking passengers for trips to Flagstaff and Tucson. He was impressed at how organized the books were. It was noted that the last overhaul had been completed a week before the accident. Repairs had been done on the fuel system. There was a signed-off section of the book with the company's address and phone. Sterling Aircraft Repair and Sales Co. had a reputation of doing good work. Their office and hangar is at Falcon Field too. They also helped their clients to sell or upgrade their airplanes. Armed with this information, Hunter decided to take Jerry with him and go over there.

They called the Sterling office and had a brief visit on the phone with the mechanic. His name was Gary Myers. He had over five years of experience and had been the primary guy taking care of the plane.

He knew the pilot well enough to describe her as conscientious and a person who did not cut corners when it came to her airplane. They set up a meeting for later that day at the Sterling hangar at Falcon Field. Hunter had some technical questions about the condition of the aircraft. Marian had not flown the airplane until after its fuel system overhaul. Some error by the mechanic or faulty part could have caused the engine failure.

Discussing the possibility of a professional mistake is a delicate issue. Hunter knew that nobody likes being accused of causing a tragic accident. Still, he had questions that needed answers. It seemed like a good idea to start the conversation with questions that would not raise a lot of defensive red flags. Gary was about thirty years old. He was of average height, thin, and wiry. He wore company white overalls that had been washed to a kind of smudgy gray. He had piercing blue eyes and wide angular features. His tanned face showed lines that indicated a man of intense emotions.

"Hello," Hunter said as he walked up to him. Gary had just turned from putting some tools away in a stand-up tool chest. He quickly walked toward Hunter.

"Are you the guys from the NTSB who called?"

"Yes, I am. My name is Agent Hunter Grayson, and this is agent Jerry Goldman." They shook hands. "You must be Gary Myers."

"That's right. You have some questions about Marian's airplane?"

"Yes, I do. I have to prepare a report on the accident, and to do that, we need to investigate anything that could be involved with the crash. Since Marian Anderson is not here to tell us, we have to figure out what happened and why it happened. I need to ask you some questions about the maintenance of the aircraft. We are not here to affix blame for the accident. We are here to determine by a careful reconstruction of the facts as best we can what caused this crash that killed two people."

Gary looked directly at Hunter. "I realize that you have a job to do. Believe me that I take my job as seriously as you do," he said with a slightly upraised chin.

"I can appreciate that," Hunter replied.

"Well then, what do you want to know?"

"Let's start with the overall condition of the airplane. How would you rate it?"

"Oh, I would say it's A+. Marian had done a lot to it. She had upgraded the radio, avionics, and the interior. She maintained it well and kept on top of things. The plane's engine was like new."

Hunter zeroed in on what he really wanted to talk about. "Her aircraft logbook said that the fuel system had been worked on the week before the crash. What was the issue that needed repair? What did you do to fix the problem?"

"Marian had taken a trip the week before. She said that the engine had felt a little rough, like it was missing every so often. She thought it might be something in the fuel system because when she made the mixture a little richer, it seemed better. I said I would look at it, and she brought it over the next day. I thought that we should replace the carburetor to be on the safe side. I got a new one in a couple of days and installed it. I did all the necessary fine tuning. It seemed to be running just perfect. I can understand how you might think that I made some mistake. Let me tell you I did not. We use only parts that are approved and inspected by the FAA," he said empathically.

"Gary, are you aware that there had been an accident several years ago that was caused by a carburetor that ran rich, which caused the engine to become overloaded with fuel, which caused the exhaust valve to stick and for the plane to lose power and crash?" Hunter recognized that Gary wanted him to just go away. Hunter was making it clear that he was claiming his territory.

"Yes, I did read about that, which is why I suggested that the carburetor be replaced. Marian was a real nice lady." Hunter could see from his body language, head looking at the floor and slumped shoulders, that Gary's feelings were genuine.

"Gary, is it possible that the part you replaced failed?"

"Well, yes, it's possible but not likely. I mean, after all, it would be very unlikely, but yes, it could happen. Do you think that is what caused this?"

"I can't answer that right now. We know several things that could point us in that direction. It might be hard to say definitively or to prove with the amount of evidence we got from the crash site. If we are concerned about the fuel system, then the carburetor would be the first place to look."

Jerry Goldman was standing slightly behind his boss. He had taken in everything that was said. He had watched for any incongruities in Gary's body language. He knew that Hunter would ask for his observations. His initial impressions were that Gary was a pretty stand-up guy. He seemed honest and liked to face things head on.

Jerry began to mull over in his mind what their report might mean. If it was determined that the carburetor was the cause of the crash, there would be consequences. He knew that what Hunter said was right; they were not trying to affix blame. It was also true that the report could be used by others to litigate those responsible: the FAA, the manufacturer, Sterling Aircraft Repair and Sales, even Gary Myers. It could be a real mess. He remembered that the pilot of the earlier crash and his passenger had barely survived with serious burns and fractures. The jury had awarded them a big settlement.

The determination of their report would be a public document. The shyster ambulance chasers would be beating down the doors of these two families to punish the culprits and build themselves a bigger bank account.

Hunter gave Gary his card. "Is there anything else that you could tell me? Sometimes, a small detail can help the investigation."

"No," Gary parried. "I think that's all I have to say." It seemed to Jerry that the mechanic hesitated. It implied nonverbally that there was something more he wanted to tell. His eyes looked away, and his voice was softer. Jerry thought there was definitely something he was protecting or felt bad about. Gary reluctantly stuck his hand out, saying, "If that's everything, I have to get back to work."

Hunter replied as he rubbed his chin, "Sure. If we need to talk any more, I'll give you a call, or you can call me on my cell phone if something comes to mind. Thank you for your time." He had to say it louder because Gary had already turned and was well on his way toward a Mooney aircraft parked in the hangar.

Hunter looked over to Jerry and gave a nod toward the door of the hangar. They both strolled silently outside toward their parked car. Hunter became aware of how blustery and dusty it had become outside. Maybe another springtime cold front was moving in. Not a good day to be flying, tough crosswind.

As I grow older I recognize the importance of…

As I grow older I see the need for…

As I grow older I understand more about…

As I grow older I wish I had…

As I grow older I regret that I never…

As I grow older I wonder why I didn't…

As I grow older I should have…

As I grow older I hope to…

As I grow older I can be more like…

As I grow older I can dream to be…

As I grow older I am…

As I grow older…

I forgot!

You Can Bank on It

Bob and David, with the time change, arrived in Pipersville well after dark. They had landed in Cleveland more or less on schedule, picked up their rental car, and made good time to their destination. They got to the motel room Bob had reserved on the internet and unpacked. It had two queen-size beds, a small table and two chairs, TV, bathroom, and computer access. It wasn't the Phoenician. The paint was chipped. The carpet was worn in the traffic areas. It had the look of being upgraded about ten years ago. The room suited its two occupants.

Bob had suggested that they head down to the motel cafe and grab a bite. There was a bar there too. Bob was going to be looking for a good watering hole. David agreed. He was feeling hungry and a little cranky. They were met at the door by a waitress wearing a hairnet and white server's dress. She was thin and looked tired and bored. She gave them a menu and pointed to the empty booths and said, "Sit wherever you like."

There were just a few patrons in the place. They sat down. The waitress came over after a few minutes and asked what they wanted to drink. Bob wanted to know if he could order from the bar. The waitress said yes. He ordered a scotch and soda. David ordered a Diet Coke. When she returned with the drinks, she took their food order, which consisted of a couple of cheese burgers and fries. It seemed to both of them that ordering anything else might be an adventure not worth trying. Now that, that was all settled, it seemed like a good time to make plans for the morning.

David started it off, "Bob, what do you think we should do tomorrow?"

"Tomorrow is Thursday, and the banks open at nine. I found out from the internet that there are six banks in town and two post offices. I suggest that we start there. We can see if the key fits any mailbox that may have belonged to your father. We have the key and the preliminary death certificate from the medical examiner's office. We have your father's recent picture and our own identification. We should be good to go if anyone has questions."

Bob continued, "I did some background research on my sister-in-law, Michael's mother, online before we left." He opened a little book from his coat pocket and began to read from it. "Her maiden name was Beth Smith. Her parents were Theresa Bell and Ronald Smith. They had no other children. The family moved from Decatur, Illinois, to Cleveland, Ohio, during the depression. They settled around there, and she went to school and graduated from high school. Two years later, she met my brother, and they were married after a short courtship. They moved to a farm near Pipersville. My brother was excluded from military service. Flat feet and a pair of arthritic knees was the reason for his deferment."

David inquired, "What did you find out about the accident?"

"The newspaper in Cleveland covered the story. It reported the facts of the case as we had been told. The fire killed Michael's two-year-old little sister, Mindy, and five-year-old brother, Samuel. The mother survived. It was determined to be an accidental fire caused by bad wiring. The house was old, and in those days, electrical codes weren't in place or enforced. Faulty work or poor materials were often behind these tragedies. The paper said that there was no evidence that suggested there was any kind of foul play.

It's really hard to draw any conclusions without the benefits of modern fire science techniques. Forensic sciences were also just in their infancy. Investigators often drew their conclusions from interviews and their own experience. The name of the investigator on the case cited in the paper was Thomas Monroe. I doubt that he is alive. He may have family still living in Pipersville. They may be able to help us find out more about the accident. We could find some evidence that might help us from your father's safe deposit box. I certainly have some unanswered questions."

David interjected, "So do I. It seems so strange to be in this town that my father knew so well. He probably rode his bike here. He went to school and attended church here. He had friends and life experiences in this place that I knew nothing about. Dad never talked about this part of his life. Now after his death, I am just now learning about him. You know, Bob, whatever happened here must have been very painful for him to go to such lengths to keep it so private."

Bob had finished his drink and was contemplating having another when the food arrived. David asked for another Diet Coke, and Bob surprised himself and asked for a cup of decaf coffee. She put the food down. It looked edible.

They started eating, and David looked up and said, "Bob, I think you're right. Let's see if we can find the safe deposit box first. It may contain all the information we need to answer the questions we have about what happened."

Bob looked up from his food too, hesitated, and replied, "It's just as possible that instead of answering our questions, we may find new ones."

"That's a possibility I guess we'll have to deal with if we find a home for this key," David said with an emphatic tone. Bob nodded his head in approval.

Dinner didn't take too long. Both men were hungry and tired. Tomorrow's opening round had been dissected and prepared. There remained only going to the room and getting some sleep.

The next day began with a windy and brisk welcome. It warmed up as the sun rose in the sky. They gulped down a continental breakfast with coffee in the motel lounge. By nine o'clock, they were out the door. Bob and David went to the two Pipersville post offices first with no success and then the town banks and fared no better. Lunchtime came around quickly, and they were both frustrated by finding nothing. They decided to go to the Dairy Queen in town and discuss the situation.

They sat outside in swivel chairs attached to a round table with an umbrella for shade, eating their cheese burgers and fries. David thought a change of diet might be a good idea. He splurged and ordered a chocolate shake, while Bob was having a large Dr. Pepper. Bob was looking out at the parking lot, watching cars come and go.

He said, "Last night, you said that your father had gone to great lengths to keep this part of his life secret. I think it doesn't fit that he would come here. There were just too many bad memories, people who would recognize him." Bob paused and tapped his finger to the side of his head. "Michael was a perfectionist. That means he was careful and methodical. Every physician needs to be a planner. What was the story he told everyone?"

David replied, "He said he was going fishing every year and staying in a cabin on a lake. He was going to be out of touch for a couple of weeks. I was angry that he took time for himself and not for me. I was never invited, nor was anyone else." David was aware that he was struggling to swallow that last bite of his burger. It felt dry in his mouth. The memories seemed to choke him, and he felt the hurt and disappointment well up in his throat. "He never made time for me. He was always about doing his own thing." It was a big confession of emotional abandonment.

Bob turned and looked directly at David. He had both hands around his milkshake like he was trying to squeeze something out of it. It got quiet.

Bob said softly, "I'm sorry about that for you, Dave. It seems that your father had a reason that you didn't know about. That's what you are here to find out. I think your father was telling the truth. He was somewhere at a cabin of some kind, probably near a lake. My guess is that if we look at a map of this state, we might find a place like he described. Let's assume that he's out here to care for his mother, who is in Hillcrest Nursing Home as Agent Goldman told you. We know there is a nursing home by that name about thirty miles from here. Let's plan on going there tomorrow. He would need someone to work with in between his yearly visits. It could be a relative or friend. No, it would probably be a professional person, say, a lawyer or somebody like that. It would have to be someone who would be expected to keep a secret and paid to keep it. A family member might not be trusted to keep such a burden. I suggest that we get a map."

"You're right, Bob. The place can't be here in Pipersville." David went on, "If we are going to find the safe deposit box, we need to start thinking like he did."

They went to a local hardware store. It had maps of the state and counties within a hundred miles of Pipersville. Upon inspection, Geauga County seemed like a perfect match. It had a rural population of Amish folks and farmers. Few, if any, of the people would have been concerned about what happened thirty miles away back then. If they read the newspaper, they would have been more interested in the obituaries. The county had lots of parks and lakes, resorts, and lodges. David was crestfallen when he realized how big the state was. Michael could have stayed anywhere. It was like trying to find a needle in a field of haystacks. He thought that since they were here, they might as well look in a few to see if they could find that pesky needle. His eyes settled on a place called Bear Lake as they scanned the map. David felt drawn to it for some reason.

He mentioned it to Bob. "Let's try there." He pointed to the spot on the map.

"You know, it's kind of funny, but I thought the same thing. I can check it out on the internet." They found out that there was a fancy lodge near the lake. It wasn't rustic at all or solitary. They decided to take a ride up there. It was only forty miles from the hotel. They could stop by the nursing home on the way back. The drive would be good for them. It was a chance to see the countryside and explore a little of the culture and build their own impressions.

They couldn't see that Ayin had suddenly joined them on their journey. Angels can break through time's temporal membrane like a fish jumping out of the water. Every so often, God gives them an assignment that requires such a leap. Human beings were always surprised by their unannounced arrival. Michael was in that spiritual cocoon being looked after and in very capable hands. Ayin knew that working with these two men in the sphere of human decisions required his care. A spiritual work was happening, which would shape the course of events in the future, affecting the outcomes of many things.

A guardian angel's assignment doesn't end when the person's fundamental option is made. It goes on well past that final choice. It reflects a time line that is acted upon by many others. Forgiveness, reconciliation, peace, love, and hope are wedded to the memory of that person. God's grace champions that holy matrimony. The angel's job is to maintain that pious recollection and guard it. Angels were always present when God's people remembered their history. Long ago, The Israelites told epic stories around the campfire and retold them to the next generation and to the one after that. Before it was written down, their angels reminded them in their hearts of their sacred encounters with God. They were not forgotten but retold, rehearsed, and kept alive. When they did come with a message from God's Spirit, it heralded in the next step of God's plan of redemption. It was birthed from the memory of His previous saving works.

Ayin knew that the purpose of this assignment was to keep Michael's memory alive. It meant that the truth was going to be told. Telling the truth in love brings to mind the value of the person's life. He knew also that the process of closure was a difficult reality for some people to face.

Ayin remained unseen in the backseat, yet he was with them. The closer they got to Bear Lake, the closer they came to the truth. He knew what awaited them; they had no idea what they were looking for or what they would find. Closer and closer they came until they drove up to the lodge where the story would begin to be told. Angels like being at epiphanies. It's the moment the light goes on for the person and truth comes in and lives. It's a special realization that heaven celebrates when the possibility dawns that God makes all things new. Here they were, and he was blessed to see it happen once again.

David and Bob drove up to the front door at "Bear Lake Lodge," the sign read in front of the big covered circular drive that invited them to stop. It was a large colonial-looking building that was designed to look older than it was. It looked to be three stories high. The grounds were immaculate. The sun was still bright in the late afternoon sky. There were a few high clouds and a slight breeze that made everything feel and look perfect. Out in the distance, you could see the blue shimmering lake. David took in a big deep breath like he wanted to take in all the view and hold it deep inside. It was such a beautiful scene, it made him feel tired, suddenly aware that he needed rest.

He got out of the car and stood there looking all around and admiring the view, waiting for Bob to walk around to his side. He heard Bob's door slam and heard his steps approaching. "Man, this is some kind of place."

Bob said, "Yeah, it's a beautiful place to relax. I wonder if your father stayed here."

"How do we find out?"

"Well, we have your father's picture. Let's see if anybody recognizes him."

They left resting against the side of the car and wandered up the three steps onto the large covered veranda with rocking chairs and small tables set all around. David opened the screen door and walked inside as Bob followed. They were greeted by an attractive young woman with long curly auburn hair and a flawless complexion standing behind a long counter. Behind her were those little boxes for the guests' keys. It was a picture right out of a Norman Rockwell painting. She looked to be about twenty years old, very pretty, and welcomed them with a big smile. "May I help you, gentlemen?" she asked.

Bob took the le ad as they both closed the distance to the counter.

"I am Robert Hughes, and this is David Turner. We are involved in settling my nephew's affairs. We think that he might have come here, or a place like it, once a year. He died tragically in a small plane crash. I brought his picture for you to look at."

She responded by interrupting and saying, "I am not the person to ask. My manager has been here a long time. You could talk to him."

"Is he here now?" David replied as he leaned upon the desk, obviously admiring the view opposite him.

"I believe that he is. If you don't mind, I'll go and see." With that, she turned around and went through an open door behind her that probably led to an office. After a few moments, a tall thin man came out followed by the woman who greeted them at the desk.

"Hello, my name is Silas Best, and I am the manager of the lodge. Is there something I can do for you?" He seemed friendly but at the same time professionally guarded. Bob stuck out his hand, and the manager responded by shaking his and then David's.

"Mr. Best, my name is Bob Hughes, and this is David Turner. We are interested in knowing if this man was a guest here over the last few years." Bob pulled out a photo of Michael from a manila folder he had brought from the car. "You see, he died quite suddenly in a small plane crash in Arizona. The family has a few loose ends to deal with because of the suddenness of the loss. He went by the name of Dr. Michael Turner, or perhaps Stephen Hughes."

Bob slid the picture across the counter to him. The manager picked it up and looked closely at it, seemingly inspecting it in great detail. There seemed to be a look of recognition that filled his face. He tapped the picture a few times and said with an air of confidence, "Gentlemen, I need some identification and some proof before we go any further into this."

Bob responded, "Of course, here is the presumptive death certificate issued by the Pinal County Medical Examiner in Arizona. The Superior Court is in the process of issuing a final death certificate."

Mr. Best scanned their driver's licenses, nodded his head, and said, "I know this person, but his name is not Michael Turner or Stephen Hughes. It's Michael Smith, or at least that's what he said. He usually came in late March or early April. He would stay with us for two weeks and then leave. He paid for everything in cash and pretty much would spend his time fishing or reading. Rarely would I see him talk to anyone. He was not one of those demanding guests. He was pleasant and private, we respected that and provided an environment where he could rest."

David was beside himself "It's incredible that we found this lodge. We came right to it. We had no idea where to look. We just took a guess, and here we are."

"That's right. Mr. Best, I'm amazed that we somehow came to the right place too. Would he go out at all?" Bob continued to inquire.

"Oh, yes, he would be gone for a day here or there. He mostly was at the lake. I think he liked to come at the off season. It was still cold and often rainy, not like the summer. It seemed that the season fit his personality."

David asked, "Mr. Best, is it possible for us to stay here tonight and meet with you tomorrow?"

"Yes," Bob interjected. "We have some more questions to ask. You could really be of great help to us. We were thinking of going back to Pipersville tonight. Finding the lodge and meeting you require a change of plans. I know this is short notice. I can appreciate that you are busy, especially at this time of year—"

Before Bob could finish the sentence, Mr. Best, thinking out loud, said, "We did have a couple that had to leave early because of a family emergency. I believe the answer is yes to both things."

I will listen for what God, the Lord, has

To Say;

Surely he will speak of peace

To his people and to his faithful.

May They not turn to foolishness!

Near indeed is his salvation for those who

fear him;

glory will dwell in our land.

Love and truth will meet;

Justice and peace will kiss.

Truth will spring up from the earth,

Justice will look down from heaven.

Yes, the Lord will grant his bounty;

Our land will yield its produce.

Justice will march before him,

And make a way for his footsteps.

(Psalm 85:9-14, The New American Bible, St. Joseph edition)

A Kiss

It wasn't difficult to notice Cindy. She made no attempt to hide her feelings; in that way, she was a refreshing person. She had no guile. She waved at Michael as she approached the big house. He was surprised that she had grown up. She was a young woman. Her hair was longer and blonder than when he saw her at the party. She'd developed a figure. She was taller by six inches. Her freckles were gone, replaced by rosy cheeks. Cindy was wearing a yellow sundress. She was as beautiful a young woman as he had ever seen. He knew that the naive little girl was gone and a mature person was taking her place. The awareness produced contradictory feelings in him. Michael was sad that the spontaneous child was absent. She would be missed. He felt happy, on the other hand, glad that she was coming into her own. Michael knew that it was a necessary step, one that he and his own children had made. She came up to the steps leading onto the porch and noticed Luke standing next to him.

"Hey, Doctor, who's your friend?" she said with a mature confidence.

"Cindy, come in, and I will introduce you."

"Sure," she said as she confidently climbed the stairs and quickly came inside the veranda. It seemed to him that she was unaware of her transformation.

"Cindy Crier, let me introduce you to Dr. Luke. He has come to help me learn the ropes here, sort of like a mentor."

Cindy reached out to Luke and shook his hand. "I am glad to meet you." She barely looked at him. She focused her attention on Michael. Cindy had an agenda of her own, and right now, she did not want any impediments. "Dr. Turner," she said in a soft yet demanding tone, "I have some personal matters that I need to discuss with you and you alone."

It was quite clear that she had no intention of discussing anything with anyone else. Michael turned to Luke, and before he could make a suggestion, Luke said, "I will wait in the living room for you after your visit."

"Yes, thank you, Dr. Luke. Cindy, let's go in to my office over here." He pointed to the first exam room.

"Okay." She followed him down the hall. They went inside, and Michael closed the door quietly behind them.

"Dr. Turner, I have to talk to someone. My mother just doesn't understand. You know that Billy and I have been seeing each other. He and his father came to see you."

"Yes, they did. I hope you know that what we discussed is private. I can't talk about any patient that would be breaking a confidence."

"Sure, I know that. Don't worry. Billy has already told me about the visit. Something strange and wonderful is happening to me. I think to Billy too. It started when he decided to hold my hand. I've had this feeling of joy and excitement. The more we've talked and been together, the more these feelings seem to grow. What do you think this is? What should I do about it?" Cindy had a confused look. He could tell by the flush in her face that there was a lot of intensity and curiosity behind her perplexed emotions.

"Cindy, what do you know about sex?" He felt awkward even bringing up the subject.

"I know about biology and all that. My mother has talked to me all about it. I don't think that things work the same way here. Anyway, that's not why I came to see you."

"It's not?" Michael was surprised by her statement.

"I want to know about all these emotions. It's like a flood of happiness that comes over me. I want more and more. Is there something wrong with me?" Her eyes were looking down at her feet as if she was embarrassed by her confession.

"Oh, no, there is nothing wrong with you. In fact, everything seems to be working quite well." He reached over and put his hand on her shoulder to reassure her.

"Billy and I almost kissed each other, and I was afraid of what it would mean and what would happen if we did." Michael could tell that there were a whole bunch of emotions associated with that possibility: guilt, excitement, danger, and risk.

"Dr. Turner, what should I do?" Cindy put her hands over her eyes and began to cry.

"Cindy, you don't have to be ashamed of your feelings. I think that Billy is a fine young man. He is very honest. If you both love each other, that's a good thing. It's not easy to make a decision or take risks that require trust. I can't tell you what to do. I believe that both of you will figure that out."

Michael thought about the preciousness of this conversation. He missed having this kind of talk with his own children. Nothing could make up for that. He reflected on his emotions. They were laced with sorrow and contrition for lost opportunities. If only he had taken the time to listen to David and Jamie. Somehow, this exchange was a recognition and opportunity to reclaim that lost experience.

He felt that a reciprocal vulnerability was called for. It was something he didn't do easily. "I have two children. I wasn't very good about helping them with these issues. I was just too busy, I told myself. I was really just afraid of getting involved. I am sorry about that. Cindy, you and Billy may need someone to support you. I will do that. I will be here for you. If you need an advocate to work with your parents and help them understand, I would be honored to help."

"Dr. Turner, thank you. Thank you so much." She sprang over to him and gave him a big hug. He was uncomfortable with her show of appreciation. He made himself stand there and decided to resist his first inclination, which was to back away.

"It's so important for me to know that somebody would be willing to help us."

When he looked at her, she had a big smile on her face. There still were leftover tears, which had the effect of making her even more radiant.

"I need to go and see Billy. Would you mind if I didn't stay to talk with your Doctor friend? I don't want to be rude, but I need to go."

Michael said, "Oh, it's okay. Dr. Luke would understand how this works better than I. Don't worry about hurting his feelings. He only wants what is best for everyone."

"Please tell him I am sorry. I will see you soon. Thank you for supporting us." With that, she brushed against him as she headed to the door, opened it, hurried down the hall, and went out through the veranda and down the path.

Michael followed her slowly. Luke joined him. There was a sense of reverence between them, as if a common cord had been struck. Nothing was being said; it didn't need to be. They just watched as Cindy walked down the path. Billy was waiting for her by the swing in his backyard. He came up to her. She put out her hand to welcome him. Then it happened. He drew close to her. Cindy put her arms around his shoulders. Billy put his arms around her waist as if they'd done it a thousand times before. It was innocent and familiar at the same time. There was a slight hesitation, and then they kissed. Where their lips met, there was a tiny pinprick of light. It began to grow brighter and brighter. Michael couldn't look at it directly. He had to close his eyes. When he opened them, they were gone. What was left behind was a feeling of consolation, a satisfied sense of well-being, such contentment Michael had never felt before. It was a beautiful revelation. He looked over at Luke. He was smiling and nodding his head.

"Where did they go?" Michael asked. He was astonished by what he had just witnessed.

Luke replied, "Where do you think?"

"I don't know. I'm asking you."

"Michael, let me ask you a question, and then you can ask me where they went."

"How do you feel?"

"I feel happy for them, contented, and satisfied. Like the best of all the 'boy gets girl' movies got rolled into one big happy ending. Luke, I think I know where they went. They went to heaven, didn't they? You don't need to tell me. I can feel it in my heart."

Luke put his hand on Michael's shoulder and thoughtfully said to him, "We have a lot ofwork to do. I must tell you that I think you've done a good job."

"Luke, what am I going to tell their parents?"

"Yes," Luke said. "We will have to deal with that."

A treasure is tomorrow. A mustard seed of possibilities

teetering with every choice this way or that.

A promise that awakens every day and draws out upon

its breath;

sighs of dreams and hopes that future inspirations

may bless.

A Contest of Wills

Jamie had been waiting for David's call. She and Mary had been hoping that he would have good news to report. When the phone rang, she hurried over and picked it up from its wireless cradle. It was David. He gave her a brief update on how they got to Bear Lake Lodge. He told her that later this morning, they were meeting with the hotel manager, who had recognized Michael's picture. He acknowledged that it was a miracle that they had discovered the right hotel.

The plan was that after interviewing the lodge's manager, he and Bob would head over to the Hillcrest Nursing Home to meet with the administrator. David had called ahead and set up the meeting. More information would make it much easier to find the safe deposit box.

She had some news to report. Jamie had received a call from Michael's attorney about the will. Since the death certificate had been issued, it was important to get the family together. They agreed on a time next week to meet at the office of Spagnolo and Huston. He would be back from his trip by then. Joseph Spagnolo was an old friend of Michael's. He had been his lawyer for most of his professional life. He had even recommended the attorney who worked on the divorce. Jamie confessed that she had met him only few times and didn't remember much about him. David's voice sounded excited when she told him about this development.

He said, "Bob and I think that Dad might have hired a lawyer to help keep his family secret. Maybe Mr. Spagnolo is the person he worked with. I'll be home in a couple of days. Why don't you call and try to see him? He might have a lot of information that could help us learn Dad's story. If you do get to see him before I get there, please ask him if he knows about Dad's situation in Ohio. Perhaps he has some of the answers we are looking for. It's possible that the key fits a box in Phoenix." Jamie realized that getting an appointment with Mr. Spagnolo needed to be first on her list of priorities.

As soon as she got off the phone, she called the law firm of Spagnolo and Huston. A pleasant woman's voice answered.

Jamie said she wished to talk to Joseph Spagnolo. The secretary asked who was calling. Jamie gave her name, and in less than a minute, he got on the line.

"Miss Turner, thank you for calling. What can I do for you?"

"I would like to make an appointment to see you." She was trying to not sound intense. She felt that rush of adrenalin. Jamie decided to take a deep breath and try to calm down. All this happened in seconds, yet she wondered if he knew. "Mr. Spagnolo, I have to talk to you about my father."

"Now, Miss Turner, I can't really discuss your father's will with you before the family meeting. It would be unethical to give anyone more information than the others."

"It's not about the will. It's about my father. I really don't want to discuss it over the phone. That is why I need to see you. I would like our meeting to take place in your office and as soon as possible."

"I don't know," he said. Jamie felt his resistance, which caused her to be even more intense. She was determined to stick to her guns. "Look, Mr. Spagnolo," she said in a resolute tone, "I am trying to learn more about my father, and there are questions about his life that I need to know. We have discovered things about Dad that are quite startling. I am asking for your help. Can we make that appointment?" There was a minute of silence, which felt uncomfortable. Finally, he said, "Yes, I suppose we can. I think that you are a very persistent young lady." She felt a sense of satisfaction that she had won the point.

"I am when I have to be," she softened her tone. "Would it be possible for us to meet tomorrow?" she asked.

"I do have some time after lunch at 1:00 p.m."

Jamie smiled and replied, "I'll be there. Thank you. I will see you tomorrow."

She felt a sense of satisfaction as she hung up the phone. It wasn't just the men going out to hunt and forage for the truth. It might be possible that she could find the safe deposit box before David and Bob, and she didn't even need to leave the state.

Jamie thought about Mr. Spagnolo's resistance. He must know something. What other explanation is there for his defensiveness? It seemed like a good idea to call her mother and go over the conversations she had with David and Mr. Spagnolo.

She dialed her number, and after a few rings, a voice came on, inviting her to leave a message after the beep.

"Mom, I have an appointment with Mr. Spagnolo tomorrow at 1:00 p.m. I know that you might not want to come. If you can think of any questions I should ask, would you write them down and e-mail me or give me a call. I don't care how late it is, just call." A few minutes later, her phone rang.

"Hi, Jamie, I got your message. I was out at the grocery store picking up a few things. What's this about you going to Phoenix to see Joe Spagnolo?"

"Mom, David called, and he has found the hotel or lodge Dad stayed at in Ohio. They are scheduled to have an interview with the manager tomorrow. From there, they're going to the Hillcrest Nursing Home to meet with the administrator. They think that Dad must have had a person help him care for his mother. I wonder if Mr. Spagnolo might know something about Dad's past."

"Jamie, please be careful. Your father trusted that man. I really never liked him. It's bad enough that we have to go to his office for the reading of the will."

"I take it, Mom, that you're not willing to go with me."

"You are right about that, Jamie. I am not interested. Whatever you're doing, I want no part of it."

She said this in a way that meant "end of discussion." Jamie had been counting on her mom's natural curiosity. There already seemed to be some water running under that bridge, more like a torrent. Jamie was tired and didn't have the energy to jump into the current. Lord knows where she might end up.

"Okay, Mom, I'll be careful. I am just going to ask him a few questions. That's all."

"Well, Jamie, my advice is to stay home. It's hard to interview a snake."

She was shocked by her mother's strong negative opinion of the man. She decided to pick up the gauntlet and said, "I can handle myself. The worse thing that can happen is that I learn nothing new about Dad. On the other hand, I might discover something that would help us put the puzzle of his life together." There was a pause and a muffled sound of crying on the phone.

"Mom, I will call you when I get back from Phoenix tomorrow."

Jamie knew from the sound that her mother's story would soon need her attention. A sense of fatigue began to fall upon her like a blanket. It suddenly felt like a good idea to get into the tub and soak out the anxiety.

She drove to Phoenix the next day. The morning air was warm and comforting. The sky was a pale blue with high clouds like twine stretched across it. The trip was uneventful. She made it to Joe Spagnolo's office with plenty of time to spare. It was not plush or imposing. It had no heavy oak overstuffed furniture. The office and the furniture were like something liberated from a motel special sale. Everything looked and felt rather common. *Strictly middle class,* she thought. *It's just like Dad to hire an attorney that is as tight with a buck as he was.* That memory made her crack a smile.

There was a receptionist sitting behind an enclosed counter. Jamie went over and introduced herself and relayed that she had an appointment with Mr. Spagnolo.

The woman replied that she would let him know she had arrived and that she could take a seat.

Jamie had fussed about what to wear for the meeting. She decided to go for the professional look. Her closet had only a couple of options. Jamie chose the gray tweed suit with matching skirt and white blouse and matching gray high heals. Mr. Spagnolo was a short man. Jamie was about his height in her stocking feet. She wanted to be a little taller and look a little older.

Mr. Spagnolo came out through a door marked "Staff Only." He was wearing a white shirt and gray pants, black shoes, and a blue tie that was loose around his collar. He was bald and had a button nose and rosy cheeks. She thought that if you put a white beard on him and some wire-rimmed glasses, he would make a great Santa. He walked over to her and said, "Miss Turner, it is nice to see you." He shook her hand. "Please, let's go into my office." With that remark, he turned, walked back to the door, and opened it for her. She was met by a narrow hallway that really could not fit both of them.

"Go to the first door on the right." He followed behind her as she walked in. He closed the door and went over to his desk, sat behind it, and motioned for her to sit in one of the two chairs across from him.

They both sat down, and he was the first to speak, "Please accept my sympathies for the tragic loss of your father. He was a good friend of mine. We worked together for many years. He was a very fine person and an excellent physician. I can't imagine how you must feel at his tragic and unexpected passing."

Jamie looked directly at him. She noticed softness in his face that indicated a real and heartfelt sorrow.

"Thank you, Mr. Spagnolo, for your kind words. I do appreciate them."

He inquired, "What can I do for you today, Miss Turner?"

"Well, after we received word of my father's death, things began to immerge about his life that we knew nothing about."

"What sort of things?"

"We found out that my father's name was Stephen Hughes before he changed it during college. Did you know about that?"

"I had made a promise to your father that I would not divulge certain facts that he wanted to keep private. Guarding secrets is often part of my job as an attorney. Your father had some things that he believed needed to be protected. Since he has passed away, I think I can tell you that I knew about his previous name."

"We also found out about the fire that killed his brother and sister and made his mother go crazy."

"You know about that?" He began to rub his forehead, and he looked a little perturbed.

Jamie answered, "Yes, we do. The NTSB, as part of their investigation into the crash, did a thorough background check. Their Agent Mr. Goldman informed us about their findings. My brother and another family member are in Ohio following up on the information they gave us."

Jamie saw a faint smile come across his face. "Well, if you have all the information you need to look into your father's history, why do you need my help?"

She had expected a little resistance from him, and she was beginning to feel it. "My brother and I know that you were his legal counsel in Phoenix. We think there was someone else he confided in, perhaps another attorney in Ohio. Do you know of someone?"

"Miss Turner, there was someone that I would occasionally be in contact with for your father. I would deal with him regarding certain financial requirements. I cannot speak to you about it until the reading of the Last Will and Testament of Dr. Turner. I have already written his name and address out for you on this paper. His name is Conner Braxton." He looked down on his desk, picked up the paper, and handed it to her.

"Is there anything else I can do for you?"

"I just have one other question. Did my father ever mention a safe deposit box or a key?"

"No, I don't know anything about a safe deposit box or a key for one that belonged to your father."

Jamie felt a coldness that convinced her on the spot that he was hiding something.

"Why? What are you looking for?"

"Oh, it's nothing." She thought that since he was being incomplete in his answers, she could avoid being honest in hers. "Just curious, I suppose." She stood up, and so did he. She shook his hand.

"Thank you for your time. I am deeply appreciative for your help. I will see you next week for the reading of my father's Will."

"Here is my card. Don't hesitate to call me if you have any other questions." There was a hint of seductiveness in his voice.

Jamie thought, *You old goat, no wonder my mother didn't trust you.*

She turned and headed out the door. She couldn't wait to get out of there. He followed her down the hall and out to the reception area. She turned, and he stood there looking at her. It was a common stare for his species.

Jamie had seen it before. It hinted, "Yes, I have information, but it requires a favor in return."

She didn't know it, but Ayin was there next to her. She decided, once she got to her car, to give David a call on her cell phone. Jamie felt pleased that she could contribute to the investigation. She knew that Connor Braxton had probably already been notified by Joe Spagnolo to expect company. She had proved the old goat had information about her father, probably more than he let on, and that there was an agent back in Ohio. Perhaps the Will would provide some answers. She had a confident feeling that somehow, more about her father would be revealed. Jamie hoped and prayed that it would be a good thing.

Before she could call David, her cellphone rang. "Hello, David. I was just about to call you. That is so weird really. I was just getting out my phone. I met with Mr. Spagnolo. Let me tell you what I found out. There is an attorney out there, his name is Connor Braxton."

In Memory of My Wife, Dorothy

God's, Grace, Given

Shared, Saved

Blessed, Born, Bride

Held, Hope, Heaven

Cared, Loved

Married, Abide

Forever!

The Promised Land

Michael realized that he was glad that Luke had shown up. This world had a whole set of different rules. What was he going to say to the parents? How can you describe the meaning of something that happened so unexpectedly? The whole thing was just too difficult for him to figure out. A wiser hand was needed, someone who had been through this before. He looked at Luke. He was staring out the open screen door down the lane. Michael was expecting Mrs. Crier or Mr. Slack or both. He turned to see what Luke was looking at. It was Delbert Finwicky quickly striding toward them. He had a walking stick with a gold handle under his arm. He was wearing a beige stovepipe hat. It was cocked to one side of his head. A blue shirt, a brown pair of knickers held up by suspenders, and a big red bowtie, with argyle socks and brown shoes-all in all, it was quiet an ensemble. It made Michel smile, although Luke said nothing. Perhaps he was just too stunned to say anything. Delbert hurriedly walked to the steps to the veranda.

He shouted loudly, "My good Doctor, it is a real pleasure to visit with you. May I come in to say hello?"

"Yes, of course. Come on in. There is someone I want you to meet."

"Gladly," he said with a wave of his hand. He walked up the steps and stood between Michael and Luke. There was awkwardness at this point. Michael was blocked by Delbert's generous frame. So he just pointed to his mentor and said, "Delbert, let me introduce to you Dr. Luke. Mr. Delbert Finwicky." They both shook hands. Delbert had a glowing smile. He looked over at Michael and said, "It is a real pleasure to make your acquaintance, Dr. Luke. May I say that we have a fine physician in our community? Dr. Turner has already helped us. Why, he hosted a wonderful party, gotten rid of Mrs. Crier's cane, found a man we didn't know existed, and helped two lovely young people just disappear. I would say that is quite a medical practice." Michael felt immediately surprised and embarrassed. There was a tone of sarcasm that Michael had never experienced from him before.

"You know about that?" he asked. "Did you see it?"

"Oh, yes, everyone saw it in their own way. I just happened to be coming over here. I was going by the Slacks' house when I witnessed their kiss. It was amazing. You know and I know that there are going to be some people who will really have trouble with all of this."

Michael felt a sense of concern about the situation. It reminded him of other unfortunate experiences from his life and his medical practice, like the time he wrote the wrong script for a patient with the same last name. It could have been serious, but the pharmacy caught it. There was that other time during one of his residency rotations; he was so tired that he completely misdiagnosed a gallbladder attack of a patient in the ER as an acute abdominal muscle strain. The attending was alert enough to take a second look and got the man to surgery. Since it was an inner city hospital, it earned him the endearing nickname "Gaulito" from his classmates and more than a few doctors and nurses. He thought he would never live it down. The memory reminded him of the embarrassment and shame that he was determined to avoid.

Delbert continued, "Might I suggest that we confront the situation like men? In other words, he said softly, let's hide."

Luke bristled, "Mr. Finwicky, you are not suggesting that we try to avoid telling what happened. I find it unacceptable to hide the facts, avoid consequences, or seek human approval."

"Dr. Luke, with the profoundest respect for your profession," Delbert continued after a short bow, "I don't believe that you know

Mrs. Odelia Crier. I can say, with the benefit of some personal experience, that if you are planning to stay here, you better build a barricade, batten down the hatches, and raise the drawbridge because you are going to need them."

Luke replied doubtfully, "Now, Mr. Finwicky, I am sure it can't be that bad." Just then, Josh walked by, pushing a little cart with a bunch of tomato plants he was taking to a small field near the house.

"Hi boys," he said. "What're you all talking about?"

Michael said, "It's too complicated to explain. Suffice to say that we expect Mrs. Crier to head this way, and she's not going to be a happy camper."

"Well, a situation like that reminds me of plants."

"What did you say?" Michael asked, totally confused and incredulous by how the present crisis was in any way like plants.

"I guess it might seem odd to you, but a plant can't help following the sun. In the morning, they face the sunrise, and by evening, they're pointed to the sunset. It's their nature. God made them that way. Odelia Crier might surprise you with how much like a plant she can be. I'll see you boys around." With that, he starting pushing his cart. He waved as he headed off to the garden.

Michael rubbed his face and said, "Does anyone understand what Josh was talking about?" They all just shook their heads and said nothing. A pregnant pause flittered in. Delbert broke the silence and said, "As I was saying to Dr. Luke, oh, yes, it can be that painful, my dear Doctor. Cindy is Odelia's alter ego. They are or were inseparable. She will be coming up that path madder than a hornet looking for someone to sting."

He pointed out the open screen door. Luke and Michael looked down the lane to see Odelia rushing toward the house. Delbert yelled, "Yikes! There she is! Just remember, men, that I am behind you all the way." He stepped back holding his cane in one hand; and in the other, his hat over his chest like a knight griping a sword and shield.

Odelia made one of her patented grand entrances, only this time, she almost fell over the last step going up to the veranda. Her face was flushed, and her hair was not in its usual impeccable order; parts of it were flying all around like she hadn't combed it lately.

She caught her balance before Michael or Luke could catch her. They had both reached out to her, only to be left holding empty right hands.

She looked up and said, "You gentlemen should be quicker than that to help a woman in distress." She straightened herself up. "Speaking of helping someone, I suppose that you are aware of the disappearance of my daughter. I saw the whole thing happen. The wall of my kitchen became somehow transparent, and I watched Billy and Cindy kiss." Her voice softened, "I was transfixed by the beauty of the experience. It shrouded me in a bright light. My whole spirit felt uplifted. It became obvious to me that they were meant to be together. A beautiful life is open for those two. I hurried over to say thank you, Dr. Turner, for caring for them. I realized in that kiss I could not hold Cindy back. I tried to control her by making her in my image. I was fearful of being left alone with no one to care for me. I understand that I may be by myself but I'm not alone. They kissed, and I said good-bye. It's a transcendent gift to give someone you love, the freedom to be who they are and carve out their own life. I will be sad if they don't come back. Perhaps my journey will lead me to them."

Michael was dumbfounded. He could not believe the profession of faith that he just heard. Even Luke seemed surprised by this change of attitude and her affectionate description. Michael felt it was incumbent for him to respond. "Odelia, I'm amazed by your attitude. I thought that you would be unhappy about Cindy's disappearance. I am pleasantly corrected by what you have just shared."

"I can tell you, Doctor, that up until that kiss, I felt very hurt and abandoned by Cindy's decision to be more and more with Billy. I was feeling jealous and angry. Something has changed in me. My previous way of acting would have required that I come here to exact some kind of vengeance for my loss."

Luke softly replied, "It is a wonderful thing to see love take root and grow. It makes new things possible and tears down things that need to be uprooted. I am very happy for you, Mrs. Crier. The kiss wasn't wasted on you. It has changed you."

"Yes, Dr. Luke, it has changed me." Odelia looked proudly at Michael and reached out her hand for Michael to kiss, which he gladly did.

"Please let me say thank you, Dr. Turner and Dr. Luke, for all your help. I shall go back to my home and ponder this experience. God bless you both." She raised her voice, suddenly acting out of character, and yelled, "God bless you too, Mr. Finwicky, hiding behind that sofa!

Gentlemen, adieu." She turned and walked out of the veranda and merrily down the lane.

Michael pivoted toward the sofa and exclaimed, "Delbert, you can come out now. She's gone."

There was another pregnant pause. From behind the sofa emerged the top of his hat, but it was not attached to his head; rather, he had his cane holding it up like a white flag of surrender. Michael could not help but laugh. It was hilarious. The hat was extended higher and higher until you could see his hand and then his arm holding the cane. Even Luke was chuckling.

Luke chimed in "Come out, man. It's quite safe."

Quickly Delbert stood up, but he dropped his hat on the floor and bent over to fetch it. He seemed to have disappeared. He stood up again and walked around the sofa.

"I dropped my hat back there, and as you could see, I needed to retrieve it. It wasn't easy. The darn thing's slippery. It's a regular 'corpus de lick' tie. I have it now safe and sound in my possession, 'non cola clement us.'" He slowly walked over to join them.

Michael decided to change the subject and relieve Delbert of any further embarrassment.

"What did you think of that?"

Luke piped up and said, "That was truly a miracle. Our friend Odelia had an epiphany that changed her world. It is a blessing not just for Cindy and Billy but for everyone."

"What do you have to say, Delbert?" Michael added.

"Gentlemen, you know how I believed that Odelia, Mrs. Crier, would deal with this situation. I am in a state of incredulity. I never entertained the slightest notion that there could be such an outcome. I was perfectly situated behind the couch to repel any attack from that woman that might require my involvement. Happily, no such methods were needed. I can see you might get the idea that I was holding back. I want to assure you that I was not fearful. I was but a valiant soldier, primed and ready to come to your aid if need be."

Michael was chuckling at this explanation and inquired, "We still have to meet with Billy's father. I wonder how that's going to work out."

"Don't be concerned, Dr. Turner," Delbert replied. "Mr. Slack is not someone to worry about. He mostly wants to be left alone. I am more concerned by Mrs. Crier. You don't think she is coming back, do you?" Michael noticed that he was standing behind them like someone taking cover behind a hedge or a fence. He was peering out around them just to make sure.

Luke replied, "Mrs. Crier is busy with other things. Come now, Mr. Finwicky. You have nothing to be concerned about either."

"Delbert," Michael interjected, "may I ask you a question about this situation?"

"Of course, Dr. Turner. Fire away."

"Well, I am wondering about how this change of Mrs. Crier will affect you?"

"What do you mean?"

"It seems that you have a way of relating to her that requires a certain, shall we say, performance. It's as if you both share parts in a play. You are the comic relief, and she is the principle antagonist. You both feed off of each other's character. I recall, the first occasion of our meeting, how you seemed to be performing for others on stage. What will happen to your play as a result of her epiphany? You would not be able to use her intractability and dominance as a foil. What would happen if you could affirm her instead of peddling her need for control? It seems that Odelia has made quite a mess for you. If she can forgive her daughter, if she can embrace a different life, what would happen to you?"

There was that pregnant pause again. It was silence, but imbedded in the quiet was a new hope. Things could change. "What you have just said does give me pause." Delbert put his hat on and leaned against his cane. "I will have to think on it. I have gotten used to her habits, you see. She always provides me with humorous material. The truth is that the only one amused is me. No one else gets to appreciate my sartorial incubations."

"Yes, Delbert, the reality of no audience must make you feel lonely and forgotten."

"You're right about that, Doctor. It does. It does." He pulled a handkerchief from his jacket pocket and loudly blew his nose. "You know, humor is in the unexpected. A slight turn of phrase that is surprising or unforeseen. A story that has a twist or a fall or a gag that stuns the audience is funny. Mrs. Crier is always so serious it's funny. That humorless quality makes it funnier-not ha-ha, but uncomfortable kind of funny. I dare say that we are much better pushing against each other than sharing our mutual qualities."

"Delbert, there are times when she gets under your skin. Still, you do love her, don't you?"

"I suppose I do. If she would only laugh at herself instead of making everything so serious and personal. She usually just rolls her eyes and dismisses my attempts to win her favor."

Michael continued, "Maybe she feels the same way about you."

"How so?" Delbert curiously asked.

"It's just as difficult to have an intimate conversation with someone who is always looking to crack a joke. Do you think that she is trying to get you to take yourself and her more seriously by exaggerating her critical opinions?"

Delbert began to laugh and laugh. "Ha-ha-ha! How ironic and funny. If what you say is true, Doctor, we have been talking past each other. Ha-ha-ha! What a joke we have played on one another."

Luke interjected, "Mr. Finwicky, my hunch is that Dr. Turner is on to something. It would be a good thing for you to provide support and caring to her as she goes through this transition without Cindy."

Delbert smiled and responded to that idea like a light had gone off and filled the whole vestibule of his mind with new possibilities.

"You know, Dr. Luke," he said, "I do believe that there is something I can do to support her in this difficult experience. I think that I will stop by her house on my way home and just let her know that I would very much like to be her friend."

"I think that is a good idea," Michael replied. "First, might I suggest that you go home and lose that silly tie and hat. Try not to make jokes but just listen."

"Dr. Turner, you have given me superb advice that I shall take to heart. Adieu, gentlemen." Delbert bowed and tipped his hat, turned, and quickly headed out the veranda and down the lane.

Michael leaned over to Luke and said quietly, "What do you think we've done?"

Luke replied with his hands on his hips, "We have either sent him into the lion's den or made it possible for those two to help each other."

Michael questioned, "I wonder which it will be."

I opened the gate and stepped inside the pen.

To tell a story that reveals the heart of my best friend

A solitary work that reflects the designs of labors

spent for greater ends

a mystery that now holds and frames my humble

verses in.

A Round Robin

ob and David had a good night's sleep at the Bear Lake Lodge. They grabbed a quick breakfast in the morning at the cafe downstairs. Their conversation began with how they were just about over the jet lag. The schedule for the day was planned. First, they would meet with Silas Best, the manager at the lodge, then pay a visit to Mr. Connor Braxton, the attorney who Jamie had found out about. Then they would stop by the Hillcrest Nursing Home to meet with the administrator there before driving back to Pipersville to spend the night. It was a full schedule to be sure. Mr. Best met them in front of the registration area and escorted them to a small conference room off the lobby. There were some comfortable padded chairs around a table that was for seven or eight people. He invited them to sit down. As they did, he closed the door. Silas was a middle-aged man, tall, with a receding hairline. He wore his age as gracefully as he wore his tailored blue suit. He had blue eyes, and his features mirrored his strong and self-assured manner. He began by saying like a teacher reviewing yesterday's class, "We were talking yesterday about our guest M r. Michael Smith. He was always a gentleman. He kept mostly to himself. He was friendly whenever we conversed. M y impressions of him were totally favorable. He paid for everything in cash and was generous to the staff."

David thought that these impressions seemed like a prepared statement. Bob quickly followed up with a question. "The last time Michael was here, did he act differently?"

"Differently?"

"Yes, I mean, did he seemed troubled or worried or out of his usual way of acting?"

Silas put his finger to his temple and softly tapped it. "Well, come to think of it, yes, he did. He was a private person, but he would talk to people. The last time he came, he was not his usual melancholy self. He was much more withdrawn. He seemed agitated and vexed, like he couldn't stay in one place. I thought that he was depressed. I was a little worried about him."

"Did you talk to him about your concern?"

"Yes, I had a short visit with him at the bar. Michael usually had a couple of scotch and sodas in the evening. I was just putting some of our bookkeeping to bed. I saw him, and I went over. We talked briefly about long days and longer nights at work, and then I asked him if he was all right. I said that I had noticed he seemed restless and sad. Was there anything I could do?

He said no, that I was perceptive, and that he had recently gone through a few personal setbacks. He went on saying that he was going to be okay and that I should not worry about him. I did not want to intrude, so we left it at that."

"How did you feel about his response?"

"I think the question you are really asking is did I think he might hurt himself?"

David interjected the question that Silas was going to answer anyway. "Well, did you?"

Silas paused and said, "I am not a trained psychologist. No, I didn't think so. I did believe that he was carefully considering making some changes in his life. What they were, he never said."

David asked as he leaned forward with his hands on the table, "Is there anything else you might share with us?"

"There is just one more thing. He left a book when he checked out. Our cleaning staff found it in the bottom of the closet, like it slipped out of something. I have it in my office. I'm sorry, but I just never got around to sending it to the forwarding address that he gave us. I'll go and get it. I'm sure he would want you to have it."

Mr. Best quickly got up, walked over to the door, and opened it. He turned and said, "I will be right back."

David and Bob just looked at each other incredulously. He returned a couple of minutes later with a small paperback book. "Ah, I found it! It's not a novel, you see, but a play," he said as he handed it to David.

He read the title out loud, *"A Long Day's journey into Night* by Eugene O'Neill. Well, gentlemen, I must get back to our guests. Again, I am sorry for your loss. Is there anything else?"

David and Bob stood up, and Bob said, "You mentioned a forwarding address. Could you get that for us?"

"Yes, Miss Parsons at the front desk can give you that information."

Handshakes were given all around, and Mr. Best escorted them to the lobby and over to the front desk. He told another older woman to find the forwarding address for Mr. Michael Smith. It took her only a few minutes to access the information on her computer, and she handed it to Bob along with a receipt for an unexpected complimentary night's stay. The address was in care of Joe Spagnolo's office in Phoenix, Arizona.

They headed out to the car. David held the book tightly in his hand. Looking over the lake and the hills beyond, he somehow knew that it was an important nugget of his father's life. He remembered Jamie telling him about attending the play at the university. Her tender recollection of his emotional response, a small curiosity had suddenly become far more important. The book raised new questions. Maybe he would find some answers up ahead.

Bob got behind the wheel, and David got into the passenger side and slammed the door. David decided to fill him in.

"Bob, there is something important about this book. Dad made a date with Jamie to take her to dinner and to see the production of this play at the university. Jamie said that he was tearful and emotional during the performance. Taking her out to dinner and going to see a play was very different behavior for him. I think that the story in this book must have been like his story in some way."

Bob started the car and headed down the street. "You don't say," he replied with a quick glance that said without words he was interested.

It took about twenty minutes to get to Connor Braxton's office. It was a small white house with green trim that had been converted into an office. It had a nice white sign with his name by the road. There was a green sign with white letters on the building. It read, "Connor Braxton, Attorney at Law." Bob turned into the small parking lot. There was a sporty Mercedes parked there already. They got out of their car and headed down the walkway to the front door. There was a step up to a small covered porch.

It was a warm and breezy day. The clouds were playing tag with the sun, and every now and then, they would catch it. The sun would disappear behind them, but they couldn't hold it for long.

There was a closed screen door and a half-opened front door behind it. Bob opened it and pushed the front door open the rest of the way and walked in as David followed. Nobody seemed to be there. There was a small waiting area with chairs and a coffee table in what probably had been a parlor before the modest remodel.

Bob called out, "Hello, anybody here?"

A voice responded from the back in a slightly higher tone, "Yeah, I'll be there in a minute. Have a seat please."

Bob looked over to David in a way that indicated he had no intention of sitting. David just shrugged his shoulders and stood there too. Besides, they had enough sitting in the car already. A couple of minutes passed and out from the back room came Mr. Conner Braxton. He was a country lawyer, and he fit all the usual stereotypes. His gray hair was unkempt. He wore a green tie that matched the sign, white shirt, gray pants, and black shoes. Bob wondered if he was in a real estate office. He realized that Braxton probably did handle real estate and probate and anything else that could help him make a buck.

"Sorry for the delay, gentlemen. I was on a phone call with a client."

Bob wondered if that was true or if he was just trying to seem busy. He looked to be in his fifties. He was of average height, slightly overweight, but not grossly. He had bags under his brown eyes and a mustache, and he smelled of tobacco, probably a cigar.

They shook hands. "I am Connor Braxton. Would you like a glass of water?" he asked more out of courtesy than concern.

They both shook their heads. "No, thanks," Bob replied. "I am Robert Hughes, and this is David Turner. We came from Phoenix to inquire after a client of yours named Dr. Michael Turner, aka Stephen Hughes, aka Michael Smith." They had decided on the ride over that Bob would be asking most of the questions since he had more experience as an investigator. David would ask follow-up questions and observe.

"Let's go into a more private place back here." He led them to a small conference room with a round table in the middle surrounded by five chairs on rollers. It probably was a bedroom at one time. It had a small window that had obviously been added to the inside wall. They sat down, and Connor quietly closed the door like he was trying not to wake the children.

Bob continued, once Connor sat down, "We got your phone number from Michael's attorney, Joseph Spagnolo, and we called and set up this appointment with you. We are very appreciative of your willingness to meet with us on such short notice."

David nodded his head in agreement. "Dr. Turner was killed in a small plane crash. David is his son, and I am his uncle. His father, William Hughes, was my older brother."

"I see," he replied. "I have had a conversation with Mr. Spagnolo, who has confirmed what you have just told me." Bob interjected, "We do have documents that you can copy. You may need for your file at some point." Connor shook his head up and down. "Yes, that might be helpful." He continued to nod his head like he wanted Bob to go on. His hands were cupped together over his mouth with his thumbs under his chin while his elbows rested on the arms of his chair.

"Information began to emerge after Michael's death that there was more to his story than the family knew."

"What kind of information?"

Bob knew that he was being interviewed. He thought that's all right for now; soon, the tables will be turned. Bob thought, *He wants to know how much information we have.*

"Well, we know, thanks to the NTSB, that Michael had a mother who he cared for out here. We know that his brother and sister were killed in a fire when he was ten. We know he lived with his grandparents and eventually took another name when he went to college and medical school. We know that you probably worked as his agent. We know what nursing home she was at and where he stayed every year when he came to see her. Since Michael is deceased, we wondered if you could help us with some of our questions."

He smiled wryly, like he had a few cards of his own, and put one hand up to the corner of his mouth. He sat back in his chair. Bob thought, *Now it's your turn.*

"We would like to know, what did you do for Dr. Turner?"

"Michael paid me a retainer every year to manage his mother's affairs. I have kept careful records of expenses and her financial requirements. He would come here every year to see her and for us to go over her needs. Michael would keep in touch with me through his attorney in Phoenix, Mr. Spagnolo. I never talked to Michael directly in Phoenix, only his attorney. I would see him, of course, when he came. I routinely would visit his mother in the nursing home and make sure any bills were paid through an account that we set up here. Michael would send the money to that account by Mr. Spagnolo. We were both signatories so I could meet her obligations."

Bob was amazed by this careful scheme. "Mr. Braxton, that's a lot of trouble to go through just to care for one old lady."

"I grant you, yes, it is. He wanted this kept in a manageable box, and that's what we did."

"Do you know any more of the history that could shed some light on this part of his life? I mean is there anything you can tell us that can explain his behavior keeping this so secret?"

"I can tell you that after the fire, he went to live with his grandparents on his mother's side. Evidently, things didn't go well. I mean, that he harbored some, shall we say, painful feelings about them. His mother was taken to the county psych hospital, where she lived for twenty years until the facility was closed and all the patients discharged because of budget cuts and given case managers. By that time, his grandparents were in poor health and unable to help her. They must have gotten in touch with Michael somehow. He took over his mother's care since she was mentally incompetent. His grandparents died that year six months apart. Michael took over the estate at that time and hired me to help him set up the foundation."

David piped up loudly, "Foundation! Did you say *foundation?*"

"Yes," Connor replied. "You didn't know about the foundation?"

Bob said, "No, we don't know what you are talking about."

"Oh," he said and paused. "Michael's grandparents took over Beth's farm after the fire. It was a small farm of 250 acres, plus there were insurance payouts for the loss of the farmhouse and the tragic loss of life. All in all, it came up to about 250,000. That was a lot of money in those days. The Smiths were good stewards and invested it for their daughter. By the time they died, the portfolio had grown to almost 500,000. They held on to the property and had it farmed by tenants and received income from that. The Smiths had their own farm. It was about 1000 acres. Since their only daughter was mentally incompetent and since Michael was their only living heir, upon their deaths, he was named the beneficiary in their Will.

"Michael was very gifted in making money. He decided to sell both properties and liquidate all the assets. The real estate market in this area was very hot at the time. He sold his mother's land to a resort for a great price. May I ask you, how did you sleep last night? How did you like Bear Lake Lodge?" Bob responded, "It was very nice, and I enjoyed the beautiful scenery. It was peaceful and elegant. How did you know we stayed there?"

"When you called yesterday, it came up on my caller ID. I'm glad you liked it so much. You see, it was where they lived. Your brother William bought it. When Beth and William divorced, Beth got the house and the property. Bill left and never came back. I guess he figured that since she got the house, that was that."

David was shocked, and so was Bob. "Why didn't the manager tell us that?"

"He has only worked there a few years. I am sure that he didn't even know. I put the deal together for Michael and the lodge. The papers were signed in this office. So were the papers for the sale of your grandparents' land for multiuse housing. The money from these two sales was the corpus of the foundation that Michael used to start the KISS Foundation, which provides medical and financial help to children who are burn victims. Joe Spagnolo, Michael, and I were the board members. We were blessed to find a great young director who was a real go-getter. We also found an honest and dependable investment consultant who gave us great financial advice. The foundation has grown with donations and fundraising and sound investments. KISS has a fantastic reputation in the state. Our office is in Cleveland. We are partners with other organizations that supports burn victims and their families.

"We started the foundation with $15 million. I think that our last financial report placed its value at around *$75* million. We have helped hundreds of children who have suffered terrible burns to get well with little or no cost to their families. We have increased our giving every year as our fund grows. KISS, at first, could only help kids who were from Geauga County. It has expanded to the whole state. David, I bet you can guess what KISS stands for. It was one of your father's favorite sayings." Suddenly, out from his unconscious, David said, "It means 'keep it simple, stupid!' Dad would say that to me whenever I had a problem that he didn't want to talk about. I hated that saying." David just shook his head. He couldn't express anything except amazement. "I can't believe all this. It's just too much." Still, a curiosity came to mind. "Why didn't Mr. Spagnolo tell my sister about this when she visited him?"

"We weren't sure that we should tell you at all. Michael was so deliberate about everything. It caused both of us some personal difficulties to maintain his desire for anonymity. Joe and I talked about it after he visited with Jamie, and we decided that you had enough information that we couldn't keep it from you. If we tried, you might begin to think that we had some kind of evil or underhanded scheme going on. It would begin to look like we were hiding something. The other reason was that Michael's vision and personal investment should be recognized, not because he needs anything that the world can give him. I'm sure he is in a better place. No, Joe and I want to tell others so that they can do the same kind of things for people."

Ayin was there. He began to feel that glowing rapture set in when a little bit of heaven's glory touches the earth. It happened in the tent of meeting in the desert and on a mountaintop in Israel, and now it was happening in a small attorney's office in Ohio.

"We knew about the fire and the loss that Michael felt and lived with. It didn't define his life. He used it to help others. That story needs to be told."

Bob responded, "I am so happy that we could be the first ones to know it."

"Believe me when I say that you are."

David quizzed, "How did you guys pull off this secret?"

"You mean how did we keep Michael's identity hidden?"

Connor replied with a tone of self-approval. "It wasn't really all that difficult. Once I hired the staff and the director, the day-to-day operation ran itself. They would call me, of course, if they had any problems, which were very rare. They filed all the reports and sent copies to me. I forwarded them to Joe, who got them to Michael. Our public relations director followed the cases that came to us for aid. Our accountant paid the bills and costs for treatment for the kids. If something required board action, Michael would use his mother's maiden name. He would come to see her once a year. The three of us would meet here during his visit. I would have a summary prepared of all the children we helped that year. It had just their first names and ages along with a brief description of how they were progressing. He would take that file and read it to his mother. He would remark that she never seemed to understand what he was saying, but he read it to her anyway."

Bob said, "Surely not every child survived."

"Yes, that's true. Our office in Cleveland has a big wall as you go in. It is the first thing you see. There is a big copper tree with copper leaves with names on them. Below it, in gold letters, are the words 'The Tree of Life.' Each name is a name of a child who died from burns. On the top of that tree are three gold leaves with the names of Samuel and Mindy and his mother, Beth. Everyone thinks that it's because they were the first ones that the foundation helped. They would be right in some respects. They are more like the roots of the foundation. They were his family."

When Braxton said that, David became unglued; he stood up red-faced, leaned over the table with locked arms on his knuckles, and glared at him. He said in a loud and angry voice that cracked like a whip, "No, we were his family, my mom and my sister and me. He never said anything about them. He never let us into his secrets. How do you think we feel about that?"

Conner was reeling back in his chair. He quickly regrouped. David's intensity had surprised him. He spoke is a softer, more deliberate, voice and said, "I am sorry. I can understand how you would feel. I apologize for being insensitive." David slowly sat down and with a few deliberate breaths, attempted to regain his emotional equilibrium.

Bob decided to step in. "Did you ever discuss letting the cat out of the bag?"

"I brought up the subject once or twice, but Michael would have no part of it. He could give you a look that said *Don't even go there.*"

David had his arms folded across his chest like he was holding an open coat together against a strong wind. He nodded his head and said, "Yeah, Dad had a way of looking at you sometimes. The closest thing I have seen to it is the look a mean bronco gets when some poor cowboy is determined to break him. Something is going to get broke all right."

Bob asked, "Who will replace Michael on the foundation?"

"It would be an issue for you to discuss. We were hoping that someone from the family would want to take his spot on the board. Michael made no provision for a replacement."

Bob continued, "It's a great thing. I feel confident that something can be worked out with the family. We are going to Hillcrest Nursing Horne from here. We want to learn more about Michael's mother. You would look in on her. What was she like?"

"She was a thin woman with white hair. She was in a world that chased out the need for anyone. She would mumble, laugh, and, at times, converse with herself. Beth had a faraway look in her eyes that made you aware that the sun had set in her mind. There was no reaching her memory. It was long darkened by that stifling gray dusk."

"They are nice people over at Hillcrest. I'm sure they can answer your questions."

"Mr. Braxton, you have been very helpful," Bob said. "We have one more thing that you might help us with."

"What's that?" He was getting tired of all the questions. "The only identifying bit of evidence from the crash site was a wallet belonging to Michael, and inside it was a key. It looks to be from a safe deposit box. Do you know anything about it?"

"A key." He paused and looked up at the ceiling, trying to bring anything to mind. "No, I have no idea about a safe deposit box either."

"Right," Bob replied. "I want to thank you for meeting with us. I am sure that we will be in touch. It has been extremely enlightening."

David nodded his head in agreement. Handshakes were exchanged, and in a few minutes, they were in the car driving down the road to the Hillcrest Nursing Home. They discussed the incredible meeting with Connor Braxton during the twenty minute drive. Some things were beginning to fall into place. There were still many other questions that needed a home.

They drove into the parking lot. Hillcrest was made of red bricks. It was a one-story building with a steep gray roof, white shutters on the windows, and a large circular driveway with a colonial façade, pillars, and capitals. It had a white sign out front that identified it as the right place.

They were met at the door by a lady wearing a white dress, which could have been a nurse's uniform. She was in her fifties, with graying hair and a figure that was like a square box with arms and hands, legs and feet, and head attached. She smiled, and her whole face seemed to gain color. It was the kind of smile that communicated a warm and caring human being. She approached them and stuck out her hand and said, "You must be Robert and David. Mr. Braxton called to let me know that you were on your way. My name is Candace Hilton.

Everyone just calls me Candy. I am the administrator. Please join me in my office." They followed her down a wide hallway into a smaller hallway that led to her rather spacious office. Her desk was at one end, and at the other was a circular table with four chairs around it.

"Can I get you anything?" she asked.

David replied, "I could use some water."

Bob added, "Make that two please."

She made a quick call to the receptionist at the front desk, who quickly brought in two plastic bottles of water.

"I hope bottles are okay for you, gentlemen."

"Yes, thank you," Bob answered.

After they all sat down, she continued, "Mr. Braxton told me about the reason you had called to inquire about Beth Hughes. If you have questions, I will do my best to answer them. He confirmed that you are the family of Michael Smith, that Michael went by other names. You knew him as Dr. Michael Turner. I am so sorry to hear that he was killed in a plane crash. He was a very nice man and saw to it that his mother was given good care."

Bob responded, "Thank you, Mrs. Hilton, for seeing us and for the water. Yes, that's all true. We do have some questions that we would like to discuss. May I ask, how long have you been with Hillcrest?"

"I think it has been about eleven years. I started out as a nurse. I decided to go back to school for an MBA. When I graduated, the company had just fired my predecessor. There was an opening. I was made interim administrator and then six months later, given the job. I have been doing this for the last four years."

"I assume that you knew Beth Hughes?"

"Oh, yes, I did. She lived here until she died last year. I took care of her when I was the nurse on her floor. I saw her every week since I took over the management of Hillcrest."

"Could you tell us about her medical condition?"

"She was diagnosed as a bipolar dementia patient. She was also psychotic. Beth was always involved with a world of her own. Narcotics seemed to calm her. Psychotropic medications didn't seem too help much. She responded to treatment by getting a little more alert. Conversely, she would get more depressed, angry, and agitated. We did look for organic causes, strokes, circulation to the brain, biochemical imbalances. Nothing really seemed to identify her problem. It was as if she had put herself in a very dark place and would not ever venture out. The goal became finding ways with medications to manage her behavior. The older she got, the more difficult that goal became."

"How did she die?" David inquired.

"We think it was a heart attack that's on the death certificate. One of our night aides found her on the floor unconscious. The paramedics were called. They could not resuscitate her because she was a DNR patient. She had a very slow heart rate and low blood pressure. She was taken to Queen of Peace Hospital, where she died. The ER doctor pronounced her. He called our physician, Dr. Carol Moore. The county coroner did not think the case required his services since Dr. Moore was willing to sign the death certificate."

David asked, "DNR-what does that mean?"

"Oh, I'm sorry. It means 'do not resuscitate.' A patient with this directive means· that no heroic measures will be taken to save their life."

"Who decides that?" David asked.

"The person who is the medical power of attorney. In this case, it was your father. He was her next of kin."

Bob interjected, "Mrs. Hilton, is there anything you can tell us about Michael that might help our family?"

"Michael came here to see his mother. He rarely spoke to anyone. My guess is that he was a man who had lots of pain. His life was broken glass. It was shattered into pieces, yet it reflected shards of an image. I'm not sure that you can put the fragments back together. What you can do is acknowledge that he was broken. God will have to help you recover the image."

Bob was aware that the conversation was sounding like a legal deposition. He felt uncomfortable about that, yet somehow, it seemed to fit the situation. Candy must have been familiar with this kind of thing. Probably other families had come looking for answers about a relative who had died. Bob knew that there were no easy answers.

Candy understood that too. She must have recognized that families trying to deal with a loss could never put all the pieces together. There were just shards of time and fragments of memories that left a partial silhouette. Her last statement felt rehearsed, like she had used it before with other families.

He found himself gazing down at the bottle of water in his hand and thinking about that. He looked up at her and said, "The only thing recovered from Michael at the crash site was a wallet that held a key. It appears to fit a safe deposit box. Would you know anything about that?"

She looked puzzled and replied, "No, did you check with Mr. Braxton?"

David interrupted before she could finish and said, "Yeah, we asked him already, and he knew nothing about it." There was a tone of frustration in his voice.

Bob knew that it had been a long day. David was on emotional overload. It was time to go. It felt a little premature and awkward to leave, but it was necessary. He stood up and said, "Thank you for your time. You have been very helpful."

David got up too. He was ready. He felt as tired as if he had spent the day moving hay into the barn. They were just about to say their final good-bye as she led them back to the front door when she stopped, turned around, and said, "I think that Michael might have had a safe deposit box someplace. I say that because he often brought a big green notebook with him when he visited his mother. It could have been a journal or something with private correspondence. I always assumed that it was kept at Mr. Braxton's office. You understand that is only my guess."

Bob replied, "Yes, thank you."

Candy gave them her card. "If there is anything further I can do, don't hesitate to call me."

Bob thought as they headed to the car, *What a day of revelations it has been. Who knows what we will uncover tomorrow?* He focused on Candy's last few sentences. *A green notebook... Hmm... I wonder...*

A furtive effort to make amends,

raises the awareness of my soul;

between incubated means and ends;

excuses are hollow sounding holes.

There is a better way than tightening my grip onto the

reluctant past.

Choose to let my hand go free, release the pain, and

enter God's rest.

Hunter's Stand

Hunter Grayson had put in another long day. The team had stayed at the same Holiday Inn that welcomed them the first day they arrived. He was getting used to living in and out of suitcases. He called Natalie and the kids earlier. They were busy with school and the duties of daily life. They adjusted to him and his suitcase being gone too. Hunter remembered the last crash he worked. It took much longer to sort out. When he came home, he had to readjust to the emotional cadence of his family. He was just beginning to get in sync when he was called to this job. Natalie and the kids quickly moved back from his pace to their comfort zone. Hopefully, this case would be over soon. The process of fitting into the daily rhythm of the family would begin again.

Yes, things were winding down. The parliamentary report would be refined and cross checked back in Washington. The cause of the crash from the limited amount of evidence recovered at the site made his job much more difficult. Putting all the pieces together seemed impossible. Hunter knew that it was like trying to pull the event backward through time. He was tugging at the facts from the moment of impact, trying to make some sense out of what happened. Conclusions usually developed from the facts, revealing the cause of the accident. They were based here, on limited gathered data. They were, without hard evidence, stretches. He had mulled that fact over in his head for several days with no sense of emerging confidence. His superiors would want answers.

They wanted something to fix so this would not happen again. Sometimes, things are just acts of God.

A hurricane or a hundred-year flood, an earthquake, a tornado are no one's fault. It just has to happen to somebody. If there are acts of God, then this crash might just fit the bill. Who would have thought that a replacement part would fail? Who would ever guess that an aircraft so meticulously cared for, with such a high safety record, would betray the trust of its pilot? The odds of this happening would be hard to count. Yet that is what happened. Hunter was reasonably sure that the carburetor had malfunctioned. The heart of the engine just quit. There was no way to resuscitate the patient. It was probably from a defective part that the mechanic had installed. Another set of odds against his best efforts to anticipate a catastrophe probably caused one instead. He couldn't put it in his report, but it seemed clear to him that their time was up. It is an undeniable truth that sometimes it's going to happen. It was in God's hands, and for some reason, He wanted them home. Affixing blame would not change the outcome. All he could do was shrug his shoulders and acknowledge to himself that it was an act of God.

If it was ultimately something that the Divine had arranged, then what was its purpose? There must be a reason to defy the probabilities and the odds of such a thing happening.

His mind was racing as he lay in his bed unable to sleep. He needed to relax, close his eyes, and drift off to wherever sleep took him. Instead, he felt twinges of anger. He was angry at being away from home, at having little evidence to work with, most of all, for not being able to find the meaning of it all. The energy was all rolled together like a fist. Hunter knew that to sleep, he had to open that fist and relax the hand that held on so tightly.

He smiled as he thought perhaps God was trying to break through to him. Maybe this case was God's way of getting his attention. It could be happening to a lot of people he didn't even know. He remembered Bob Hughes, that insurance investigator. He didn't know about his nephew, his family, and his own feelings of how the accident affected him; now he does. It could be that Bob uncovered something about his brother that needed resolution.

Perhaps it took a tragedy like this crash to bring him into the light of some new self-discovery. He finally began to feel sleepy. Talking to God must be relaxing. He was left with one fundamental truth-only God knows why this happened. The question of faith rests on the belief that God knows best and that sometimes, that is all there is to hold on to.

Oh well, tomorrow, he and the team would pack up their equipment and board a flight back to Washington. His boss, John Tyler, had already reviewed his report. He would not be very happy. His old friend Ed Fox will be armed with those arrows of disapproval. He loved having his own zingers to fire off now and then. Hunter had no defense. He couldn't use the unscientific 'act of God' argument. He'd immediately find himself sitting behind a desk filling reports for other agents. No, he would explain as best he could how a new carburetor put into a perfectly good Lycoming engine caused a crash that killed a pilot and a passenger. Just great! All he could do was throw himself on the mercy of the court and say the circumstantial evidence points to only one possible conclusion-that the failure of the carburetor led to the crash. All this angst led to a release of adrenalin, which had him wide awake again.

We laid the child beneath the tree;

away from the tangled roots of pain.

Near the ends of the outstretched branches

the good earth purges what remains.

A gentle breeze rustles the new leaves.

Welcoming springs return again.

The Smith Saga

Michael looked over at Luke and said, "You know, there are two people that I really haven't visited. Why don't we go down to the Smiths' place and make a friendly house call? Shouldn't they receive a little of their doctor's medical attention?"

Luke chuckled. "Yes, I think that's a good idea. Let's go!"

They found themselves down the path in no time. The Smiths' house was a little more weathered than most of the others. It needed a fresh coat of paint. It wasn't in disrepair; there was a green lawn and small garden. The place had that feeling of being lived in. It also felt like it was stuck in a rut, as if the mundane had become a way of life.

Luke and Michael walked up to the front door. He felt a sense of resistance in the air. It was somehow evident to him that any conversation that emerged would be difficult.

Michael hesitated, took a deep breath, and knocked on the door. It opened and a smiling John Smith greeted them.

"Gentlemen, it is a real pleasure to have you come visit us. We don't have many people come by." There was a hint of disappointment in his voice. "Please come in." He opened the door wider and motioned them to enter the house.

Michael replied, "Yes, thank you. I didn't have a chance to visit much with you and your wife during our little party. Please let me introduce Dr. Luke, who has accompanied me." Handshakes were passed, and they walked into the parlor. "I thought that we would stop by to get better acquainted."

"That's very nice of you. I will tell Mary. I'm sure that she would very much like to be a part of our conversation. Please sit down while I go and get her. Feel free to make yourselves comfortable." With that statement, he left the room and went down a hall that probably led to a bedroom.

Michael looked around the parlor. It seemed to fit the Smiths' personalities. It was very nice, all in dark cherry wood. The chairs were all straight back, which made you sit up straight. The couch and dining room table all revealed a similar elegant yet—uncomfortable style. Michael's impressions of Mr. Smith were much the same. He seemed affable enough, but there was also a feeling of discomfort. The skin of his face seemed too tight. Most people had little laugh lines around their eyes and lips. John Smith had no such facial characteristics. His brown eyes melted into an ordinary face that was easy to forget. His white shirt and black pants were starched and pressed just like he appeared to be.

Michael turned to Luke. They both decided to sit on the couch. The feeling of frustration crept into his consciousness. Things were not as they seemed. Michael looked up as John Smith led his wife, Mary, by the hand into the room. She was smiling, yet she was also slightly leaning back against his momentum. She obviously was not real happy about being there.

"Gentlemen, let me introduce my wife, Mary. This is Dr. Turner and Dr Luke, my dear. They have come to pay us a visit."

Mary was a plain-looking woman. She had her long brown hair pulled back into a ponytail. She had a small round head with a sharp turned-up nose, brown eyes, and a chin that almost melted into a long feminine neck. She wore a blue dress with long sleeves and a high neckline with black schoolteacher shoes.

They took their seats in two straight-backed chairs across from their guests interposed by a big heavy coffee table. There was an uncomfortable silence.

Michael decided to say something first even if it felt awkward. "You have a lovely home. Thank you for your hospitality. Mrs. Smith, I was saying to your husband that Dr. Luke and I really didn't have much of an opportunity to get acquainted with you at the party. I thought that it might be a nice thing to stop by."

Mary smiled and nodded her head while her eyes darted over to her husband, looking for reassurance.

John spoke up and said, "I-I mean, we are happy for your attention. We discussed that we should stop by and see you. It seems that you have made the first overture."

Michael knew that he needed to get a patient history. He was also sensitive to the danger of being interrogating and curious. He didn't want to spark a defensive battle of avoidance or hostility. He decided to ask an open-ended question to see where it would lead.

"You know that I don't remember much about how I got here. I remember flying with a friend of mine. The plane had some problem, and we were going to crash, and the next thing I know, an angel is escorting me here. Did something like that happen to you?"

John replied, "Something like that I suppose. When Mary and I arrived here, she was expecting, and was pretty far along in her pregnancy. We were very excited about having the baby. Mary was so happy and literally full of life. I remember that it was dark outside. She began to have contractions. We didn't know what to do. Mary was in pain, and we were both afraid. A young doctor had arrived and was living at the big house, where you live now. I didn't want to leave her alone to go get the doctor. Then that man showed up."

"What man was that?" Michael inquired.

"We hadn't seen him again until the party at your house. He lives in the shadows. You introduced him as Mr. Bradley Schley. He never told us his name. He had been watching and listening to my cries for help. He knocked on the door and told us that he would go get the Doctor. They were here in no time at all."

Mary began to sob. "Oh, John, must you talk about this? You know the pain it causes me."

"Mary, these two Doctors have come to hear our story. Maybe they can help us through our grief and sorrow."

Mary had buried her head in her hands and was bent over, rocking in a chair that did not cooperate. "No, John, nothing can help. Nothing can change what is gone." Mary said with a hopeless tone that also carried a note of anger with it.

Luke intervened with his best fatherly voice, "I know that this is difficult for both of you. Sometimes, letting the memories come out can help. If you want to, please go on."

Mary interrupted, "I will not hear any more of this." Sobbing, she got up and ran down the hallway and slammed the bedroom door.

There was a long pause, and John gave out a big sigh. "Dr. Turner, I am sorry for my wife's behavior. I'm tired of our conflict over this subject. I'm tired of the endless grieving over a broken heart and broken memories. I need to get on with my life, and so does Mary."

"Could you tell me what happened once the doctor arrived?"

"He did an examination and said to me that he could not hear any fetal heart tones in his stethoscope. He worked feverishly to get the baby delivered. He said it was dead and couldn't be resuscitated. The doctor said it was a perfect little boy, except it had a blue dusky color."

"What happened after that?"

"He cleaned up the baby and wrapped it in a new blanket and gave it to Mary. She really didn't want to hold it, but I insisted. Maybe I shouldn't have done that. Anyway, Josh made a little coffin out of wood for it. Josh and I said some prayers. I think our friend Mr. Schley was there in the background. We buried the baby under this great big old tree by this cave."

"What happened to the young physician?" Michael asked.

"You know, he just disappeared. Maybe he gave up medicine or just went up to heaven or somewhere else. I don't know what happened to him."

"I'm so sorry for you and your wife."

"Doctor, I have to tell you that I'm worn out by all this." John was bent over with his elbows resting on his legs, looking at the palms of his hands. "We tried to grieve the loss. All we have left is grieving the grief. I can't talk to her anymore about it, and yet that's all we talk about. We have drifted farther and farther apart. Can you help us?"

"I can try, John. It sounds like your wife is stuck in this spiral of pain. I get the impression that you want to get past this compulsive agony. Is that how you feel?"

"Yes, Doctor, I want to experience a different kind of life."

Michael asked, "Do you think that Mary would talk to me?"

"I think she needs to talk to somebody. Talking to me just makes her feel worse. I could suggest that a visit with you might help her. I could encourage her to see you and get an objective medical opinion. She just might go for that."

"She would have to make the first step. I'm usually home. All she has to do is to decide to walk up the path."

"I will see what I can do to nudge her in that direction. Thank you for your visit."

It was a clear sign to Michael and Luke that John had experienced enough intensity.

"Of course," Michael said as they shook hands and John led them to the front door.

They found themselves walking up the path from the Smiths' house. Luke seemed deep in thought. Michael looked over at him and said, "There is something I don't understand about our conversation with Mr. Smith."

Luke stopped and looked at Michael. "You're wondering about the dead baby."

"Yes, I am," he replied. ".All the people who live here are transitioning. I know that I am alive. How could a child die here? I mean a baby would be alive, not buried in the ground under some tree."

"You're correct. If what you say is true, then what is it that died? Maybe it wasn't a baby but something like an infant."

"You're speaking in riddles, Luke. What exactly are you saying?"

"There are many things that seem fragile like a baby. An idea or a new concept can be talked about as if it was 'my baby.' A child is more than a combination of genetic material. It's the fruit of the couple's relationship, of their communion. It's *our* baby. Making a life together or building a dream begins with communion. Maybe what died wasn't really ever alive. Something that was necessary to bring it to birth was missing. Perhaps it was just too fragile to survive."

"Luke, you are getting very esoteric. How can a baby not be a baby?"

Luke responded, "I don't know how to answer that riddle. I think that Mrs. Smith knows something about the answer. When she comes to see you, it would be good to consider that possibility."

They had arrived at the veranda of the big house. There were a couple of rocking chairs, and they both sat down.

Luke continued, "Whatever happens, the real story will eventually be told."

Michael inquired, "What is the real story?"

"I don't know for sure." Luke closed his eyes. "I do believe that we will find out."

The olive is a bitter pill to chew without a vinegar bath,

so is the nectar of oil squeezed out its purpose clear.

We press upon its comfort the oil to cook

and dip the bread;

a dish Mary tasted bitter, preserved by briny tears.

Forgiveness

Jamie had just put down the phone after a long visit with David. He had told her about their conversations with Mr. Best from the Bear Lake Lodge, Mr. Braxton, and Candice Hilton. She had been dumbfounded by what he'd said. It was overwhelming. Her father had started a foundation for burned children? David was possibly feeling the same way. Over the phone, he sounded like he was trying to catch his breath. He told her that he was feeling confused and was beginning to see his father in a different light. He was a much deeper and more complex person than he'd realized. It was very hard for him not to resent his dad for all the things that he'd hidden about himself. Most boys want to be like their dads. He evidently knew very little about his father. He was becoming aware that there was blame for that on both sides.

David wanted something from his old man, but he wasn't real sure what it was. Then it hit him. He had wanted his father's trust and affection. Most of all, he wanted his approval. David told Jamie that just before the call ended. It would require some follow-up questions later. She thought that he wasn't ready to discuss the answers. She knew that his self-discovery had stirred a big pot of disappointment. It would need to be shared at a time when both of them could sit down together.

Jamie concluded that she would have to talk to her mother about what Bob and David had found out. It wouldn't be easy. Her mother had built a protective wall around her heart after the divorce so that she could move forward in her life. It seemed that all the revelations about Michael were puncturing that wall little by little. It would remind Mary about how much the building blocks of their relationship had crumbled. Jamie already knew that going there would be difficult for her mom.

She decided to give her a call and set up a time for them to talk. It would have to be soon, before the formal reading of the Will Thursday afternoon. Jamie had made up her mind that she wanted to be the one to tell the story. She didn't want a bunch of secrets to be flaunted around by that creepy Mr. Spagnolo. She felt sure that if parts of her dad's life are going to be exposed, that meant that her mom would need to be prepared. Living in the same city made setting up their meeting easier. She picked up the phone. It didn't ring long before Mary answered.

"Hi, Mom."

"Hi, Jamie, how are you?"

"I'm okay. Is there a good time for me to come over and have a visit with you?"

"Is everything all right?" Mary asked.

"Oh yeah, it's good, but I have heard from David, and I thought I could come by and share what he told me." Jamie was aware that she was working at sounding undisturbed or intense. There was no need to alarm her with only part of the information.

"Why don't you plan to come over tonight for dinner? I was going to call you. I have some chicken that I picked up at the store, and we can make a salad."

"Sounds great, Mom. What time?"

"How about 5:00 p.m."

"Super. I'll see you later."

That was easy, she thought. It might not be so easy when she has to talk about some things that her mother should have known and her dad kept secret.

Jamie got a few errands finished: dropped off some dry cleaning, went to the bank, and bought some chilled Sutter Home Chardonnay at the store. A couple of glasses at dinner might be good for both of them. Before she knew how the time went by, she was standing outside her mother's house, using the key she gave her to open the door.

"Hi, Mom, I'm here," she said loudly.

Mary quickly popped her head around the kitchen wall and said, "I'm in here."

Jamie walked into the kitchen holding the bottle of wine, which she held up, and said, "Look what I found on my way over."

Mary smiled and kissed her on the cheek and replied, "That's a good idea. Dinner is almost ready. I just have to cut up the tomatoes."

Jamie noticed her mother was dressed in a comfortable blue top with tan pants.

"Oh, I like your top. It's really cute."

"Thank you. I got it the other day. The store was having a sale. I think you look very stylish too. I love that white blouse. Don't leave it here. You may never see it again."

The finishing touches were made for dinner. The final preparations included small talk about the weather and traffic and their latest shopping adventure. Mary bowed her head after they sat down and said a little prayer thanking God for the food. Jamie replied with a strong amen. They had similar tastes; some came from parental approval, but Jamie didn't mind. They both liked ranch dressing, which they applied more liberally than they should have. Jamie had already opened the wine, and she poured it into a couple of crystal goblets.

"So, Jamie, what is it that you need to tell me?" she had asked the question just as Jamie had put a fork full of salad in her mouth. She couldn't respond. All she could do was to vigorously wave her other hand back and forth in front of her mouth. They both found it funny. Mary could laugh. Jamie had to mumble and try not to, which made it funnier.

She took a big swallow with some wine as a chaser and cleared her throat.

"Uha, one of these days, I am going to have to get that swallowing thing perfected. Mom, I heard from David today. He had a lot of information about Dad."

"What did he say?"

"They went to this lodge on a hunch that Dad might have stayed there. It was close to the nursing home where his mother lived. David said it felt like they were led there. He said it was like a God thing. Anyway, they met the manager of the lodge, and he recognized Dad from the picture they brought, only he didn't use Turner or Hughes as his name. He knew him as Mr. Michael Smith, which was his mother's maiden name.

"Some things that Dad said were true. He really lived with his grandparents. They both died. He never mentioned that he inherited his mother's farm and their estate. He sold both of the properties and made a lot of money. He used the proceeds to start a foundation for burned children in Ohio. It's called the KISS Foundation. David and Bob learned about this when they visited with an attorney Mr. Connor Braxton. He met with Dad every year when he went out there to see his mother. David said that Mr. Braxton and Mr. Spagnolo along with dad, of course, were the board of directors. Braxton and Spagnolo hired the staff and made sure things went smoothly. The value of KISS has grown by donations and by good investments. It is now worth about $70 million."

Mary started to laugh. She just shook her head. "This has to be some kind of joke!"

Jamie was surprised by her mother's response. "No, Mom, these are the facts. According to David, the foundation has done a lot of good over the years. You will never guess why Dad wanted the name KISS. It stands for 'keep it simple, stupid'." When Jamie said that, Mary started to laugh even harder. It was contagious. She started laughing too.

Mary lifted her glass and said, "I'll drink to that."

Jamie did likewise. They clinked their glasses together. She said, "Me too."

There was a tipping point, however, when the laughter became painful and serious. Somehow, they found themselves crying. A torrent of emotion had run past the reality. It led them down a dim alley of "why didn't we know about this?" Mary wiped the tears from her eyes and said, "That was one of Michael's favorite sayings. Every time he used it, I thought it was just to change the subject or block an uncomfortable conversation. Boy, did he have me fooled."

Jamie chimed in, "Me too, Mom. They were given a book from the hotel manager that Dad had left behind. It was A *Long Day's Journey into Night*. David said that they had not found what the key was for. Bob had a few ideas about that, which they were going to follow up with before they had to catch their flights.

"They met with the administrator of the Hillcrest Nursing Home, where Dad's mom, Beth Hughes, died. She filled in some of the details about Dad's mother. I guess that she was really sick and in her own world. She died of a heart attack."

Mary continued to slowly shake her head. "This is such an elaborate ruse. Why did he go to such lengths to keep this hidden?"

"Mom, David and Bob think that the fire was so painful for him. He lost his mother, brother, and sister, and his father who abandoned them. He just couldn't face it. There is another explanation, that he was so shamed by what people thought about his mother being possibly responsible for the fire in some way that he wanted no part of the family name."

Mary looked up and said, "I suppose that these are possible reasons. It just seems to me that there is something more to it."

Jamie thought now might be a good time to discuss her mother's feelings about Mr. Spagnolo.

"Mom, when you told me the other day that you did not like or trust Mr. Spagnolo, what was your reason for saying that?"

Mary began to stare as if she was focusing on the opposite wall. "Your father and I went to a party at a friend's house. I can't remember where. Mr. Spagnolo was your father's attorney, and we were just starting out in practice. I went over to the table where the punch bowl was. Mr. Spagnolo followed me. He came up behind me. He whispered in my ear that I should go over to his office to get better acquainted. It felt like he was making a pass at me. I was just floored. It was totally inappropriate. I was angry, hurt, and confused."

Jamie replied, "Well, evidently, the old creep hasn't changed much. He tried to flirt with me when I went to see him. Then what happened?"

"When your father and I got home, I told him about it. You know what he said? He told me to just stay away from him. I shouldn't worry about it. Mr. Spagnolo was his business attorney. He was in no position to find another. I should leave it at that. There should be no reason for me to see him."

"How did you feel about that?"

"I was very disappointed and hurt by your father's reaction. He was not going to defend me. I felt alone, like I had to take care of myself because Michael wouldn't or couldn't. It seemed to me then that Mr. Spagnolo had something on your father. I guess he did."

Jamie looked at her mother and said, "Maybe it was the foundation, Mom. I'm wondering if Mr. Spagnolo and Dad thought this little diversion up as a way to keep you from sticking your nose in their business. Think about it. Dad knew that you would tell him about the incident. He gave you directions that kept you out of Mr. Spagnolo's office. It all furthered Dad's desire to keep his past and the foundation private. He probably didn't understand how deeply hurt you were by his little pretend intrigue."

"I never thought about it that way. It did have the desired effect of keeping me away from their business," she said sarcastically. "It caused a rift on our relationship that I haven't been able to talk about until now. Jamie, it may seem to you that I didn't know him very well. I have pondered this lately. I knew parts of your father's personality very well. I know that he could be controlling and, at times, manipulative. He could be gentle and reflective. Michael was very intelligent. Getting too close or vulnerable, he thought, was dangerous and unpredictable. I can understand why he believed that now. I thought it was because of my faults. Maybe David thinks it's because of his problems. I believe that in his own way, he loved us." Tears began to roll down her cheeks. She continued, "I wish he had trusted me enough to have introduced me to this other world. It's very hard to admit that I missed so many things now the whole story is coming out."

Ayin was there in the kitchen, invisible, ministering to their hearts, whispering one small word over and over. "Forgive."

"I think you're right, Mom, there is more to this. I think it has something to do with the key. Why would he carry that in his wallet? It is important. The key fits something that either holds a treasure or something painful, maybe both.

"Oh, there is one more thing that will give you a kick. David and Bob stayed one night at the Bear Lake Lodge. David said the surroundings are very beautiful. The lodge had been built years ago. The property that the lodge sits on belonged to his mother, Beth Hughes. Dad sold it to them since his mother was incompetent. It's a strange turn of providence that they would spend time on the land that was Dad's boyhood home. The fire destroyed the original house. I think it's very interesting that Dad stayed there every year."

"Well, I am sure that your father had worked out a good deal to stay there. I should have mentioned before what you already know. He was frugal." They both had a good laugh over that.

Dinner was winding down. They got up and put the dishes in the sink to be loaded in the dishwasher. Jamie was getting tired. It had been a very emotional time for both of them. They had some coffee and said their good-byes.

Jamie found herself walking back to her car much like how she found herself walking up to the front door, feeling tense and insecure. The night air was still balmy and the breeze stirred up some thoughts in her head.

"There will be a time when all of us will have to forgive him. It won't be easy. Maybe not today or tomorrow but soon, when all the truth comes out." She heard her bed calling; time to lie down, to rest, to sleep, and to put the anxiety on hold until tomorrow.

Jamie started the car and headed home. What a day. She had her own little secret. A smile lifted the corners of her mouth. That nice Officer Jesse Hernandez had called. He had asked her on a date for Saturday night. She wasn't entirely aware of it, but she had hoped he would.

I recline beneath a shady tree.

It's a locus of contentment for me.

A captivating moment alone without a thing to do,

admires visions, thoughts, and seasons changing hues.

I wonder about all the days

to come and all that have been so far full of stress.

They are distant measures, now that I can rest.

A Schley Confession

Michael and Luke were sitting in the parlor talking about the huge leaps that science had made in treating illnesses. Michael heard the squeaky screen door open, and Josh walked in. Michael immediately got up and walked over to meet him.

"Josh, it's good to see you." He was surprised at how quickly a feeling of happiness flooded his senses. "Do you know Dr. Luke?"

"No, I haven't met him yet."

"Well, let me introduce you two. Dr. Luke, this is Josh, our caretaker and all-around great guy."

"Why, thank you, Dr. Turner," Josh replied. "It's good to meet you, Dr. Luke. Please forgive me if I don't shake hands. My gloves are pretty muddy, and taking them off would just mess up the place. That's why I left my boots outside on the veranda." He was dressed in his usual work clothes—jeans and blue chambray shirt. He was in his stocking feet. The big toe on the left foot was sticking out of his sock.

"What have you been doing?" Michael asked.

"You know that little spring behind the big house here. I thought it might be easier to water the cows if we cleaned out the bushes and reeds."

"I think that's a great idea. Do you need some help?"

"Oh, no, sir, that's my job. Besides you and Dr. Luke here need to see your patients. It's the reason I stopped by. I haven't seen Mr. Schley since the party. He usually is hiding somewhere that I can see him. Lately, I haven't spied him around at all. I guess I'm worried about him. I think y'all should go and check on him. He might need your help. Brad Schley reminds me of an old mule I had. That mule was stubborn like a lot of people, I suppose. It just wouldn't move sometimes. It would plant its behind on the ground, and you couldn't move it. I used to carry a little whip for moments like that. I never did hit that mule. I would just crack it near its ear, and off it would go. That's because that old mule couldn't remember from the last time. People are different though. They do remember. It seems sooner or later, they're going to test you to see if you really would use that whip or not."

This little story made Michael shake his head. "Josh, you are a good friend, but I don't get what you're saying," Michael said with a tone of frustration.

"You know, Dr. Turner, it's no fun at all if I spell it out for you."

"I have to admit Josh that it's probably a good idea to go and pay a visit to Mr. Schley. You don't mind if I'm not excited though. He is a difficult person to try to help. I have had a few patients in my day. If they didn't want to get well, take the prescribed medication, rest, and take care of themselves, they just wouldn't heal, no matter how hard I tried working with them."

Josh got a big grin on his face. "Like that old mule of mine."

Michael was completely surprised, and he let out a big laugh. "Yeah, just like your old mule," he playfully repeated.

"Okay, I get it. We have to show him that we are serious and resolute no matter what decisions he may make."

"Something like that," Josh replied. "I will keep you boys in my prayers." He tipped his hat, turned and headed back through the veranda, grabbed his boots, and went outside.

"Luke, my recollection tells me that he likes to hang out by this huge old tree. Let's take a walk down there and see if we can find him."

Luke nodded his head, and off they went. As they walked, looming up ahead was that tree. Its branches reached above the leafy canopy, as if it stretched up to claim the largest portion of the sky. Michael hadn't realized before how dominating in size and beauty it was. The closer they came to it, the more it grabbed his attention. He just stopped and stared at it. Michael pointed and said to Luke, "The last time I came here, Brad was hiding in the shade of that tree. Maybe we can find him there. I was told by my angel, Ayin, not to go into that cave over there." He pointed to the hillside next to the tree. "It leads to a bad place."

"Oh, yes, I know," replied Luke. "Everyone has been told to stay away from there. I sure hope that your patient Mr. Schley hasn't gone in that direction."

"Me too. I think we should just stand here and observe the shadows. I'll call out to see if he's around."

Michael put his cupped hand to the side of his mouth and yelled, "Bradley Schley, this is Dr. Turner and Dr. Luke. We've come to see how you are doing. Please come out so we can see you."

Nothing happened; Michael had the feeling that something would. Sure enough, a shadow seemed to move and slowly stand up away from the tree. He knew that it was Bradley Schley. Michael felt a sense of apprehension well up in his stomach. It made him acutely aware that it was going to be a difficult conversation.

"Well, well, Dr. Turner, what a surprise to see you out here," he said in a gravelly voice.

Luke and Michael walked toward him. Once they got into the shade of the tree, his features emerged. He had a floppy hat covering his eyes. He was wearing an old pair of jeans with holes in the knees and a khaki long-sleeved shirt.

"You know that I make house calls. Since you don't have a house, I have to come out here to find you."

Bradley put his hands on his hips and said, "Well, you found me. You can just go back to where you came from."

Michael did not like being told what to do. After all, he was the Doctor, and he's the one who wrote the orders. He thought better of reacting with anger. "Luke and I came by for a friendly visit. Josh told us that he hadn't seen you lately. I was wondering how you're doing and if you enjoyed the party."

"I'm all right. What do you want me to say? You know that the angel Ayin made me go. Who's your quiet friend?" Bradley asked.

"Oh, yes, let me introduce Dr. Luke. This is Bradley Schley."

Luke looked straight at Bradley and said in a strong voice, "I am very pleased to meet you."

"Thank you, Doctor. I must confess that most people are not so inclined when they see me. Pardon me if I'm a little doubtful," Bradley said sarcastically.

Michael followed up with a question. "I talked to the Smiths, and they told me how you helped them. They mentioned that you showed up and tried to support them."

"I didn't do anything except go get the doctor. It turned out that the baby could not be saved, so I really didn't do much good at all."

Michael approached him and said, "You were there, and just being there can give support." Bradley's eyes darted from side to side. He was obviously uncomfortable with being affirmed.

"Look," he replied, "I don't bother anyone, and all I ask is to be left alone."

Michael got a little closer and asked, "Isn't being left by your self lonely and isolating? I wonder if you just say that to keep people away. What is really bothering you? Is there something you need to talk about that might release some of your pain?"

"Life is a miserable place. Just look at the Smiths. They lost their only child. Is that fair? Is that the way we exist, by being in agony? Look at them. They still haven't gotten over it. What chance do I have?" he said in almost a whisper.

"What do you mean 'what chance do I have'?"

"I mean that everybody has stuff that they are protecting. It happens when someone tells them not to tell anyone. You surely know about secrets in your profession. I'm sure, Doctor, that you have to protect your patients by keeping their confidences. I have a few confidences to keep too. If I gave them up, some people around here would be hurt. Sometimes, I think that they would forget about me completely if they could."

"You know, Bradley, you have made that real easy for them. Until the party, no one except the Smiths even knew you existed. How could anyone ever miss you if they hadn't ever met you?"

"You're right about that. I'm the invisible man. It's a role that I have to play. Maybe I will just take myself down that hole there." He pointed to the cave in the hillside that Ayin told Michael about.

"No, that's no place for you," Michael said forcefully. "It leads to Perdition. That is no place for you or anyone."

"It might be the best place for me. No one could ever find me there, and my secrets would be safe forever. Besides, no one cares about me anyway."

"The fact that Luke and I have come here to see you shows that we care about you."

"It does not!" Bradley blurted out. "It means nothing! Why, I bet if I went down into that cave, you wouldn't try to rescue me. No, sir, you would say what most Doctors say to the family after an operation went bad. 'We did our best. We are very sorry but the patient died.' Dr. Turner, you and your friend would wash your hands and bow to the inevitable. Some people die despite our best efforts. You wouldn't give me another thought. You would just move on to the next patient."

Michael was hurt by what Bradley was saying, yet deep inside, he knew that he was right.

"Let's face it, Doctor. I'm expendable. I have seen your operation, and I know what I've seen with my own eyes. Why, you can triage me right out of sight and be no worse for it. Heck, you might be doing that right now."

It got quiet. Michael took in a deep breath. In the old days of his practice, he would have thrown out the little twerp and told him to find another Doctor. He felt the anger rise up, but then something amazing happened. It shocked him much more than Bradley's condemnation.

Michael quietly said, "Bradley you're probably right about my past medical practice. That is not the issue here. I don't know what I would do if you decided to go down into that cave, perhaps to be lost forever. Such a choice, on your part, would be an eternal nightmare for you. I really don't want to have to find out what I would do or not do to rescue you. I think the best course of action is for neither of us to have to deal with such a desperate choice. It would be far better for you to make a decision that makes healing possible. Are you interested in that?"

"I'll tell you what, Doc. I will think about it," Bradley said softly.

"I want you to know that my office is always open. Come by any time. You're always welcome." Michael tried to summon up all the conviction behind the invitation that he could muster, hoping that Bradley would take advantage of it.

Bradley slowly moved backward into the shadow of the tree and disappeared into its charcoal pigment. Michael and Luke turned and headed back to the big house.

"What did you think of that conversation, Dr. Luke?"

"I think that there is a good chance that despite our best efforts, that young man might end up outside of our help. I believe that it's still possible for him to change his direction. Will he make that choice? I just don't know."

Michael replied, "He is a very disturbed person, that's for sure. He had me feeling angry there. Something happened that I have not experienced very often. Instead of staying mad at him, I felt a real care and concern for him. Bradley has become part of my community, and what happens to him matters to me. I think that it affects all of us no matter what he says about not being noticed, wanted, or important."

Michael desired to explore that subject some more. His thoughts were interrupted by Luke pointing toward the veranda of the big house.

He pressed, "Look, my dear colleague, I think there is another person already on the steps of the veranda wanting to visit you."

Time is a treasure never possessed, held, or bound.

It flees the scene just in a second.

It bears no contempt or judgment.

It only asks to be found.

It consists of the sameness; it magnifies the differenced.

It has no sorrows or laments; bears no regrets.

Time is the measure of movement and swiftness of going

forward, backward, up or down.

It parades ever onward, admires the moment,

the second, the hour, the day,

the week, the month, the year.

When it runs out,

What treasure shall appear?

A Brand New Day

David and Bob had decided to stay their last night in Bear Lake Lodge. It was a change of plans. They agreed that they could drive into Cleveland from there tomorrow. It would take them a little longer. They had one other place to stop on their way to the airport. Bob got an idea, another inspiration. He wanted to find out where Beth Smith was buried. They'd called Connor Braxton on his cell phone, and he gave them the name "Greenwood Cemetery." They called the Greenwood mortuary and got the afterhours operator, who told them that someone should be there after 8:00 a.m. They decided to head over there early the next morning. Their plane didn't take off until 1:00 and 1:40 p.m. Bob would catch a flight directly to Dallas, Texas, to meet up with his wife and his grandkids. David would be heading back to Tucson.

David was getting sleepy with the droning sound of the car engine. He was very tired. The day had been full of discoveries— some good and some curious. All of them were intense. It was dusky gray outside when they pulled into the front parking lot of the lodge. You could hear the loud quacking and screeching sounds of geese, ducks, coots, and other birds lifting up their voices for a final symphony before the curtain of darkness closed the stage. They rolled out of the car and headed up to the lodge and went to the front desk. The manager had already gone home. He had kept their room for them in case they needed to stay another night, again with his compliments.

Bob suggested that they go down to the bar and get a couple of drinks and have a couple of sandwiches to decompress and discuss the day's events. David nodded his head and followed Bob, who already knew how to find a good scotch and soda.

They located a tall table with a couple of stools and sat down.

David spoke up and asked, "You didn't say much about going to the cemetery. Why do you want to go there?"

Bob had picked up some popcorn that was sitting in the middle of the table and shoved a small handful into his mouth as their drinks quickly arrived.

"It just occurred to me that Michael had spent a lot of emotional and financial energy around the care of his mother. I thought that maybe there would be something more we can learn at her graveside. Mr. Braxton said that she was cremated. They had a short committal service for her at the columbarium at the cemetery. Call it another hunch, but I feel that we need to check it out before we head off on our separate ways tomorrow."

David took a big swig of his beer. "Sounds okay to me. Heck, even if we don't find anything, we can at least pay our respects. Besides, I don't think I can take any more surprises, at least not today."

"You're right about that, David. It has been a big day of amazing developments. Your father was a man full of surprises."

"The most amazing thing is that I never knew it. He would go to work, come home, sometimes take late-night call, and start all over again the next day. He was a man of routine and predictability. He fashioned reality around the things he could control. I suppose that's why we fought so much. I was determined not to be under his thumb. I thought I was being so independent, so right in my own opinions. I never saw the man behind the curtain, the man that was in pain."

David didn't see Ayin standing behind him with his hand on his shoulder softly whispering, "Forgive."

Bob looked up from his drink. "David, he didn't make it easy for anyone to see that side of him. He had a very wellrehearsed façade. I think my brother did too. He is part of this story. Bill is the forgotten man, the escape artist who wanted to bond but never really knew how. You know my family has very few pictures of him after he left home. He was always going somewhere else. I think both men were alike in that way—your father running from the past, my brother running from the future."

They had both ordered their usual cheeseburgers, and just then, they arrived. The food at the lodge was really wholesome, and portions were large. They were both ready to have their appetites satisfied. David looked up at the waitress and noticed how cute she was. She had a peaches-and-cream complexion, light brown hair in a ponytail, and a long athletic build that was not enhanced by the white short-sleeved lodge uniform that she wore.

She smiled and said, "Is there anything else I can get you, gentlemen? David looked at her, trying to draw out a memory. His mind was slow to move in that direction.

"Didn't I see you before at the front desk? Were you working there?"

"Why, yes I was," she replied with a coquettish smile.

"What's your name, may I ask?"

"My name is Theresa Best."

"Are you related to the manager, Silas Best?" He felt embarrassed by his own question.

"He's my dad. I've worked at the lodge for several years, helping wherever I'm needed. I have had every job here. Of course, except manager, at least that's what Dad says."

"I'm David Turner." He straightened himself up in the chair. "This is Bob Hughes."

"Yes, I know."

David was at a loss for words, and there was an uncomfortable silence.

"Your hair was different."

Theresa made a slight smile, which indicated she liked being noticed. "That's right. I had it curled and down when you saw me before." David smiled back, and Bob knew that their conversation was over. Someone new had stepped in.

He was right. The rest of dinner was basically small talk. It consisted of Bob watching David watch Theresa and smiling every time she walked by.

He thought that David might benefit from a little encouragement. He leaned over and said quietly, "You are obviously taken by that charming young lady. You haven't been able to look at anything else or think of anything else." He pointed at David's half-eaten hamburger. "I suggest that before you decide to leave, you ask for her number and e-mail address. We're going to be leaving tomorrow. Who knows, something may develop that would require your attention back here. They are going to need a new board member for KISS. You might as well begin to work on that possibility. Charming name for it, isn't it?" He chuckled.

David chuckled back and said, "It's pretty obvious."

Bob just nodded his head and rolled his eyes. "I have the impression that the feelings are mutual."

"You do?" David found himself blushing despite his best efforts to keep cool.

"Look, I am too old and tired to find this little flirtation exciting or interesting. You, my young friend, do not suffer from my condition. I am going to take my rather substantial frame up to our room and enjoy one more drink before I drift off to sleep. Please be moderately quiet when you turn in for the night." Bob got up and with the wave of his hand, headed out of the Bar and Grille.

He left David holding the bill, which was a good reason to talk to Theresa. He put down his credit card and waited for her to come pick it up.

Theresa was surprised to see David by himself. She came over and picked up the credit card with the bill.

"Thank you. Was everything all right?"

"It was very good except one thing."

"Oh, what was that?" she replied curiously.

"I looked very carefully, but there was nothing on that piece of paper that told me how to get in touch with you and when you get off work."

"Tabs at the bar and food bills generally don't include that kind of information."

David pressed on, "Well, I think they should, especially in your case."

"Really? Why?"

"Well, how is a guy like me going to find out that information if it's not written down somewhere? It leaves me with only one other option. I'll just have to ask you. It could be risky. You might not be willing to tell me, but I hope you will."

"Since you asked, Mr. Turner, I get off in an hour, and if you would like, we could get better acquainted and perhaps exchange information. Of course, I assume that it's not past your bedtime."

"Let me tell you, Miss Best, that since I met you, I have gotten my second wind. You need to add a cup of coffee to that." He pointed to the bill in her hand. They both had a good chuckle. "I'll wait." He said with a big smile.

The new day was ushered in by the opening chorus of quacks, hoots, whistles, and cackles, like an orchestra tuning up. Birds of every kind all seemed to be roused to song or, in most cases, noise. It woke Bob up from a restless sleep. David had come in late and in the dark, announced himself by running into the corner of his bed. The verbal display that followed reminded Bob that David had acquired a rather colorful vocabulary. He was sorry that it would be necessary to wake him up. They had agreed to get an early start; there was no time like the present.

"Rise and shine, cowboy," Bob bellowed out as he shook the corner of David's bed with a joyful sense of retribution.

Forty minutes later, they were cleaned up, packed, and ready to head off after a quick cup of coffee and a couple of donuts from the continental breakfast in the lobby.

They dropped off their room keys at the front desk and headed out to Greenwood Cemetery. The sun was trying to peak over the tree line. It was going to be another lovely spring day. It was still brisk in the morning with a hint of warmth filtering into the day as the shadows melted away. David was aware that he needed some more sleep. Two hours of talking with Theresa had made him feel recharged somehow. He hoped that he could get a nap on the plane, as if that ever happened.

Bob as usual broke the silence. "Well, David, how did it go with the beautiful Miss Best?"

"I think that you have described her perfectly. We exchanged phone numbers and e-mail addresses. We talked and laughed. I had a great time. She is as beautiful on the inside as she is to look at. She has had a couple of boyfriends, but they all went to the university. She stayed here to help her family. I think she has high standards. I'm not sure I can measure up." David fixed his eyes out the car window as Bob drove on.

Bob slightly elevated his voice. "Nonsense, you should not allow yourself to let your thoughts slide downward. What do you have to offer? What do you have to give?" he said with a sense of determination.

David looked back at him. "I don't know," David said softly.

"Sure you do. Say it out loud."

There was a pause, and then David said, "Well, I am honest and self-reliant."

"There you go. What else? Say it louder."

David replied confidently, "I am generous, kind, and I have a good sense of humor."

With each affirmation, David's voice grew in self-assurance.

"That's it, David. I am going to give you a little advice. If you are serious about pursuing this young woman, you are going to have to charge ahead into life. No more running away from your father or your problems. Your father, rest his soul, is dead. He lived his life. You need to embrace yours. Sink your spurs into life, and let it take you for a ride. If you get bucked off every once in a while, jump right back on. My god, man, make your mark. Look, I'm old, and I am more designed for sitting in a recliner. Not you, no, sir."

David became instantly aware that this old distant relative was giving him what his own father couldn't give. He was teaching him about growing up. No more child's play by disengaging or avoiding commitments. Winning the heart of Theresa Best would mean being responsible and embracing life in a mature way. He closed his eyes and took some deep breaths. Bob shook him back into the moment when he said, "Look, here we are." Time had flown by. They drove in and parked in front of the Glenwood Cemetery. It was a red brick building that looked to have been built in the sixties. It was early. The hours posted on the door said that the office wasn't going to open for another half hour. There were gardeners working the grounds. They got out of the car and headed to the closest worker they could see. He was just about to start up a riding lawn mower. David hailed him as Bob tried to catch up. Those fifty yards seemed like an eternity. He got there out of breath and flushed. David was already talking to the man.

David said, "Can you direct us to the columbarium?"

"Oh, yes, I show you," he replied with a heavy Italian accent. "You come to give respects to someone?"

"Yes, my grandmother, Beth Smith."

"You Michael Smith's son?"

David nodded. "My name is David, and this is our relative Bob Hughes."

"My name is Giuseppe." He pounded his hand on his chest. "He never said he had a son."

"I only recently found out about my grandmother. My father was killed in a plane crash."

"I know your father very well. I am very sorry to hear he die. He give money for the columbarium and everything. I do a lot of the work. He was a very nice man, your father. Come, I show you. Come."

Giuseppe was a short bald man with a rather round frame that was as solid as the granite used for the markers. He moved at a pace that didn't seem fast until you tried to match it. Bob slowed down. It was better than having a heart attack trying to keep up with those two. He decided instead to consider it a leisurely stroll in the park. They moved toward a small building sitting alone in a corner of the cemetery. It was like a tiny A-frame cabin surrounded by some boulders and a fountain at its entrance. They approached the front, which had a walkway around it. There was a wall of little square plates. A few had names under them. Across from the wall was a marble bas-relief of a beautiful virgin with child. She held out the baby as if to invite the admirer to hold him. The child Jesus had his arms outstretched too, reaching out to be held.

Bob caught up with them and overheard what they were saying. Giuseppe was showing David the niche for Beth Smith. He was pointing to it as he said, "This Michael's mother's place. He paid for building the whole columbarium. He had a special one made just for her ashes. I leave you now. I go get back to work. God bless you. God bless you both." He turned and headed back to his mower.

Bob carefully looked at the plate, which, upon closer inspection, was really a small hinged brass door. It was about twenty-four inches wide and twenty-four inches high. The door was beautifully cast in bronze with a dove hovering over an inscription that read, "Beth Smith, God's Child." It reminded Bob of an ambry from his altar boy days at St. Monica's Episcopal Church. He noticed the lock on the right side of the door.

Bob said excitedly, "I wonder…David, let's see if the key from your father fits this lock."

David drew closer and stared. "You know, Bob, it just might," David said enthusiastically.

He nervously opened his coat pocket and retrieved the key that he had in an envelope.

He put it in his hand and pushed it into the lock. It slipped in perfectly. He turned the key. The door opened.

I held the urn tightly so it would be secure.

I opened the tempered top of the jar grace preserved.

I tightly grasped the prize He won; so its memory

would endure.

I let go of my anger when you sinned.

I extended my hand when you returned.

I opened my heart and waved "come in."

Blest Be the Tie That Binds

Michael and Luke approached his residence. It was clear to him that Odelia Crier was waiting for them. She waved as they approached. She walked down the steps to meet them. Michael noticed that she was not bent over or grimacing in pain. She had a youthful sense about her. There was a transformation taking place. Odelia had gotten younger. It was a process that took Michael by surprise. He just had to stop and admire the change. She was wearing a pair of jeans with a short-sleeved red blouse. She had a pair of sneakers on her feet. Her hair, which had been gray, was a beautiful auburn color.

She had her hands on her hips and twirled as she said, "What do you think, Doctor? How do I look?"

"Odelia, I am stunned. I just cannot explain your transformation."

She said, "You know, Doctor, I can't explain it either. I've decided to just enjoy it. All my life, I've had to be the mature adult, setting goals and making sure things followed a tight schedule. All I had to show for it was my sore hips and joints. I'm tired of setting the pace, being the one in charge, meting out the discipline. Do you know who is helping me discover my emancipation?" Michael shook his head. "It's Delbert Finwicky. He's that wonderful little man that you sent my way. I began to see him not as a buffoon. I realize that Delbert is a man with many fine characteristics. I think his best virtue is his ability to be keenly aware of what is going on around him." Michael had to hold back the laughter that was rising in his throat. All he could see was Delbert hiding behind the couch in fear of Odelia Crier as they walked up the steps.

"Oh, yes," Michael replied. "I would say that he has an uncanny awareness of most situations. Do you like his sense of humor?" he asked with some incredulity.

"It has taken me some effort, but I think I'm actually learning to enjoy it."

Luke chimed in, "I suppose that for a woman like you, he can seem capricious."

"True, Doctor. I admit that I have had to modify some of my judgments. It's not an easy thing for me to change my opinions. I like predictability and sameness. I know that I'm safe when I can arrange the players on stage. I have recently discovered that there is another hand that can be played." She looked down and slowly paced the floor. It was as if she was trying to dictate a thought that needed to emerge. She continued, "Delbert has a real talent in making the ordinary an adventure. Where I revel in predictability, Delbert feels most himself in the world of spontaneity. I used to look down my nose at his useless fretting, slap stick, and silly humor."

Michael quipped, "I take it that something has changed?"

"Yes, it has. I am changing. I don't limp or hurt anymore. I can listen to Delbert and appreciate his unique slant on things. Since your arrival, Dr. Turner, many things have changed. I think the changes are for the good. I came by to thank both of you. I know that Delbert feels a deep sense gratitude for your help and friendship. He has told me that you were the first person to seek his opinion. It made it easier for him to talk to me. He confessed that he was afraid of me. Can you imagine that?" She turned her head and flashed Michael a coquettish grin. It made him smile. Her reaction was so out of character that it made the conversation lighter and far more interesting.

"You said things have changed. What specifically has changed in your world?"

"I have changed my compulsive perfectionism. It may have served me in the past, but it also robbed me of something. It made me a difficult person to be around. Delbert keeps reminding me that life can be 'fun.' I am still trying to understand what that term means. Delbert seems to know a lot about having 'fun.' Perhaps I can learn from him."

Michael agreed, "I think that he can be a good teacher. I believe that you have a few things to teach him too."

"I do?"

"Oh, yes, like how to dress."

Michael scrunched his forehead and started to laugh; so did Odelia.

"You really need to help that man even if he puts up resistance."

Odelia came closer to him and put her hand on his shoulder. "I have already begun his wardrobe reclamation," she said playfully.

"It sounds like an exciting adventure is developing for both of you."

"Yes, Doctor, I would say that new possibilities are emerging as we get to know one another better." She put her hand on her hip and raised an eyebrow. It was not overtly flirtatious, but it could have been read that way.

Michael and Luke both enjoyed the mixed message. It seemed that Delbert's comedic sense of irony and timing had already worn off on her.

They had not been aware that Delbert had walked down the path looking for Odelia. He was already on the steps to the veranda when Michael realized that someone was there.

Delbert spoke up in a loud voice, "It is I, Delbert Finwicky, looking for that lovely creature Odelia Crier. I see that my quest has been rewarded. Here she is." Delbert stepped inside the veranda and walked toward Michael to shake his hand. If he hadn't identified himself, Michael would never have recognized him. He seemed to have gotten several inches taller; or was it that he was just walking straighter? His bald head had brown hair that filled in the vacant spots. His round face was younger and thinner. So was his round belly, which had a much flatter landscape. He was dressed in a pair of tan pants and a red short-sleeved shirt. He wore brown dress shoes and a tan wide-brimmed hat. His attire showed that Odelia had been doing some wardrobe reclamations indeed.

Michael said, "Delbert, it is a pleasure to see you. It is very apparent that you both have experienced something rather transformative."

"I would say so, Dr. Turner. We have, or are, going through an incredible metamorphosis. I can only chalk it up to this beautiful lady. I am so glad that I took your advice. I can truly say that although we had been acquainted, we didn't really know each other."

Odelia walked over to Delbert and took his hand, which he offered with prideful delight. Delbert patted her hand with his other hand and gestured for them to head down the path.

"We must say adieu, Doctors. Odelia and I are going for a walk and some conversation. My dear, after you." She nodded in agreement and walked through the open screen door and down the steps as Delbert followed. Then she took his arm, and they paraded down the path together. Well, at least they tried to walk arm and arm. Odelia was taller than Delbert, and he had to take more steps to keep up with her gait. Looking at the pair from the back was funny. Delbert was kicking up dust trying to match her steps and almost falling all over himself and her. Michael heard them laughing at their uncoordinated attempt at togetherness.

He looked over and saw that Luke had the biggest grin. He was smiling too. Both men felt a similar sense of enjoyment and mystery. No one would have expected this incredible change, yet there it was.

Then it happened. It wasn't an earthquake or a lightning bolt but a soft florescent light. It was like a glow around everything, a wonderful brilliance that visited everywhere. It was diffuse, then it began to gather into a ball of light and settled on Delbert and Odelia. They became dazzling white. The light faded, and the colors and background emerged, and they were gone.

Michael found himself transfixed. His mind was so still. It didn't want to move from its place of rest. There was a captivating sense of wonder and awe. Nothing needed to be said. Nothing could be said. It was an experience that transcended the event. A profound feeling of joy and satisfaction grew in his chest and pushed out to the edges of his soul. He seemed to have discovered a new center of gravity. It flooded his mind with tenderness and resonated in a sound like a thousand voices all in harmony and yet each one unique. Somehow, he was aware that two voices had been added. Two new choir members had swelled the ranks. What followed was a feeling beyond contentment.

He had found a pearl of great price. It wasn't about possessing it or hoarding it. He felt complete in being in the experience. His usual response to mystery was to run, avoid, or hide. There was none of that for him now. Being present was all that mattered. Being touched and having his soul's hardness tenderized was far more important and far better.

Slowly, Michael came back to himself. Things around him came into focus. He felt different. The transformation of Delbert and Odelia had started something deep inside him. Michael realized that he was changing. Other things were changing too.

He knew that Luke was leaving. The stillness had told him. Quietly, it had played a melody of contentment and peace. It was a new tune for him. It was a tender song that sprang up and resonated in his heart. He reached out his arms, and Luke embraced him and said, "I know that my work here is done. There are still a few challenges ahead of you. They are the most difficult. You have the strength to rise to those challenges. I have every confidence that you can become that caring physician that God wants you to be."

"Luke, I can see that this is a necessary step. I was not a very accepting student at our introduction. I am sorry about that. I have come to appreciate your influence in my practice. I have felt your care and support. Thank you for your help. I guess this is a kind of graduation, at least I feel like it is."

Michael's attention was diverted when Josh walked by carrying a long rope wrapped around his shoulder. "Is that you, Doc?" he loudly asked.

"Yes, I'm here with Dr. Luke."

"Who?"

"My mentor, Dr. Luke."

"Sorry, Doc, but I don't see anybody there but you."

Michael turned toward an empty spot where Luke had been.

He was gone. He wasn't surprised. It just made him feel a bit vulnerable. He knew that a bridge had been crossed, which put him in a more fragile and demanding country. He was on is own. Josh had come up the steps and was in the veranda doorway.

He looked sweaty. He'd been working hard outside.

Michael inquired, "What's the rope for?"

Josh looked directly at Michael with a tired expression. "A rope can come in handy. A man never knows when he might need one. This is a really good rope. I can tell you from experience. Why, it can be used for pulling livestock from holes, rescue a person, carry a load, or pull out a stump or rock. You want to always remember where you put it. You might just need it in a crisis. Yes, sir, there is nothing on this farm as necessary as a good long rope. I thought that I would take it with me over by that big tree. I have some brush that needs cleaning out. I just might need it.

"That reminds me of a story. It seems that there was this rancher. He lived in South Dakota. They were having a huge blizzard. It was so bad that you couldn't see your hand in front of your face. The temperature got to forty below. Well, sir, he had stretched a rope from the barn to the ranch house on some fence posts to hold on to get to the barn. You see, he had to check on the livestock and feed them every day. His wife insisted that he should also have a rope tied around his waist so they could pull him in if something happened. He disagreed with her, saying he didn't need anything like that.

"She would not relent and demanded he have a lifeline. Women seldom lose those kinds of arguments. Something did happen that afternoon. On his way back, from the barn, the wind blew fiercely. It was so bad that he lost his grip on the rope and fell down. The visibility was so awful that he couldn't find it. He thanked God that he had that rope around his waist. He pulled against it and got himself up. Reinforcements had arrived by that time, and they brought him safely home."

"That's a good story, Josh. What are you saying?"

"What do you think it means, Doc?"

"If you have to take the risk of saving someone, be sure you have as many lifelines as you can get. You might need them all." Michael became aware that he was being taught by this interpretation of the story. He had rescued lots of people in his career. It had taken on a new meaning for him. Saving people from death was a skill that he carried with him just like Josh carried that rope. He had been that lifeline for many people even if he hadn't acknowledged it. His skill had reached out to his patients with that cord of hope. He'd forgotten. He'd been too busy or too tired to remember.

"Josh, let me tell you, if I keep up this pace, you and I will be the only ones left here.

What will we do then?"

"Don't worry about that, Doc. There's always some work that needs to be done. I believe that God will think of something creative to keep us occupied."

"Maybe I'll get some new patients to work with?" Michael said excitedly.

"That is a possibility, Doc. Right now, though, I think you better focus on the ones you're caring for. Like those two coming up the path." Josh pointed to the two people coming swiftly toward them. "Doc, I will be seeing you." With that and a tip of his hat, Josh stepped down to the ground and went off in the direction of the big tree.

Here is my servant, whom I uphold,

My chosen one with whom I am well pleased.

Upon him I have put my spirit;

He shall bring forth justice to the nations

He will not cry but, nor shout,

nor make his voice heard in the street.

A bruised reed he will not break,

and a dimly burning wick he will not quench.

(Isaiah 42:1-3, New American Bible)

Reflections

David pushed himself into the seat of the plane. He felt the adrenalin start to back off. He could relax. Bob's flight was leaving later, heading off to Dallas. David had barely made his flight. Getting through security had taken forever. The line just seemed to never move. He had brought a carry-on, his black duffel bag. It was too large for what little he packed. David had zipped it open and taken out two green notebooks before he stored it in the overhead compartment. The plane was taxing down the runway. Instead of looking out the window, he was transfixed, thinking about what he and Bob discovered.

They had opened Beth Smith's niche in the cemetery's columbarium. Inside was the urn of her ashes and two large green notebooks. It had been quite a find. Both books contained his history. The larger one had the clients that the KISS Foundation had helped. The other one was the most interesting. It had some family pictures of his mother, grandparents, and of his father, William Hughes. They were mostly old black-and-white photos. Michael had arranged them by years. There was a special eight-by-twelve picture of his mother, Beth, from her graduation.

She was attractive but not beautiful. Her teeth were a little crowded into her mouth. They were scrunched together, which was a distraction from an otherwise-pleasant face. Her dark hair was shoulder length. She seemed to be forcing a smile, like she was all too aware of the liability of those teeth. Was it something deeper?

She looked to be self-conscious like some young women who are very aware of their liabilities and not too familiar with their assets. Her parents were farmers after all. What in the world would she need straight teeth for? That was for city folks who had lots of money and time on their hands. Her world didn't have much spare time; keeping up with the demands of the farm saw to that. David knew about the long days of caring for livestock.

Funny, he thought it interesting that he should be drawn to ranching. Looking at her picture made him realize the strength of her tug into his life. Without knowing, he was following a pattern that came through her family. Was it genetic, or was it a spiritual thing? He didn't know, but looking at these snapshots made him wonder.

His father had written reflections on his life between sections of pictures. Was it a journal, or was it history? It seemed to lack any personal depth. He referred to the memories as factually as possible—"Went fishing on Bear Lake" or something like that in these pictures of his childhood. David noticed that these photos were always with his mother, brother, and sister or with his grandparents, the Smiths. Many of them seemed stiff and staged. There were a few pictures of Michael's father. He seemed affable and was the only one who appeared to be spontaneous. In every picture, he was trying to catch someone off guard or being silly. There was an understandable empty section probably because of the fire.

The next group of pictures was about Michael as a teenager working on the tractor or laboring on an old car. It was clear that the Smiths valued hard work. Michael was photographed always doing something useful. Then David came across this surprising entry. It was handwritten on lined paper and said,

How I hated working that farm. I was determined to get out of there when I graduated from high school. My grandparents wanted me to spend the rest of my life being a slave doing all the work. I studied hard, and I got good grades. No girls, no life, just work and study until that day of freedom arrived. When I threw my graduation cap in the air, I knew that my feet were not far behind. I designed a delicate plan of escape. I had told them that it was a long shot but I was going to try for a scholarship. They begrudgingly filled out their part of the paperwork for Ohio University. I explained that it was a long shot. I felt confident, however, that it would work out based on my excellent high school grades and good recommendations from my teachers. Sure enough, it did. When I got that letter from the university giving me a partial scholarship. I was beside myself. I knew that I could always find work, and along with my scholarship, I would have enough money to get by. I downplayed it to the Smiths. I told them that if it didn't work out, I could always come back to the farm. They decided that since I would need bus money to return, they would send me a few dollars each month in case I needed to come home. Little did they know that I had no plans of ever coming back. They were true to their word. They send me $50.00 each month until I graduated and went to medical school. I decided then and there to change my name. I arranged it with the bank so that I could deposit their check under my old name. I believed that they owed me that and much, much more for all my free work. I never looked back until I had to.

David was floored. His father was frugal and self-motivated and expected everyone else to be. He could understand why. He had to be calculating to be independent and self-sufficient. David had never understood why his father seemed so determined, so driven; he needed to be. Michael learned how to set goals and accomplish things. David already knew that his father never did anything without a plan. The entry made it so much easier to understand his dad's stoicism. It was born out of necessity. Tempered with overcoming adversity, it was his singular accomplishment. He could see that his father must have come to this realization much earlier in his life. Perhaps it dawned on him while he lived with the Smiths. His dad felt alone, and for that to change, he desperately needed to leave the farm. David knew about feelings of aloneness. He had decided to leave home too. Just like his father, he was determined to chart his own course. Michael had learned that lesson so well; he lived in an isolated condition that no one was able to penetrate until now.

David could see that the plane was full of passengers. He couldn't see Ayin with his hand on his shoulder whispering, "Believe." He couldn't see any of it. Yet in this fragile moment, he had a singular experience of contemplation. The sound of the engines droned into nothingness, as did the sound of the passengers coughing or moving around; the sound of the crying babies faded. His usual restless eyes settled into a state of repose. There was no noise; there was nothing to see. He was alone with his thoughts. Then the word got through. "Believe." Before he could even ask a question, the grace of God echoed in his heart, "Believe in My love for you. Believe that your father loved you. Believe that you can love others. Believe that I am bringing about what is best for you. Believe!" Then silence.

His hands were the first to acknowledge that it was the time to begin to move. They passed over the open pages of the green notebook in his lap. Then he moved his head slowly from side to side. He heard the sounds of a planeload of people pressing upon his ears like pressure. He looked around and saw that there was a rather large man sitting next to him. He looked like a business man wearing gray slacks, white shirt, and a blue striped tie that was open in the collar. He could evidently fall asleep without much help. The man had his mouth open and was rhythmically snoring. David looked at his watch to see how long he had been doing whatever that was. They had been in the air for over an hour.

"Was I sleeping?" he asked himself. "No, I was awake. I don't know what happened. Maybe I don't have to know. I am going to do exactly as God instructed. I am going to believe!" David realized that there was a lot more to digest from his father's notebook. He probably would find some of his father's memories hard to swallow. He was determined that whatever would come of it, he would believe that it would work out for the best.

The rest of the flight was uneventful. His plane landed at Sky Harbor. Jamie was going to meet him. They would go and stay at his father's place since the day after, they would all meet at Mr. Spagnolo's office in Phoenix.

Jamie was so glad to see David as she drove up to the terminal. She pulled over and popped the trunk from inside her car. He put his duffel bag in it and slammed it shut. She noticed he was carrying a large green notebook. He got into the car. Her voice crackled with excitement as she asked, "Is that the notebook you found at the cemetery?"

"Yeah, it sure is."

"What does it say?"

David could see that Jamie needed to pay attention on getting out of the airport. Sky Harbor can be a difficult task if you concentrate; focusing on something else made it impossible.

"Look, Jamie, I will fill you in when we get out of this traffic at the airport. So do you know how to get out of here?"

"Don't worry, David. I have been here a few times."

After a few fancy maneuvers, they managed to get on a road that didn't require as much attention. They were finally on the right road, going in the right direction. Talking became a little easier. David broke the quiet concentration.

"Jamie, it was an interesting experience. You know, Bob was a real help. It seemed that he knew just where to go and what leads to follow. It was more than that too. I think some divine hand was guiding us. I can't explain it. Dad had really worked to keep this part of his world secret. Now that it's coming to light, I think that I understand him better. He had some deep childhood hurts that he lived with. Dad couldn't bring himself to talk about them with anyone because the pain was so bad. I can see how this alter ego he created hid his brokenness. I don't like that he shut us out. All he did was make the wound deeper. I've been trying to forgive him. I still have a ways to go on that score."

Jamie looked across at him for a quick minute before she turned and focused back on the road. "The notebook says all that?"

"Not directly, but yes, it does. I know that Dad never intended anyone to see it. Who would have looked in the cemetery to find it? It was almost like he was putting it away. He buried his history so deep that he couldn't be reminded about it anymore. The death of his mother sealed the gravity of it all."

"Did you find out what *The Long Day's journey into Night* had to do with his story?"

David responded, "Not actually, but I think we could make some assumptions about that from some of the material in the notebook. Dad lost his entire family. His brother and sister died in the fire. His father had left the family around that time, and his mother went crazy. His only option was to stay with his grandparents. They really used him for working the farm. The notebook doesn't say it, but when you read his letter we found and read between the lines, it comes out. I think he felt somehow responsible, like he was to blame for what happened somehow."

Jamie replied with a puzzled tone, "Do you mean that he blamed himself? How is that possible, David? He wasn't even there."

"I know," David said. "It's just our impression. Bob wondered, 'Why would he go to such trouble to hide all this if he didn't feel guilty in some strange way?' It's possible the root of his guilt or fear, or whatever you call it, probably was the cause of his secretive ways. He never was really able to get close to anyone. He felt guilty or angry or confused when any kind of vulnerability was required. It does mirror the play. Dad had an amazing defense system. How was he able to keep the two worlds from running into each other?"

Jamie said quietly, "Well, at least until now."

"Yeah, that's right. You went to the theater with him. Did you notice anything odd about the play?"

"Yes, I did, and I haven't wanted to talk about it." Tears were welling up in Jamie's eyes. She quickly pulled the car over and parked in a Safeway parking lot. She turned off the engine and unbuckled her seat belt and turned toward David. She bested her left arm on the steering wheel and said, "You haven't read the play. The mother's name is Mary, and the elder son's name is Jamie. I just thought it was a coincidence about the names. Now I am not so sure. The story is about the mother's addiction and the family's dysfunction. How everyone in the family revolves around her. There is a husband named Tyrone and another son named Edmund. Do you think that

Dad was so moved by the play because it was like our family?" She had a worried look on her face.

David replied, "I'm not sure, but I don't think it was about our family as much as it was about his family growing up. His mother was a fragile woman, and she may have been addicted to codeine. She had recently gone through a divorce. She was having a hard time coping. I think that he felt the problems with his family were similar to the play." David was aware that he was trying to protect Jamie. She had been close to her father, and all this new information was a shock. It would have been insensitive and hurtful to throw a few well-placed doubts. He had to confess in his own mind that he had been guilty of those doubts. He decided to change the subject.

"How's Mom taking all of this?"

Jamie turned her head and looked out the front window. "She is not taking it well. I have given her little status reports about what you and Bob have discovered. She just nods her head and doesn't say much. It's like she's emotionally numb. Talking about it seems to make the numbness worse. Dad's death was so unexpected that just grieving the loss hasn't left much emotional energy to deal with the information you guys have discovered. I think not having a body, something tangible, has made it more difficult. Dad's passing seemed so unreal that it was easy to deny."

"How are you doing?"

"I don't know, David. Right now, I am trying to understand what happened. I will have to sort out my feelings when I have time to think about all that. *A Long Day's Journey into Night* is a good title for how I feel about life. I believe that there is a light somewhere, maybe at the end of the tunnel, but I just can't locate it. How about you? How are you feeling?"

"Finding the notebook was a complete miracle. It has made me aware of how helpful God can be." David got quiet like his words were to be carefully held and could be dropped and easily damaged. "I guess that I feel sad that he and I spent so much time and energy fighting. Sometimes, the biggest conflicts are the ones encased in silence. We just didn't know how to resolve our pain. I sincerely hope that Dad has figured that out with God."

"God? What do you mean 'God'?" Jamie said with incredulity. "You have never been a person who held out much hope for God's help before."

"That's right. I haven't been much of a fan. I have somehow experienced a change of heart. Maybe it's the journey I've been on, or it could be that I am beginning to develop some adult tendencies. I can't explain it, but I have come to believe in God. I don't feel religious or something like that. I believe that I've had an experience that cannot be described any other way. Bob and I, for example, on this trip, without knowing, stayed at the very hotel that was built right over the spot of the fire. I met this most wonderful young lady named Theresa Best. I plan to go back as soon as things with the Will and funeral get settled. If I had not been on this journey, if we had never been given the key, I would never have met her. I don't know if Dad's around, but somebody is. I think it's a God thing."

Jamie was speechless. David had never talked like this before. He was always so self-assured. He prided himself that he didn't need anyone. All that pride had evaporated.

Jamie admitted to herself that she didn't know who he was anymore. He had changed, and that meant their relationship would change too.

David sensed her resistance and discomfort. She started the car and drove out of the parking lot without saying a word.

"David, I don't know what to say. It's your business." She paused and said, "I am going to take us to Dad's apartment. We can stay there tonight and see Mr. Spagnolo for the reading of the Will tomorrow."

He could tell that she was upset by how she had changed the subject. David decided that not saying anything more about God would be a good idea. It seemed that, for some reason, Jamie had her own bruised resentment. The idea that she was nursing it surprised him.

I have done what is just and right;

do not deliver me to my oppressors.

Be surety for your servant's good;

Let not the proud oppress me.

My eyes have failed from watching for your salvation

and for your righteous promise.

Deal with your servant according to your

loving-kindness

and teach me your statutes

(Psalm 119:121-124, New Revised Standard Version)

A Time for Planting

ichael had looked up to see the Smiths walking up to the veranda. They seemed more agitated with each other. He could still feel that cloud of pain that sucked up the energy around them muscle its way toward him.

"Dr. Turner, it's nice to see you." John stuck out his hand, and Michael grasped it.

"It's nice to see you and Mary too. It's good that you decided to come and see me." He was aware that John had made it seem like the roles were reversed.

"Oh yes, thank you."

Michael inquired, "What can I do for you?"

"We—that is, Mary and I—thought it might be a good thing, that is, if Mary could see you as a patient." John was very agitated and was trying to pick his words carefully, only to come across as awkward.

Michael responded brightly, "Why, of course. That is, if the patient really wants to see me as her doctor. Is that what you want, Mary?"

She was looking down. Her arms were wrapped around her bosom as if she was protecting it. "Why, yes, yes, I would like to see you on a professional basis. It appears that the way people are disappearing around here, I shouldn't need an appointment," she said sarcastically.

He felt a little embarrassed. "Why, yes, I think I can fit you in," he said lightly. He chose not to be offended. "Please come with me. We can chat in here." Mary nodded and followed him to the first door. Michael opened it and motioned for her to go inside.

John spoke up and said, "Should I go in too?"

"I think Mary and I should meet first," Michael replied. He gave John a look that could only be translated as a no.

"Oh, that's okay. I'll wait out here in the living room."

Michael closed the door and remarked, "Why don't you sit on the exam table, and I will take your blood pressure and check your other vital signs?"

Mary looked at him and said very matter-of-factly, "That won't be necessary. We both know that there is nothing wrong with me." She took a seat in a small chair in the corner of the room.

Mary was wearing a long short-sleeved dress with a scoop neck; without a belt, it looked too large for her tiny frame. Michael thought it looked like an old maternity dress. She had her hands folded on her lap. She haltingly continued as she softly said, "Doctor, you need to know that there was no baby. I was never pregnant. I wanted to be, and I convinced myself that I was expecting. It was a pretense. I faked the contractions even to myself. When the young physician came to deliver my child that night, he knew right away that I was not going to have a baby. He knew that it was a false pregnancy. He told everyone to leave the room. He said that he had delivered the child and it died. It needed to be kept wrapped in the blanket since it was premature. He encouraged my husband to play along and say how beautiful it was. No one actually ever saw it. If they had, they would have seen that it was nothing but a small bag of flour from the pantry."

"Why would the young Doctor do that?"

"He did it to spare me the embarrassment."

"Oh yes, of course." Michael was not surprised. Many of his patients had lied to him. They would swear that they did not do drugs. Then the blood work would come back showing high levels of alcohol or street drugs. They would explain that they were taking their insulin and not drinking when it was patently obvious that they were drinking. Being a Doctor leads you to hear every kind of human subterfuge. He had never run into a case of pseudocyesis in all his years in practice. He was surprised that the correct medical term had come so quickly to his mind. "I don't understand. What possible reason do you have, given this way out of the situation, to continue to grieve the loss of your baby? Don't you know that your husband has had it with the grieving? Have you thought about how this has affected him?"

"What's the difference if I lost a real child or I lost the idea of a child? What I have gone through is far worse. If you have a child and it dies, you have been able at least to hold it, and for a time, even briefly, you know it's real. The sadness and grief will pass. Eventually, life will go on. I've never conceived, in fact, the experience of holding, cooing with, or caressing my baby. I've only had the faint hope of a child. I've only had the imagination of a new life. The suffering of that absence is far more painful. Why shouldn't my husband be familiar with my world, where the absence of something removes my hope? He did make a vow to be with me in good times and in bad. Why should he complain? After all, he is my husband. He is the father!" She cried empathically.

Michael could see that he was up against a seasoned pro. He appreciated how adeptly she twisted words to affirm her grief and isolation.

"Mary, you have a wonderful circular argument going. It doesn't recognize the feelings of your husband. John is not having nearly as much fun grieving as you are. I would say that he is contemplating making changes to your relationship."

"What changes are you talking about?"

"Mary, the stress of being in constant grief is too emotionally demanding for him. Have you ever thought of telling him the truth?"

"No, if I confessed to him what I have done, he would leave me for sure. The only way to assure that he stays is to continue with the grieving."

"Mary, what makes you think that he has not already checked out?"

"What do you mean?"

Michael pressed on, "What makes love so difficult for you that you have to substitute grief and loss for it?"

"It's the risk," Mary replied forcefully. "You never know what to expect with love. If I was to tell John, I would be risking losing him. I'm not prepared for that possibility."

Michael rubbed his hand over his brow and said, "I am sorry, Mary, but what if you have already lost him? It could be possible that he already suspects that it was a false pregnancy. It could be that he had hoped you would come to your senses and think of him and his needs for a change. Maybe he is about to give up that hope. My guess is that when the hope is all gone, he will be too."

Mary jumped up from her chair and yelled, "No, no, don't say that! I won't listen to that. He wouldn't leave me." She began to sob.

Michael came closer to her and put his hand on her shoulder. "You and John need to face the truth. It's a risk for both of you. Taking such a risk could make love possible. Without it, there is only more emotional separation."

"Doctor, what should I do? I'm frightened."

"You should be. It's a risk to love someone. It's also a great joy and happiness. I can't tell you what to do. I can only say that whatever it is, let it be the truth." Michael pointed to the closed door. "John is out there waiting. I can send him in to talk to you if you want me to. I will be here in the parlor if you need me."

She was still standing in the middle of the room with her hand clenched together. Mary nodded her head and said, "Yes, Dr. Turner, please ask him to come in."

Michael turned and opened the door and walked out to the parlor. John was sitting in one of the overstuffed chairs. When Michael came out, John stood up and walked toward him. His eyes darted from side to side and seemed to be full of questions. Michael put his hand on his shoulder and walked him to the doorway of the room.

"John, your wife and I have been talking, and she has something she needs to tell you. Please go in. I will be right outside if you need me." Before John could respond, Michael led him to the room and closed the door.

Michael found himself not knowing what to do. He became aware that there was something… He could pray. He believed that only God could make this work out. He sat down in the overstuffed chair. It felt comfortable. He just talked to God from his heart, asking him to make these two people happy together and to bless them with love for each other. He felt a familiar presence next to him with his hand on his arm. He looked up, and there was Ayin joining him in this devotion. He was surrounded by an incandescent glow of light. It was bleach white. Then it parted into every color imaginable. The colors began to shimmer and dance. Michael stood up to dance with the light. He laughed and laughed as joy enveloped his soul. He raised his arms higher and higher; his hands outstretched like the light would carry him and the joy would lift him up. Michael wanted to go on with that dance forever. The room slowly returned to its dimensions and color. He found himself alone, sitting back in the chair. He turned his head to look at the door to the exam room. It was open. He walked over and peered in and found it empty.

He sighed. *Where did they go?* he thought. Michael turned and walked out toward the veranda, and there were John and Mary hugging each other. It wasn't a desperate kind of hug; it looked natural and easy. John must have seen him coming. He left Mary and walked toward him and welcomed Michael and robustly shook his hand.

"Dr. Turner, thank you so much for your help. Mary and I have had quite a conversation. We've talked about many things. Some of them were hard to face. She told me the truth about her pregnancy. She was not pregnant at all. I told Mary that I had suspected that. I was afraid to face it, just like she was. I thought that I had failed her because I wasn't able to give her something she wanted so badly. I felt as tied to my sense of failure as she felt grief over what she couldn't have. We were both heart sick."

Michael replied, "Truth can be a powerful medicine if it's administered in love." He wondered, *Where did that piece of wisdom come from?*

Mary walked over and took John's hand. She smiled. "I'm beginning to realize just how important truth is for there to be real love. Thank you, Dr. Turner. John and I feel a sense of relief. I know him better, and he knows me too. What we were doing to each other was holding us in an unhealthy pattern of fear and pain. We both think that we can move forward with God's help. We don't know exactly what that means, but we are willing to take the risk and find out."

Michael gave them both a hug. A strong wind whipped through the veranda. The screen door slapped against the casing. The wind made a sound like a high, soft woman's voice. It wasn't harsh or shrill. It was soothing like when his mother hummed a lullaby to him when he was a small child. Funny, he thought, that he should be remembering that now. He looked back at John and Mary because he had diverted his eyes with the wind. Only they were gone.

He felt a deep sense of peace and contentment flutter around him. He recalled fleeting moments when the world was not such a bad place. Working his boyhood farm had produced some of those memories every now and then. It was sated with hardship and toil, yet it bore in its recollection the gleam of creation. Time stood still in that place even in the midst of activity. Michael knew the experience of the territory of the good earth. It held the sweet smell of the ground and the sound of nature's rhythms. It absorbed all the nutrients of past plantings like a phoenix to rise and produce a new and abundant harvest. He remembered those rare moments when life wasn't a chore but a gift, the produce of a loving divine gardener.

It left him with questions: would he ever get to heaven? Would he have to settle for only a glimpse like this?

Let The Truth Sink In

Death is not in charge; we are not the prisoners of

pain or fear.

Let The Truth Sink In

Sorrow is not our fate; doubt is not the cynical reality

of life.

Let The Truth Sink In

Despair and hopelessness do not manage our hearts

resources.

Let The Truth Sink In Jesus is alive!

Hide and Seek

The day to meet with Mr. Spagnolo and go over Michael's Will had finally arrived. The meeting was scheduled for 10:00 a.m. at his office. Jamie and David had arrived there together. Mary was driving up from Tucson. The day was rather gray and overcast. It seemed to foreshadow a difficult meeting ahead. It didn't feel like a storm, but all that was needed was a little cold air. Mary arrived just before the meeting started. Mr. Spagnolo directed them to a small conference room that had a square table and six chairs. He sat at the head of the table and passed around to everyone a two page copy of Michael's Will. David thought it was just like his dad to keep the document short and to the point. Once they were all seated, Mr. Spagnolo began to address the family.

"Michael was a really a good friend. The Will, as you can see, names me as its executer. Please read it over, then I will go over it with you point by point." There was a five-minute pause, then he continued.

"Let me summarize where we stand right now." He put on a pair of small reading glasses and looked a little self-conscious at having to use them. "Most of this you may already know. Michael was killed in a small plane crash. The accident was investigated by the NTSB. They issued a preliminary report. The Pinal County Sheriff's department also did an investigation. They determined that Dr. Turner was the passenger in the plane and that both he and the pilot Marian Anderson died in the accident. The Pinal County medical examiner has now issued a death certificate on the determination of the superior court. The circumstances of the crash have also touched off several investigations by insurance companies that have policies with Dr. Turner. The nature of the accident has fallen within the guidelines of several policies—namely, an accidental death policy that Michael had. It will pay 500,000 and a term life insurance policy for 200,000. It also includes the policy that the pilot Marian Anderson had on the plane and any passengers. It will pay a 100,000 benefit. The total amount comes to 800,000. The Will says that any money obtained by insurance payouts would be split evenly between David and Jamie. I expect that those funds will be available in the next couple of months. Michael put together a trust for his children's college education. It is to be used for that purpose. Any monies leftover or not used can be designated by them for their children's education. Right now, that trust's principle is 125,000.

"Mary, Michael wanted you to get the benefit of his investments and all the monies not spent on his funeral costs, including liquidation of assets and the sale of his practice are to go to you. I am designated to arrange for the sale of those things and the transfer of the assets after taxes and my fees to you.

"Finally, you know about Michael's other interests with the KISS Foundation. There are no liabilities or assets that the family needs to be concerned about. I do want to invite any one of you to take his place on the board of directors. It's my opinion that he would approve of a replacement from the family." With this last statement, Mr. Spagnolo looked up from his paperwork on the table and fixed his gaze for the first time on those present.

He asked, "Are there any questions?"

David spoke up, "Mr. Spagnolo, is there anything you can tell us? I mean, my father kept a part of his life very hidden from us. I appreciate what my dad is giving to us after he's gone. I never really wanted that. It's occurred to me that you knew a part of him that we have only recently discovered. What are your impressions of who he was?"

"I think your father was a very good man. He helped a lot of people, not just in his practice or by the KISS foundation. He tried to make a difference for good, and I think he succeeded more than he failed. He was also a troubled man, as you have discovered.

"Please understand I am not being critical of him. It is obvious, however, that he went to great lengths to keep a secret. He took different names, covered over his whereabouts, and walled off himself from those who tried to get too close. He got Mr. Braxton and me to play along with his game.

"The attorney-client relationship is a trusting one built on confidential requirements. I must confess to you that I tried on a number of occasions to encourage him to let you know about his hidden world. He would just patronize me and say, "Let's just leave things the way they are for now. Maybe someday, I will tell them." The day I hoped for sadly never came until after he passed away. Now you know what I knew and had to carry all these years. I must tell you that although I have lost a friend, I also have been relieved of a heavy burden."

David could see his bottom lip quiver and a glistening of tears at the edges of his eyes. It seemed that there was more to be said but a reluctance to say it, so he decided to prompt him. "Mr. Spagnolo…"

Mr. Spagnolo reached into his pocket and blew his nose and said, "Please call me Joe."

"All right, Joe, I think there is something more you want to say."

"Well, yes, there is, but now may not be the time. After all, we are here about Michael's Will, not about the feelings of some old lawyer."

Jamie replied, "Look, Mr. Spagnolo, you have given us the terms of my father's Will, and we all understand them. I think you have something you need to say and now is as good a time as any," she said with an air of demand.

Mary stood up quickly with her fists on the table and her arms locked. "I don't care what Mr. Spagnolo has to say. I've already heard enough" She looked at the little man with a mean contempt. It was quite out of character for Mary. There was a history of pain behind those words. David looked over at her to soften what he had seen and heard as rude and hostile.

"Mom," he said loudly over her anger, "what's going on?"

"David, this is between Mr. Spagnolo and me. You better just stay out of it."

David gave him a puzzled look. Joe remained focused on his papers. David could see that his hands were trembling although his face was exactly unmoved.

Joe Spagnolo's eyes darted back and forth like he was having a discussion with himself.

After a few minutes, he said, "Very well, Mrs. Turner, I had hoped to discuss this with you in private."

She glared back and said sarcastically, "I bet you did!" Her face was flushed.

"It is obvious that the conversation will happen now." He turned to look at David, and he remained sitting as he also peered over at Jamie. "Twenty years ago, I made a pass at your mother while we were at a party. I'm very sorry about it. Michael didn't want any of his family looking into his affairs. We had just started the foundation, and he was determined to keep it a secret. He thought up this little scenario to keep you away, Mary." He looked back over to her and said quietly and deliberately, "He didn't want you checking up on his financial or legal dealings."

Mary sat back down in her chair. She was shaking her head side to side as if by doing so, she could clear her mind. She murmured, "No, no, no. I don't believe you."

"He knew that you would turn me down and tell him about it. How right he was. You did exactly as he expected. He said that you just needed to stay away from me. I had some information that could prove to be, shall we say, difficult. That was true since I knew about the fire and his previous name. Michael was quite pleased with himself that our little charade had worked so well. You did stay away.

"I think Michael knew that his response to you about my silly attempt at seduction had probably hurt you. He unfortunately discounted that concern. He thought you would get over it. The things you have said indicate that you've not gotten over it at all. You might wonder why I went along with him. I've asked myself that question many times. I was a young lawyer in those days with few clients. Michael's business was the foundation to build my future.

I've never been successful enough to have a wealthy practice, but I have been steady."

"Do you expect me to believe that?" Mary charged. "Come, come, Mary, I love my wife and our three children and our five grandchildren. I honestly have no interest in anyone else, nor have I ever had those feelings."

She began to sob, embarrassed by this revelation. She covered her eyes with her hands. The truth had come out, and it was obvious to everyone.

Jamie said to him, "Why did you come on to me when I visited you last week?"

"I decided to maintain the same ruse because Mr. Braxton and I had not discussed this new development. We knew you. had information that we had tried to keep quiet. We weren't sure if our confidentiality was still warranted. We decided that telling you was a better course of action. So here we are. I'm very sorry to have to tell you. I assure you that it's the truth."

David was floored by this development. He got up and went over to his mother and wrapped his arm around her shoulders. There was a silence that nestled itself into her memory and blanked out the anger and pain. It was a momentary hush because there was nothing left to say.

Mr. Spagnolo looked at her with a very sympathetic nod of his head. He stood up and said, "There is just one more thing left to do." He pulled an envelope from the inside breast pocket of his jacket.

"I am to give you this envelope after the terms of the Will had been discussed." Mr. Spagnolo walked over to where Mary was sitting and handed the envelope to her.

"What's this?"

"I don't know. I was instructed to give it to you, and now I have done so."

Mary stared down at the envelope in her hand. She was confused. Should she open it and read it in front of everyone, or should she wait until she was alone? Anyway, there it was. Now what to do?

We are crowned by intellect and skill;

with habits of independence and thought.

We walk and move and run;

carrying the genetic palate of our world.

A noble metaphor a hodgepodge

of mysteries providence has overcome.

Potpourri

Bob Hughes had spent an enjoyable few days with his family in Dallas. He and his wife, Janice, had just returned to Phoenix. Bob knew about the meeting at Mr. Spagnolo's office with the Turner family. He was curious about how it had gone. He decided to give David a call. Odd, he thought that while he was in Ohio, he had no memory lapses. Maybe he was allergic to Phoenix or to something in his home. He decided it must be the coffeemaker's fault. The darn thing never worked for him the way it was supposed to.

There are mysteries in life. He smiled. Perhaps nothing helped him focus like a good old-fashioned treasure hunt. A puzzle had a riveting effect when combined with family characters and secrets. It even helped sharpen his mind. He felt more alert and engaged in things.

He liked David. It was refreshing to find a young man who admitted he didn't know everything. He hadn't learned yet that he could avoid answering some questions. David only knew how to give straightforward answers. He was humble enough to be teachable. It seemed that his father Michael was quite different. He didn't know how to be forthcoming or engaged. He had mastered the art of misdirection and avoidance. It probably stemmed back to the fire and its aftermath. Bob felt sure the way Michael treated others—keeping them at arm's length—was a predictor of how he treated himself. Having all his secrets was normal for him. Most people would have to work hard at maintaining such a bifurcated life. It would have been too taxing for anyone to try to carry it off and not give it away at some unguarded moment. Not for Michael. No, sir, for him, it was normal.

Bob's mind settled on Michael's history. He and David has stopped on the way to the airport and made a copy of both notebooks. Some of the photos didn't come out well, but he could still make them out. The pictures of his older brother were quite compelling. It was a revelation to know that he was a bit of a ham and could play practical jokes on people. Bob only remotely remembered his brother Bill. What he did recall tended to create a tapestry of a serious yet unreliable person. Bob found himself feeling relief at the idea that Bill was capable of having fun.

He realized that Michael's personality was far more serious. His thoughts skipped back to the play *A Long Day's Journey into Night.* It was about family's dysfunctional attempts at relationship. Michael must have seen some similarities in his own experience. Which family was it? Was it his father, Bill, and Beth and his brother and sister, Samuel and Mindy? Was it his grandparents John and Theresa Smith and his mother Beth? Was it his own family—Mary, Jamie, and David? Was it possible that his reaction to the play and its characters were like a composite of all his familial relationships? Bob was sure that it had to do with guilt. Michael was hiding something that he was ashamed about. Why would he go to such lengths to start a foundation and build it to help burn victims, specifically children? Why would he keep it so secret if he was not ashamed about something he did or failed to do? It comes down to Michael's story, and there were some significant holes that needed to be explored—the determination of those who investigated that the cause of the fire was poor wiring. What if Michael knew about the wiring or saw something that made him aware that it was a dangerous house? What if the cause of his secretive other life was because he felt ashamed by something he had done to start the fire? It could be possible that he blamed his mother; like in the play, she was emotionally absent because of her depression and addiction.

Michael had to shoulder the load of the family once his father left. That's a lot for a ten-year-old boy to have to face. His mother was probably relying on him for a lot of the work. Whatever their relationship, it probably robbed him of elements of his childhood.

It was a missing part of him that was more about an absence than a presence. Something should have been there but would never be known or felt or even missed. It was absent nonetheless. Living with the Smiths and the loss of his family was a "double down" of pain upon his fragile nature. No comfort there, only chains of chores and his solitary dream of a future away from the memories, away from the shame, away from the rural life and the empty past.

Bob could see it all in the notebook. Like looking at an impressionist painting, standing too close only confused the eye and the mind. Standing back and thinking about it brought the scene into focus. A figure emerged within the landscape of Michael's choices. Bob felt a sudden admiration for him. Michael had risen above his circumstances. He had shown great courage to pull and tug at life on its terms. He'd gone to college and medical school, had excelled and prospered. He'd raised a family and made contributions to society and been a good citizen. Yet the emptiness remained. He knew it even though he never directly said it in his journal. Every page seemed to hint at it. The death of his mother and divorce of his wife must have been powerful punches that would have stopped most fights. Still, Michael hadn't curled up in a ball and died or thrown in the towel. He went on, perhaps not knowing why, without a purpose or destination until God or fate rang the bell and stopped it. He was gone just like his brother Bill. Neither one could come back and fill in all the gaps. Looking at the copy of the notebook in his hands made him wonder, why did he write this at all?

He could have been looking for something or trying to understand his motives. Maybe he was trying to forgive his mother or himself. Maybe he just needed to write it down, to get it out of his system. Isn't that what Eugene O'Neill was doing, exposing his own dysfunctional past to bring it to consciousness? Perhaps the same can be said for any author. They all write their own story through the characters they create. When those stories are true, they resonate with everyone who reads them. That's what makes them so powerful. Michael, however, wanted no audience, no readers or publishers. He wanted his book to be buried with his mother's ashes in the past and kept there. It was a solitary book of a solitary life. Bob couldn't help but see the sadness in it. The irony was that despite his best efforts to keep it secret, the story was being told. Michael's calculated efforts to keep his own confidence had failed. It was, instead, as if some provident hand was intent on unmasking the real person.

He knew that David and the family should be back in Tucson at Mary's condo by now. Bob had their number, and he decided to get up from his leather recliner, which was no easy task, and give him a call. He was curious how the meeting with the attorney had gone. Bob wondered if there were any unexpected developments with Michael's estate.

He was surprised that after a couple of rings, David's voice said, "Hello."

"Hi, David, it's Bob. How are you doing?"

"I'm great, Bob. Everything is just real good."

Bob could hear the excitement and satisfaction m his voice. "It sounds like ·you were pleased by the meeting with the attorney."

"Oh yeah, the Will is very fair and generous to all three of us."

"David, I am curious if there were any other developments?"

"There were a few things that were very important. It might be good if you could come down to the condo on Saturday, if that's possible. I think we should discuss these things in person." There was a hint of caution in his tone.

"Yes, I think that will work. I could bring Janice. She hasn't met you and your family. I think she would like that too."

"Okay, Bob, that sounds great. I'll let everybody know the two of you are coming."

"We will look forward to getting together on Saturday."

David hung up the phone and walked over to the couch and lay down with his head on the armrest. He had felt more than a little confused by the meeting with Joe Spagnolo. He thought overall, things had gone over pretty well. The major details of who got what were settled. He never allowed himself to think of his father's estate. He really didn't want his money. What he wanted, he could never have. He'd have to settle for the financial part instead of what he really needed. Michael had always been able to give money when his interpersonal skills failed. David knew when his mind started chasing after itself, he usually ended up in the parched land of regret and angry disappointment. He resisted that journey, choosing to put a different spin on his judgments. His dad wasn't without his flaws, but so is everyone. He decided to give him some grace. He hadn't walked in his skin. Who was he to judge? If anything had shown that to be true, it was his trip to Ohio.

He closed off that line of thought and decided to wander over to the letter that Michael left his mother. Mary had decided to read the letter alone. Perhaps sometime she might share what was in it. It was a private matter, and asking her about it would be very inappropriate. She would have to decide if and when she was ready to discuss the letter with her family.

He reviewed the decisions that had been made since their return from Phoenix. It felt good to put his hands together over his heart lying there on the couch. The family decided that the memorial service for his dad would be held in Phoenix. All his friends, patients, and collogues lived there. The couple had built their family and made their life there. Mary had called Good Shepherd Anglican Church and arranged for the service. His mom knew the old pastor. They had gone to Good Shepherd mostly on holy days or for some special event. Both he and his sister had been baptized there.

Jamie was busy preparing the obituary to go in the newspaper in Phoenix and Tucson. She had a couple of nice photographs of Michael that were taken recently. There was no body, or even remains, to bury. David felt the absence again when he thought about that. It was so like his father to skip out from the final act. No bows or curtain calls. No big deal. Just keep it simple. A smile reluctantly filtered across his face. "Dad, it is so true to form, standing back in the shadows." It was then, thinking about that solitary figure, that the tears began to come. Someone looking at him might have thought he was laughing. It was an odd emotional release of sadness and irony. He said out loud, "How can I say good-bye to you, Dad?" He thought, *I'll have to do the best I can. As usual, you have not given me a lot to work with.*

Mary was busy making plans for the reception after the service. It couldn't be held outside; it could be just too hot. The evening temperature might be uncomfortable.

She decided to have it downtown, not far from the church, at the Hyatt Hotel. The time for the funeral mass was ten on Saturday, June 30. She had no idea how many to plan for. It was decided that a buffet would be the best way to go. She had called the florist. She and Jamie were going over later this afternoon to pick out the arrangements for the church and the reception. Mary was glad for the busy details, which kept her occupied. They provided some respite from the thoughts of the meeting with Joe Spagnolo. She was grateful that Michael had been so generous. It was true that he'd always provided well for the family.

She sat on the edge of her bed with the letter loosely held in her right hand. It was quiet. The moment seemed right to read it. She carefully pulled and tore the envelope open. She took out a single page from inside. Her hands trembled as she carefully unfolded the letter. It was in Michael's handwriting and was difficult to read. He was a Doctor with the usual proclivities for speed writing. She could see that he had tried to make the words more legible.

Dear Mary,

If you are reading this letter, then I have left this world. I need to tell you that I love you and Jamie and David. I think that I have left your with resources that should help you live comfortably. I know that I have not been what you wanted in a husband. I know that I left too many things on the back burner for too long. If a had been able to share more of myself with you, perhaps you would have still been my wife. I do not have the heart of a poet. I wish I could have told you a million things. I just never took the risk. Maybe wherever end up, I will find out why. Pray for me, forgive me, and think of me now and then.

With Much Love Always,
Michael

Tears began to roll down her face. It was a letter from a subscriber to melancholy. It gave several clues but no direct evidence. Mary felt the same old battle lines of fear. She realized that despite her tears, she was really angry at him. He knew how to bring out her hostility with a feigned remark of hopeless inevitability. He did ask for her forgiveness. That was something new for him. He usually just said he was sorry. Michael would then shrug his shoulders and walk away. He would discount her feelings by saying, "Women!" and shaking his head as if some mysterious force was now in charge of the conversation. Her feelings were far too complex and difficult for someone of his sex to understand. It had been a well-worn path of escape for both of them.

She wadded up the letter in as tight a ball as she could. If she could have strangled it to death, she would have. She threw it against the wall, hoping it would disappear and take with it all the pain. It landed on the floor, and despite her intentions, there it was. Mary lay back and rolled onto her side ori the bed and stayed in a fetal position. She quietly sobbed. The emotional intensity slowly drained away, leaving her exhausted. Her breathing became rhythmic and deeper as she went to sleep. Ayin was there, quietly speaking words of comfort in her ear.

Jamie had been out getting a few things at the store. They needed milk, ice, water, and some paper stuff. David got up from the couch and met her at the door to help unload the car. She was wearing a tight pair of jeans, white sneakers, and a white cotton top. She had gotten more than a few looks at the store. The thought of that attention made her smile. Jamie felt good about her dad's Will. It was fair to everyone. She hauled the last plastic bag full of groceries onto the kitchen countertop. David told her that Bob and his wife, Janice, were coming over on Saturday. She was happy to hear it. Jamie was feeling confused by the many facets of the situation surrounding Michael's death. Bob had a way of looking at the parts and seeing how they fit. She had decided that whatever came of piecing the puzzle together, she would be a willing partner. The door to her mother's bedroom was closed. *Well,* she thought, *Mom is probably taking an afternoon nap.* She put away the last box of Kleenex and walked over to the couch and lay down. David had gone down the hall and into the office to work on the computer. Jamie felt a relaxing little nap coming on too. It had been a busy last couple of days. It was time to let go of all the intensity, if only for an hour or so.

Her father had been a difficult person to get to know; that's why he had so few friends and an ex-wife. Jamie knew that she loved her dad. She had always been the one offering support by giving him an ever-so-slight ray of hope with a hug or a smile. She thought that if only dad and God could talk it out, healing would come into his fractured heart. She smiled at that idea. Her father would have a million questions. He would keep God very busy. Slowly, she relaxed and dropped off into that world where the music of her heartbeat played and where dreams lived.

"In the covert of the cliff,

let me see your face,

let me hear your voice;

For your voice is sweet,

and your face lovely,

Catch us the foxes,

the little foxes,

that ruin the vineyards—

for our vineyards are in

blossom."

(Song of Solomon 2:14b-15, NRSV)

Slack Time Out

Michael was feeling pretty good about his work. Caring for people seemed to be coming easier for him. Almost all the people he helped disappeared into heaven. He was happy in knowing that in some way or another, they moved on to a fuller life. He felt a tug in his heart to join them. He thought, *It might be a good idea to go check up on Morgan Slack.*

He took a few steps down from the veranda and, walking down the path, headed over to his house. The air, which had been warm and mild with a slight breeze, began to feel a little heavy and muggy as he got closer to the house. He could see Morgan sitting in an old wooden rocking chair on his porch, reading a book.

"Hi, Morgan," Michael said loudly as he waved his hand above his head. He didn't want to startle him, so he decided to give him fair warning that he was approaching.

Morgan just raised his hand and waved back. He didn't take his eyes off the book but continued reading as Michael got closer. He noticed that Morgan had a younger-looking face if not younger, then at least more peaceful and less intense.

"What are you reading?" he said as he arrived at the porch.

"Oh, it's not a book but a play entitled *A Long Day's Journey into Night* by Eugene O'Neill. Have you read it?"

"Yes, I have, and I saw the play once."

Morgan stopped rocking and looked up and said, "It's a sad story, isn't it? About a family that are mostly toxic to each other. It doesn't seem like anything I would read. It's not a scientific journal or a book on physics or chemistry. It does say a lot about the human condition. We are such fragile creatures. We often make our small part of the world a very difficult place."

"You're probably right. It's a play that would make some people uncomfortable."

Michael continued, "You see the mother is a drug addict and the family revolves around her use of 'medicine.' It isn't one of those happy-ending plays. It really is about how broken people tend to maintain patterns of distrust and pain."

"You see, Doctor, it struck me. I mean, I finally figured it out. We are here in this place. There is no time here, wherever this is." He waved his hand in a circle around his head. "No time means there is no materiality and, if that's true, no motion. Scientific inquiry requires change and measurements and motion. There's no need for science here. It's a futile effort to try to even be involved in the process of scientific inquiry. If the nature of this place is timeless, then what are we to do here? I think the answer is, since scientific study is not necessary, that leaves only one other option—that is to explore the nature of relationships. There's no need to be obsessed with answers that cloud our minds with proving or disproving our latest theories of the universe. It's melted down into this reality. What matters forever is what we care about. Take away time and the light of God can emerge from behind the cloud of our intellectual vanity. Many people don't believe because they are addicted to the notions that time provides. It's a false god because it cannot be sustained. They defend time's power and value. Who needs God when human beings find time and motion far more intellectually stimulating? When time runs out, as it does for everyone, that false god must end with it. We are left with the naked truth of God's goodness and love forever."

Michael sat down on the porch with his hand on his chin and his elbow on his leg. "Are you saying that we are to stay here forever? I mean it's an okay place, and I think it beats some of the alternatives. Still, there must be more."

"Oh, yes, Doctor, there is more. Billy and Cindy discovered it when they grew to love each other. I'm becoming aware of what really matters here. Before I could see it, I had to give up the quest of finding a scientific explanation. There is none because there's no need for science in this place. There is only one thing that matters, and that's love and caring."

"I think I understand, Morgan. I know too that things here seem real enough and solid to the touch and comparable to what I knew."

"Yes, Doctor, that's true. There is something different though. It's as if God placed us in parts of this precious world to transition into His. I want to thank you for your help." Morgan's tone was softer and compelling. "I would have never come to know this without your guidance."

Michael was shocked by this compliment. He was expecting Morgan to be unhappy and disagreeable. Instead, he was teaching him and giving him encouragement.

"How did I do that?"

"When I dragged Billy to see you, I was looking for you to agree with me. You did something different. You listened to both of us. I realized then that I should be doing the same."

"Billy is a fine young man. He is committed to telling the truth. Why not? He learned that virtue from his father," Michael replied.

Morgan began a chuckle that built up to a cascade of laughter. Ha-ha-ha! It made his shoulders go up and down and his eyes bug out. He coughed and took a deep breath. Michael laughed too.

"This is funny. Look, here we are, in a place that seems solid and real to us. It feels like we are living and moving and changing. We are in a dimension where existence isn't defined by measurable time frames. I have to tell you that it makes no intellectual sense. That is the beauty of it, and that's what's funny."

"What do you mean?" Michael asked with a tone of curiosity.

"I mean there is no need for an intellectual defense. Many people use science or something like it as a way of being in control of their environment. It works most of the time, except when machines break down or when nature does something unexpected. Science will fall short. Timelessness will eventually exert its real dominance. Even though we know that it will, we are determined to trust in ourselves.

We have no need for an outmoded idea like God to fracture our fantasy. We believe that we can do quite well on our own since we can't prove His existence anyway. Thank the god of science that it came along just in time to rescue us from our consciences. We think that if science fosters knowledge of any kind, it must be good. We blindly worship at the altar of our limited reason. That's what I've done. I kept everyone at arm's length. I developed my scientific mind as a hedge against my heart. I manipulated Billy to be just like me. I have little to do with anyone. I am an intellectual hermit. I believed that my knowledge and education made me better than everyone. I would never admit to that attitude, but that's what I believed. A sophisticated defense like mine is well guarded and hard to confront personally and publicly."

"So what are you going to do about it?"

"I've decided to give my intellectual doubt a rest."

"What do you mean?'

Morgan stood up and stretched. He put the book down on the seat of the rocker. "I am going to change my attitude. It doesn't seem like a big thing, but it is. I intend to put aside my denial and pride and discover who God is on His terms. I've decided to stop trying to explain everything and instead let God reveal Himself as He wants."

Michael stood up too and approached Morgan and put his hand on his shoulder and said with a serious tone, "What if He takes you up on that offer?"

Morgan looked back at Michael, studying his face close up. "Well then, Doctor," he said with a chuckle, "the adventure would begin. I don't think He would be impressed with my degrees or how many books I've read or classes I've taken and taught. I did enjoy them. I realize that in the area of love and caring, I have a lot to learn."

Morgan began to walk off the porch and around toward the back of his house. There was a tree back there that had an old tire hanging from a rope attached to a limb. Michael walked with him. Morgan scrunched into the tire and gently swung back and forth.

"I think the first thing I'm going to do, Dr. Turner, is try out this old swing. Billy loved to come back here and do this."

"It looks like fun," Michael replied.

Michael heard his name being called. The voice sounded like Josh. He turned and looked up the path. He saw him running up to the big house. Michael looked at Morgan, who had a look of delight on his face as he swung back and forth.

Michael said, "It sounds like Josh is looking for me. I need to get to the office. Please excuse me. I have to go."

"Oh, that's okay. I think I'll enjoy the experience and just swing here."

Michael said good-bye and hurried up the path. He looked back and knew what he would see. The swing was still moving, but Morgan had disappeared. *I guess,* he thought, *God accepted his offer.*

He waved and shouted. Josh turned and saw him coming up the path. They met just in front of the main house. Josh was hot and sweaty. Something was bothering him.

"You need to come with me. I have to show you something very important." Michael had never seen him so concerned.

"Sure, I'll follow you."

Trying to catch his breath, Josh replied, "Well, let's go then."

Canyons bright with

color, filled with glory

Arizona!

Colossal majesty,

with splendor,

stilled with ecstasy

Arizona!

Mountains Height

and copper, mined

with subtlety,

Arizona, my home!

Memories

David had brought the two green notebooks back from Ohio. Everyone had a chance to go through them on their own. Each time David studied them, he seemed to feel a little more at peace with his father. He had to admit that his dad had left behind quite a legacy—his own adult children, a foundation to help burn victims in Ohio—a successful medical practice, financial resources for his family, and even a few good childhood memories. Ayin, who was standing next to him, nodded and smiled with each recollection.

David was startled by the doorbell even though he expected company. He went and opened the front door. It was Bob and Janice Hughes. David was happy and excited to see Bob and meet Janice. He welcomed them and gave Bob a hug and Janice a kiss on the cheek. He felt a sense of family with them even though he had just met Janice. They fit together like a pair of well-worn gloves.

She had graying hair and a triangular face with brown eyes and a broad well-practiced smile. She was not beautiful, but she was attractive. Janice was dressed in a casual style. She wore a red blouse with a scoop neckline and tan slacks with brown shoes. Her taste in jewelry was a bit ostentatious—big earrings and a large amber necklace. She talked with her hands; motion and communication seemed to be the same thing. David's found her to be delightful. Bob could be a grouch, but Janice made up for him with her bubbly personality. He could see that they balanced each other's weaknesses with their own strengths.

David thought of the romantic e-mails he and Theresa were exchanging and hoped that they would be a couple like Bob and Janice years down the road. Jamie entered the room first. Mary made her entrance a few minutes later. The introductions were made, and drink orders were filled. It didn't take long before the men set off together and the ladies gathered in their circle. David thought how funny it was that this mutual segregation happened without any prompting. Bob came up and said, "Well, I see it's time for us to talk about guy stuff."

"Bob, you must have been reading my mind. There has to be some magic signal that they all know. I think it is a relational equation unknown to men. The number of women multiplied by the number of men divided by two times squared equals time. It determines the exact ratio that requires separation and grouping."

Bob looked over at the ladies, who were laughing and talking about some kind of sale on shoes. He let out a big sigh and shook his head. He looked at the beer in his hand and asked, "So what's going on with the estate? How is everyone doing?"

"I think my father was very fair. Jamie and I will receive about $400,000 each. Mom's to get the proceeds from selling Dad's practice and the properties. It hasn't been determined yet, but it will probably be more for her. Dad also left behind a generous educational trust for us and our children."

"Gee, that's great, Dave. There must have been something more to the reading of the Will because you wanted to talk about it in person."

David sat down on a chair near the rarely used fireplace. Bob sat down opposite him in an oak rocker. "Yes, several things were very surprising."

Bob asked curiously, "Like what?"

"Well, Mr. Spagnolo, at one point, confessed that although he had made a pass at my mother years ago, it was my father's idea so that she would not find out about the foundation. They had rehearsed and planned it out. My father would just tell her to stay away from him. My mother interpreted his advice as abandonment. Dad probably didn't know the emotional price they both paid. The second thing was that Mr. Spagnolo gave Morn a letter from Dad to be read by her alone on the event of his death. I don't know for sure if she even read it or what's in it. The contents of the letter were meant to be private, unless Morn chooses to share them."

Bob rubbed his face with his right hand. He turned his head up and looked at the ceiling as if somehow an answer would be found up there. "A wise man told me that you cannot not tell your story. It means that this is a story about Michael. Things that have happened are pieces of the story that are trying to be told, and will be told, if we listen."

David said, "That's interesting, Bob. What are you suggesting?"

"Dave, let me first say that what I am going to propose is only a theory. I think it explains a few things. I mean no disrespect to your father's memory. These things have been floating around in my mind. Most of this case revolves around your father's pain and guilt. It must have been a terrible thing for him to lose his brother, sister, and, mentally, his mother to the fire. The foundation was a way to get some redemption from the suffering he felt. I think that Michael knew something about the reason for the fire. I don't think he purposely did anything to cause it. I think that he may have suspected something or should have intervened in some way.

"The fact that he buried the memories of his family with his mother's ashes tells me how intense the secret was, and the metaphor of ashes points to the fire. It was put in a place to be forgotten and hidden away forever. The fixation on the play isn't so much about his family being like the Tyrones. Although there is definitely some of that. It's more about the frailty of the human condition. The way people block real communication. We discover in the play that Edmund, the son, has consumption TB. He tries desperately to tell his mother. She is locked into a world of addiction and avoidance. You keep hoping that she will listen to his pain. She never does. Maybe Michael had something he wanted to tell his mother, something important about the fire, but his mother's mental state never let him. Like the play, she was so disconnected and into her own reality. I found this picture in the notebook. It was taken when Michael was a young boy." Bob took out a small photo from his shirt pocket. In the picture, Michael was holding his mother's hand out by the screen door on the porch of their house. "See, you can't make out if they are going somewhere or coming back from somewhere." Underneath it were these words, 'If only I could get you to listen.' Bob continued 1 "What was it that he needed or wanted to tell her?"

"How would we be able to find that out? Dad is not here to tell us. Besides even if we did find out, what difference would it make?"

Quickly, Bob interrupted before David could formulate the next question. "It's important because it was so huge an influence in your father's life. It might help you understand what motivated him."

"I don't even know if I want to understand the whole story. There are a lot of loose ends that are hard to make sense of." Thinking about his father's double life only confused and angered him. "There are a lot of half truths to deal with. It's like Dad had a part-time life," David angrily replied.

Bob bent over and put his hand of David's shoulder. Speaking softly, he said, "Nobody chows down on a lie that is obviously untrue. We swallow it one small bite at a time. Usually, such a diet produces a sour stomach. Believe me. I know something about that kind of nausea. When the truth comes out, I've noticed that there is a sense of relief. There's a craving for a new opportunity. I hope discovering the whole story will help all of us. We may be able to move past the grief and experience healing and even redemption."

David made no reply except to nod his head and agree. Bob knew that David's acknowledgement meant he had signed on.

The ladies had decided it was time to include the men in their discussion. Jamie glided over and invited David and Bob to join them. The women resumed the conversation about the funeral service. Bob looked over at David and gave him a nod. (It suggested, *Let's keep this under our hats for now.)* David shook his head and mouthed the word *okay.*

The funeral was a week away. The plans were well organized and moving forward. David feigned interest. His mind was still spinning back to what Bob had said. He tried to stay focused on the conversation, attempting to look involved. He was having no success. His mind returned to the puzzle of the fire, Michael, and his mother. He had a hunch that somehow, more of his father's story would come to light.

Ayin stood invisibly next to him and smiled, nodding his head as if to say yes.

Jamie came over to David and offered him a drink of white wine. She looked like a woman with something on her mind. She whispered, "Let's take a walk out to the backyard. I need to talk with you."

"Sure." David took her arm and guided her to the back door and into the backyard. "What would you like to talk about?"

"The Dark Night of the Soul"

St. John of the Cross

One dark night,

fired with love's urgent longings

—ah, the sheer grace!—

I went out unseen,

My house being now all stilled.

In darkness, and secure

by the secret ladder, disguised,

—ah the sheer grace—

in darkness and concealment,

my house being now all stilled.

On that clad night,

in secret, for no one saw me,

nor did I look at anything,

with no other light to guide

than the one that burned in my heart.

The Dark Night

Josh led the way, and Michael followed right behind. They got to the big old tree near the cave that led to Perdition. When they arrived, Michael suspected that something had happened to Mr. Schley.

"Look here!" Josh yelled and waved for Michael to come where he was bending down.

Michael went over to him. "What is it, Josh?"

"See these muddy footprints?" He stood up and pointed. "They lead right to that cave." Josh was visibly upset and concerned. "I have looked everywhere, and I have not found Bradley Schley."

Michel saw the muddy footprints leading directly to the cave. "Oh no!" he exclaimed. "What will happen to him? What can we do?"

"Dr. Turner, I don't think there is anything to do. He decided on his own to go down there."

"Josh, he's my patient, and I have to do everything I can to save him."

"I can't let you go down there by yourself. We might lose you too. No, sir, you're not going down there."

Michael took a deep breath and asked, "Would you go down there with me?"

"Dr. Turner, a lot of bad stuff could happen down there. I don't think it's a good idea."

Michael interrupted, "Josh, if the two of us go, it would be easier to get him and ourselves out."

"Doctor, what will we do if the man doesn't want to be rescued?"

"I don't know, Josh. I just believe that he does even if he doesn't know it. A lot of people who go to the Doctor don't know what they need. They have tried everything to get themselves better. Nothing has worked so they come to see me. Patients go to the Doctor not because they know what they need but because they don't. Bradley Schley has made a poor choice. He may not know he needs saving, but I do because I am a Doctor."

"Doc, since you put it that way, I think we have to at least try." Josh looked directly at him.

Michael asked, "What are we going to need to get down there?"

"Not too much. A good strong rope. I have that over by the big tree. We're going to need something for light. I have a couple of oil lamps that I always keep around. They are over there, too under the big tree. There's a lot of oil in them. They should be long lasting enough for our needs."

"Well then, Josh," Michael said with a tone that exuded command, "let's get down there." He knew this would be difficult. It was risky, and he was fearful. Having Josh go with him made it feel less intimidating.

Josh went into action. He tied one end of the rope around the old tree. He made a special knot that would have made any sailor smile with pride. He collected the two lanterns and returned to Michael.

Josh wrapped the rope around his waist and tied the end around Michael. "You're going to have to take this lantern and lead the way down. I will be behind you to pull you up if something happens. If we find him, I'll help pull you both up. You might have to carry him. If we take it a little at a time, we should be all right. One thing, Doc, it is windy and noisy and dark. Be sure of your footing, and don't let go of the lantern. Do you understand that?"

"Yes, I understand."

"Okay then, you go first since you're the Doctor." Josh smiled and pointed to the cave's entrance.

Michael shook his head and ambled over to the mouth of the cave. It was the closest he had ever been to it. He could hear the wind howling like a low growling animal. It scared him. His legs felt rubbery and resistant to go on. He decided to hold on to the hope that something good could happen even in this place. It was strewn with large boulders that he had to negotiate to get inside. He looked intently down into the darkness. He checked back to see Josh about ten feet behind him.

He yelled out, "Josh, what if we run out of rope?"

"Don't worry about that. It should be long enough."

"Okay, if you say so."

Michael started to go down into the darkness. He was aware that the cave was going down. It wasn't steep but gradual at first. The most pressing thing he noticed was the wind whipping against his clothes. It was creepy and cold. It made a sound that grew louder the further into the cave they went. His lantern was affected too. It produced light, but the darkness was pervasive and resistant to it. He could only make out an area around his feet. That's why after walking some distance, they did not hear or see the large barred metal gate close and lock behind them.

Michael looked back to see if he could spot Josh. He could make out the movement of his lantern like a fuzzy smudge of light. It was pointless to call out. He would never hear him. He began to think how stupid he was for this hairbrained idea. He should have stayed in safety. Now he was in real trouble. What if he could never get out of here? He said to himself, "I was the guy that said if someone didn't want help, leave him alone. Here I am, the great Dr. Turner, looking for someone who's not worth the risk or the trouble." Then it hit him. This place is affecting me with self-doubt and fear. It was surrounding and coxing him with anger and inevitability.

The cave reminded him of something. It was that same feeling of being lost, of envelopment and isolation that he felt before the plane crash. That moment when hope was almost obliterated, he cried out to God for help. It was like his soul was being overcome by the darkness too. He had seen a cave then. Could this be the same one? He held on more tightly to the lantern, clinging to what little light it provided. "I still have to find him. I have to find Bradley

Schley," he yelled at the top of his voice. The putrid wind crushed the words as soon as they left his mouth.

His foot slipped. He regained his balance. The rocks under his feet had become slippery. Some kind of slime covered everything. He didn't want to know what it was. He chose not to look. Judging by the rankness of the air, it was not good. It smelled like some of the surgical cases he observed during his residency when a limb had to be amputated or an infected wound debrided. The memory was nauseating.

He took another step, slipped again, and, this time, fell sliding down into the cave. He suddenly stopped. He grabbed on to a slimy rock outcropping. "Thank God for Josh. He saved me," he sighed out loud. Michael managed to hold on to his lantern. Amazingly, the light hadn't gone out. He reached around the outcropping that helped stop his fall. He tried to get a better grip before deciding his next move. Maybe they had gone as far as they could go. Maybe it was too late to help Mr. Schley. He prayed, "Good Lord, it would be wonderful if this hurricane would let up."

He felt something touch the top of his hand. It startled him. He had not seen any indication that something or someone else was there. He had visions of ugly demons or ghosts. He was terrified to look and find out. He held up his lantern and gazed at the creature that he shared the same big couple of boulders with.

Shivering in the darkness was Bradley Schley. He was scrunched up in a fetal position, knees under his chin, with his back against the rocks. He was dirty and squinted his eyes when Michael brought the lantern closer.

Bradley motioned for him to move so he could talk directly into his ear. Michael slid his body to his left until they were shoulder to shoulder. Bradley cupped his hands and put them up against his head like a small megaphone to talk into.

"Dr. Turner," he yelled into his ear, "what are you doing here?"

Suddenly, the howling winds quieted. They were still there, but it was like someone put a big blanket over them. Michael took the opportunity to check in with Josh instead.

He yelled, half expecting the wind and noise to return, "Josh, are you there?"

"Yes, sir, I am here, about ten yards behind you."

"Thanks for holding on to the rope. I was sliding pretty fast. I don't know what would have happened if you hadn't been able to stop my fall. Hey, guess what. I have Bradley with me. We've found him."

Josh replied excitedly, "That's great. It's not going to be easy getting out of here."

Michael responded, "I will let you know when we are ready to climb out."

"Okay. Just say when."

Michael inquired, "Bradley, can you walk?"

"I don't know. I started sliding, and I was able to grab on to this rock. Don't ask me how. I just did." Michael picked up a tone in his voice that indicated feelings of relief. "Did you come down here to find me?" he asked with a sense of disbelief.

"Yes, Brad, we both did."

"Why?"

"You are my patient, and I have a responsibility to do everything I can to help you. God gave you to me to care for, and I intend to do just that."

"Look, Doctor, I deserve to be in this place. It's my fate. It's inevitable. Nobody can change that."

"That's not true," Michael replied with frustration. "We haven't given up on you. We came down here to save you. It's going to take your participation for all three of us to climb out of here. I don't think you really want to be here for all eternity because you clung on to this rock so tightly."

"Dr. Turner, I want to go with you. But you don't understand. I know things, dark and hidden things. I have done terrible, harmful, and hurtful deeds. How can I go with you, back into the light? What would happen to me if I gave up my secrets? Who would I be without them? I've carved out an identity that suits me and makes me feel cozy in the shadows. How can I give it up? For what?"

"Brad, you were not created to live in the dark. You fear being destroyed if you came face-to-face with the light of love. That's why we came down here to get you, to tell you that you won't get annihilated by the light. You can become a free person. If you give up the fear, something wonderful will take its place. Look at where fear has brought you. Life is so much more than this. Come with us, and find out how wonderful it can be."

"Yes, Dr. Turner, I want to go with you and Josh. My legs are too weak. I can't even get up. You will have to help me."

"Brad, I will help you, but you have to try to push forward too. Thank God the wind and the noise have, for some reason, backed off. I think we need to leave now. Let's try to stand first." Michael pushed himself up against the rock and stood up. Bradley needed a hand. Michael grabbed his arm and pulled while Bradley pushed up with his other hand and used his knees to straighten up. He was standing too. He leaned against Michael.

"I am too unsteady. I need your support," he said in a raspy voice.

Michael yelled out, "Josh, we are ready to try to take some steps. I need some rope to wrap around him in case we should fall."

"Okay, Doc, here is some slack."

Michael wrapped the rope around Bradley and tied a knot. "Okay," Josh yelled back. "I will back up as you come forward. Take it easy. Try to keep the rope tight. Don't let it get too much slack."

Michael turned and put his left arm around Bradley, and in the other held on to the lantern. He said, "Let's get going, Brad." The first steps they took were to leave the safety of the rocks. They both stumbled, yet they managed to take a few steps and not fall.

The ground was slippery and steep. Josh continued to pull them along, and Michael and Bradley, at times, half crawled, going very slowly and deliberately.

The cave was filled with difficult obstacles. They became a little easier to negotiate without the wind and with Josh's help. Mr. Schley was still having a hard time. He fell and landed on his side. Michael fell too trying to hold on to him.

"Dr. Turner, I can't go on. I just don't have the strength. You and Josh can leave me here and save yourselves."

"No, Brad, we are going to get out of here together, even if I have to carry you."

Bradley looked over at Michael with tears in his eyes. "I think that's what it will take because I can't even get up."

"Okay then, that's what we will do."

Michael yelled out to Josh, "Bradley can't go on. He's too weak. I am going to carry him on my back. Is that okay with you?"

Josh yelled back out of the darkness, "It sure is. Be careful that somebody holds the lantern. Don't lose it." His voice sounded encouraging and concerned.

"Yeah, I got that, Josh." Michael looked over at Bradley. He motioned with his head to get Brad's approval of this idea. Brad nodded and tried to feign a smile.

They managed to help each other stand. Michael had him take a couple of steps on the side of a boulder. Michael backed up to him and gave him the lantern to hold. Bradley maneuvered so that he could put his arms around Michael's neck. Michael put his hands around Brad's legs. The old crab carry.

Michael remembered how he would carry Jamie and David around the house when they were little, and they would laugh and laugh and laugh. He felt sad for all the special times he missed with Mary and the children. How he wanted those times back to do over. God would forgive him. He prayed that they would too. Somehow, when he remembered those few glorious days, Bradley felt lighter and easier to carry.

He saw that there was one light in the darkness like a star, and as they ascended, it began to grow larger. He called out to Josh, "What's that star up there? It seems to be getting bigger."

"That is the entrance to the cave. We're getting closer to getting out."

Michael was excited by that news. "Do you hear that, Brad? We are almost home."

He just made a groaning sound.

Michael adjusted his grip and continued to climb. He realized that Bradley seemed smaller and lighter. Each step made him feel happier. Each step took them closer to safety. The star burned brighter and brighter, flooding the cave with light. Michael's mind reached back to his childhood, remembering that story about the star that led the way to Bethlehem. The world was in darkness waiting for a new beginning. Now it was here. He could almost touch it. A new beginning was waiting for him in that universe of light and glory. *Follow that star. We are home free. Nothing can stop us now!*

He could easily make out the edges of the cave. It was hard to look at the light directly. He looked down or to the right or left. It would take effort for his sight to return. That's why he didn't see the closed gate. It was right in front of him. If Josh hadn't said something, he would have run right into it.

"Hold up, Dr. Turner," Josh commanded.

"Josh, what's the matter? Why aren't you up ahead?" Michael stopped, looked at Josh, and realized that there was a locked gate in front of them. "What's this?" He put Bradley down in a pocket of the cave. He didn't notice anything different about him. He was focused on getting out of Perdition.

"It's locked, Doc," Josh replied.

"What do you mean locked?" he exclaimed.

"I mean we can't get out of here without the key to unlock that door."

"Josh, we can't stay in this awful place. We need to open that gate!"

Bradley said, "It's impossible to get out of here without the key."

Michael's hopes fell. He grabbed the gate and shook it. Nothing happened, except he made himself feel more helpless and angry. He asked in a way that said he was open to suggestions, "How do we get out of here?"

I live, in a universe of fractured space.

We rely, upon the mystery of God's grace.

I move, among the fragments of old time.

We grow, together as love's refined.

Fragments

It was obvious by the way Jamie almost pushed him outside that she had something on her mind. The air was hot and breezy, and it caught his attention. She was concerned about the letter her mother received from Michael. Mary hadn't said anything about it. Jamie was worried about her mother's emotional well-being.

Her mother had gone through a lot: the divorce, Michael's death, the revelations about him, and now the letter. She grabbed David's arm and said, "I am worried about Mom." Her face had little furrows on her forehead. She had a glistening of tears close to the edges of her eyes. He was aware that she felt vulnerable.

"What concerns you about Mom?"

"She hasn't dealt with her feelings about Dad's death. She's busy making plans for the funeral. It's like she is so busy she won't allow herself to grieve. I'm afraid that when all this hits her, it could be very devastating. Emotionally, I don't think she's in a good place."

David tried to give her a reassuring look coupled with a pat on her shoulder. "I hear you about that. She has been distant and private. Those types of qualities are more in keeping with Dad's personality than with hers. Should one of us try to talk to her and see if she will open up?" David asked.

"I don't think that you or I should ask her. She knows us too well. We are her kids. It should be somebody else. Maybe Bob could talk to her."

David explained, "He would like to talk to Mom. I know that he has some questions that she could answer about the fire and Dad's childhood."

"What could Mom tell him about that?" she replied with a look of confusion.

"It might have something to do with the letter. If Bob could see it, who knows, there might be something in it that could explain more about Dad's story."

"David, I don't know if she wants to talk about that. She hasn't been very supportive about looking into Dad's past. The whole fiasco with the attorney Joe Spagnolo comes to mind," she said with a note of sarcasm.

"Look, Jamie, if you're so concerned about Mom, then something has to be done to help her get this stuff off her chest. I can't make her talk to Bob, but I think she should."

She was feeling torn about the idea and sorry she brought it up. "David, I think she needs a therapist, not an investigator."

"You are probably right about the therapist, but she might need an investigator too."

"Why?"

"Because Bob might help her get to the facts. Mom is going to have to face them sooner or later so she can grieve Dad's death."

Jamie stood there with her arms across her chest. She said nothing for a few minutes.

"Okay, David, if you think it will help. I'll mention the idea to her and see what she says. Don't be surprised if she turns it down."

Jamie waited till an opportunity presented itself for the two of them to talk. She didn't have to wait long. Mary got up from her chair to put on a sweater. She was feeling cold because David had set the air conditioner lower than how she liked it. Jamie got up at the same time and followed her into the bedroom.

David was busy having a political discussion with Bob, and Janice was trying to keep it from becoming personal. It would probably go on for a while.

Jamie came up behind Mary and said, "Mom, I think we need to visit."

Mary turned and faced her and asked, "About what?"

"David and I think that you might feel better if you talked to Bob about the letter."

"What! Why should I talk to him about that? He's a stranger to me. I don't talk to strangers about personal things like that." Her face and tone had an edge of hostility and disapproval.

"Mom, when someone needs health care, they go to the emergency room for help. They get a doctor or nurse they never met before. We think that Bob has some of the facts that might help you grieve through this. David and I aren't interested in seeing the letter. We only want what's best for you."

Mary was full of contradictory feelings. It was as if the anger, hurt, and pain had tied a knot that looped around her heart and began to squeeze. "Let's sit down on the bed for a minute," she said while taking a few deep breaths.

"Are you all right?" Jamie put her arm around her. She felt a wave of guilt for raising the subject.

"Yes, I'll be okay. I just was having an anxiety attack. Since the divorce, I've had these every so often. Your analogy of the emergency room was apropos. I've had a recent visit to the ER thinking I was having a heart attack."

"What did the doctors say?" Jamie was surprised that her mother had never mentioned this.

Mary took Jamie's hand and patted it. "They gave me some medication and wanted me to stay away from stress and do yoga or some such thing." Mary began to laugh, and so did Jamie. It broke the tension. "What possible reason should I have to be stressed?"

They laughed together.

"Darling," she said softly, "have I been unbearable to be with?"

"No, not unbearable, but you seem on edge and defensive. You don't share your feelings, and you avoid any discussion having to do with Dad."

"I was the one who divorced him. I'm not sure where I fit into your investigation into your father's past. Michael tended to place value on tangible things. He didn't ever talk about feelings. They were the enemy. I guess that I have fallen into that trap too. Regret and hurt tend to affect a person. It's easier to say nothing sometimes than to get noticed saying the wrong things. I am sorry."

"Mom, would you talk to Bob Hughes?"

"Okay," Mary replied with a nod.

They both got up from the edge of the bed and walked into the living room. Bob and David were still trying to solve the world's problems. It was obvious that they had not arrived at any agreement on how to fix them. Mary led the way, and Jamie followed right behind her. She reached her hand out to Jamie, looking for support. She took her hand as they walked up to Bob. Mary broke into the discussion and said, "Mr. Hughes, can I tear you away for a few moments? I need some insight into my ex-husband's history. You might be able to help me. I also received, at the reading of the Will, a letter that Michael wrote to me. It might have something in it that could help you."

"Sure," Bob replied. "Where would you like to meet?"

"Let's go into the study. We can have a little chat, if that is all right with you, Mrs. Hughes." Janice nodded her head in agreement.

Bob got up and followed Mary into a room that was off from the living room. It was probably meant to be another bedroom. It had a big desk and computer, a copier, and two office chairs that could be easily moved. Bob scooted one of them to be directly across from her. They both sat down.

Mary started out speaking very matter-of-factly, "Mr. Hughes, it has been suggested to me by my children that we should talk."

He interrupted her, "Please call me Bob."

"Oh yes, of course, and you can call me Mary. Now as I was saying, it seems that my family thinks that there is something to be gained by us putting our heads together."

"Okay," Bob curiously replied.

"I know about most of Michael's history and his family. What I want to know is why. I don't believe that you can answer that question. The only one who can is not alive to be interviewed."

"I wouldn't say that. I think that we can rebuild his story and find out from the facts what Michael's life has been trying to tell us."

"What do you mean by that?" she asked feeling frustrated.

"I mean every person's story is about redemption, loss, victories and defeats, moments of excitement, and hopelessness. I think you are aware of the basic facts about Michael's hidden life."

"Yes, I am."

"Well then the question that is begging to be answered is obvious. Why was it so important to hide this from you and the family?"

"Let me tell you, Mr. Hughes, I have wondered about that and spent many sleepless nights trying to figure that out. I have finally given up trying. I have accepted the fact that we will never know why."

"Mary, in some cases, I might agree with you, but not in this case. I think that Michael couldn't help it. Unconsciously, he was telling it all along. We just couldn't see it. He had a lot of guilt and shame tied up in this whole façade. I think it all goes back to the fire. Something happened there that he felt responsible for. Do you have the letter you received at Mr. Spagnolo's office?"

Mary thought how carefully he conducted himself. He was professional and impartial. She felt secure that he could be trusted. It was obvious that he would not be easily shocked.

"Yes, I do." She went over to the desk, opened the middle drawer, and pulled out a pale-green envelope. She held it up, walked over to him, and gave it to him.

"Would you mind if I read it?"

"No," Mary said. "You can look at it if you promise to give it back."

"Yes, of course, along with the original green notebook I need to borrow."

He quickly opened the envelope since it already had been opened and pulled out a crumpled and flattened letter. He said nothing about the letter's condition as he read. He looked up after a few minutes and said, "Yes, Mary, there is something here that could explain a lot of things. I will need to get back to Phoenix and investigate this further. Would you make me a copy?" He looked over at the copier.

"Yes, I will. Please try to protect my privacy as you go forward with this," she said with a resolute tone in her voice.

Bob got up, shook her hand, and gave her a peck on her cheek.

Mary was surprised by his quick movement to pursue something he found in the letter. It must be very important for him to mobilize that big frame of his so fast.

She asked, "What is it?"

"It could be significant. I will get back to you as soon as I find out."

With that, he turned and left the room. Ayin invisibly stood next to Mary. He had a big glowing smile on his face.

I will not leave you orphaned; I am coming to you. In

a little while the world will no longer see me, but you

will see me; because I live, you also will live. On that

day you will know that I am in my Father, and you in

me, and I in you. (John 14:18-21, nrsv)

Communion

Michael didn't know what to do. His only hope was that Josh might have an idea.

Josh looked down at his belt. He said dryly. "You know, you're only locked out by a gate like that if you don't have a key. Let me see here. I think I've got one that will fit. Yeah, here it is." He pulled off his right glove so he could get the key off his key chain. That's when Michael saw the hole in his wrist. At first, he thought that Josh had been hurt pulling them out of the cave. No, he realized that He had been hurt thousands of years ago.

Josh got the key and held it in his hand. He reached it out to him and asked, "Do you recognize it?"

Michael studied both the hand and the key. "Yes, I think I do know this key. It's the key to my mother's ashes. I know whose wound this is too. I think you have one on the other wrist and two in your feet and one in your side, don't you."

Softly and tenderly, Josh said, "Yes, I do."

Michael was in awe. He tried to formulate words to say. "You have been with me all along."

"Oh yes, I have always been with you."

He felt bathed in an experience of love and peace. "What about our friend over there, Mr. Schley? Have you been with him too?"

"Oh yes, him most of all," Josh said, turning and looking at the person huddled in a fetal position up against a rock where Michael put him down.

Josh continued, "Why don't you pick him up and carry him out while I open the gate."

Josh turned, put the key in the rusty lock, and turned it. The gate made a creaking sound as he pushed it back. The wind howled back a wailing reply that sounded like "Nooo, noooo, nooooo." It gained momentum faster and faster until it sounded like one constant roar. Michael picked up Bradley and put him over his shoulder. He picked up the lantern in the other hand and, following Josh, carried him over and around some boulders and past the entrance to the cave.

Michael had such a feeling of relief. He had rescued Mr. Schley. He was proud of himself not one of his patients had been lost. Thanks to him, they had moved on to their eternal reward. He had become a caring Doctor at last. He felt a sense of accomplishment like when he got his license to practice medicine. Michael put Bradley down on the green grass under the big old tree. The air was clean and fresh. A slight breeze surrounded them. It was the combination of all the best spring days of his life. It flooded his memory with a fondness for the world and God's purpose in creating it. He basked in the light of his success.

Josh came over and untied the rope around him and Bradley. Michael was so happy and excited, "We did it! We did it! We rescued him, and we're safe."

Josh looked at him in a way that checked his enthusiasm. "What did we do?"

"Why, we saved Mr. Schley over there." He pointed to Bradley under the tree.

"Did we?" Josh asked. "You better go over to him and look again."

"Sure," Michael replied. "I'll go over and check him out." He was thinking like a Doctor. There must be something wrong with him. Of course, why else would he be too weak to walk without being carried.

Bradley had his back to him as if he was trying to hide his face. That was not new behavior; Bradley liked being hidden. He walked around and knelt in front of him. Bradley was not there. The person Michael saw was a young boy. He looked to be about ten years old. The boy said nothing. Michael was surprised and thought that somehow Bradley had become a boy. The youngster looked familiar to him.

Michael yelled over to Josh, "Bradley isn't here. There is a boy in his place. Is this Bradley Schley when he was young?"

Josh said as he wrapped up the rope. "Why don't you ask him?"

Michael bent over closer to him and asked, "Who are you, son? What's your name?"

The boy said nothing, except he began to cry softly. Michael decided to respond to his tears with something new for him, empathy. He said, "Look, son, I won't hurt you. I want to be your friend."

The boy slowly began to sit up and looked directly into Michael's eyes. Then he knew that he recognized him.

"My name is Stephen Hughes," he said. "Why did you rescue me? Don't you know that I deserve to be in hell for what I've done? Don't you know that it was all my fault?"

"What was your fault?"

"Everything is my fault. My father left us because of me. He didn't want to be around me anymore." Big tears were flowing down his cheeks. "I killed them, my brother and sister. I killed them. Everyone blamed my mother, but I did it. I did it!" He was weeping and shaking.

"What do you mean you killed them?"

"My mother didn't feel well most mornings. She was always sick and needed her medicine. She depended on me to feed the kids' breakfast. I always fed my sister, Mindy, in the morning by getting a bottle ready before I went to school. My brother, Samuel, and I had cereal. He must have gone back to bed after I left. I brought my sister her bottle upstairs, and she usually drank it in her crib. I didn't mean to, but I left the water boiling on the stove. I caused the fire that killed them. It's *all* my fault."

Michael felt the tears well up inside him. "No, no, no, it's not your fault. The fire started upstairs. The wiring was bad, the report said. It wasn't your fault. It wasn't!" he yelled.

The boy glared back at him angrily and with a look of certitude. "I'm guilty. I know I am. Nothing you say can change it. You have said it to me thousands of times, and it hasn't helped one bit."

Michael felt fearful of him and, at the same time, pity for him. The boy was inconsolable. Michael cried out, "Oh, Jesus, what do I say to him? How can I relieve his pain?"

Jesus walked over to them. "Does it matter if he's right or wrong? Stephen believes that he needs forgiveness for what happened. I forgave him years ago, but it's not enough. You must forgive him too. You need to forgive yourself. You can do it."

"How do you know that?"

"I know you can because at the farm parts of yourself have begun to fit back together. Mrs. Crier, Cindy, Billy, Morgan, Delbert, and the Smiths are all parts of your soul. They all existed here for you to care about and love. They have been waiting for you to come back to them. Their disappearance meant that they had become integrated inside your heart. That's where heaven is and where I am. Caring for each one made you stronger and drew you deeper into the love I have for you. Then you chose to make a sacrifice, to take a risk. You chose to rescue the most broken part of yourself. You decided to save our friend Mr. Schley, Stephen. Ayin told you that there can be no secrets in glory, not from my Father or from Me or from yourself."

Michael was shocked and amazed. He asked humbly, "Who is Luke?"

"Luke is all the great men and women in your profession that taught you how to care for others. They have given you an eternal resource planted in your soul that points to My Father's goodness and grace."

"Then I am that young doctor too?"

"Yes, you are."

Michael was still kneeling next to Stephen. "What do I need to do for him?"

"What do you think?"

Michael wrapped his arms around the boy. Hugged him and said, "In the name of Jesus, I forgive you. I forgive you for all the loneliness and pain you plied into this heart. I forgive you for the judgments of blame and guilt that concealed the light of God's truth and love. I forgive you for the ponderous chain of shame that locked you in fear. I forgive you for the belief that inevitability would overshadow love and care. I absolve you of all your sins in the name of the Father and the Son and the Holy Spirit." Tears were streaming down Michael's cheeks. They were not of sorrow of pain but of release. They were tears of a deep, profound litany of new life and newfound peace. He looked down, and the boy was gone. Then there was a rumbling sound from the mouth of the cave. Rocks and dirt collapsed and filled the air with a musty-smelling dust. When it cleared, there was no trace of the cave, just a verdant hillside with a small burbling brook. Only he remained. He stood up, and Jesus came near and put his hand on his shoulder.

Michael put his hand on top and took Jesus's hand, bowed down, and kissed it as he said, "My Lord and my God, thank you."

Jesus opened his other hand, and inside was the key. "What do you want to do with this?"

Michael replied with a smile from ear to ear, "My Lord, you take it and do with it as you think best."

Jesus said, "Michael, there are some people who want to be here with us."

He was looking into those loving brown eyes of the Lord. He focused so intently that he didn't see the people gather around him. There was Ayin. He came up to him.

Michael said, "Ayin, you know that I am sorry of hurting my family and that my prayers go out to them, David and Jamie, but most of all, for Mary. I withheld so much of myself from her when she needed my love and support. I so wish that I could tell them how much I love them and ask their forgiveness."

Ayin touched his arm and replied, "Don't worry about that. Our Heavenly Father has been doing his work of redemption and reconciliation. The light has begun to shine on your life, and grace and truth have come from it."

He turned and saw his mother, Beth, his brother, Samuel, his sister, Mindy, and Marian Anderson. His brother and sister, grownup and brilliant like diamonds, and many others who had been his patients and friends. They reached out to him like spokes on a wheel. He knew and felt their love. The light around them began to glow as they sang the song of God's redemption. Colors brighter than hundreds of rainbows shimmered around him. It was a dazzling fountain of love that embraced every part of his soul. It filled him with *glory.*

Something small can make a big difference.

Don't gloss over the tiny in significance.

Or settle for in complete and fractured moments,

that imperfect creatures causally inhabit.

Matted colors brush against the garish

"Father, into your hands I commit my spirit."

New Jerusalem Bible, Luke 23: 46

A Small Mystery

Hunter had delivered his report to his boss, John Tyler, after he returned from Arizona. To his surprise, John was not dismissive of his diagnosis of the carburetor as being the culprit. John called him into his office. He was a pear shaped person, balding with a short nose and ruddy complexion. He looked like Winston Churchill without the cigar.

John motioned for Hunter to sit down. He looked at Hunter's report on his desk.

"I read over your report. I intend to study it more carefully later this afternoon. I think it is very well thought out, but I have a few ideas and questions. I think it needs to go further into the causes of the carburetor failure. For example, why don't you check up on the number of carburetor failures in the last ten years? I remember there was another case of a family in the Midwest that died in a small plane crash that had a similar possible cause. Check with the FAA and see if they have anything more to tell us. Hunter, if what you suggest is true, something doesn't pass the smell test. Find out who manufactured the carburetor that was installed in this plane."

"John," Hunter replied, "I did that when I interviewed the mechanic in Mesa. He told me where he got the part, and I called them. They assured me that they had no complaints since they made changes to the float in the carburetor. It seems that the metal ones leaked and the malfunction caused the carburetor to be saturated by fuel. That flooded the engine. They had to be redesigned using plastic ones, which corrected the problem. He said that they have been in use since 1992. It's all in my report."

John leaned back in his office chair with his hands cupped behind his head like a cradle. After a pause, he said, "They're hiding something."

Hunter responded, "If they are, it's probably so they won't get sued."

"You're right about that. Is it possible that they delivered a carburetor that had a metal float? It could happen. Maybe it happened in this case. Hunter, you have done some good work in this investigation. I want you to follow up on this. It could keep the flying public safer."

Hunter put his hand out to shake John's and said, "I will get busy on this and check back with you next week."

John stood up from behind his desk and clasped his hand while he steadied himself, putting his weight on the other. Hunter was just about to leave John's office when he asked him, "Oh, how did Jerry and Brenda work out?"

Hunter smiled and replied, "They were good. I think it was a learning experience for them. They faced a very difficult situation and adapted pretty well. Jerry got hurt, but he's mostly recovered from a bad ankle sprain. I sent you an e-mail about it."

"I know you did. Thanks, Hunter. By all means, let's get together next week. Check with Judy, my secretary, and get on my calendar. Sounds like we have a mystery, and you know how I love a mystery."

Hunter let out a sigh of relief after he closed John's door. He didn't think I was crazy. On the contrary, he was quite *supportive.* He realized that he had accepted the manufacture's explanation about the carburetor far too readily. John's line of thought had opened a new view of things. His suspicions had rubbed off on him. He wanted to dig deeper. Maybe there was a solution to the puzzle after all. He knew that John loved to find out about something that the FAA should have known. In that way, the mystery was also the chase. He so enjoyed being the one to find that the FAA had missed something. Hunter knew that John was an honorable public servant whose main goal was to make flying safer. He also knew that John would enjoy dirtying the FAA's noses at the same time.

He thought, *Oh well, what's wrong with a little friendly competition?*

The next few days were filled with a concentrated examination of the company that made the carburetors and checking them against the FAA and NTSB databases. Once the serial numbers on the older carburetors were contrasted against the newer ones, it became obvious that somehow, they'd shipped an old carburetor with the metal float instead of a carburetor with the newer plastic one. It was, in Hunter's mind, a negligent act by the company. He had all the facts to back up his hypothesis. The mechanic Gary Myers was probably hiding the fact that he should have caught the problem, but he didn't. For some reason, he either failed to remember the recall or just missed it. He felt ready to discuss his findings with John.

He had made an appointment with John's secretary, Judy. She welcomed him and told him that Mr. Tyler would be with him in a few minutes. Hunter remained standing and tried to keep from pacing. He noticed that Judy was a woman who took her job seriously. She wore a gray two-piece suit with a white blouse. Her hair was a little to short and curly for his taste. She looked to be about fifty years old and had some gray highlights in her brown hair. Her appearance contrasted against John's frumpy, thrown-together style. He thought, *They probably work well together being so different.*

Bob opened the door and motioned Hunter to come into his office. They shook hands, and John led him in and invited him to take a seat.

"What did you find out?" he asked curiously.

Hunter replied, "The bottom line is this. Several of the crashes, including this one, were the result of a mix-up in sending out old parts instead of new ones. The old parts are new, in the sense that they have never been used. However, a critical element was changed in 1992 and replaced by a plastic float. The old carburetors had a metal one. The manufacturer doesn't want to acknowledge the mistake, but we have evidence in the part numbers and the manufacturing dates."

"That's great work, Hunter," John exclaimed as he clasped his hands together. "I think we can save a few lives with this information."

"John, the FAA will need to be brought in on this so that the flying public can be notified and changes made to keep this from happening again. The company, Imperial Aircraft Inc., should have made a recall of these carburetors, but they were unwilling because of the cost."

"Yeah, Hunter, you're right. Hey, you have all the data to support this finding. Let's give the FAA a call on speaker phone. There has to be somebody working over there. You have the facts to e-mail them today, don't you?"

"Oh, sure I do."

John looked at him with a big smile and a sense of satisfaction and said, "I do love solving a mystery."

Jesus said, "I thank you, Father, Lord of heaven and earth, because you have hidden these things from the wise and the intelligent and have revealed them to infants; yes, Father, for such was your gracious will. All things have been handed over to me by my Father, and no one knows the Son except the Father, and no one knows the Father except the Son and anyone to whom the Son chooses to reveal him. Come to me, all you that are weary and are carrying heavy burdens, and I will give you rest. Take my yoke upon you, and learn from me; for I am gentle and humble in heart, and you will find rest for your souls. For my yoke is easy, and my burden is light."

(Matthew 11:25-30, New Revised Standard Version)

Tides

The Reverend Samuel Waters had come over to meet with the family Thursday evening. They picked out the readings and went over the service and the music. They had some decaf coffee with some poppy seed cake that Jamie bought. The pastor was an elderly gentleman with snow white hair. He was short and stocky, affable, and outgoing. His face seemed to brighten every time he smiled. Mary had attended Good Shepherd about once a month, and Michael had usually tagged along at Christmas and Easter, at least when the kids were little.

David thought the visit was awkward. The rector had never come over to their house. Now that his dad had died, there he was, like an expectant interloper. He felt angry about that, like their bastion of privacy had been intruded upon. David was aware that this was not their house but his dad's condo. It wasn't the house he grew up in. It was the three-bedroom, two-bath condo of a man who'd lived alone. It made him feel sad. It felt surreal. Perhaps they should have stayed at a hotel, at least until after the funeral. Mary wanted to get an idea of what needed to be done to identify stuff that needed to be sold or given to goodwill.

They had come up from Tucson on Wednesday afternoon. Everyone had a bedroom, except David. He stayed in his father's office. Thank God it was big enough for the Hide-A Bed that his father kept there. The condo was Spartan, clean, and had a touch of what a man becomes when there is no woman around to check his inclinations for just the essentials. David had gone to the refrigerator Friday morning, looking for something to eat. Food was as Spartan as the furnishings, just some frozen dinners in the freezer. He found some oatmeal that he could put on the stove or the microwave. He went hunting in the cabinets for a saucepan to boil some water. Odd, to his surprise, he found no skillets or frying pans, nothing to cook with. It struck him as strange that his dad didn't have any pans at all. He remembered that his father never wanted to cook. It must have been hard for him to live alone since his mom always made the meals. It was like a thing with him. He would never even get close to the stove.

He used to say, "I'm allergic to cooking."

Of all his father's foibles, that was the one that stood out the most. *Funny,* he almost said out loud, *that I should be thinking about that.*

Since there was so little food in the house, David took orders and drove over to the closest McDonalds, just down the street. He had managed to get the coffee going in his father's coffeemaker before he left. He loudly announced to everyone that he was back.

Everybody must have been as hungry as he was, because they arrived at the table before he could take the food out of the bag. He thought that sitting together with food and fresh coffee might make this a good time to explore things a little more.

"Mom, I know Dad didn't like to cook. I wonder what that was about."

"Your father just refused to cook. He didn't want to learn even though I offered to teach him. When your father made up his mind, there was no changing it."

"That's so true," Jamie interjected. ".And I don't think Dad wanted to go out to dinner as much as he did. He just didn't want to cook, and that's the price he had to pay."

David replied, "Well, as I recall, there were more than a few times that the price was pretty high."

Mary laughed and laughed. "It's true he was so tight with his money, but when it came to food, 'survival,' he had to pay the piper."

David changed the subject. "Since we are all sitting together, there is something I want to tell you. I have invited a new friend of mine to come to the funeral. Her name is Theresa Best. She is flying in later today, and I am going to pick her up at the airport."

Mary interrupted, "She's the young woman you met in Ohio."

"Yes, she's coming here and will be staying at the Hyatt, and then we are going back to Ohio together. She has become very special to me."

"I think it's great that she's coming, but do you think a funeral is the right time?" Jamie said with a puzzled look on her face.

"Well, I think so, Jamie," David replied with a demonstrative tone. "She's coming at my request. It will be comforting for me to have her here and to meet all of you too."

Jamie said with a hint of feigned acceptance, "Well, I guess it's settled."

Just then, there was a loud knock at the door. David went over and opened it.

There stood Bob Hughes. He looked hot and slightly out of breath. David ushered him into the dining room.

"Welcome, Bob," David said. "What brings you over? I didn't think we would see you until the service tomorrow morning."

"Well, I came up with some ideas that I need to talk to all of you about. It has to do with your father and the fire when he was a child."

David said, "I made some coffee. Let's go to the table. We just ate some McDonalds. Please sit down." There was an open chair for Bob to sit in.

Jamie and Mary were still in their nightgowns and robes.

Mary interjected hurriedly, "I need to get dressed."

"No, you're fine. It's okay," Bob said reassuringly.

Jamie piped up, "So what's going on, Bob?"

"I think that I have put a few things together that, taken separately, don't mean much, but you put them together, something begins to emerge. We have a series of clues to what happened to cause the fire. As you know, the investigator found that it was faulty wiring in the upstairs that shorted and caused it. I think there is more to the story. Michael's father, my brother, had left the home for greener pastures. Stephen was left to do things that adults usually did. His mother was not well. It's difficult to say that she was addicted to codeine, but she probably was. He was expected to feed the kids before he left for school."

Mary asked, "How did you get that idea?"

"I got it from you, Mary. You shared with me the quote from the letter he wrote you. It said he left too many things on the back burner. I thought that was an odd thing to say. It seemed like a Freudian slip. Then when I went home and looked carefully in his notebook, I found this newspaper clipping under a photo. He circled it. The picture was taken after the fire. Look closely. I'll pass it around. The only thing left standing is the stove, and look what's on it."

David had gotten the picture first. It was yellow with age, but you could clearly see that there was a saucepan on the stove.

David sucked in a big breath of air and said, "Oh, God!"

David looked over at Jamie and said, "There is not one pan to cook with in this house. Dad said he had an allergy about cooking."

Mary replied with astonishment, "I used to think that Michael just didn't want to be saddled with the chore of cooking. This seems to say that he was terrified about cooking because of his past."

Bob continued, "That fits with everything else. You see, Michael probably blamed himself for everything. His father's leaving. Children often blame themselves for parental abandonment. They think unconsciously that there is something wrong with them. That somehow, they caused the divorce.

"I think that day of the fire, he made Mindy's bottle and took it up to her, and Samuel went back to bed upstairs after breakfast. He probably forgot to shut off the stove. Later, his mother came downstairs and noticed the stove still on and shut it off. She went to the couch and went to sleep. I doubt that she heard the children. They were probably slowly suffocated by the smoke. When she did wake up, it was too late. The fire was already raging in the house."

David shook his head. "Dad had to know that the fire was caused by the bad wiring."

Bob went on quickly, "He may have known intellectually, but in that place in his soul where that ten-year-old boy lived, he was to blame. Why else would he go to such great lengths to hide what happened from everyone? Why would he build a new identity unless he was ashamed and covered with guilt. The other part of that was, many people thought that his mother had set the fire. He believed it was his fault, yet he said nothing. His personal shame kept him from defending her. He probably considered himself a coward since he took no responsibility for the tragedy."

Bob went on, "Here's a ten-year-old boy that lost not just his father but his brother and sister and his mother too. He was left to live with his grandparents, who really didn't want him. They used him as a hired hand, but there is no evidence that they loved him. I'm sure in his mind he was being severely punished by God for his crime."

Jamie interrupted and loudly cried, "But he didn't do anything wrong."

Bob continued, "You're right about that, Jamie, but try convincing that little boy. Don't you see? He had to take on a different name so that he could survive. He had to keep those two worlds separate so that he could function."

Mary had her arms around her waist and quietly asked, "Why do you think it was so important for him to go back there every year?"

Bob looked over at her and replied sympathetically, "I have thought a lot about that question. It's obvious that after the County Psych Hospital closed, he felt some responsibility to take care of his mother. I don't believe it was just out of guilt or duty but out of hope."

"What do you mean 'hope'?" David asked.

"Each year, he would check on things at the foundation and his mother's care. Then he would go and sit with her with the hope that she could come to her senses long enough to answer his most important question. Was it my fault? That's why he went to the play *A Long Day's journey into Night* and read it so carefully. It prepared him to face the fact, like Edmund in the play, that his mother would never be free to acknowledge his suffering. She would always be in a world that had no answers for him. He would have to live with the inevitably of never knowing the truth."

Mary began to cry. "What you are telling us is a very sad story." Ayin was next to her, invisibly stroking her hair with reassurance and forgiveness.

David interrupted her sorrow. "I don't think that's it at all, Mom. Bob's interpretation of the facts seems likely. It explains a lot of things. Dad overcame tremendous personal deprivations. Did he have a difficult time bonding? Yes, he did. He had a deficit that we all know about. I think he was an exceptional person. In spite of all his pain, he did a lot of good for people. I never thought that before. For him to move through life and do the things he did in spite of those blind spots in his perception makes his story remarkable."

Jamie leaned over and put her hand on Mary's shoulder. "Mom, he tried to be what you needed. He just didn't know how. I don't know how you can forgive him, but you need to somehow."

David looked over at Bob and said, "Mom, it's possible to forgive him because I have."

Jamie chimed in and said, "So have I, Mom."

Bob added, "I've had to forgive my brother for his abandoning me too."

Mary looked at everyone and said, "I'm not ready to do that now. I know that you're right. I don't like being the odd person out, but I'm not there yet. Maybe when I am alone, that can happen but not right now. Please be patient with me."

"It's okay, Mom," David replied. "It will happen when you're ready and not till then."

A little while later, Bob went home. David had picked up Theresa at Sky Harbor Airport. Her flight had been delayed because of severe thunderstorms in the Cleveland Metropolitan area. She'd arrived at 9:00 p.m. David had taken her to the Hyatt after they had a small supper at the hotel restaurant. He would pick her up before the service early enough to meet the family.

Saturday morning, Mary walked into the church just as David and this beautiful young woman did. She was tall with light brown hair. Mary could tell they were an item by the way she had her arm through his. They already had mastered somehow that ability of walking together without bumping or tripping each other. They approached Mary. David did the introductions. He was beaming with the look of a man who had found a great treasure.

Jamie came over to meet Theresa Best. The four of them gathered in a little circle and chitchatted about her flight and the terrible weather in Cleveland.

Mary noticed that Jamie seemed to be looking around as if she was trying to find something. People had begun to filter into the church. Mary was happy that so many people, friends, and patients were there. She was busy welcoming the guests. They all expressed sympathy at her loss and theirs too.

Jamie had evidently found what she was looking for. She came up holding this young man's hand. He looked familiar. Mary had met him before. He was a little taller than Jamie. He had coal-black hair and a football player's build. She said, "Mom, this is Jesse Hernandez. He's the officer who came and told me about Dad. Remember, he came over to your house with the agent from the NTSB. We have become friends, and I would like him to sit with me. Is that okay?"

"Of course, it's good to see you again." Mary extended her hand. He had big hands, but he tenderly took hers and sincerely looked at her and offered his sympathy with genuine and heartfelt emotion. Time passed by so quickly that before she could take a deep breath, it was time to take their places in the front row. Mary wasn't sure how she got there, but somehow, she did. Father Samuel started down the center aisle wearing a white alb and stole preceded by an altar boy in a black cassock and white surplus carrying a lighted candle. Father was reading from the 1979 Book of Common Prayer.

"Everyone the Father gives to me will come to me," he said in a booming voice.

Mary suddenly felt a sense of peace flood her heart.

"I will never turn away anyone who believes in me."

She closed her eyes. The tide of forgiveness began to come in.

"He who raised Jesus Christ from the dead will also give new life to our mortal bodies through his indwelling Spirit."

The waters rushed over the sediments of hurt and covered them. The tidal waters rushed into the vacant places of hopelessness.

"My heart, therefore is glad, and my spirit rejoices. My body also shall rest in hope."

She opened her eyes and looked to her left. There was David and Theresa. She looked to the right. There was Jamie and Jesse. She looked around the church and saw a congregation full of people.

Father Samuel came closer down the aisle. Each word raised the tide of forgiveness higher. "You will show me the path of life. In your presence there is fullness of Joy. And in your right hand are pleasures for evermore."

Then suddenly, she knew that she could forgive him. The tide had come in, and it gave her soul strength. All the little boats of a bright future were floating, and she was buoyed with hope. Mary closed her eyes and prayed. It reached into all her pain and sorrow. It touched all the places of disappointment and fractured promises.

"Michael, I forgive you," she said as she moved her lips, and the whispered sound echoed in her heart. "I absolve you in my heart and in the love of Jesus." Ayin was standing next to her, and he lifted his arms and unfurled his wings in *praise.*

Reprise

Hunter was getting dressed for another day at work. His mind focused on the case that he had just put to bed. To its credit, the FAA had followed up right away on the information of his report. They had found the company negligent of not maintaining quality standards of carburetor replacement parts in the Lycoming engine. Bulletins were issued to owners and mechanics about the metal floats. Recalls, when needed, were initiated.

He sat at the edge of his bed and bent over to tie his shoes. He sat there for a moment and thought about the odds of that crash happening.

"Somehow, as tragic as it was, something good came out of it. The good Lord knows how many lives were saved."

He smiled when he remembered that trip to the Superstitions.

Maybe he would go hiking back there someday,
and see if he could find
the old Lost Dutchman's Mine.

Finis